BEST STORIES
of
SARAH ORNE
JEWETT

BEST STORIES *of* SARAH ORNE JEWETT

EDITED BY CHARLES G. WAUGH,
MARTIN H. GREENBERG
AND JOSEPHINE DONOVAN

WITH AN INTRODUCTION BY
JOSEPHINE DONOVAN

ILLUSTRATED BY PETER FARROW

LANCE TAPLEY, PUBLISHER

No part of this book may be reproduced or transmitted in any form or by any means, electronic or mechanical, including photocopying, recording or by any information storage or retrieval system, without the written permission of the publisher, except by a reviewer quoting brief passages in a magazine, newspaper, or broadcast. Address inquiries to Lance Tapley, Publisher, P.O. Box 2439, Augusta, Maine 04330.

Designed by Lisa Lyons
Typeset by Sandau Type and Design
Printed in the United States of America

Back cover photograph of Sarah Orne Jewett courtesy of Special Collections, University of New Hampshire Library .

Library of Congress Cataloging-in-Publication Data
Jewett, Sarah Orne. 1849-1909.
    [Short stories. Selections]
    The best stories of Sarah Orne Jewett/edited by Charles G. Waugh, Martin H. Greenberg & Josephine Donovan; introduction by Josephine Donovan; illustrated by Peter Farrow.
    p. cm.
    I. Waugh, Charles. II. Greenberg, Martin Harry. III. Donovan, Josephine, 1941- . IV. Title.
PS2131.W38 1988 813'.4—dc19   88-15955 CIP
ISBN 0-912769-33-5; $10.95

CONTENTS

NOTE ON THE TEXT

In the attempt to render Sarah Orne Jewett's work faithfully and accurately, this book reproduces the original spelling and punctuation of the first published versions of each of these stories.

A Way of One's Own:
The Writings of Sarah Orne Jewett

Josephine Donovan

S arah Orne Jewett, who lived from 1849 to 1909, stood at the confluence of two great literary traditions: one was the indigenous current of women's "local color" literature of the mid-nineteenth century, springing primarily from Harriet Beecher Stowe and Rose Terry Cooke. The other issued from the British and European realists Flaubert, Thackeray, Turgenev, Tolstoi, and George Sand. This tradition stretched back to the late seventeenth and early eighteenth century, to the origins of the novel.

Jewett herself often invoked Laurence Sterne as a literary model, particularly his satirical novel *A Sentimental Journey*, which she said her father had commended to her with the injunction to "tell things *just as they are!*"

She held to this realist doctrine of mimesis throughout her career; on numerous occasions Jewett counseled younger writers that the artist's duty is to transcribe reality directly with as little doctoring up as possible. She told aspiring writer John Thaxter not to "write a 'story' but just *tell the thing!*"[1] And she advised Willa Cather, then beginning her literary career, "Don't try to write the kind of short story that this or that magazine wants—write the truth and let them take it or leave it." She added: "Write it as it is, don't try to make it like this or that. You can't do it in anybody else's way—you will have to make a way of your own."[2]

In reflecting upon the achievement of Sarah Orne Jewett, one is struck by the strength of her determination to make a way of her own. This unusual self-confidence may explain how she was able to create stories that rank with the masterpieces of the genre. For the "best" short stories of Sarah Orne Jewett remain among the best short stories in English.

The story form that Jewett inherited came from Harriet Beecher Stowe and Rose Terry Cooke. Their local color school, an outgrowth of the Romantic movement in literature, was in part a rebellion against the homogenizing tendencies of the Industrial Revolution and the emergence of mass communication and transportation. These writers sought to capture the precious particulars of their region, fearing they would soon be erased by the uniformity dictated by mechanization and modern bureaucracy.

Several of Jewett's characters lament that people are growing more and more alike, that the rough edges of rural and personal eccentricity are being shaved off as national molds are imposed upon regional difference. As Mrs. Goodsoe remarks in "The Courting of Sister Wisby," "In old times . . . [people] stood in their lot an' place, and were n't all just alike, either, same as pine spills." And Jewett herself once commented, on hearing of a plan to subdivide the banks of the Piscataqua River, separating Maine and New Hampshire, that such development gave her "a hunted feeling like the last wild thing that is left in the fields."[3]

The local colorists used regional particularities in dialect, clothes, settings, customs, and characters. The author who appears to have originated the tradition in English, and who had a great influence on early nineteenth-century American women writers, was Irish writer Maria Edgeworth, who lived from 1767 to 1849. Also important was a younger contemporary, Mary Russell Mitford, who developed the "village sketch" format used so heavily by the American women, including Jewett. In this genre a narrator typically wanders through her own village as a kind of tour guide, introducing the reader to various village eccentrics, sometimes conversing with them to hear their latest "news" or "stories," and spending a considerable amount of time describing local birds, animals, and vegetation. There is little or no plot, though the possibility is there for a plot to emerge in the narrations of the village characters to the author-narrator.

Jewett used this format repeatedly—perhaps even more than the other local colorists. In this collection, "A Bit of Shore Life," "An Autumn Holiday," "The Courting of Sister Wisby," and "The Foreigner" are particularly good examples of the device. "An Autumn Holiday" opens with a young woman meandering through the countryside. During the course of her wanderings the rural environment is described in great detail. She finally reaches a cottage where two women are spinning; in their chatting with the narrator the central story eventually emerges, the comic predicament of Daniel Gunn, a one-time militia captain who "got sun-struck" and thought he was a woman. (This story, by the way, was originally entitled "Miss Daniel Gunn," but cautious editors or perhaps Jewett herself evidently decided that this title was too outrageous.)

Jewett acknowledged the influence of her local-colorist foremothers, particularly Harriet Beecher Stowe, who first published New England stories in the 1830s, eventually collected as *The Mayflower; or, Sketches of Scenes and Characters among the Descendents of the Pilgrims* (1843). It was Stowe's great local-color novels, *The Minister's Wooing* (1859), *The Pearl of Orr's Island* (1862), and *Oldtown Folks* (1869)—all set in New England—that had the most influence.

Jewett singled out *The Pearl of Orr's Island* as a work that greatly influenced her in her youth. In the second preface to *Deephaven* (1893), Jewett's first collection of stories (originally published in 1877), Jewett remarked:

> It was, happily, in the writer's childhood that Mrs. Stowe had
> written of those who dwelt along the wooded seacoast and by
> the decaying, shipless harbors of Maine. The first chapters of
> *The Pearl of Orr's Island* gave the younger author of *Deephaven*
> to see with new eyes, and to follow eagerly the old shore paths
> from one gray, weather-beaten house to another where Genius
> pointed her the way.[4]

Later, on rereading Stowe's novel, Jewett commented that she still found it "just as clear and perfectly original and strong as it seemed to me in my thirteenth or fourteenth year, when I read it first."[5] This book, still eminently readable, is set off the coast of Maine near Brunswick. It is clear that Stowe's descriptions of Maine characters and her use of a real Maine setting helped the young Jewett to realize that her own locale might provide the materials of literature. Within a decade after reading Stowe's novel, Jewett was publishing her own stories of Maine life. The first of these, "The Shore House," which is set along the coast in the York region, was published in the *Atlantic Monthly* in September, 1873. It was later divided into two stories, "Kate Lancaster's Plan" and "The Brandon House and the Lighthouse," when published as part of *Deephaven*, which includes a series of sketches published in the *Atlantic* in the 1870s—all set in the York area.

The other major influences upon Jewett were the European realists. Not surprisingly, she thought Flaubert's *Madame Bovary* a "wonderful" and "great" book, though she found herself exasperated with the title character for failing to recognize "what there was in that dull little village! She is such a lesson to dwellers in country towns who drift out of relation to their surroundings, not only social but the very companionships of nature, unknown to them."[6] Jewett here is commenting on modern rootlessness and alienation from nature, and affirming the merits of provincial life, especially its rootedness and closeness to nature—a typical assertion of the local color vision.

This moral perspective pervades Jewett's work. The realists she most admired, Thackeray and Tolstoi, were those whose works (as she noted of *Vanity Fair*) "were full of splendid scorn for meanness and wickedness...."[7] While Jewett's own works are not satirical in this sense, they nevertheless in many cases have a moral depth worthy of these great realists. "Miss Tempy's Watchers" in this volume, for example, while on the surface a comic tale about two women dozing at a friend's wake, is a powerful and subtle story about the enriching waves of goodness that continue to ripple from Miss Tempy's generous engagement in life. Like the old quince-tree that she "expected" "into bloomin,' " Miss Tempy's example seems to resurrect the spirit of compassion in the watchers at her wake. It is this level of moral seriousness that gives Jewett's work an interest beyond that of local-color oral history, carrying it into the realm of great literature.

Jewett was born September 3, 1849, in South Berwick, Maine, a town on the southern border of the state, on the Piscataqua River about ten miles inland from the Atlantic Ocean, and about sixty-five miles from Boston. It was through her access to Boston publishers that she was able to achieve literary success at an early age. Boston was the publishing hub of the nation. The house in which she was born and lived most of her life is a large and handsome Georgian structure in the center of South Berwick, cared for by the Society for the Preservation of New England Antiquities. It is open to the public in summers.

Jewett's parents were Caroline Frances Perry (1820-1891) and Theodore Herman Jewett (1815-1878), a physician. Through her mother, Jewett was connected to the Perry and Gilman families of Exeter, New Hampshire. By way of the Gilman family, Sarah was related to two other well-known American women writers, the seventeenth-century poet Anne Bradstreet and novelist Tabitha Tenney. The latter wrote an amusing satirical novel, *Female Quixotism* (1801), which is reminiscent of Sterne's *Sentimental Journey* and anticipates the comic flavor of some of Jewett's own work. "The Dulham Ladies," for example, pokes fun at the vanities of two elderly women who adorn themselves with then-fashionable "frisettes," or wigs, which only serve to make them look ridiculous. *Female Quixotism* similarly satirizes a woman's vain pretensions; indeed, there is a comparably farcical scene with a wig. It is not known whether Jewett read Tenney's novel or knew of Tenney, though the latter seems probable. In any event, there may well have been a family style of humor that both writers drew upon. On her paternal side, Jewett's grandfather was Theodore Furber Jewett (1787-1860), a prosperous shipowner and merchant in the West Indies trade. It was his financial success that established the family economically and meant that Sarah never had to worry about income. Indeed, she once remarked that, for her, writing was never a "bread and butter affair."[8] Her grandmother was Sarah Orne (1794-1819), for whom she was named (although her first given name was Theodora, after her father and grandfather, she never used it). From her grandparents, who were born in the last decades of the eighteenth century, Sarah would have heard New England oral history dating back to pre-Revolutionary times. Her last novel, *The Tory Lover* (1901), is set during the Revolution in South Berwick.

Sarah had two sisters, Mary Rice and Caroline. Caroline's son, Theodore Herman Jewett, was the last member of the immediate family when he died in 1930. At that time Sarah's manuscripts, correspondence, and much of her library were bequeathed to the Houghton Library at Harvard, where they remain. There are also substantial collections of Jewett materials at the Society for the Preservation of New England

Antiquities in Boston and at the Colby College Library in Waterville, Maine.

As a child Sarah appears to have been something of a maverick, probably like the character Nan Prince in Jewett's autobiographical novel *A Country Doctor* (1884). Nan is a wayward tomboy who is more comfortable in the fields than in the drawing room, and who definitely has a mind of her own. A neighbor complains, "She won't go to bed till she 's a mind to . . . she 'd be'n up into . . . oaks, trying to catch a little screech owl. She belongs with the wild creatur's . . . just the same natur'."[9] Nan conceives the unorthodox plan of becoming a physician, and is encouraged in her ambitions by her foster father, who is a country doctor undoubtedly modeled on Jewett's own father. One suspects that the latter encouraged Sarah to become a writer in much the same way as Dr. Leslie urges Nan to become a doctor.

Jewett readily acknowledged the influence of her father; as a child she accompanied him on house calls where she heard some of the stories and met some of the people transfigured in her fiction. On their rides Dr. Jewett also instructed Sarah about local vegetation; her work reflects a detailed knowledge of New England plants and herbs. Less is known about Sarah's relationship with her mother; while we know that it was intense, Sarah rarely mentioned her mother in her writings, and this remains an unfortunate blank in our understanding of the writer. Sarah was also close to her sisters; a voluminous correspondence remains between her and Mary Rice Jewett.

Jewett's writing career began under the aegis of William Dean Howells, who was an associate editor at the *Atlantic Monthly* in 1869 when Jewett submitted her story "Mr. Bruce." Howells accepted it and encouraged her to send him stories that realistically reflected her Maine locale. This she did in the sketches that were published in the *Atlantic* in the 1870s, collected (after Howells's suggestion) as *Deephaven* in 1877.

The editor-in-chief of the *Atlantic* at this time was James T. Fields, probably the most powerful publisher in the country. It was through Fields and especially his wife, Annie Adams, who lived from 1834 to 1915, that Jewett gained entrée to the Boston literary world. Annie Fields had by this time turned the Fieldses' townhouse on Charles Street into America's most famous literary salon. Nearly all the literary lions of the day—Dickens, Holmes, Hawthorne, Lowell, Longfellow, Emerson, Whittier, and Arnold—passed through. Annie also provided a haven for a number of women writers; Harriet Beecher Stowe, Celia Thaxter, Rebecca Harding Davis, Louisa May Alcott, Elizabeth Stuart Phelps, Willa Cather, as well as Jewett, found emotional support and professional encouragement from Annie, who often served as an unofficial editor for her husband.

After James's death in 1881, Annie's relationship with Sarah intensified. They came to form what was then called a "Boston marriage," a life-long commitment between two women. This was undoubtedly the most important relationship of Sarah's (and possibly of Annie's) adult life. Such commitments were not unusual in the nineteenth century, as Carroll Smith-Rosenberg and other scholars have discovered,[10] and, while it is anachronistic to use the twentieth-century term lesbian to describe them, it is clear that the emotional intensity of these relationships was such that they would be so labeled today (we, of course, do not know what the physical character of these "romantic friendships" was). Scores of letters remain documenting the devotion of Sarah and Annie to one another; they were treated as a couple by numerous correspondents.

By the 1880s, Sarah's life was divided between Boston and South Berwick. She spent part of the year in the city, part in the country (and part at Manchester-by-the-Sea, Massachusetts, at Annie's summer home). The geographical partition in Jewett's life between the urban and rural worlds is reflected as a tension in her fiction of the period.

"A White Heron," for example, perhaps Jewett's single greatest story and certainly the one most anthologized and analyzed (scarcely a year goes by without a new interpretation by scholars), is built upon the clash between rural and urban civilization. What makes this ostensibly simple story so powerful and rich is that it seems to symbolize a number of historical conflicts that were occurring in late nineteenth-century America. Like *Huckleberry Finn*, which was published the same year (1886), the story hinges upon the question of the betrayal of personal friendship to abstractions that purport to have higher claims. In Twain's novel it is whether Huck will betray his black friend Jim, thus obeying the Fugitive Slave Law, which mandated that escaped slaves be returned to their owners; in Jewett's case it is whether the girl Sylvia will betray her woodland "friend," the heron, which an ornithologist wishes to kill and stuff for his collection. The tension in the Jewett story is between the claims of science and patriarchal authority, and the integrity of the natural world and the "feminine" emotional engagement of the girl in that world.

The gun the ornithologist carries in "A White Heron" symbolizes masculine dominance as well as industrial imperialism (when she accompanies the hunter in the woods Sylvia "did not lead the guest, she only followed, and there was no such thing as speaking first"), and so Sylvia's resistance can be seen as a feminist act preserving the matriarchal woodland sanctuary where she and her grandmother live peaceably with the beasts. In both works, the story turns out "happily" for most readers; betrayal is resisted and the claims of impersonal abstractions are rejected.

The matriarchal character of Jewett's vision is apparent in a number of stories: for example, "Miss Tempy's Watchers," "In Dark New England Days," "The Flight of Betsey Lane," "Martha's Lady," and "The Foreigner" in the stories collected here. In these, the rural world is dominated by powerful women characters who seem at times to exude an almost supernatural strength. ("The King of Folly Island," conversely, presents a powerful critique of patriarchal tyranny.) But it is in her masterpiece, the book *The Country of the Pointed Firs*, that Jewett brings this vision to culmination. There the powerful witch-herbalist Almira Todd reigns supreme over a rural sanctuary that becomes redemptive for the tired woman narrator who has come back to Maine jaded from the city, seeking rejuvenation and reinspiration. The rural world in Jewett's final vision becomes a source of spiritual energy, contrasted to the alienating, deadening world of urban industry.

Jewett once advised Willa Cather that a writer had to see the world before she could describe the parish. It was advice she herself had followed. As a youth she traveled to New York, Philadelphia, Cincinnati, Chicago, and Wisconsin. As an adult she traveled widely with Annie Fields. Their trips included four voyages to Europe (in 1882, 1892, 1898, and 1900), a Caribbean cruise in 1896, and domestic trips to Florida and Chicago (to attend the 1893 World's Fair). On her trips to Europe, Jewett met many of the great writers of the day, including Christina Rossetti, Alfred Lord Tennyson, Mark Twain, Henry James, and Rudyard Kipling. She visited most of the European countries and made pilgrimages to the graves of the Bronte sisters in England and Madame de Sevigne in France. Jewett's greatest works benefit from the perspective gleaned from her travels; she saw the people of rural Maine in the larger context of Western history and culture. In *The Country of the Pointed Firs*, for example, Jewett describes a procession at a family reunion:

... we might have been a company of ancient Greeks going to celebrate a victory, or to worship the god of harvests ... we were no more a New England family celebrating its own existence. ... We possessed the instincts of a far, forgotten childhood. ...[11]

In addition to several collections of short stories (listed in the Bibliography), Jewett wrote three novels—*A Country Doctor* (1884), *A Marsh Island* (1885), and *The Tory Lover* (1901)—as well as the hybrid works—*Deephaven* and *Pointed Firs*—that are a cross between a novel and a short-story collection. In 1902 she was thrown from a carriage and suffered severe spinal injuries from which she never recovered. On June 24, 1909, she died of a cerebral hemorrhage in South Berwick, where she is buried.

Willa Cather, who was the writer perhaps most influenced by Jewett (a series of extraordinary letters remain between the two), singled out *The Country of the Pointed Firs* as one of three works of American literature destined for immortality (the others being *Huckleberry Finn* and *The Scarlet Letter*). Today we might want to add some of Jewett's stories—those collected here, for example—and some of Cather's own works—especially *My Antonia*, written under a strong Jewett influence—to the list.

It was her style, that "very personal quality of perception," Cather noted, that made Jewett's works stand out. "Among fifty thousand books," she observed, "you find very few writers who ever achieved a style at all." But Jewett's faithfulness to her "individual voice"—her determination to forge a way of her own—established the integrity that created, as Cather noted, "almost flawless examples of literary art."[12]

Samples of Jewett's magnificent style can be selected at random from throughout this volume. In "A Bit of Shore Life," for example, one of Jewett's early stories, the narrator observes of the seacoast early in the morning that "the world just then was like the hollow of a great pink seashell." Or, in "A White Heron," as Sylvia is contemplating whether to reveal the bird's whereabouts to the ornithologist:

The murmur of the pine's green branches is in her ears, she remembers how the white heron came flying through the golden air and how they watched the sea and the morning together, and Sylvia cannot speak; she cannot tell the heron's secret and give its life away.

Phrases such as "came flying through the golden air" stand with the greatest achievements in the English language.

Cather dedicated one of her novels, O *Pioneers!* (1912), to her mentor. The dedication succinctly sums up Jewett's accomplishment. It reads:

To the memory of

SARAH ORNE JEWETT

in whose beautiful and delicate work

there is the perfection

that endures.

NOTES

[1] Richard Cary, ed., *Sarah Orne Jewett Letters*, rev. and enl. ed. (Waterville, Me.: Colby College Press, 1967), p. 120.

[2] "Willa Cather Talks of Work," *Philadelphia Record*, 9 August 1913, in *The Kingdom of Art: Willa Cather's First Principles and Critical Statements 1893-1896*, ed. Bernice Slote (Lincoln: University of Nebraska Press, 1966), p. 449.

[3] Annie Fields, ed., *Letters of Sarah Orne Jewett* (Boston: Houghton, Mifflin Co., 1911), p. 90.

[4] Sarah Orne Jewett, *Deephaven and Other Stories*, ed. Richard Cary (New Haven: College and University Press, 1966), p. 32.

[5] Fields, ed., *Letters*, p. 47. Jewett did, however, criticize the novel for its lack of structural integrity.

[6] Ibid., pp. 82-83.

[7] Ibid., p. 55.

[8] Cary, ed., *Letters*, p. 30.

[9] Sarah Orne Jewett, *A Country Doctor* (Boston: Houghton, Mifflin Co., 1884), p. 61.

[10] Carroll Smith-Rosenberg, "The Female World of Love and Ritual: Relations between Women in Nineteenth-Century America," *Signs* 1, no. 1 (Autumn 1975):1-29; Lillian Faderman, *Surpassing the Love of Men* (New York: Morrow, 1981), pp. 197-203; Josephine Donovan, "The Unpublished Love Poems of Sarah Orne Jewett," *Frontiers* 4, no. 3 (Fall 1979); rpt. in *Critical Essays on Sarah Orne Jewett*, ed. Gwen L. Nagel (Boston: G. K. Hall, 1984), pp. 107-17.

[11] Sarah Orne Jewett, *The Country of the Pointed Firs* (Boston: Houghton, Mifflin Co., 1896), p. 163.

[12] Cather's comments are found in her 1925 preface to the *Best Stories of Sarah Orne Jewett*, (Boston: Houghton, Mifflin Co., 1925), reprinted as *The Country of the Pointed Firs and Other Stories*, (New York: Doubleday Anchor, 1956), and in *Not under Forty* (New York: Knopf, 1936), p. 95.

MISS SYDNEY'S FLOWERS

However sensible it may have been considered by other people, it certainly was a disagreeable piece of news to Miss Sydney, that the city authorities had decided to open a new street from St. Mary Street to Jefferson. It seemed a most unwarrantable thing to her that they had a right to buy her property against her will. It was so provoking, that, after so much annoyance from the noise of St. Mary Street during the last dozen years, she must submit to having another public thoroughfare at the side of her house also. If it had only been at the other side, she would not have minded it particularly; for she rarely sat in her drawing-room, which was at the left of the hall. On the right was the library, stately, dismal, and apt to be musty in damp weather; and it would take many bright people, and a blazing wood-fire, and a great deal of sunshine, to make it pleasant. Behind this was the dining-room, which was really bright and sunny, and which opened by wide glass doors into a conservatory. The rattle and clatter of St. Mary Street was not at all troublesome here; and by little and little Miss Sydney had gathered her favorite possessions from other parts of the house, and taken one end of it for her sitting-room. The most comfortable chairs had found their way here, and a luxurious great sofa which had once been in the library, as well as the bookcase which held her favorite books.

The house had been built by Miss Sydney's grandfather, and in his day it had seemed nearly out of the city: now there was only one other house left near it; for one by one the quiet, aristocratic old street had seen its residences give place to shops and warehouses, and Miss Sydney herself had scornfully refused many offers of many thousand dollars for her home. It was so changed! It made her so sad to think of the dear old times, and to see the houses torn down, or the small-paned windows and old-fashioned front-doors replaced with French plate-glass to display better the wares which were to take the places of the quaint furniture and well-known faces of her friends! But Miss Sydney was an old woman, and her friends had diminished sadly. "It seems to me that my invitations are all for funerals in these days," said she to her venerable maid Hannah, who had helped her dress for her parties fifty years before. She had given up society little by little. Her friends had died, or she had allowed herself to drift away from them, while the acquaintances from whom she might have filled their places were only acquaintances still. She was the last of her own family, and, for years before her father died, he had lived mainly in his library, avoiding society and caring for nothing but books; and this, of course, was a check upon his daughter's enjoyment of visitors. Being left to herself, she finally became content with her own society, and since his death, which followed a long illness, she had refused all invitations; and with the exception of the interchange of occasional ceremonious calls with perhaps a dozen families, and her pretty constant attendance at church, you rarely were reminded of her existence. And I must tell the truth: it was not easy to be intimate with her. She was a good woman in a negative kind of way. One never heard of any thing wrong she had done; and if she chose to live alone, and have nothing to do with people, why, it was her own affair. You never seemed to know her any better after a long talk. She had a very fine, courteous way of receiving her guests,—a way of making you feel at your ease more than you imagined you should when with her,—and a stately kind of tact that avoided skilfully much mention of personalities on either side. But mere hospitality is not attractive, for it may be given grudgingly, or, as in her case, from mere habit; for Miss Sydney would never consciously be rude to any one in her own house—or out of it, for that matter. She very rarely came in contact with children; she was not a person likely to be chosen for a confidant by a young girl; she was so cold and reserved, the elder ladies said. She never asked a question about the winter fashions, except for her dressmaker, and she never met with reverses in housekeeping affairs, and these two facts rendered her unsympathetic to many. She was fond of reading, and enjoyed heartily the pleasant people she met in books. She appreciated their good qualities, their thoughtfulness, kindness, wit, or sentiment; but the thought never suggested itself to her mind that there were living people not far away, who could give her all this, and more.

If calling were not a regulation of society, if one only went to see the persons one really cared for, I am afraid Miss Sydney would soon have been quite forgotten. Her character would puzzle many people. She put no visible hindrance in your way; for I do not think she was consciously reserved and cold. She was thoroughly well-bred, rich, and in her way charitable; that is, she gave liberally to public subscriptions which came under her notice, and to church contributions. But she got on, somehow, without having friends; and, though the loss of one had always been a real grief, she learned without much trouble the way of living the lonely, comfortable, but very selfish life, and the way of being the woman I have tried to describe. There were occasional days when she was tired of herself, and life seemed an empty, formal, heartless discipline. Her wisest acquaintances pitied her loneliness; and busy, unselfish people wondered how she could be deaf to the teachings of her good clergyman, and blind to all the chances of usefulness and happiness which the world afforded her; and others still envied her, and wondered to whom she meant to leave all her money.

I began by telling you of the new street. It was suggested that it should bear the name of Sydney; but the authorities decided finally to compliment the country's chief magistrate, and call it Grant Place. Miss Sydney did not like the sound of it. Her family had always been indifferent to politics, and indeed the kite of the Sydneys had flown for many years high above the winds that affect commonplace people. The new way from Jefferson Street to St. Mary was a great convenience, and it seemed to our friend that all the noisiest vehicles in the city had a preference for going back and forth under her windows. You see she did not suspect, what afterward became so evident, that there was to be a way opened into her own heart also, and that she should confess one day, long after, that she might have died a selfish old woman, and not have left one sorry face behind her, if it had not been for the cutting of Grant Place.

The side of her conservatory was now close upon the sidewalk, and this certainly was not agreeable. She could not think of putting on her big gardening-apron, and going in to work among her dear plants any more, with all the world staring in at her as it went by. John the coachman, who had charge of the greenhouse, was at first very indignant; but, after he found that his flowers were noticed and admired, his anger was turned into an ardent desire to merit admiration, and he kept his finest plants next to the street. It was a good thing for the greenhouse, because it had never been so carefully tended; and plant after plant was forced into luxuriant foliage and blossom. He and Miss Sydney had planned at first to have close wire screens made to match those in the dining-room; but now, when she spoke of his hurrying the workmen, whom she supposed had long since been ordered to make them, John said, "Indeed, mum, it would be the ruin of the plants shutting out the light; and they would all be rusted with the showerings I gives them every day." And Miss Sydney smiled, and said no more.

The street was opened late in October, and, soon after, cold weather began in real earnest. Down in that business part of the city it was the strangest, sweetest surprise to come suddenly upon the long line of blooming plants and tall green lily-leaves under a roof festooned with roses and trailing vines. For the first two or three weeks, almost everybody stopped, if only for a moment. Few of Miss Sydney's own friends even had ever seen her greenhouse; for they were almost invariably received in the drawing-room. Gentlemen stopped the thought of business affairs, and went on down the street with a fresher, happier feeling. And the tired shop-girls lingered longest. Many a man and woman thought of some sick person to whom a little handful of the green leaves and bright blossoms, with their coolness and freshness, would bring so much happiness. And it was found, long months afterward, that a young man had been turned back from a plan of wicked mischief by the sight of a tall, green geranium, like one that bloomed in his mother's sitting-room way up in the country. He had not thought, for a long time before, of the dear old woman who supposed her son was turning his wits to good account in the city. But Miss Sydney did not know how much he wished for a bit to put in his buttonhole when she indignantly went back to the dining-room to wait until that impertinent fellow stopped staring in.

II

It was just about this time that Mrs. Marley made a change in her place of business. She had sold candy round the corner in Jefferson Street for a great many years; but she had suffered terribly from rheumatism all the winter before. She was nicely sheltered from too much sun in the summer; but the north winds of winter blew straight toward her; and after much deliberation, and many fears and questionings as to the propriety of such an act, she had decided to find another stand. You or I would think at first that it could make no possible difference where she sat in the street with her goods; but in fact one had regular customers in that business, as well as in the largest wholesale enterprise. There was some uncertainty whether these friends would follow her if she went away. Mrs. Marley's specialty was molasses-candy; and I am sure, if you ever chanced to eat any of it, you would look out for the old lady next time you went along the street. Times seemed very hard this winter. Not that trade had seriously diminished; but still the out-look was very dark. Mrs. Marley was old, and had been so for some years, so she was used to that; but somehow this fall she seemed to be growing very much older all of a sudden. She found herself very tired at night, and she was apt to lose her breath if she moved quickly; besides this, the rheumatism tortured her. She had saved only a few dollars, though she and her sister had had a comfortable living,—what they had considered comfortable, at least, though they sometimes had been hungry, and very often cold. They would surely go to the almshouse sooner or later,—she and her lame old sister Polly.

It was Polly who made the candy which Mrs. Marley sold. Their two little rooms were up three flights of stairs; and Polly, being too lame to go down herself, had not been out of doors in seven years. There was nothing but roofs and sky to be seen from the windows; and, as there was a manufactory near, the sky was apt to be darkened by its smoke. Some of the neighbors dried their clothes on the roofs, and Polly used to be very familiar with the apparel of the old residents, and exceedingly interested when a strange family came, and she saw something new. There was a little bright pink dress that the trig young French woman opposite used to hang out to dry; and somehow poor old Polly used always to be brightened and cheered by the sight of it. Once in a while she caught a glimpse of the child who wore it. She hardly ever thought now of the outside world when left to herself, and on the whole she was not discontented. Sister Becky used to have a great deal to tell her sometimes of an evening. When Mrs. Marley told her in the spring twilight that the grass in the square was growing green, and that she had heard a robin, it used to make Polly feel homesick; for she was apt to think much of her childhood, and she had been born in the country. She was very deaf, poor soul, and her world was a very forlorn one. It was nearly always quite silent, it was very small and smoky out of doors, and very dark and dismal within. Sometimes it was a hopeless world, because the candy burnt; and if there had not been her Bible and hymn-book, and a lame pigeon that lit on the window-sill to be fed every morning, Miss Polly would have found her time go heavily.

One night Mrs. Marley came into the room with a cheerful face, and said very loud, "Polly, I 've got some news!" Polly knew by her speaking so loud that she was in good-humor. When any thing discouraging had happened, Becky spoke low, and then was likely to be irritated when asked to repeat her remark.

"Dear heart!" said Mrs. Marley, "now I am glad you had something hot for supper. I was turning over in my mind what we could cook up, for I feel real hollow. It 's a kind of chilly day." And she sat down by the stove, while Polly hobbled to the table, with one hand to her ear to catch the first sound of the good news, and the other holding some baked potatoes in her apron. That hand was twisted with rheumatism, for the disease ran in the family. She was afraid every day that she should have to give up making the candy on the next; for it hurt so to use it. She was continually being harrowed by the idea of its becoming quite useless, and that the candy might not be so good; and then what would become of them? Becky Marley was often troubled by the same thought. Yet they were almost always good-natured, poor old women; and, though Polly Sharpe's pleasures and privileges were by far the fewest of anybody's I ever knew, I think she was as glad in those days to know the dandelions were in bloom as if she could see them; and she got more good from the fragments of the Sunday-morning sermon that sister Becky brought home than many a listener did from the whole service.

The potatoes were done to a turn, Mrs. Marley shouted; and then Polly sat down close by her to hear the news.

"You know I have been worrying about the cold weather a-coming, and my rheumatics; and I was afeared to change my stand, on account of losing custom. Well, to-day it all come over me to once that I might move down a piece on Grant Place,—that new street that's cut through to St. Mary. I've noticed for some time past that almost all my reg'lar customers turns down that way, so this morning I thought I'd step down that way too, and see if there was a chance. And after I gets into the street I sees people stopping and looking at something as they went along; and so I goes down to see; and it is one of them hothouses, full of plants a-growing like it was mid-summer. It belongs to the big Sydney house on the corner. There's a good place to sit right at the corner of it, and I'm going to move over there to-morrow. I thought as how I wouldn't leave Jefferson Street to-day, for it was too sudden. You see folks stops and looks at the plants, and there was n't any wind there to-day. There! I wish you could see them flowers."

Sister Polly was very pleased, and, after the potatoes and bread were eaten, she brought on an apple pie that had been sent up by Mrs. Welch, the washer-woman who lived on the floor next but one below. She was going away for three or four days, having been offered good pay to do some cleaning in a new house, and her board besides, near her work. So you see that evening was quite a jubilee.

The next day Mrs. Marley's wildest expectations were realized; for she was warm as toast the whole morning, and sold all her candy, and went home by two o'clock. That had never happened but once or twice before. "Why, I should n't wonder if we could lay up considerable this winter," said she to Polly.

Miss Sydney did not like the idea of the old candy-woman's being there. Children came to buy of her, and the street seemed noisier than ever at times. Perhaps she might have to leave the house, after all. But one may get used to almost any thing; and as the days went by she was surprised to find that she was not half so much annoyed as at first; and one afternoon she found herself standing at one of the dining-room windows, and watching the people go by. I do not think she had shown so much interest as this in the world at large for many years. I think it must have been from noticing the pleasure her flowers gave the people who stopped to look at them that she began to think herself selfish, and to be aware how completely indifferent she had grown to any claims the world might have upon her. And one morning, when she heard somebody say, "Why, it's like a glimpse into the tropics! Oh! I wish I could have such a conservatory!" she thought, "Here I have kept this all to myself for all these years, when so many others might have enjoyed it too!" But then the old feeling of independence came over her. The greenhouse was out of people's way; she surely could n't have let people in whom she did n't know; however, she was glad, now that the street was cut, that some one had more pleasure, if she had not. After all, it was a satisfaction to our friend; and from this time the seeds of kindness and charity and helpfulness began to show themselves above the ground in the almost empty garden of her heart. I will tell you how they grew and blossomed; and as strangers came to see her real flowers, and to look in at the conservatory windows from the cold city street, instead of winter to see a bit of imprisoned summer, so friend after friend came to find there was another garden in her own heart, and Miss Sydney learned the blessedness there is in loving and giving and helping.

For it is sure we never shall know what it is to lack friends, if we keep our hearts ready to receive them. If we are growing good and kind and helpful, those who wish for help and kindness will surely find us out. A tree covered with good fruit is never unnoticed in the fields. If we bear thorns and briers, we can't expect people to take very great pains to come and gather them. It is thought by many persons to be not only a bad plan, but an ill-bred thing, to give out to more than a few carefully selected friends. But it came to her more and more that there was great selfishness and short-sightedness in this. One naturally has a horror of dragging the secrets and treasures of one's heart and thought out to the light of day. One may be willing to go without the good that may come to one's own self through many friendships; but, after all, God does not teach us, and train our lives, only that we may come to something ourselves. He helps men most through other men's lives; and we must take from him, and give out again, all we can, wherever we can, remembering that the great God is always trying to be the friend of the least of us. The danger is, that we oftenest give out friendship selfishly; we do not think of our friends, but of ourselves. One never can find one's self beggared; love is a treasure that does not lessen, but grows, as we spend it.

The passers-by seemed so delighted with some new plants which she and John had arranged one day, that, as she was going out in the afternoon to drive, she stopped just as she was going to step into the carriage, and said she thought she would go round and look at the conservatory from the outside. So John turned the horses, and followed. It was a very cold day, and there were few people in the street. Every thing was so cheerless out of doors, and the flowers looked so summer-like! No wonder the people liked to stop, poor souls! For the richer, more comfortable ones lived farther up town. It was not in the shopping region; and, except the businessmen who went by morning and evening, almost every one was poor.

Miss Sydney had never known what the candy-woman sold before, for she could not see any thing but the top of her rusty black bonnet from the window. But now she saw that the candy was exactly like that she and her sister used to buy years upon years ago; and she stopped to speak to the old woman, and to buy some, to the utter amazement of her coachman. Mrs. Marley was excited by so grand a customer, and was a great while counting out the drumsticks, and wrapping them up. While Miss Sydney stood there, a thin, pitiful little girl came along, carrying a clumsy baby. They stopped, and the baby tried to reach down for a piece. The girl was quite as wistful; but she pulled him back and walked on to the flowers. "Oh! pitty, pitty!" said the baby, while the dirty little hands patted the glass delightedly.

"Move along there," said John gruffly; for it was his business to keep that glass clean and bright.

The girl looked round, frightened, and, seeing that the coachman was big and cross-looking, the forlorn little soul went away. "Baby want to walk? You 're so heavy!" said she in a fretful tired way. But the baby was half crying, and held her tight. He had meant to stay some time longer, and look at those pretty, bright things, since he could not have the candy.

Mrs. Marley felt as if her customer might think her stingy, and proceeded to explain that she could n't think of giving her candy away. "Bless you, ma'am, I would n't have a stick left by nine o'clock."

Miss Sydney "never gave money to street-beggars." But these children had not begged, and somehow she pitied them very much, they looked so hungry. And she called them back. There was a queer tone to her voice; and she nearly cried after she had given the package of candy to them, and thrown a dollar upon the board in front of Mrs. Marley, and found herself in the carriage, driving away. Had she been very silly? and what could John have thought? But the children were so glad; and the old candy-woman had said, "God bless you, mum!"

After this, Miss Sydney could not keep up her old interest in her own affairs. She felt restless and dissatisfied, and wondered how she could have done the same things over and over so contentedly for so many years. You may be sure, that, if Grant Place had been unthought of, she would have lived on in the same fashion to the end of her days. But after this she used to look out of the window; and she sat a great deal in the conservatory, when it was not too warm there, behind some tall callas. The servants found her usually standing in the dining-room; for she listened for footsteps, and was half-ashamed to have them notice that she had changed in the least. We are all given to foolish behavior of this kind once in a while. We are often restrained because we feel bound to conform to people's idea of us. We must be such persons as we imagine our friends think us to be. They believe that we have made up our minds about them, and are apt to show us only that behavior which they think we expect. They are afraid of us sometimes. They think we cannot sympathize with them. Our friend felt almost as if she were yielding to some sin in this strange interest in the passers-by. She had lived so monotonous a life, that any change could not have failed to be somewhat alarming. She told Bessie Thorne afterward, that one day she came upon that verse of Keble's Hymn for St. Matthew's Day. Do you remember it?—

"There are, in this loud, stunning tide
       Of human care and crime,
With whom the melodies abide
       Of the everlasting chime;
Who carry music in their heart
Through dusky lane and wrangling mart,
       Plying their daily task with busier feet
       Because their secret souls a holy strain repeat."

It seemed as if it were a message to herself, and she could not help going to the window a few minutes afterward. The faces were mostly tired-looking and dissatisfied. Some people looked very eager and hurried, but none very contented. It was the literal daily bread they thought of; and, when two fashionably-dressed ladies chanced to go by the window, their faces were strangely like their poorer neighbors in expression. Miss Sydney wondered what the love for one's neighbor could be; if she could ever feel it herself. She did not even like these people whom she watched, and yet every day, for years and years, she had acknowledged them for brothers and sisters when she said, "Our Father who art in heaven."

It seemed as if Miss Sydney, of all people, might have been independent and unfettered. It is so much harder for us who belong to a family for we are hindered by the thought of people's noticing our attempts at reform. It is like surrendering some opinion ignominiously which we have fought for. It is a kind of "giving in." But when she had acknowledged to herself that she had been in the wrong, that she was a selfish, thoughtless old woman, that she was alone, without friends, and it had been her own fault, she was puzzled to know how to do better. She could not begin to be very charitable all at once. The more she realized what her own character had become, the more hopeless and necessary seemed reform.

Such times as this come to many of us, both in knowing ourselves and our friends. An awakening, one might call it,—an opening of the blind eyes of our spiritual selves. And our ears are open to some of the voices which call us; while others might as well be silent, for all the heed we give them. We go on, from day to day, doing, with more or less faithfulness, that part of our work we have wit enough to comprehend; but one day suddenly we are shown a broader field, stretching out into the distance, and know that from this also we may bring in a harvest by and by, and with God's help.

Miss Sydney meant to be better,—not alone for the sake of having friends, not alone to quiet her conscience, but because she knew she had been so far from living a Christian life, and she was bitterly ashamed. This was all she needed, —all any of us need,—to know that we must be better men and women for God's sake; that we cannot be better without his help, and that his help may be had for the asking. But where should she begin? She had always treated her servants kindly, and they were the people she knew best. She would surely try to be more interested in the friends she met; but it was nearly Christmas time, and people rarely came to call. Every one was busy. Becky Marley's cheery face haunted her; and one day after having looked down from the window on the top of her bonnet, she remembered that she did not get any candy, after all, and she would go round to see the old lady again, she looked poor, and she would give her some money. Miss Sydney dressed herself for the street, and closed the door behind her very carefully, as if she were a mischievous child running away. It was very cold, and there were hardly a dozen persons to be seen in the streets, and Mrs. Marley had evidently been crying.

"I should like some of your candy," said our friend. "You know I did n't take any, after all, the other day." And then she felt very conscious and awkward, fearing that the candy-woman thought she wished to remind her of her generosity.

"Two of the large packages, if you please. But, dear me! are n't you very cold, sitting here in the wind?" and Miss Sydney shivered, in spite of her warm wrappings.

It was the look of sympathy that was answered first, for it was more comforting than even the prospect of money, sorely as Mrs. Marley needed that.

"Yes, mum, I 've had the rheumatics this winter awful. But the wind here!—why, it ain't nothing to what it blows round in Jefferson Street, where I used to sit. I should n't be out to-day, but I was called upon sudden to pay my molasses bill, when I 'd just paid my rent; and I don't know how ever I can. There 's sister Polly—she 's dead lame and deaf. I s'pose we 'll both be in the almshouse afore spring. I 'm an old woman to be earning a living out o' doors in winter weather."

There was no mistaking the fact that Miss Sydney was in earnest when she said, "I 'm so sorry! Can't I help you?"

Somehow she did not feel so awkward, and she enjoyed very much hearing this bit of confidence.

"But my trade had improved wonderful since I came here. People mostly stops to see them beautiful flowers; and then they sees me, and stops and buys something. Well, there 's some days when I gets down-hearted, and I just looks up there, and sees them flowers blooming so cheerful, and I says, 'There! this world ain't all cold and poor and old, like I be; and the Lord he ain't never tired of us, with our worrying about what he 's a-doing with us; and heaven 's a-coming before long anyhow!'" And the Widow Marley stopped to dry her eyes with the corner of her shawl.

Miss Sydney asked her to go round to the kitchen, and warm herself; and, on finding out more of her new acquaintance's difficulties, she sent her home happy, with money enough to pay the dreaded bill, and a basket of good things which furnished such a supper for herself and sister Polly as they had not seen for a long time. And their fortunes were bettered from that day. "If it had n't been for the flowers, I should ha' been freezing my old bones on Jefferson Street this minute, I s'pose," said the Widow Marley.

Miss Sydney went back to the dining-room after her *protégée* had gone, and felt a comfortable sense of satisfaction in what she had done. It had all come about in such an easy way too! A little later she went into the conservatory, and worked among her plants. She really felt so much younger and happier; and once, as she stood still, looking at some lilies-of-the-valley that John had been forcing into bloom, she did not notice that a young lady was looking through the window at her very earnestly.

III

That same evening Mrs. Thorne and Bessie were sitting up late in their library. It was snowing very fast, and had been since three o'clock; and no one had called. They had begun the evening by reading and writing, and now were ending it with a talk.

"Mamma," said Bessie, after there had been a pause, "whom do you suppose I have taken a fancy to? And do you know, I pity her so much!— Miss Sydney."

"But I don't know that she is so much to be pitied," said Mrs. Thorne, smiling at the enthusiastic tone. "She must have every thing she wants. She lives all alone, and has n't any intimate friends, but, if a person chooses such a life, why, what can we do? What made you think of her?"

"I have been trying to think of one real friend she has. Everybody is polite enough to her, and I never heard that any one disliked her; but she must be forlorn sometimes. I came through that new street by her house to-day: that's how I happened to think of her. Her greenhouse is perfectly beautiful, and I stopped to look in. I always supposed she was cold as ice (I 'm sure she looks so); but she was standing out in one corner, looking down at some flowers with just the sweetest face. Perhaps she is shy. She used to be very good-natured to me when I was a child, and used to go there with you. I don't think she knows me since I came home: at any rate, I mean to go to see her some day."

"I certainly would," said Mrs. Thorne. "She will be perfectly polite to you, at all events. And perhaps she may be lonely, though I rather doubt it; not that I wish to discourage you, my dear. I have n't seen her in a long time, for we have missed each other's calls. She never went into society much; but she used to be a very elegant woman, and is now, for that matter."

"I pity her," said Bessie persistently. "I think I should be very fond of her if she would let me. She looked so kind as she stood among the flowers to-day! I wonder what she was thinking about. Oh! do you think she would mind if I asked her to give me some flowers for the hospital?"

Bessie Thorne is a very dear girl. Miss Sydney must have been hard-hearted if she had received her coldly one afternoon a few days afterward, she seemed so refreshingly young and girlish a guest as she rose to meet the mistress of that solemn, old-fashioned drawing-room. Miss Sydney had had a re-action from the pleasure her charity had given her, and was feeling bewildered, unhappy, and old that day. "What can she wish to see me for, I wonder?" thought she, as she closed her book, and looked at Miss Thorne's card herself, to be sure the servant had read it right. But, when she saw the girl herself, her pleasure showed itself unmistakably in her face.

"Are you really glad to see me?" said Bessie in her frankest way, with a very gratified smile. "I was afraid you might think it was very odd in me to come. I used to like so much to call upon you with mamma when I was a little girl! And the other day I saw you in your conservatory, and I have wished to come and see you ever since."

"I am very glad to see you, my dear," said Miss Sydney, for the second time. "I have been quite forgotten by the young people of late years. I was sorry to miss Mrs. Thorne's call. Is she quite well? I meant to return it one day this week, and I thought only last night I would ask about you. You have been abroad, I think?"

Was not this an auspicious beginning? I cannot tell you all that happened that afternoon, for I have told so long a story already. But you will imagine it was the beginning of an intimacy that gave great pleasure, and did great good, to both the elder woman and the younger. It is hard to tell the pleasure which the love and friendship of a fresh, bright girl like Bessie Thorne, may give an older person. There is such a satisfaction in being convinced that one is still interesting and still lovable, though the years that are gone have each kept some gift or grace, and the possibilities of life seem to have been realized and decided. There are days of our old age when there seems so little left in life, that living is a mere formality. This busy world seems done with the old, however dear their memories of it, however strong their claims upon it. They are old: their life now is only waiting and resting. It may be quite right that we sometimes speak of second childhood, because we must be children before we are grown; and the life to come must find us, will find us, ready for service. Our old people have lived in the world so long; they think they know it so well: but the young man is master of the trade of living, and the old man only his blundering apprentice.

Miss Sydney's solemnest and most unprepared servant was startled to find Bessie Thorne and his mistress sitting cozily together before the dining-room fire. Bessie had a paper full of cut flowers to leave at the Children's Hospital on her way home. Miss Sydney had given liberally to the contribution for that object; but she never had suspected how interesting it was until Bessie told her, and she said she should like to go some day, and see the building and its occupants for herself. And the girl told her of other interests that were near her kind young heart,—not all charitable interests,—and they parted intimate friends.

"I never felt such a charming certainty of being agreeable," wrote Bessie that night to a friend of hers. "She seemed so interested in every thing, and, as I told you, so pleased with my coming to see her. I have promised to go there very often. She told me in the saddest way that she had been feeling so old and useless and friendless, and she was very confidential. Imagine her being confidential with me! She seemed to me just like myself as I was last year,—you remember,—just beginning to realize what life ought to be, and trying, in a frightened, blind kind of way, to be good and useful. She said she was just beginning to understand her selfishness. She told me I had done her ever so much good; and I couldn't help the tears coming into my eyes. I wished so much you were there, or some one who could help her more; but I suppose God knew when he sent me. Doesn't it seem strange that an old woman should talk to me in this way, and come to me for help? I am afraid people would laugh at the very idea. And only to think of her living on and on, year after year, and then being changed so! She kissed me when I came away, and I carried the flowers to the hospital. I shall always be fond of that conservatory, because, if I hadn't stopped to look in that day, I might never have thought of her.

"There was one strange thing happened, which I must tell you about, though it is so late. She has grown very much interested in an old candy-woman, and told me about her; and do you know that this evening uncle Jack came in, and asked if we knew of anybody who would do for janitress—at the Natural History rooms, I think he said. There is good pay, and she would just sell catalogues, and look after things a little. Of course the candy-woman may not be competent; but, from what Miss Sydney told me, I think she is just the person."

The next Sunday the minister read this extract from "Queen's Gardens" in his sermon. Two of his listeners never had half understood its meaning before as they did then. Bessie was in church, and Miss Sydney suddenly turned her head, and smiled at her young friend, to the great amazement of the people who sat in the pews near by. What *could* have come over Miss Sydney?

"The path of a good woman is strewn with flowers; but they rise *behind* her steps, not before them. 'Her feet have touched the meadow, and left the daisies rosy.' Flowers flourish in the garden of one who loves them. A pleasant magic it would be if you could flush flowers into brighter bloom by a kind look upon them; nay, more, if a look had the power not only to cheer but to guard them. This you would think a great thing? And do you think it not a greater thing that all this, and more than this, you can do for fairer flowers than these,—flowers that could bless you for having blessed them, and will love you for having loved them,—flowers that have eyes like yours, and thoughts like yours, and lives like yours?"

A BIT OF
SHORE LIFE

I often think of a boy with whom I made friends last summer, during some idle, pleasant days that I spent by the sea. I was almost always out of doors, and I used to watch the boats go out and come in; and I had a hearty liking for the good-natured fishermen, who were lazy and busy by turns, who waited for the wind to change, and waited for the tide to turn, and waited for the fish to bite, and were always ready to gossip about the weather, and the fish, and the wonderful events that had befallen them and their friends.

Georgie was the only boy of whom I ever saw much at the shore. The few young people there were all went to school through the hot summer days at a little weather-beaten schoolhouse a mile or two inland. There were few houses to be seen, at any rate, and Georgie's house was the only one so close to the water. He looked already nothing but a fisherman; his clothes were covered with an oil-skin suit, which had evidently been awkwardly cut down for him from one of his father's, of whom he was a curious little likeness. I could hardly believe that he was twelve years old, he was so stunted and small; yet he was a strong little fellow; his hands were horny and hard from handling the clumsy oars, and his face was so brown and dry from the hot sun and chilly spray, that he looked even older when one came close to him. The first time I saw him was one evening just at night-fall. I was sitting on the pebbles, and he came down from the fish-house with some lobster-nets, and a bucket with some pieces of fish in it for bait, and put them into the stern of one of the boats which lay just at the edge of the rising tide. He looked at the clouds over the sea, and at the open sky overhead, in an old, wise way, and then, as if satisfied with the weather, began to push off his boat. It dragged on the pebbles; it was a heavy thing, and he could not get it far enough out to be floated by the low waves, so I went down to help him. He looked amazed that a girl should have thought of it, and as if he wished to ask me what good I supposed I could do, though I was twice his size. But the boat grated and slid down toward the sand, and I gave her a last push as the boy perched with one knee on her gunwale and let the other foot drag in the water for a minute. He was afloat after all; and he took the oars, and pulled manfully out toward the moorings, where the whale-boats and a sail-boat or two were swaying about in the wind, which was rising a little since the sun had set. He did not say a word to me, or I to him. I watched him go out into the twilight,—such a little fellow, between those two great oars! But the boat could not drift or loiter with his steady stroke, and out he went, until I could only see the boat at last, lifting and sinking on the waves beyond the reef outside the moorings. I asked one of the fishermen whom I knew very well, "Who is that little fellow? Ought he to be out by himself, it is growing dark so fast?"

"Why, that's *Georgie!*" said my friend, with his grim smile. "Bless ye! he's like a duck; ye can't drown him. He won't be in until ten o'clock, like's not. He'll go way out to the far ledges when the tide covers them too deep where he is now. Lobsters he's after."

"Whose boy is he?" said I.

"Why, Andrer's, up here to the fish-house. *She's* dead, and him and the boy get along together somehow or 'nother. They 've both got something saved up, and Andrer's a clever fellow; took it very hard, losing of his wife. I was telling of him the other day: 'Andrer,' says I, 'ye ought to look up somebody or 'nother, and not live this way. There's plenty o' smart, stirring women that would mend ye up, and cook for ye, and do well by ye.'—'No,' says he; 'I've hed my wife, and I've lost her.'— 'Well, now,' says I, 'ye've shown respect, and there's the boy a-growin' up, and if either of you was took sick, why, here ye be.'—'Yes,' says he, 'here I be, sure enough;' and he drawed a long breath, 's if he felt bad; so that's all I said. But it's no way for a man to get along, and he ought to think of the boy. He owned a good house about a half mile up the road;

but he moved right down here after she died, and his cousin took it, and it burnt up in the winter. Four years ago that was. I was down to the Georges Banks."

Some other men came down toward the water, and took a boat that was waiting, already fitted out with a trawl coiled in two tubs, and some hand-lines and bait for rock-cod and haddock, and my friend joined them; they were going out for a night's fishing. I watched them hoist the little sprit-sail, and drift a little until they caught the wind, and then I looked again for Georgie, whose boat was like a black spot on the water.

I knew him better soon after that. I used to go out with him for lobsters, or to catch cunners, and it was strange that he never had any cronies, and would hardly speak to the other children. He was very shy; but he had put all his heart into his work,—a man's hard work, which he had taken from choice. His father was kind to him; but he had a sorry home, and no mother,—the brave, fearless, steady little soul!

He looked forward to going one day (I hope that day has already dawned) to see the shipyards at a large seaport some twenty miles away. His face lit up when he told me of it, as some other child's would who had been promised a day in fairy-land. And he confided to me that he thought he should go to the Banks that coming winter. "But it 's so cold!" said I: "should you really like it?"—"Cold!" said Georgie. "Ho! rest of the men never froze." That was it,—that "rest of the men;" and he would work until he dropped, or tend a line until his fingers froze, for the sake of that likeness,—the grave, slow little man, who has so much business with the sea, and who trusts himself with touching confidence to its treacherous keeping and favor.

Andrew West, Georgie's father, was almost as silent as his son at first, but it was not long before we were very good friends, and I went out with him at four o'clock one morning, to see him set his trawl. I remember there was a thin mist over the sea, and the air was almost chilly; but, as the sun came up, it changed the color of every thing to the most exquisite pink,—the smooth, slow waves, and the mist that blew over them as if it were a cloud that had fallen down out of the sky. The world just then was like the hollow of a great pink sea-shell; and we could only hear the noise of it, the dull sound of the waves among the outer ledges.

We had to drift about for an hour or two when the trawl was set; and after a while the fog shut down again gray and close, so we could not see either the sun or the shore. We were a little more than four miles out, and we had put out more than half a mile of lines. It is very interesting to see the different fish that come up on the hooks,—worthless sculpin and dog-fish, and good rock-cod and haddock, and curious stray creatures which often even the fishermen do not know. We had capital good luck that morning, and Georgie and Andrew and I were all pleased. I had a hand-line, and was fishing part of the time, and Georgie thought very well of me when he found I was not afraid of a big fish, and, besides that, I had taken the oars while he tended the sail, though there was hardly wind enough to make it worth his while. It was about eight o'clock when we came in, and there was a horse and wagon standing near the landing; and we saw a woman come out of Andrew's little house. "There 's your aunt Hannah a'ready," said he to Georgie; and presently she came down the pebbles to meet the boat, looking at me with much wonder as I jumped ashore.

"I sh'd think you might a' cleaned up your boat, Andrer, if you was going to take ladies out," said she graciously. And the fisherman rejoined, that perhaps she would have thought it looked better when it went out than it did then; he never had got a better fare o' fish unless the trawls had been set over night.

There certainly had been a good haul; and, when Andrew carefully put those I had caught with the hand-line by themselves, I asked his sister to take them, if she liked. "Bless you!" said she, much pleased, "we could n't eat one o' them big rock-cod in a week. I 'll take a little ha'dick, if Andrer 'll pick me one out."

She was a tall, large woman, who had a direct, business-like manner,—what the country people would call a master smart woman, or a regular driver,—and I liked her. She said something to her brother about some clothes she had been making for him or for Georgie, and I went off to the house where I was boarding for my breakfast. I was hungry enough, since I had had only a hurried lunch a good while before sunrise. I came back late in the morning, and found that Georgie's aunt was just going away. I think my friends must have spoken well of me, for she came out to meet me as I nodded in going by, and said, "I suppose ye drive about some? We live right 'mongst the woods; it ain't much of a place to ask anybody to." And she added that she might have done a good deal better for herself to have staid off. But there! they had the place, and she supposed she and Cynthy had done as well there as anywhere. Cynthy—well, she was n't one of your pushing kind; but I should have some flowers, and perhaps it would be a change for me. I thanked her, and said I should be delighted to go. Georgie and I would make her a call together some afternoon when he was n't busy; and Georgie actually smiled when I looked at him, and said, "All right," and then hurried off down the shore. "Ain't he an odd boy?" said Miss Hannah West, with a shadow of disapproval in her face. "But he 's just like his father and grandfather before him; you would n't think they had no gratitude nor feelin', but I s'pose they have. They used to say my father never 'd forgit a friend, or forgive an enemy. Well, I 'm much obliged to you, I 'm sure, for taking an interest in the boy." I said I liked him; I only wished I could do something for him. And then she said good-day, and drove off. I felt as if we were already good friends. "I 'm much obliged for the fish," she turned round to say to me again, as she went away.

One morning, not very long afterward, I asked Georgie if he could possibly leave his business that afternoon, and he gravely answered me that he could get away just as well as not, for the tide would not be right for lobsters until after supper.

"I should like to go up and see your aunt," said I. "You know she asked me to come the other day when she was here."

"I 'd like to go," said Georgie sedately. "Father was going up this week; but the mackerel struck in, and we could n't leave. But it 's better 'n six miles up there."

"That 's not far," said I. "I 'm going to have Captain Donnell's horse and wagon;" and Georgie looked much interested.

I wondered if he would wear his oil-skin suit; but I was much amazed, and my heart was touched, at seeing how hard he had tried to put himself in trim for the visit. He had on his best jacket and trousers (which might have been most boys' worst), and a clean calico shirt; and he had scrubbed his freckled, honest little face and his hard little hands, until they were as clean as possible; and either he or his father had cut his hair. I should think it had been done with a knife, and it looked as if a rat had gnawed it. He had such a holiday air! He really looked very well; but still, if I were to have a picture of Georgie, it should be in the oil-skin fishing-suit. He had gone out to his box, which was anchored a little way out in the cove, and had chosen two fine lobsters which he had tied together with a bit of fish-line. They were lazily moving their claws and feelers; and his father, who had come in with his boat not long before, added from his fare of fish three plump mackerel.

"They're always glad to get new fish," said he. "The girls can't abide a fish that's corned, and I have n't had a chance to send 'em up any mackerel before. Ye see, they live on a cross-road, and the fish-carts don't go by." And I told him I was very glad to carry them, or any thing else he would like to send. "Mind your manners, now, Georgie," said he, "and don't be forrard. You might split up some kindlin's for y'r aunts, and do whatever they want of ye. Boys ain't made just to look at, so ye be handy, will ye?" And Georgie nodded solemnly. They seemed very fond of each other, and I looked back some time afterward to see the fisherman still standing there to watch his boy. He was used to his being out at sea alone for hours; but this might be a great risk to let him go off inland to stay all the afternoon.

The road crossed the salt-marshes for the first mile, and, when we had struck the higher land, we soon entered the pine-woods, which cover a great part of that country. It had been raining in the morning for a little while; and the trunks of the trees were still damp, and the underbrush was shining wet, and sent out a sweet, fresh smell. I spoke of it, and Georgie told me that sometimes this fragrance blew far out to sea, and then you knew the wind was north-west.

"There's the big pine you sight Minister's Ledge by," said he, "when that comes in range over the white schoolhouse, about two miles out."

The lobsters were clashing their pegged claws together in the back of the wagon, and Georgie sometimes looked over at them to be sure they were all right. Of course I had given him the reins when we first started, and he was delighted because we saw some squirrels, and even a rabbit, which scurried across the road as if I had been a fiery dragon, and Georgie something worse.

We presently came in sight of a house close by the road,—an old-looking place, with a ledgy, forlorn field stretching out behind it toward some low woods. There were high white-birch poles holding up thick tangles of hop-vines, and at the side there were sunflowers straggling about as if they had come up from seed scattered by the wind. Some of them were close together, as if they were whispering to each other; and their big, yellow faces were all turned toward the front of the house, where people were already collected as if there were a funeral.

"It's the auction," said Georgie with great satisfaction. "I heard 'em talking about it down at the shore this morning. There's 'Lisha Downs now. He started off just before we did. That 's his fish-cart over by the well."

"What is going to be sold?" said I.

"All the stuff," said Georgie, as if he were much pleased. "She 's going off up to Boston with her son."

"I think we had better stop," said I, for I saw Mrs. 'Lisha Downs, who was one of my acquaintances at the shore, and I wished to see what was going on, besides giving Georgie a chance at the festivities. So we tied the horse, and went toward the house, and I found several people whom I knew a little. Mrs. Downs shook hands with me as formally as if we had not talked for some time as I went by her house to the shore, just after breakfast. She presented me to several of her friends with whom she had been talking as I came up. "Let me make you acquainted," she said; and every time I bowed she bowed too, unconsciously, and seemed a little ill at ease and embarrassed, but luckily the ceremony was soon over. "I thought I would stop for a few minutes," said I by way of apology. "I did n't know why the people were here until Georgie told me."

"She 's going to move up to Boston 'long of her son," said one of the women, who looked very pleasant and very tired. "I think myself it 's a bad plan to pull old folks up by the roots. There 's a niece o' hers that would have been glad to stop with her, and do for the old lady. But John, he 's very high-handed, and wants it his way, and he says his mother sha'n't live in no such a place as this. He makes a sight o' money. He 's got out a patent, and they say he 's just bought a new house that cost him eleven thousand dollars. But old Mis' Wallis, she 's wonted here; and she was telling of me yesterday she was only going to please John. He says he wants her up there, where she 'll be more comfortable, and see something."

"He means well," said another woman whom I did not know; "but folks about here never thought no great of his judgment. He 's put up some splendid stones in the burying-lot to his father and his sister Miranda that died. I used to go to school 'long of Miranda. *She 'd* have been pleased to go to Boston; she was that kind. But there! mother was saying last night, what if his business took a turn, and he lost every thing. Mother 's took it dreadfully to heart; she and Mis' Wallis was always mates as long ago as they can recollect."

It was evident that the old widow was both pitied and envied by her friends on account of her bettered fortunes, and they came up to speak to her with more or less seriousness, as befitted the occasion. She looked at me with great curiosity, but Mrs. Downs told her who I was, and I had a sudden instinct to say how sorry I was for her, but I was afraid it might appear intrusive on so short an acquaintance. She was a thin old soul who looked as if she had had a good deal of trouble in her day, and as if she had been very poor and very anxious. "Yes," said she to some one who had come from a distance, "it does come hard to go off. Home is home, and I seem to hate to sell off my things; but I suppose they *would* look queer up to Boston. John says I won't have no idea of the house until I see it;" and she looked proud and important for a minute, but, as some one brought an old chair out at the door, her face fell again. "Oh, dear!" said she, "I should like to keep that! it belonged to my mother. It 's most wore out anyway. I guess I 'll let somebody keep it for me;" and she hurried off despairingly to find her son, while we went into the house.

There is so little to interest the people who live on those quiet, secluded farms, that an event of this kind gives great pleasure. I know they have not done talking yet about the sale, of the bargains that were made, or the goods that brought more than they were worth. And then the women had the chance of going all about the house, and committing every detail of its furnishings to their tenacious memories. It is a curiosity one grows more and more willing to pardon, for there is so little to amuse them in every-day life. I wonder if any one had not often been struck, as I have, by the sadness and hopelessness which seems to overshadow many of the people who live on the lonely farms in the outskirts of small New England villages. It is most noticeable among the elderly women. Their talk is very cheerless, and they have a morbid interest in sicknesses and deaths; they tell each other long stories about such things; they are very forlorn; they dwell persistently upon any troubles which they have; and their petty disputes with each other have a tragic hold upon their thoughts, sometimes being handed down from one generation to the next. Is it because their world is so small, and life affords so little amusement and pleasure, and is at best such a dreary round of the dullest housekeeping? There is a lack of real merriment, and the fun is an odd, rough way of joking; it is a stupid, heavy sort of fun, though there is much of a certain quaint humor, and once in a while a flash of wit.

I came upon a short, stout old sister in one room, making all the effort she possibly could to see what was on the upper shelves of a closet. We were the only persons there, and she looked longingly at a convenient chair, and I know she wished I would go away. But my heart suddenly went out toward an old dark-green Delft bowl which I saw, and I asked her if she would be kind enough to let me take it, as if I thought she were there for the purpose. "I 'll bring you a chair," said I; and she said, "Certain, dear." And I helped her up, and I'm sure she had the good look she had coveted while I took the bowl to the window. It was badly cracked, and had been mended with putty; but the rich, dull color of it was exquisite. One often comes across a beautiful old stray bit of china in such a place as this, and I imagined it filled with apple-blossoms or wild roses. Mrs. Wallis wished to give it to me, she said it wasn't good for any thing; and, finding she did not care for it, I bought it; and now it is perched high in my room, with the cracks discreetly turned to the wall. "Seems to me she never had thrown away nothing," said my friend, whom I found still standing on the chair when I came back. "Here 's some pieces of a pitcher: I wonder when she broke it! I 've heard her say it was one her grandmother give her, though. The old lady bought it to a vandoo down at old Mis' Walton Peters's after she died, so Mis' Wallis said. I guess I 'll speak to her, and see if she wants every thing sold that 's here."

There was a very great pathos to me about this old home. It must have been a hard place to get a living in, both for men and women, with its wretched farming-land, and the house itself so cold and thin and worn out. I could understand that the son was in a hurry to get his mother away from it. I was sure that the boyhood he had spent there must have been uncomfortable, and that he did not look back to it with much pleasure. There is an immense contrast between even a moderately comfortable city house and such a place as this. No wonder that he remembered the bitter cold mornings, the frost and chill, and the dark, and the hard work, and wished his mother to leave them all behind, as he had done! He did not care for the few plain bits of furniture; why should he? and he had been away so long, that he had lost his interest in the neighbors. Perhaps this might come back to him again as he grew older; but now he moved about among them, in his handsome but somewhat flashy clothes, with a look that told me he felt conscious of his superior station in life. I did not altogether like his looks, though somebody said admiringly, as he went by, "They say he 's worth as much as thirty thousand dollars a'ready. He 's smart as a whip."

But, while I did not wonder at the son's wishing his mother to go away, I also did not wonder at her being unwilling to leave the dull little house where she had spent so much of her life. I was afraid no other house in the world would ever seem like home to her: she was a part of the old place; she had worn the doors smooth by the touch of her hands, and she had scrubbed the floors, and walked over them, until the knots stood up high in the pine boards. The old clock had been unscrewed from the wall, and stood on a table; and when I heard its loud and anxious tick, my first thought was one of pity for the poor thing, for fear it might be homesick, like its mistress. When I went out again, I was very sorry for old Mrs. Wallis; she looked so worried and excited, and as if this new turn of affairs in her life was too strange and unnatural; it bewildered her, and she could not understand it; she only knew every thing was going to be different.

Georgie was by himself, as usual, looking grave and intent. He had gone aloft on the wheel of a clumsy great ox-cart in which some of the men had come to the auction, and he was looking over people's heads, and seeing every thing that was sold. I saw he was not ready to come away, so I was not in a hurry. I heard Mrs. Wallis say to one of her friends, "You just go in and take that rug with the flowers on 't, and go and put it in your wagon. It 's right beside my chist that 's packed ready to go. John told me to give away any thing I had a mind to. He don't care nothing about the money. I hooked that rug four years ago; it 's most new; the red of the roses was made out of a dress of Miranda's. I kept it a good while after she died; but it was no use to let it lay. I 've given a good deal to my sister Stiles: she was over here helping me yesterday. There! it 's all come upon me so sudden! I s'pose I shall wish, after I get away, that I had done things different; but, after I knew the farm was goin' to be sold, I didn't seem to realize I was goin' to break up, until John came, day before yesterday."

She was very friendly with me, when I said I should think she would be sorry to go away; but she seemed glad to find I had been in Boston a great deal, and that I was not at all unhappy there. "But I suppose you have folks there," said she, "though I never supposed they was so sociable as they be here, and I ain't one that 's easy to make acquaintance. It 's different with young folks; and then in case o' sickness I should hate to have strange folks round me. It seems as if I never set so much by the old place as I do now I'm goin' away. I used to wish 'he' would sell, and move over to the Port, it was such hard work getting along when the child'n was small. And there 's one of my boys that run away to sea, and never was heard from. I 've always thought he might come back, though everybody give him up years ago. I can't help thinking what if he should come back, and find I wa'n't here! There! I 'm glad to please John: he sets everything by me, and I s'pose he thinks he's going to make a spry young woman of me. Well, it 's natural. Every thing looks fair to him, and he thinks he can have the world just as he wants it; but I know it 's a world o' change,—a world o'change and loss. And, you see, I shall have to go to a strange meetin' up there.—Why, Mis' Sands! I am pleased to see you. How did you get word?" And then Mrs. Wallis made another careful apology for moving away. She seemed to be so afraid some one would think she had not been satisfied with the neighborhood.

The auctioneer was a disagreeable-looking man, with a most un-pleasant voice, which gave me a sense of discomfort, the little old house and its surroundings seemed so grave and silent and lonely. It was like having all the noise and confusion on a Sunday. The house was so shut in by the trees, that the only outlook to the world beyond was a narrow gap in the pines, through which one could see the sea, bright, blue and warm with sunshine, that summer day.

There was something wistful about the place, as there must have been about the people who had lived there; yet hungry and unsatisfied as her life might have been in many ways, the poor old woman dreaded the change.

The thought flashed through my mind that we all have more or less of this same feeling about leaving this world for a better one. We have the certainty that we shall be a great deal happier in heaven; but we cling despairingly to the familiar things of this life. God pity the people who find it so hard to believe what he says, and who are afraid to die, and are afraid of the things they do not understand! I kept thinking over and over of what Mrs. Wallis had said: 'A world of change and loss!' What should we do if we did not have God's love to make up for it, and if we did not know something of heaven already?

It seemed very doleful that everybody should look on the dark side of the Widow Wallis's flitting, and I tried to suggest to her some of the pleasures and advantages of it, once when I had a chance. And indeed she was proud enough to be going away with her rich son; it was not like selling her goods because she was too poor to keep the old home any longer. I hoped the son would always be prosperous, and that the son's wife would always be kind, and not be ashamed of her, or think she was in the way. But I am afraid it may be a somewhat uneasy idleness, and that there will not be much beside her knitting-work to remind her of the old routine. She will even miss going back and forward from the old well in storm and sunshine; she will miss looking after the chickens, and her slow walks about the little place, or out to a neighbor's for a bit of gossip, with the old brown checked handkerchief over her head; and when the few homely, faithful old flowers come up next year by the doorstep, there will be nobody to care any thing about them.

I said good-by, and got into the wagon, and Georgie clambered in after me with a look of great importance, and we drove away. He was very talkative; the unusual excitement of the day was not without its effect. He had a good deal to tell me about the people I had seen, though I had to ask a good many questions.

"Who was the thin old fellow, with the black coat, faded yellow-green on the shoulders, who was talking to Skipper Downs about the dog-fish?"

"That 's old Cap'n Abiah Lane," said Georgie; "lives over toward Little Beach,—him that was cast away in the fog in a dory down to the Banks once; like to have starved to death before he got picked up. I 've heard him tell all about it. Don't look as if he 'd ever had enough to eat since!" said the boy grimly. "He used to come over a good deal last winter, and go out after cod 'long o' father and me. His boats all went adrift in the big storm in November, and he never heard nothing about 'em; guess they got stove against the rocks."

We had still more than three miles to drive over a lonely part of the road, where there was scarcely a house, and where the woods had been cut off more or less, so there was nothing to be seen but the uneven ground, which was not fit for even a pasture yet. But it was not without a beauty of its own; for the little hills and hollows were covered thick with brakes and ferns and bushes, and in the swamps the cat-tails and all the rushes were growing in stiff and stately ranks, so green and tall; while the birds flew up, or skimmed across them as we went by. It was like a town of birds, there were so many. It is strange how one is always coming upon families and neighborhoods of wild creatures in the unsettled country places; it is so much like one's going on longer journeys about the world, and finding town after town with its own interests, each so sufficient for itself.

We struck the edge of the farming-land again, after a while, and I saw three great pines that had been born to good luck in this world, since they had sprouted in good soil, and had been left to grow as fast as they pleased. They lifted their heads proudly against the blue sky, these rich trees, and I admired them as much as they could have expected. They must have been a landmark for many miles to the westward, for they grew on high land, and they could pity, from a distance, any number of their poor relations who were just able to keep body and soul together, and had grown up thin and hungry in crowded woods. But, though their lower branches might snap and crackle at a touch, their tops were brave and green, and they kept up appearances, at any rate; these poorer pines.

Georgie pointed out his aunts' house to me, after a while. It was not half so forlorn-looking as the others, for there were so many flowers in bloom about it of the gayest kind, and a little yellow-and-white dog came down the road to bark at us; but his manner was such that it seemed like an unusually cordial welcome rather than an indignant repulse. I noticed four jolly old apple-trees near by, which looked as if they might be the last of a once flourishing orchard. They were standing in a row, in exactly the same position, with their heads thrown gayly back, as if they were all dancing in an old-fashioned reel; and, after the forward and back, one might expect them to turn partners gallantly. I laughed aloud when I caught sight of them: there was something very funny in their looks, so jovial and whole-hearted, with a sober, cheerful pleasure, as if they gave their whole minds to it. It was like some old gentlemen and ladies who catch the spirit of the thing, and dance with the rest at a Christmas party.

Miss Hannah West first looked out of the window, and then came to meet us, looking as if she were glad to see us. Georgie had nothing whatever to say; but, after I had followed his aunt into the house, he began to work like a beaver at once, as if it were any thing but a friendly visit that could be given up to such trifles as conversation, or as if he were any thing but a boy. He brought the fish and lobsters into the outer kitchen, though I was afraid our loitering at the auction must have cost them their first freshness; and then he carried the axe to the wood-pile, and began to chop up the small white-pine sticks and brush which form the summer fire-wood at the farm-house,—crow-sticks and underbrush, a good deal of it,—but it makes a hot little blaze while it lasts.

I had not seen Miss Cynthia West, the younger sister, before, and I found the two women very unlike. Miss Hannah was evidently the capable business-member of the household, and she had a loud voice, and went about as if she were in a hurry. Poor Cynthia! I saw at first that she was one of the faded-looking country-women who have a hard time, and who, if they had grown up in the midst of a more luxurious way of living, would have been frail and delicate and refined, and entirely lady-like. But, as it was, she was somewhat in the shadow of her sister, and felt as if she were not of very much use or consequence in the world, I have no doubt. She showed me some pretty picture-frames she had made out of pine-cones and hemlock-cones and alder-burs; but her chief glory and pride was a silly little model of a house, in perforated card-board, which she had cut and worked after a pattern that came in a magazine. It must have cost her a great deal of work; but it partly satisfied her great longing for pretty things, and for the daintiness and art that she had an instinct toward, and never had known. It stood on the best-room table, with a few books, which I suppose she had read over and over again; and in the room, beside, were green paper curtains with a landscape on the outside, and some chairs ranged stiffly against the walls, some shells, and an ostrich's egg, with a ship drawn on it, on the mantel-shelf, and ever so many rugs on the floor, of most ambitious designs, which they had made in winter. I know the making of them had been a great pleasure to Miss Cynthia, and I was sure it was she who had taken care of the garden, and was always at much pains to get seeds and slips in the spring.

She told me how much they had wished that Georgie had come to live with them after his mother died. It would have been very handy for them to have him in winter too; but it was no use trying to get him away from his father; and neither of them were contented if they were out of sight of the sea. "He 's a dreadful odd boy, and so old for his years. Hannah, she says he 's older now than I be," and she blushed a little as she looked up at me; while for a moment the tears came into my eyes, as I thought of this poor, plain woman, who had such a capacity for enjoyment, and whose life had been so dull, and far apart from the pleasures and satisfactions which had made so much of my own life. It seemed to me as if I had had a great deal more than I deserved, while this poor soul was almost beggared. I seemed to know all about her life in a flash, and pitied her from the bottom of my heart. Yet I suppose she would not have changed places with me for any thing, or with anybody else, for that matter.

Miss Cynthia had a good deal to say about her mother, who had been a schoolmate of Mrs. Wallis's—I had been telling them what I could about the auction. She told me that she had died the spring before, and said how much they missed her; and Hannah broke in upon her regrets in her brusque, downright way: "I should have liked to kep' her if she 'd lived to be a hundred, but I don't wish her back. She 'd had considerable many strokes, and she could n't help herself much of any. She 'd got to be rising eighty, and her mind was a good deal broke," she added conclusively, after a short silence; while Cynthia looked sorrowfully out of the window, and we heard the sound of Georgie's axe at the other side of the house, and the wild, sweet whistle of a bird that flew overhead. I suppose one of the sisters was just as sorry as the other in reality.

"Now I want you and Georgie to stop and have some tea. I 'll get it good and early," said Hannah, starting suddenly from her chair, and beginning to bustle about again, after she had asked me about some people at home whom she knew. "Cynthy! Perhaps she 'd like to walk round out doors a spell. It 's breezing up, and it 'll be cooler than it is in the house.—No: you need n't think I shall be put out by your stopping; but you 'll have to take us just as we be. Georgie always calculates to stop when he comes up. I guess he 's made off for the woods. I see him go across the lot a few minutes ago."

So Cynthia put on a discouraged-looking gingham sun-bonnet, which drooped over her face, and gave her a more appealing look than ever, and we went over to the pine-woods, which were beautiful that day. She showed me a little water-fall made by a brook that came over a high ledge of rock covered with moss, and here and there tufts of fresh green ferns. It grew late in the afternoon, and it was pleasant there in the shade, with the noise of the brook and the wind in the pines, that sounded like the sea. The wood-thrushes began to sing,—and who could have better music?

Miss Cynthia told me that it always made her think of once when she was a little girl to hear the thrushes. She had run away, and fallen into the ma'sh; and her mother had sent her to bed quick as she got home, though it was only four o'clock. And she was so ashamed, because there was company there,—some of her father's folks from over to Eliot; and then she heard the thrushes begin to call after a while, and she thought they were talking about her, and they knew she had been whipped and sent to bed. "I 'd been gone all day since morning. I had a great way of straying off in the woods," said she. "I suppose mother was put to it when she see me coming in, all bog-mud, right before the company."

We came by my friends, the apple-trees, on our return, and I saw a row of old-fashioned square bee-hives near them, which I had not noticed before. Miss Cynthia told me that the bee money was always hers; but she lost a good many swarms on account of the woods being so near, and they had a trick of swarming Sundays, after she 'd gone to meeting; and, besides, the miller-bugs spoilt 'em; and some years they did n't make enough honey to live on, so she did n't get any at all. I saw some bits of black cloth fluttering over the little doors where the bees went in and out, and the sight touched me strangely. I did not know that the old custom still lingered of putting the hives in mourning, and telling the bees when there had been a death in the family, so they would not fly away. I said, half to myself, a line or two from Whittier's poem, which I always thought one of the loveliest in the world, and this seemed almost the realization of it. Miss Cynthia asked me wistfully, "Is that in a book?" I told her yes, and that she should have it next time I came up, or had a chance of sending it. "I 've seen a good many pieces of poetry that Mr. Whittier wrote," said she. "I 've got some that I cut out of the paper a good while ago. I think every thing of 'em."

"I put the black on the hives myself," said she. "It was for mother, you know. She did it when father died. But when my brother was lost, we did n't, because we never knew just when it was; the schooner was missing, and it was a good while before they give her up."

"I wish we had some neighbors in sight," said she once. "I 'd like to see a light when I look out after dark. Now, at my aunt's, over to Eliot, the house stands high, and when it 's coming dark you can see all the folks lighting up. It seems real sociable."

We lingered a little while under the apple-trees, and watched the wise little bees go and come; and Miss Cynthia told me how much Georgie was like his grandfather, who was so steady and quiet, and always right after his business. "He never was ugly to us, as I know of," said she; "but I was always sort of 'fraid of father. Hannah, she used to talk to him free 's she would to me; and he thought, 's long 's Hannah did any thing, it was all right. I always held by my mother the most; and when father was took sick,—that was in the winter,—I sent right off for Hannah to come home. I used to be scared to death, when he 'd want any thing done, for fear I should n't do it right. Mother, she 'd had a fall, and could n't get about very well. Hannah had good advantages. She went off keeping school when she was n't but seventeen, and she saved up some money, and boarded over to the Port after a while, and learned the tailoress trade. She was always called very smart,—you see she 's got ways different from me; and she was over to the Port several winters. She never said a word about it, but there was a young man over there that wanted to keep company with her. He was going out first mate of a new ship that was building. But, when she got word from me about father, she come right home, and that was the end of it. It seemed to be a pity. I used to think perhaps he 'd come and see her some time, between voyages, and that he 'd get to be cap'n, and they 'd go off and take me with 'em. I always wanted to see something of the world. I never have been but dreadful little ways from home. I used to wish I could keep school; and once my uncle was agent for his district, and he said I could have a chance; but the folks laughed to think o' me keeping school, and I never said any thing more about it. But you see it might 'a' led to something. I always wished I could go to Boston. I suppose you 've been there? There! I could n't live out o' sight o' the woods, I don't believe."

"I can understand that," said I, and half with a wish to show her I had some troubles, though I had so many pleasures that she did not, I told her that the woods I loved best had all been cut down the winter before. I had played under the great pines when I was a child, and I had spent many a long afternoon under them since. There never will be such trees for me any more in the world. I knew where the flowers grew under them, and where the ferns were greenest, and it was as much home to me as my own house. They grew on the side of a hill, and the sun always shone through the tops of the trees as it went down, while below it was all in shadow— and I had been there with so many dear friends who have died, or who are very far away. I told Miss Cynthia, what I never had told anybody else, that I loved those trees so much that I went over the hill on the frozen snow to see them one sunny winter afternoon, to say good-by, as if I were sure they could hear me, and looked back again and again, as I came away, to be sure I should remember how they looked. And it seemed as if they knew as well as I that it was the last time, and they were going to be cut down. It was a Sunday afternoon, and I was all alone, and the farewell was a reality and a sad thing to me. It was saying good-by to a great deal besides the pines themselves.

We stopped a while in the little garden, where Miss Cynthia gave me some magnificent big marigolds to put away for seed, and was much pleased because I was so delighted with her flowers. It was a gorgeous little garden to look at, with its red poppies, and blue larkspur, and yellow marigolds, and old-fashioned sweet, straying things,—all growing together in a tangle of which my friend seemed ashamed. She told me that it looked as ordered as could be, until the things begun to grow so fast she could n't do any thing with 'em. She was very proud of one little pink-and-white verbena which somebody had given her. It was not growing very well; but it had not disappointed her about blooming.

Georgie had come back from his ramble some time before. He had cracked the lobster which Miss Hannah had promptly put on to boil, and I saw the old gray cat having a capital lunch off the shells; while the horse looked meeker than ever, with his headstall thrown back on his shoulders, eating his supper of hay by the fence; for Miss Hannah was a hospitable soul. She was tramping about in the house, getting supper, and we went in to find the table already pulled out into the floor. So Miss Cynthia hastened to set it. I could see she was very much ashamed of having been gone so long. Neither of us knew it was so late. But Miss Hannah said it did n't make a mite o' difference, there was next to nothing to do, and looked at me with a little smile, which said, "You see how it is. I 'm the one who has faculty, and I favor her."

I was very hungry; and, though it was not yet six, it seemed a whole day since dinner-time. Miss Hannah made many apologies; and said, if I had only set a day, she would have had things as they ought to be. But it was a very good supper, and she knew it! She did n't know but I was tired o' lobsters. And when I had eaten two of the biscuit, and had begun an attack on the hot gingerbread, she said humbly that she did n't know when she had had such bad luck, though Georgie and I were both satisfied. He did not speak more than once or twice during the meal. I do not think he was afraid of me, for we had had many a lunch together when he had taken me out fishing; but this was an occasion, and there was at first the least possible restraint over all the company, though I 'm glad to say it soon vanished. We had two kinds of preserves, and some honey beside, and there was a pie with a pale, smooth crust, and three cuts in the top. It looked like a very good pie of its kind; but one can't eat every thing, though one does one's best. And we had big cups of tea; and, though Miss Hannah supposed I had never eaten with any thing but silver forks before, it happened luckily that I had, and we were very merry indeed. Miss Hannah told us several stories of the time she kept school, and gave us some reminiscences of her life at the Port; and Miss Cynthia looked at me as if she had heard them before, and wished to say, "I know she 's having a good time." I think Miss Cynthia felt, after we were out in the woods, as if I were her company, and she was responsible for me.

I thanked them heartily when I came away, for I had had such a pleasant time. Miss Cynthia picked me a huge nosegay of her flowers, and whispered that she hoped I would n't forget about lending her the book. Poor woman! she was so young,—only a girl yet, in spite of her having lived more than fifty years in that plain, dull home of hers, in spite of her faded face and her grayish hair. We came away in the rattling wagon. Georgie sat up in his place with a steady hand on the reins, and keeping a careful lookout ahead, as if he were steering a boat through a rough sea.

We passed the house where the auction had been, and it was all shut up. The cat sat on the doorstep waiting patiently, and I felt very sorry for her; but Georgie said there were neighbors not far off, and she was a master hand for squirrels. I was glad to get sight of the sea again, and to smell the first stray whiff of salt air that blew in to meet us as we crossed the marshes. I think the life in me must be next of kin to the life of the sea, for it is drawn toward it strangely, as a little drop of quicksilver grows uneasy just out of reach of a greater one.

"Good-night, Georgie!" said I; and he nodded his head a little as he drove away to take the horse home. "Much obliged to you for my ride," said he, and I knew in a minute that his father or one of the aunts had cautioned him not to forget to make his acknowledgments. He had told me on the way down that he had baited his nets all ready to set that evening. I knew he was in a hurry to go out, and it was not long before I saw his boat pushing off. It was after eight o'clock, and the moon was coming up pale and white out of the sea, while the west was still bright after the clear sunset.

I have a little model of a fishing dory that Georgie made for me, with its sprit-sail and killick and painter and oars and gaff all cleverly cut with the clumsiest of jack-knives. I care a great deal for the little boat; and I gave him a better knife before I came away, to remember me by; but I am afraid its shininess and trig shape may have seemed a trifle unmanly to him. His father's had been sharpened on the beach-stones to clean many a fish, and it was notched and dingy; but this would cut; there was no doubt about that. I hope Georgie was sorry when we said good-by. I 'm sure I was.

A solemn, careful, contented young life, with none of the playfulness or childishness that belong to it,—this is my little fisherman, whose memory already fades of whatever tenderness his dead mother may have given him. But he is lucky in this, that he has found his work and likes it; and so I say, 'May the sea prove kind to him! and may he find the Friend those other fishermen found, who were mending their nets on the shores of Galilee! and may he make the harbor of heaven by and by after a stormy voyage or a quiet one, whichever pleases God!'

AN AUTUMN
HOLIDAY

I had started early in the afternoon for a long walk;
it was just the weather for walking, and I went
across the fields with a delighted heart. The wind
came straight in from the sea, and the sky was
bright blue; there was a little tinge of red still lingering on the maples, and
my dress brushed over the late golden-rods, while my old dog, who
seemed to have taken a new lease of youth, jumped about wildly and raced
after the little birds that flew up out of the long brown grass—the constant
little chickadees, that would soon sing before the coming of snow. But this
day brought no thought of winter; it was one of the October days when to
breathe the air is like drinking wine, and every touch of the wind against
one's face is a caress: like a quick, sweet kiss, that wind is. You have a sense
of companionship; it is a day that loves you.

I went strolling along, with this dear idle day for company; it was a
pleasure to be alive, and to go through the dry grass, and to spring over the
stone walls and the shaky pasture fences. I stopped by each of the stray
apple-trees that came in my way, to make friends with it, or to ask after its
health, if it were an old friend. These old apple-trees make very charming
bits of the world in October; the leaves cling to them later than to the
other trees, and the turf keeps short and green underneath; and in this
grass, which was frosty in the morning, and has not quite dried yet, you
can find some cold little cider apples, with one side knurly, and one shiny

bright red or yellow cheek. They are wet with dew, these little apples, and a black ant runs anxiously over them when you turn them round and round to see where the best place is to bite. There will almost always be a bird's nest in the tree, and it is most likely to be a robin's nest. The prehistoric robins must have been cave dwellers, for they still make their nests as much like cellars as they can, though they follow the new fashion and build them aloft. One always has a thought of spring at the sight of a robin's nest. It is so little while ago that it was spring, and we were so glad to have the birds come back, and the life of the new year was just showing itself; we were looking forward to so much growth and to the realization and perfection of so many things. I think the sadness of autumn, or the pathos of it, is like that of elderly people. We have seen how the flowers looked when they bloomed and have eaten the fruit when it was ripe; the questions have had their answer, the days we waited for have come and gone. Everything has stopped growing. And so the children have grown to be men and women, their lives have been lived, the autumn has come. We have seen what our lives would be like when we were older; success or disappointment, it is all over at any rate. Yet it only makes one sad to think it is autumn with the flowers or with one's own life, when one forgets that always and always there will be the spring again.

I am very fond of walking between the roads. One grows so familiar with the highways themselves. But once leap the fence and there are a hundred roads that you can take, each with its own scenery and entertainment. Every walk of this kind proves itself a tour of exploration and discovery, and the fields of my own town, which I think I know so well, are always new fields. I find new ways to go, new sights to see, new friends among the things that grow, and new treasures and pleasures every summer; and later, when the frosts have come and the swamps have frozen, I can go everywhere I like all over my world.

That afternoon I found something I had never seen before—a little grave alone in a wide pasture which had once been a field. The nearest house was at least two miles away, but by hunting for it I found a very old cellar, where the child's home used to be, not very far off, along the slope. It must have been a great many years ago that the house had stood there; and the small slate head-stone was worn away by the rain and wind, so there was nothing to be read, if indeed there had been any letters on it. It had looked many a storm in the face, and many a red sunset. I suppose the woods near by had grown and been cut, and grown again, since it was put there. There was an old sweet-brier bush growing on the short little grave, and in the grass underneath I found a ground-sparrow's nest. It was like a little neighborhood, and I have felt ever since as if I belonged to it; and I wondered then if one of the young ground-sparrows was not always sent to take the nest when the old ones were done with it, so they came back in the spring year after year to live there, and there were always the stone and the sweet-brier bush and the birds to remember the child. It was such a lonely place in that wide field under the great sky, and yet it was so comfortable too; but the sight of the little grave at first touched me strangely, and I tried to picture to myself the procession that came out from the house the day of the funeral, and I thought of the mother in the evening after all the people had gone home, and how she missed the baby, and kept seeing the new grave out here in the twilight as she went about her work. I suppose the family moved away, and so all the rest were buried elsewhere.

I often think of this place, and I link it in my thoughts with something I saw once in the water when I was out at sea: a little boat that some child had lost, that had drifted down the river and out to sea; too long a voyage, for it was a sad little wreck, with even its white sail of a hand-breadth half under water, and its twine rigging trailing astern. It was a silly little boat, and no loss, except to its owner, to whom it had seemed as brave and proud a thing as any ship of the line to you and me. It was a ship-wreck of his small hopes, I suppose, and I can see it now, the toy of the great winds and waves, as it floated on its way, while I sailed on mine, out of sight of land.

The little grave is forgotten by everybody but me, I think: the mother must have found the child again in heaven a very long time ago: but in the winter I shall wonder if the snow has covered it well, and next year I shall go to see the sweet-brier bush when it is in bloom. God knows what use that life was, the grave is such a short one, and nobody knows whose little child it was; but perhaps a thousand people in the world to-day are better because it brought a little love into the world that was not there before.

I sat so long here in the sun that the dog, after running after all the birds, and even chasing crickets, and going through a great piece of affectation in barking before an empty woodchuck's hole to kill time, came to sit patiently in front of me, as if he wished to ask when I would go on. I had never been in this part of the pasture before. It was at one side of the way I usually took, so presently I went on to find a favorite track of mine, half a mile to the right, along the bank of a brook. There had been heavy rains the week before, and I found more water than usual running and the brook was apparently in a great hurry. It was very quiet along the shore of it; the frogs had long ago gone into winter-quarters, and there was not one to splash into the water when he saw me coming. I did not see a musk-rat either, though I knew where their holes were by the piles of fresh-water mussel shells that they had untidily thrown out at their front door. I thought it might be well to hunt for mussels myself, and crack them in search of pearls, but it was too serene and beautiful a day. I was not willing to disturb the comfort of even a shell-fish. It was one of the days when one does not think of being tired: the scent of the dry everlasting flowers, and the freshness of the wind, and the cawing of the crows, all come to me as I think of it, and I remember that I went a long way before I began to think of going home again. I knew I could not be far from a cross-road, and when I climbed a low hill I saw a house which I was glad to make the end of my walk—for a time, at any rate. It was some time since I had seen the old woman who lived there, and I liked her dearly, and was sure of a welcome. I went down through the pasture lane, and just then I saw my father drive away up the road, just too far for me to make him hear when I called. That seemed too bad at first, until I remembered that he would come back again over the same road after a while, and in the mean time I could make my call. The house was low and long and unpainted, with a great many frost-bitten flowers about it. Some hollyhocks were bowed down despairingly, and the morning-glory vines were more miserable still. Some of the smaller plants had been covered to keep them from freezing, and were braving out a few more days, but no shelter would avail them much longer. And already nobody minded whether the gate was shut or not, and part of the great flock of hens were marching proudly about among the wilted posies, which they had stretched their necks wistfully through the fence for all summer. I heard the noise of spinning in the house, and my dog scurried off after the cat as I went in the door. I saw Miss Polly Marsh and her sister, Mrs. Snow, stepping back and forward together spinning yarn at a pair of big wheels. The wheels made such a noise with their whir and creak, and my friends were talking so fast as they twisted and turned the yarn, that they did not hear my footstep, and I stood in the doorway watching them, it was such a quaint and pretty sight. They went together like a pair of horses, and kept step with each other to and fro. They were about the same size, and were cheerful old bodies, looking a good deal alike, with their checked handkerchiefs over their smooth gray hair, their dark gowns made short in the skirts, and their broad little feet in gray stockings and low leather shoes without heels. They stood straight, and though they were quick at their work they moved stiffly; they were talking busily about some one.

"I could tell by the way the doctor looked that he did n't think there was much of anything the matter with her," said Miss Polly Marsh. " 'You need n't tell me,' says I, the other day, when I see him at Miss Martin's. 'She 'd be up and about this minute if she only had a mite o' resolution;' and says he, 'Aunt Polly, you 're as near right as usual;' " and the old lady stopped to laugh a little. "I told him that wa'n't saying much," said she, with an evident consciousness of the underlying compliment and the doctor's good opinion. "I never knew one of that tribe that had n't a queer streak and was n't shif'less; but they 're tougher than ellum roots;" and she gave the wheel an emphatic turn, while Mrs. Snow reached for more rolls of wool, and happened to see me.

"Wherever did you come from?" said they, in great surprise. "Why, you was n't anywhere in sight when I was out speaking to the doctor," said Mrs. Snow. "Oh, come over horseback, I suppose. Well, now, we 're pleased to see ye."

"No," said I, "I walked across the fields. It was too pleasant to stay in the house, and I have n't had a long walk for some time before." I begged them not to stop spinning, but they insisted that they should not have turned the wheels a half-dozen times more, even if I had not come, and they pushed them back to the wall before they came to sit down to talk with me over their knitting—for neither of them were ever known to be idle. Mrs. Snow was only there for a visit; she was a widow, and lived during most of the year with her son; and Aunt Polly was at home but seldom herself, as she was a famous nurse, and was often in demand all through that part of the country. I had known her all my days. Everybody was fond of the good soul, and she had been one of the most useful women in the world. One of my pleasantest memories is of a long but not very painful illness one winter, when she came to take care of me. There was no end either to her stories or her kindness. I was delighted to find her at home that afternoon, and Mrs. Snow also.

Aunt Polly brought me some of her gingerbread, which she knew I liked, and a stout little pitcher of milk, and we sat there together for a while, gossiping and enjoying ourselves. I told all the village news that I could think of, and I was just tired enough to know it, and to be contented to sit still for a while in the comfortable three-cornered chair by the little front window. The October sunshine lay along the clean kitchen floor, and Aunt Polly darted from her chair occasionally to catch stray little wisps of wool which the breeze through the door blew along from the wheels. There was a gay string of red peppers hanging over the very high mantel shelf, and the wood-work in the room had never been painted, and had grown dark brown with age and smoke and scouring. The clock ticked solemnly, as if it were a judge giving the laws of time, and felt itself to be the only thing that did not waste it. There was a bouquet of asparagus and some late sprigs of larkspur and white petunias on the table underneath, and a Leavitt's Almanac lay on the county paper, which was itself lying on the big Bible, of which Aunt Polly made a point of reading once to come into the best room, but I like the old kitchen best. "Who was it that you were talking about as I came in?" said I. "You said you did n't believe there was much the matter with her." And Aunt Polly clicked her knitting-needles faster, and told me that it was Mary Susan Ash, over by Little Creek.

"They 're dreadful nervous, all them Ashes," said Mrs. Snow. "You know young Joe Adam's wife, over our way, is a sister to her, and she 's forever a-doctorin'. Poor fellow! *he 's* got a drag. I 'm real sorry for Joe; but, land sakes alive! he might 'a known better. They said she had an old green bandbox with a gingham cover, that was stowed full o' vials, that she moved with the rest of her things when she was married, besides some she car'd in her hands. I guess she ain't in no more hurry to go than any of the rest of us. I 've lost every mite of patience with her. I was over there last week one day, and she 'd had a call from the new supply—you know Adam's folks is Methodists—and he was took in by her. She made out she'd got the consumption, and she told how many complaints she had, and what a sight o' medicine she took, and she groaned and sighed, and her voice was so weak you could n't more than just hear it. I stepped right into the bedroom after he 'd been prayin' with her, and was taking leave. You 'd thought, by what he said, she was going right off then. She was coughing dreadful hard, and I knew she had n't no more cough than I had. So says I, 'What 's the matter, Adaline? I 'll get ye a drink of water. Something in your throat, I s'pose. I hope you won't go and get cold, and have a cough.' She looked as if she could 'a bit me, but I was just as pleasant 's could be. Land! to see her laying there, I suppose the poor young fellow thought she was all gone. He meant well. I wish he had seen her eating apple dumplings for dinner. She felt better 'long in the first o' the afternoon before he come. I says to her, right before him, that I guessed them dumplings did her good, but she never made no answer. She will have these dyin' spells. I don't know's she can help it, but she need n't act as if it was a credit to any body to be sick and laid up. Poor Joe, he come over for me last week another day, and said she'd been havin' spasms, and asked me if there wa' n't something I could think of. 'Yes,' says I; 'you just take a pail o' stone-cold water, and throw it square into her face; that'll bring her out of it;' and he looked at me a minute, and then he burst out a-laughing—he could n't help it. He 's too good to her; that 's the trouble."

"You never said that to her about the dumplings?" said Aunt Polly, admiringly. "Well, I should n't ha' dared;" and she rocked and knitted away faster than ever, while we all laughed. "Now with Mary Susan it 's different. I suppose she does have the neurology, and she 's a poor broken-down creature. I do feel for her more than I do for Adaline. She was always a willing girl, and she worked herself to death, and she can't help these notions, nor being an Ash neither."

"I'm the last one to be hard on anybody that's sick, and in trouble," said Mrs. Snow.

"Bless you, she set up with Ad'line herself three nights in one week, to my knowledge. It 's more 'n I would do," said Aunt Polly, as if there were danger that I should think Mrs. Snow's kind heart to be made of flint.

"It ain't what I call watching," said she, apologetically. "We both doze off, and then when the folks come in in the morning she'll tell what a sufferin' night she's had. She likes to have it said she has to have watchers."

"It 's strange what a queer streak there is running through the whole of 'em," said Aunt Polly, presently. "It always was so, far back 's you can follow 'em. Did you ever hear about that great-uncle of theirs that lived over to the other side o' Denby, over to what they call the Denby Meadows? We had a cousin o' my father's that kept house for him (he was a single man), and I spent most of a summer and fall with her once when I was growing up. She seemed to want company; it was a lonesome sort of a place."

"There! I don't know when I have thought o' that," said Mrs. Snow, looking much amused. "What stories did you use to tell, after you come home, about the way he used to act! Dear sakes! she used to keep us laughing till we was tired. Do tell her about him, Polly; she'll like to hear."

"Well, I 've forgot a good deal about it: you see it was much as fifty years ago. I was n't more than seventeen or eighteen years old. He was a very respectable man, old Mr. Dan'el Gunn was, and a cap'n in the militia in his day. Cap'n Gunn, they always called him. He was well off, but he got sun-struck, and never was just right in his mind afterward. When he was getting over his sickness after the stroke he was very wandering, and at last he seemed to get it into his head that he was his own sister Patience that died some five or six years before: she was single too, and she always lived with him. They said when he got so 's to sit up in his arm-chair of an afternoon, when he was getting better, he fought 'em dreadfully because they fetched him his own clothes to put on; he said they was brother Dan'el's clothes. So, sure enough, they got out an old double gown, and let him put it on, and he was as peacable as could be. The doctor told 'em to humor him, but they thought it was a fancy he took, and he would forget it; but the next day he made 'em get the double gown again, and a cap too, and there he used to set up alongside of his bed as prim as a dish. When he got round again so he could set up all day, they thought he wanted the dress; but no; he seemed to be himself, and had on his own clothes just as usual in the morning; but when he took his nap after dinner and waked up again, he was in a dreadful frame o' mind, and had the trousers and coat off in no time, and said he was Patience. He used to fuss with some knitting-work he got hold of somehow; he was good-natured as could be, and sometimes he would make 'em fetch the cat, because Patience used to have a cat that set in her lap while she knit. I was n't there then, you know, but they used to tell me about it. Folks used to call him Miss Dan'el Gunn.

"He 'd been that way some time when I went over. I 'd heard about his notions, and I was scared of him at first, but I found out there was n't no need. Don't you know I was sort o' 'fraid to go, 'Lizabeth, when Cousin Statiry sent for me after she went home from that visit she made here? She 'd told us about him, but sometimes, 'long at the first of it, he used to be cross. He never was after I went there. He was a clever, kind-hearted man, if ever there was one," said Aunt Polly, with decision. "He used to go down to the corner to the store sometimes in the morning, and he would see to business. And before he got feeble sometimes he would work out on the farm all the morning, stiddy as any of the men; but after he come in to dinner he would take off his coat if he had it on, and fall asleep in his arm-chair, or on a l'unge there was in his bedroom, and when he waked up he would be sort of bewildered for a while, and then he'd step round quick's he could, and get his dress out o' the clothes-press, and the cap, and put 'em on right over the rest of his clothes. He was always small-featured and smooth-shaved, and I don' know as, to come in sudden, you would have thought he was a man, except his hair stood up short and straight all on top of his head, as men-folks had a fashion o' combing their hair then, and I must say he did make a dreadful ordinary-looking woman. The neighbors got used to his ways, and, land! I never thought nothing of it after the first week or two.

"His sister's clothes that he wore first was too small for him, and so my cousin Statiry, that kep' his house, she made him a linsey-woolsey dress with a considerable short skirt, and he was dreadful pleased with it, she said, because the other one never would button over good, and showed his wais'coat, and she and I used to make him caps; he used to wear the kind all the old women did then, with a big crown, and close round the face. I've got some laid away up-stairs now that was my mother's—she wore caps very young, mother did. His nephew that lived with him carried on the farm, and managed the business, but he always treated the cap'n as if he was head of everything there. Everybody pitied the cap'n; folks respected him; but you couldn't help laughing, to save ye. We used to try to keep him in, afternoons, but we could n't always."

"Tell her about that day he went to meeting," said Mrs. Snow.

"Why, one of us always used to stay to home with him; we took turns; and somehow or 'nother he never offered to go, though by spells he would be constant to meeting in the morning. Why, bless you, you never'd think anything ailed him a good deal of the time, if you saw him before noon, though sometimes he would be freaky, and hide himself in the barn, or go over in the woods, but we always kept an eye on him. But this Sunday there was going to be a great occasion. Old Parson Croden was going to preach; he was thought more of than anybody in this region: you've heard tell of him a good many times, I s'pose. He was getting to be old, and did n't preach much. He had a colleague, they set so much by him in his parish, and I did n't know's I'd ever get another chance to hear him, so I did n't want to stay to home, and neither did Cousin Statiry; and

Jacob Gunn, old Mr. Gunn's nephew, he said it might be the last time ever he 'd hear Parson Croden, and he set in the seats anyway; so we talked it all over, and we got a young boy to come and set 'long of the cap'n till we got back. He had n't offered to go anywhere of an afternoon for a long time. I s'pose he thought women ought to be stayers at home according to Scripture.

"Parson Ridley—his wife was a niece to old Dr. Croden—and the old doctor they was up in the pulpit, and the choir was singing the first hymn—it was a fuguing tune, and they was doing their best: seems to me it was 'Canterbury New.' Yes, it was; I remember I thought how splendid it sounded, and Jacob Gunn he was a-leading off; and I happened to look down the aisle, and who should I see but the poor old cap'n in his cap and gown parading right into meeting before all the folks! There! I wanted to go through the floor. Everybody 'most had seen him at home, but, my goodness! to have him come into meeting!"

"What did you do?" said I.

"Why, nothing," said Miss Polly; "there was nothing to do. I thought I should faint away; but I called Cousin Statiry's 'tention, and she looked dreadful put to it for a minute; and then says she, 'Open the door for him; I guess he won't make no trouble,' and, poor soul, he did n't. But to see him come up the aisle! He'd fixed himself nice as he could, poor creature; he 'd raked out Miss Patience's old Navarino bonnet with green ribbons and a willow feather, and set it on right over his cap, and he had her bead bag on his arm, and her turkey-tail fan that he 'd got out of the best room; and he come with little short steps up to the pew; and I s'posed he 'd set by the door; but no, he made to go by us, up into the corner where she used to set, and took her place, and spread his dress out nice, and got his handkerchief out o' his bag, just 's he'd seen her do. He took off his bonnet all of a sudden, as if he'd forgot it, and put it under the seat, like he did his hat—that was the only thing he did that any woman would n't have done—and the crown of his cap was bent some. I thought die I should. The pew was one of them up aside the pulpit, a square one, you know, right at the end of the right-hand aisle, so I could see the length of it and out of the door, and there stood that poor boy we 'd left to keep the cap'n company, looking as pale as ashes. We found he 'd tried every way to keep the old gentleman at home, but he said he got ferce as could be, so he did n't dare to say no more, and Cap'n Gunn drove him back twice to the house, and that's why he got in so late. I did n't know but it was the boy that had set him on to go to meeting when I see him walk in, and I could 'a wrung his neck; but I guess I misjudged him; he was called a stiddy boy. He married a daughter of Ichabod Pinkham's over to Oak Plains, and I saw a son of his when I was taking care of Miss West last spring through that lung fever—looked like his father. I wish I 'd thought to tell him about that Sunday. I heard he was waiting on that pretty Becket girl, the orphan one that lives with Nathan Becket. Her father and mother was both lost at sea, but she 's got property."

"What did they say in church when the captain came in, Aunt Polly?" said I.

"Well, a good many of them laughed—they could n't help it, to save them; but the cap'n he was some hard o' hearin', so he never noticed it, and he set there in the corner and fanned him, as pleased and satisfied as could be. The singers they had the worst time, but they had just come to the end of a verse, and they played on the instruments a good while in between, but I could see 'em shake, and I s'pose the tune did stray a little, though they wen' through it well. And after the first fun of it was over, most of the folks felt bad. You see, the cap'n had been very much looked up to, and it was his misfortune, and he set there quiet, listening to the preaching. I see some tears in some o' the old folks' eyes; they hated to see him so broke in his mind, you know. There was more than usual of 'em out that day; they knew how bad he 'd feel if he realized it. A good Christian man he was, and dreadful precise, I 've heard 'em say."

"Did he ever go again?" said I.

"I seem to forget," said Aunt Polly. "I dare say. I was n't there but from the last of June into November, and when I went over again it was n't for three years, and the cap'n had been dead some time. His mind failed him more and more along at the last. But I'll tell you what he did do, and it was the week after that very Sunday, too. He heard it given out from the pulpit that the Female Missionary Society would meet with Mis' William Sands the Thursday night o' that week—the sewing society, you know; and he looked round to us real knowing; and Cousin Statiry, says she to me, under her bonnet, 'You don't s'pose he 'll want to go?' and I like to have laughed right out. But sure enough he did, and what do you suppose but he made us fix over a handsome black watered silk for him to wear, that had been his sister's best dress. He said he 'd outgrown it dreadful quick. Cousin Statiry she wished to heaven she 'd thought to put it away, for Jacob had given it to her, and she was meaning to make it over for herself; but it did n't do to cross the cap'n and Jacob Gunn gave Statiry another one—the best he could get, but it was n't near so good a piece, she thought. He set everything by Statiry, and so did the cap'n, and well they might.

"We hoped he'd forget all about it the next day; but he did n't; and I always thought well of those ladies, they treated him so handsome, and tried to make him enjoy himself. He did eat a great supper; they kep' a-piling up his plate with everything. I could n't help wondering if some of 'em would have put themselves out much if it had been some poor flighty old woman. The cap'n he was as polite as could be, and when Jacob come to walk home with him he kissed 'em all round and asked 'em to meet at his house. But the greatest was—land! I don't know when I've thought so much about those times—one afternoon he was setting at home in the keeping-room, and Statiry was there, and Deacon Abel Pinkham stopped in to see Jacob Gunn about building some fence, and he found he'd gone to mill, so he waited a while, talking friendly, as they expected Jacob might be home; and the cap'n was as pleased as could be, and he urged the deacon to stop to tea. And when he went away, says he to Statiry, in a dreadful knowing way, 'Which of us do you consider the deacon come to see?' You see, the deacon was a widower. Bless you! when I first come home I used to set everybody laughing, but I forget most of the things now. There was one day, though"—

"Here comes your father," said Mrs. Snow. "Now we must n't let him go by or you'll have to walk 'way home." And Aunt Polly hurried out to speak to him, while I took my great bunch of golden-rod, which already drooped a little, and followed her, with Mrs. Snow, who confided to me that the captain's nephew Jacob had offered to Polly that summer she was over there, and she never could see why she did n't have him: only love goes where it is sent and Polly was n't one to marry for what she could get if she did n't like the man. There was plenty that would have said yes, and thank you too, sir, to Jacob Gunn.

That was a pleasant afternoon. I reached home when it was growing dark and chilly, and the early autumn sunset had almost faded in the west. It was a much longer way home around the road than by the way I had come across the fields.

TOM'S HUSBAND

 **I** shall not dwell long upon the circumstances that led to the marriage of my hero and heroine; though their courtship was, to them, the only one that has ever noticeably approached the ideal, it had many aspects in which it was entirely commonplace in other people's eyes. While the world in general smiles at lovers with kindly approval and sympathy, it refuses to be aware of the unprecedented delight which is amazing to the lovers themselves.

But, as has been true in many other cases, when they were at last married, the most ideal of situations was found to have been changed to the most practical. Instead of having shared their original duties, and, as school-boys would say, going halves, they discovered that the cares of life had been doubled. This led to some distressing moments that instead of dwelling in heaven they were still upon earth, and had made themselves slaves to new laws and limitations. Instead of being freer and happier than ever before, they had assumed new responsibilities; they had established a new household, and must fulfill in some way or another the obligations of it. They looked back with affection to their engagement; they had been longing to have each other to themselves, apart from the world, but it seemed that they never felt so keenly that they were still units in modern society. Since Adam and Eve were in Paradise, before the devil joined them, nobody has had a chance to imitate that unlucky couple. In some respects they told the truth when, twenty times a day, they said that life had never been so pleasant before; but there were mental reservations on either side which might have subjected them to the accusation of lying. Somehow, there was a little feeling of disappointment, and they caught themselves wondering—though they would have died sooner than confess it—whether they were quite so happy as they had expected. The truth was, they were much happier than people usually are, for they had an uncommon capacity for enjoyment. For a little while they were like a sail-boat that is beating and has to drift a few minutes before it can catch the wind and start off on the other tack. And they had the same feeling, too, that any one is likely to have who has been long pursuing some object of his ambition or desire. Whether it is a coin, or a picture, or a stray volume of some old edition of Shakespeare, or whether it is an office under government or a lover, when fairly in one's grasp there is a loss of the eagerness that was felt in pursuit. Satisfaction, even after one has dined well, is not so interesting and eager a feeling as hunger.

My hero and heroine were reasonably well established to begin with: they each had some money, though Mr. Wilson had most. His father had at one time been a rich man, but with the decline, a few years before, of manufacturing interests, he had become, mostly through the fault of others, somewhat involved; and at the time of his death his affairs were in such a condition that it was still a question whether a very large sum or a moderately large one would represent his estate. Mrs. Wilson, Tom's step-mother, was somewhat of an invalid; she suffered severely at times with asthma, but she was almost entirely relieved by living in another part of the country. While her husband lived, she had accepted her illness as inevitable, and rarely left home; but during the last few years she had lived in Philadelphia with her own people, making short and wheezing visits only from time to time, and had not undergone a voluntary period of suffering since the occasion of Tom's marriage, which she had entirely approved. She had a sufficient property of her own, and she and Tom were independent of each other in that way. Her only other step-child was a daughter, who had married a navy officer, and had at this time gone out to spend three years (or less) with her husband, who had been ordered to Japan.

It is not unfrequently noticed that in many marriages one of the persons who choose each other as partners for life is said to have thrown himself or herself away, and the relatives and friends look on with dismal forebodings and ill-concealed submission. In this case it was the wife who might have done so much better, according to public opinion. She did not think so herself, luckily, either before marriage or afterward, and I do not think it occurred to her to picture to herself the sort of career which would have been her alternative. She had been an only child, and had usually taken her own way. Some one once said that it was a great pity that she had not been obliged to work for her living, for she had inherited a most uncommon business talent, and, without being disreputably keen at a bargain, her insight into the practical working of affairs was very clear and far-reaching. Her father, who had also been a manufacturer, like Tom's, had often said it had been a mistake that she was a girl instead of a boy. Such executive ability as hers is often wasted in the more contracted sphere of women, and is apt to be more a disadvantage than a help. She was too independent and self-reliant for a wife; it would seem at first thought that she needed a wife herself more than she did a husband. Most men like best the women whose natures cling and appeal to theirs for protection. But Tom Wilson, while he did not wish to be protected himself, liked these very qualities in his wife which would have displeased some other men; to tell the truth, he was very much in love with his wife just as she was. He was a successful collector of almost everything but money, and during a great part of his life he had been an invalid, and he had grown, as he laughingly confessed, very old-womanish. He had been badly lamed, when a boy, by being caught in some machinery in his father's mill, near which he was idling one afternoon, and though he had almost entirely outgrown the effect of his injury, it had not been until after many years. He had been in college, but his eyes had given out there, and he had been obliged to leave in the middle of his junior year, though he had kept up a pleasant intercourse with the members of his class, with whom he had been a great favorite. He was a good deal of an idler in the world. I do not think his ambition, except in the case of securing Mary Dunn for his wife, had ever been distinct; he seemed to make the most he could of each day as it came, without making all his days' works tend toward some grand result, and go toward the upbuilding of some grand plan and purpose. He consequently gave no promise of being either distinguished or great. When his eyes would allow, he was an indefatigable reader; and although he would have said that he read only for amusement, yet he amused himself with books that were well worth the time he spent over them.

The house where he lived nominally belonged to his step-mother, but she had taken for granted that Tom would bring his wife home to it, and assured him that it should be to all intents and purposes his. Tom was deeply attached to the old place, which was altogether the pleasantest in town. He had kept bachelor's hall there most of the time since his father's death, and he had taken great pleasure, before his marriage, in refitting it to some extent, though it was already comfortable and furnished in remarkably good taste. People said of him that if it had not been for his illnesses, and if he had been a poor boy, he probably would have made something of himself. As it was, he was not very well known by the townspeople, being somewhat reserved, and not taking much interest in their every-day subjects of conversation. Nobody liked him so well as they liked his wife, yet there was no reason why he should be disliked enough to have much said about him.

After our friends had been married for some time, and had outlived the first strangeness of the new order of things, and had done their duty to their neighbors with so much apparent willingness and generosity that even Tom himself was liked a great deal better than he ever had been before, they were sitting together one stormy evening in the library, before the fire. Mrs. Wilson had been reading Tom the letters which had come to him by the night's mail. There was a long one from his sister in Nagasaki, which had been written with a good deal of ill-disguised reproach. She complained of the smallness of the income of her share in her father's estate, and said that she had been assured by American friends that the smaller mills were starting up everywhere, and beginning to do well again. Since so much of their money was invested in the factory, she had been surprised and sorry to find by Tom's last letters that he had seemed to have no idea of putting in a proper person as superintendent, and going to work again. Four per cent. on her other property, which she had been told she must soon expect instead of eight, would make a great difference to her. A navy captain in a foreign port was obliged to entertain a great deal, and Tom must know that it cost them much more to live than it did him, and ought to think of their interests. She hoped he would talk over what was best to be done with their mother (who had been made executor, with Tom, of his father's will).

Tom laughed a little, but looked disturbed. His wife had said something to the same effect, and his mother had spoken once or twice in her letters of the prospect of starting the mill again. He was not a bit of a business man, and he did not feel certain, with the theories which he had arrived at of the state of the country, that it was safe yet to spend the money which would have to be spent in putting the mill in order. "They think that the minute it is going again we shall be making money hand over hand, just as father did when we were children," he said. "It is going to cost us no end of money before we can make anything. Before father died he meant to put in a good deal of new machinery, I remember. I don't know anything about the business myself, and I would have sold out long ago if I had had an offer that came anywhere near the value. The larger mills are the only ones that are good for anything now, and we should have to bring a crowd of French Canadians here; the day is past for the people who live in this part of the country to go into the factory again. Even the Irish all go West when they come into the country, and don't come to places like this any more."

"But there are a good many of the old work-people down in the village," said Mrs. Wilson. "Jack Towne asked me the other day if you were n't going to start up in the spring."

Tom moved uneasily in his chair. "I 'll put you in for superintendent, if you like," he said, half angrily, whereupon Mary threw the newspaper at him; but by the time he had thrown it back he was in good humor again.

"Do you know, Tom," she said, with amazing seriousness, "that I believe I should like nothing in the world so much as to be the head of a large business? I hate keeping house,—I always did; and I never did so much of it in all my life put together as I have since I have been married. I suppose it is n't womanly to say so, but if I could escape from the whole thing I believe I should be perfectly happy. If you get rich when the mill is going again, I shall beg for a housekeeper, and shirk everything. I give you fair warning. I don't believe I keep this house half so well as you did before I came here."

Tom's eyes twinkled. "I am going to have that glory,—I don't think you do, Polly; but you can't say that I have not been forbearing. I certainly have not told you more than twice how we used to have things cooked. I 'm not going to be your kitchen-colonel."

"Of course it seemed the proper thing to do," said his wife, meditatively; "but I think we should have been even happier than we have if I had been spared it. I have had some days of wretchedness that I shudder to think of. I never know what to have for breakfast; and I ought not to say it, but I don't mind the sight of dust. I look upon housekeeping as my life's great discipline;" and at this pathetic confession they both laughed heartily.

"I 've a great mind to take it off your hands," said Tom. "I always rather liked it, to tell the truth, and I ought to be a better housekeeper,—I have been at it for five years; though housekeeping for one is different from what it is for two, and one of them a woman. You see you have brought a different element into my family. Luckily, the servants are pretty well drilled. I do think you upset them a good deal at first!"

Mary Wilson smiled as if she only half heard what he was saying. She drummed with her foot on the floor and looked intently at the fire, and presently gave it a vigorous poking. "Well?" said Tom, after he had waited patiently as long as he could.

"Tom! I 'm going to propose something to you. I wish you would really do as you said, and take all the home affairs under your care, and let me start the mill. I am certain I could manage it. Of course I should get people who understood the thing to teach me. I believe I was made for it; I should like it above all things. And this is what I will do: I will bear the cost of starting it, myself,—I think I have money enough, or can get it; and if I have not put affairs in the right trim at the end of a year I will stop, and you may make some other arrangement. If I have, you and your mother and sister can pay me back."

"So I am going to be the wife, and you the husband," said Tom, a little indignantly; "at least, that is what people will say. It 's a regular Darby and Joan affair, and you think you can do more work in a day than I can do in three. Do you know that you must go to town to buy cotton? And do you know there are a thousand things about it that you don't know?"

"And never will?" said Mary, with perfect good humor. "Why, Tom, I can learn as well as you, and a good deal better, for I like business, and you don't. You forget that I was always father's right-hand man after I was a dozen years old, and that you have let me invest my money and some of your own, and I have n't made a blunder yet."

Tom thought that his wife had never looked so handsome or so happy. "I don't care, I should rather like the fun of knowing what people will say. It is a new departure, at any rate. Women think they can do everything better than men in these days, but I 'm the first man, apparently, who has wished he were a woman."

"Of course people will laugh," said Mary, "but they will say that it's just like me, and think I am fortunate to have married a man who will let me do as I choose. I don't see why it is n't sensible: you will be living exactly as you were before you married, as to home affairs; and since it was a good thing for you to know something about housekeeping then, I can't imagine why you should n't go on with it now, since it makes me miserable, and I am wasting a fine business talent while I do it. What do we care for people's talking about it?"

"It seems to me that it is something like women's smoking: it is n't wicked, but it is n't the custom of the country. And I don't like the idea of your going among business men. Of course I should be above going with you, and having people think I must be an idiot; they would say that you married a manufacturing interest, and I was thrown in. I can foresee that my pride is going to be humbled to the dust in every way," Tom declared in mournful tones, and began to shake with laughter. "It is one of your lovely castles in the air, dear Polly, but an old brick mill needs a better foundation than the clouds. No, I 'll look around, and get an honest, experienced man for agent. I suppose it's the best thing we can do, for the machinery ought not to lie still any longer; but I mean to sell the factory as soon as I can. I devoutly wish it would take fire, for the insurance would be the best price we are likely to get. That is a famous letter from Alice! I am afraid the captain has been growling over his pay, or they have been giving too many little dinners on board ship. If we were rid of the mill, you and I might go out there this winter. It would be capital fun."

Mary smiled again in an absent-minded way. Tom had an uneasy feeling that he had not heard the end of it yet, but nothing more was said for a day or two. When Mrs. Tom Wilson announced, with no apparent thought of being contradicted, that she had entirely made up her mind, and she meant to see those men who had been overseers of the different departments, who still lived in the village, and have the mill put in order at once, Tom looked disturbed, but made no opposition; and soon after breakfast his wife formally presented him with a handful of keys, and told him there was some lamb in the house for dinner; and presently he heard the wheels of her little phaeton rattling off down the road. I should be untruthful if I tried to persuade any one that he was not provoked; he thought she would at least have waited for his formal permission, and at first he meant to take another horse, and chase her, and bring her back in disgrace, and put a stop to the whole thing. But something assured him that she knew what she was about, and he determined to let her have her own way. If she failed, it might do no harm, and this was the only ungallant thought he gave her. He was sure that she would do nothing unladylike, or be unmindful of his dignity; and he believed it would be looked upon as one of her odd, independent freaks, which always had won respect in the end, however much they had been laughed at in the beginning. "Susan," said he, as that estimable person went by the door with the dust-pan, "you may tell Catherine to come to me for orders about the house, and you may do so yourself. I am going to take charge again, as I did before I was married. It is no trouble to me, and Mrs. Wilson dislikes it. Besides, she is going into business, and will have a great deal else to think of."

"Yes, sir; very well, sir," said Susan, who was suddenly moved to ask so many questions that she was utterly silent. But her master looked very happy; there was evidently no disapproval of his wife; and she went on up the stairs, and began to sweep them down, knocking the dust-brush about excitedly, as if she were trying to kill a descending colony of insects.

Tom went out to the stable and mounted his horse, which had been waiting for him to take his customary after-breakfast ride to the post-office, and he galloped down the road in quest of the phaeton. He saw Mary talking with Jack Towne, who had been an overseer and a valued workman of his father's. He was looking much surprised and pleased.

"I was n't caring so much about getting work, myself," he explained; "I 've got what will carry me and my wife through; but it 'll be better for the young folks about here to work near home. My nephews are wanting something to do; they were going to Lynn next week. I don't say but I should like to be to work in the old place again. I 've sort of missed it, since we shut down."

"I 'm sorry I was so long in overtaking you," said Tom, politely, to his wife. "Well, Jack, did Mrs. Wilson tell you she 's going to start the mill? You must give her all the help you can."

"'Deed I will," said Mr. Towne, gallantly, without a bit of astonishment.

"I don't know much about the business yet," said Mrs. Wilson, who had been a little overcome at Jack Towne's lingo of the different rooms and machinery, and who felt an overpowering sense of having a great deal before her in the next few weeks. "By the time the mill is ready, I will be ready, too," she said taking heart a little; and Tom, who was quick to understand her moods, could not help laughing, as he rode alongside. "We want a new barrel of flour, Tom, dear," she said, by way of punishment for his untimely mirth.

If she lost courage in the long delay, or was disheartened at the steady call for funds, she made no sign; and after a while the mill started up, and her cares were lightened, so that she told Tom that before next pay day she would like to go to Boston for a few days, and go to the theater, and have a frolic and a rest. She really looked pale and thin, and she said she never worked so hard in all her life; but nobody knew how happy she was, and she was so glad she had married Tom, for some men would have laughed at it.

"I laughed at it," said Tom, meekly. "All is, if I don't cry by and by, because I am a beggar, I shall be lucky." But Mary looked fearlessly serene, and said that there was no danger at present.

It would have been ridiculous to expect a dividend the first year, though the Nagasaki people were pacified with difficulty. All the business letters came to Tom's address, and everybody who was not directly concerned thought that he was the motive power of the reawakened enterprise. Sometimes business people came to the mill, and were amazed at having to confer with Mrs. Wilson, but they soon had to respect her talents and her success. She was helped by the old clerk, who had been promptly recalled and reinstated, and she certainly did capitally well. She was laughed at, as she had expected to be, and people said they should think Tom would be ashamed of himself; but it soon appeared that he was not to blame, and what reproach was offered was on the score of his wife's oddity. There was nothing about the mill that she did not understand before very long, and at the end of the second year she declared a small dividend with great pride and triumph. And she was congratulated on her success, and every one thought of her project in a different way from the way they had thought of it in the beginning. She had singularly good fortune: at the end of the third year she was making money for herself and her friends faster than most people were, and approving letters began to come from Nagasaki. The Ashtons had been ordered to stay in that region, and it was evident that they were continually being obliged to entertain more instead of less. Their children were growing fast, too, and constantly becoming more expensive. The captain and his wife had already begun to congratulate themselves secretly that their two sons would in all probability come into possession, one day, of their uncle Tom's handsome property.

For a good while Tom enjoyed life, and went on his quiet way serenely. He was anxious at first, for he thought that Mary was going to make ducks and drakes of his money and her own. And then he did not exactly like the looks of the thing, either; he feared that his wife was growing successful as a business person at the risk of losing her womanliness. But as time went on, and he found there was no fear of that, he accepted the situation philosophically. He gave up his collection of engravings, having become more interested in one of coins and medals, which took up most of his leisure time. He often went to the city in pursuit of such treasures, and gained much renown in certain quarters as a numismatologist of great skill and experience. But at last his house (which had almost kept itself, and had given him little to do beside ordering the dinners, while faithful old Catherine and her niece Susan were his aids) suddenly became a great care to him. Catherine, who had been the main stay of the family for many years, died after a short illness, and Susan must needs choose that time, of all others, for being married to one of the second hands in the mill. There followed a long and dismal season of experimenting, and for a time there was a procession of incapable creatures going in at one kitchen door and out of the other. His wife would not have liked to say so, but it seemed to her that Tom was growing fussy about the house affairs, and took more notice of those minor details than he used. She wished more than once, when she was tired, that he would not talk so much about the housekeeping; he seemed sometimes to have no other thought.

In the early days of Mrs. Wilson's business life, she had made it a rule to consult her husband on every subject of importance; but it had speedily proved to be a formality. Tom tried manfully to show a deep interest which he did not feel, and his wife gave up, little by little, telling him much about her affairs. She said that she liked to drop business when she came home in the evening; and at last she fell into the habit of taking a nap on the library sofa, while Tom, who could not use his eyes much by lamp-light, sat smoking or in utter idleness before the fire. When they were first married his wife had made it a rule that she should always read him the evening papers, and afterward they had always gone on with some book of history or philosophy, in which they were both interested. These evenings of their early married life had been charming to both of them, and from time to time one would say to the other that they ought to take up again the habit of reading together. Mary was so unaffectedly tired in the evening that Tom never liked to propose a walk; for, though he was not a man of peculiarly social nature, he had always been accustomed to pay an occasional evening visit to his neighbors in the village. And though he had little interest in the business world, and still less knowledge of it, after a while he wished that his wife would have more to say about what she was planning and doing, or how things were getting on. He thought that her chief aid, old Mr. Jackson, was far more in her thoughts than he. She was forever quoting Jackson's opinions. He did not like to find that she took it for granted that he was not interested in the welfare of his own property; it made him feel like a sort of pensioner and dependent, though, when they had guests at the house, which was by no means seldom, there was nothing in her manner that would imply that she thought herself in any way the head of the family. It was hard work to find fault with his wife in any way, though, to give him his due, he rarely tried.

But, this being a wholly unnatural state of things, the reader must expect to hear of its change at last, and the first blow from the enemy was dealt by an old woman, who lived near by, and who called to Tom one morning, as he was driving down to the village in a great hurry (to post a letter, which ordered his agent to secure a long-wished-for ancient copper coin, at any price), to ask him if they had made yeast that week, and if she could borrow a cupful, as her own had met with some misfortune. Tom was instantly in a rage, and he mentally condemned her to some undeserved fate, but told her aloud to go and see the cook. This slight delay, besides being killing to his dignity, caused him to lose the mail, and in the end his much-desired copper coin. It was a hard day for him, altogether; it was Wednesday, and the first days of the week having been stormy the washing was very late. And Mary came home to dinner provokingly good-natured. She had met an old school-mate and her husband driving home from the mountains, and had first taken them over her factory, to their great amusement and delight, and then had brought them home to dinner. Tom greeted them cordially, and manifested his usual graceful hospitality; but the minute he saw his wife alone he said in a plaintive tone to rebuke, "I should think you might have remembered that the servants are unusually busy to-day. I do wish you would take a little interest in things at home. The women have been washing, and I 'm sure I don't know what sort of a dinner we can give your friends. I wish you had thought to bring home some steak. I have been busy myself, and could n't go down to the village. I thought we would only have a lunch."

Mary was hungry, but she said nothing, except that it would be all right,—she did n't mind; and perhaps they could have some canned soup.

She often went to town to buy or look at cotton, or to see some improvement in machinery, and she brought home beautiful bits of furniture and new pictures for the house, and showed a touching thoughtfulness in remembering Tom's fancies; but somehow he had an uneasy suspicion that she could get along pretty well without him when it came to the deeper wishes and hopes of her life, and that her most important concerns were all matters in which he had no share. He seemed to himself to have merged his life in his wife's; he lost his interest in things outside the house and grounds; he felt himself fast growing rusty and behind the times, and to have somehow missed a good deal in life; he had a suspicion that he was a failure. One day the thought rushed over him that his had been almost exactly the experience of most women, and he wondered if it really was any more disappointing and ignominious to him than it was to women themselves. "Some of them may be contented with it," he said to himself, soberly. "People think women are designed for such careers by nature, but I don't know why I ever made such a fool of myself."

Having once seen his situation in life from such a stand-point, he felt it day by day to be more degrading, and he wondered what he should do about it; and once, drawn by a new, strange sympathy, he went to the little family burying-ground. It was one of the mild, dim days that come sometimes in early November, when the pale sunlight is like the pathetic smile of a sad face, and he sat for a long time on the limp, frost-bitten grass beside his mother's grave.

But when he went home in the twilight his step-mother, who just then was making them a little visit, mentioned that she had been looking through some boxes of hers that had been packed long before and stowed away in the garret. "Everything looks very nice up there," she said, in her wheezing voice (which, worse than usual that day, always made him nervous); and added, without any intentional slight to his feelings, "I do think you have always been a most excellent housekeeper."

"I 'm tired of such nonsense!" he exclaimed, with surprising indignation. "Mary, I wish you to arrange your affairs so that you can leave them for six months at least. I am going to spend this winter in Europe."

"Why, Tom, dear!" said his wife, appealingly. "I could n't leave my business any way in the"—

But she caught sight of a look on his usually placid countenance that was something more than decision, and refrained from saying anything more.

And three weeks from that day they sailed.

A WHITE HERON

The woods were already filled with shadows one June evening, just before eight o'clock, though a bright sunset still glimmered faintly among the trunks of the trees. A little girl was driving home her cow, a plodding, dilatory, provoking creature in her behavior, but a valued companion for all that. They were going away from the western light, and striking deep into the dark woods, but their feet were familiar with the path, and it was no matter whether their eyes could see it or not.

There was hardly a night the summer through when the old cow could be found waiting at the pasture bars; on the contrary, it was her greatest pleasure to hide herself away among the high huckleberry bushes, and though she wore a loud bell she had made the discovery that if one stood perfectly still it would not ring. So Sylvia had to hunt for her until she found her, and call Co'! Co'! with never an answering Moo, until her childish patience was quite spent. If the creature had not given good milk and plenty of it, the case would have seemed very different to her owners. Besides, Sylvia had all the time there was, and very little use to make of it. Sometimes in pleasant weather it was a consolation to look upon the cow's pranks as an intelligent attempt to play hide and seek, and as the child had no playmates she lent herself to this amusement with a good deal of zest. Though this chase had been so long that the wary animal herself had given an unusual signal of her whereabouts, Sylvia had only laughed when she came upon Mistress Moolly at the swamp-side, and urged her affectionately homeward with a twig of birch leaves. The old cow was not inclined to wander farther, she even turned in the right direction for once as they left the pasture, and stepped along the road at a good pace. She was quite ready to be milked now, and seldom stopped to browse.

Sylvia wondered what her grandmother would say because they were so late. It was a great while since she had left home at half-past five o'clock, but everybody knew the difficulty of making this errand a short one. Mrs. Tilley had chased the horned torment too many summer evenings herself to blame any one else for lingering, and was only thankful as she waited that she had Sylvia, nowadays, to give such valuable assistance. The good woman suspected that Sylvia loitered occasionally on her own account; there never was such a child for straying about out-of-doors since the world was made! Everybody said that it was a good change for a little maid who had tried to grow for eight years in a crowded manufacturing town, but, as for Sylvia herself, it seemed as if she never had been alive at all before she came to live at the farm. She thought often with wistful compassion of a wretched dry geranium that belonged to a town neighbor.

"'Afraid of folks,'" old Mrs. Tilley said to herself, with a smile, after she had made the unlikely choice of Syvia from her daugher's houseful of children, and was returning to the farm. "'Afraid of folks,' they said! I guess she won't be troubled no great with 'em up to the old place!" When they reached the door of the lonely house and stopped to unlock it, and the cat came to purr loudly, and rub against them, a deserted pussy, indeed, but fat with young robins, Sylvia whispered that this was a beautiful place to live in, and she never should wish to go home.

The companions followed the shady wood-road, the cow taking slow steps, and the child very fast ones. The cow stopped long at the brook to drink, as if the pasture were not half a swamp, and Sylvia stood still and waited, letting her bare feet cool themselves in the shoal water, while the great twilight moths struck softly against her. She waded on through the brook as the cow moved away, and listened to the thrushes with a heart that beat fast with pleasure. There was a stirring in the great boughs overhead. They were full of little birds and beasts that seemed to be wide awake, and going about their world, or else saying good-night to each other in sleepy twitters. Sylvia herself felt sleepy as she walked along.

However, it was not much farther to the house, and the air was soft and sweet. She was not often in the woods so late as this, and it made her feel as if she were a part of the gray shadows and the moving leaves. She was just thinking how long it seemed since she first came to the farm a year ago, and wondering if everything went on in the noisy town just the same as when she was there; the thought of the great red-faced boy who used to chase and frighten her made her hurry along the path to escape from the shadow of the trees.

Suddenly this little woods-girl is horror-stricken to hear a clear whistle not very far away. Not a bird's-whistle, which would have a sort of friendliness, but a boy's whistle, determined, and somewhat aggressive. Sylvia left the cow to whatever sad fate might await her, and stepped discreetly aside into the bushes, but she was just too late. The enemy had discovered her, and called out in a very cheerful and persuasive tone, "Halloa, little girl, how far is it to the road?" and trembling Sylvia answered almost inaudibly, "A good ways."

She did not dare to look boldly at the tall young man, who carried a gun over his shoulder, but she came out of her bush and again followed the cow, while he walked alongside.

"I have been hunting for some birds," the stranger said kindly, "and I have lost my way, and need a friend very much. Don't be afraid," he added gallantly. "Speak up and tell me what your name is, and whether you think I can spend the night at your house, and go out gunning early in the morning."

Sylvia was more alarmed than before. Would not her grandmother consider her much to blame? But who could have foreseen such an accident as this? It did not seem to be her fault, and she hung her head as if the stem of it were broken, but managed to answer "Sylvy," with much effort when her companion again asked her name.

Mrs. Tilley was standing in the doorway when the trio came into view. The cow gave a loud moo by way of explanation.

"Yes, you 'd better speak up for yourself, you old trial! Where 'd she tucked herself away this time, Sylvy?" But Sylvia kept an awed silence; she knew by instinct that her grandmother did not comprehend the gravity of the situation. She must be mistaking the stranger for one of the farmer-lads of the region.

The young man stood his gun beside the door, and dropped a lumpy game-bag beside it; then he bade Mrs. Tilley good-evening, and repeated his wayfarer's story, and asked if he could have a night's lodging.

"Put me anywhere you like," he said. "I must be off early in the morning, before day; but I am very hungry, indeed. You can give me some milk at any rate, that 's plain."

"Dear sakes, yes," responded the hostess, whose long slumbering hospitality seemed to be easily awakened. "You might fare better if you went out on the main road a mile or so, but you 're welcome to what we 've got. I 'll milk right off, and you make yourself at home. You can sleep on husks or feathers," she proffered graciously. "I raised them all myself. There 's good pasturing for geese just below here towards the ma'sh. Now step round and set a plate for the gentleman, Sylvy!" And Sylvia promptly stepped. She was glad to have something to do, and she was hungry herself.

It was a surprise to find so clean and comfortable a little dwelling in this New England wilderness. The young man had known the horrors of its most primitive housekeeping, and the dreary squalor of that level of society which does not rebel at the companionship of hens. This was the best thrift of an old-fashioned farmstead, though on such a small scale that it seemed like a hermitage. He listened eagerly to the old woman's quaint talk, he watched Sylvia's pale face and shining gray eyes with ever growing enthusiasm, and insisted that this was the best supper he had eaten for a month; and afterward the new-made friends sat down in the door-way together while the moon came up.

Soon it would be berry-time, and Sylvia was a great help at picking. The cow was a good milker, though a plaguy thing to keep track of, the hostess gossiped frankly, adding presently that she had buried four children, so Sylvia's mother, and a son (who might be dead) in California were all the children she had left. "Dan, my boy, was a great hand to go gunning," she explained sadly. "I never wanted for pa'tridges or gray squer'ls while he was to home. He 's been a great wand'rer, I expect, and he 's no hand to write letters. There, I don't blame him, I 'd ha' seen the world myself if it had been so I could."

"Sylvy takes after him," the grandmother continued affectionately, after a minute's pause. "There ain't a foot o' ground she don't know her way over, and the wild creaturs counts her one o' themselves. Squer'ls she 'll tame to come an' feed right out o' her hands, and all sorts o' birds. Last winter she got the jay birds to bangeing here, and I believe she 'd 'a' scanted herself of her own meals to have plenty to throw out amongst 'em, if I had n't kep' watch. Anything but crows, I tell her, I 'm willin' to help support—though Dan he had a tamed one o' them that did seem to have reason same as folks. It was round here a good spell after he went away. Dan an' his father they did n't hitch,—but he never held up his head ag'in after Dan had dared him an' gone off.''

The guest did not notice this hint of family sorrows in his eager interest in something else.

"So Sylvy knows all about birds, does she?" he exclaimed, as he looked round at the little girl who sat, very demure but increasingly sleepy, in the moonlight. "I am making a collection of birds myself. I have been at it ever since I was a boy." (Mrs. Tilley smiled.) "There are two or three very rare ones I have been hunting for these five years. I mean to get them on my own ground it they can be found."

"Do you cage 'em up?" asked Mrs. Tilley doubtfully, in response to this enthusiastic announcement.

"Oh, no, they 're stuffed and preserved, dozens and dozens of them," said the ornithologist, "and I have shot or snared every one myself. I caught a glimpse of a white heron three miles from here on Saturday, and I have followed it in this direction. They have never been found in this district at all. The little white heron, it is," and he turned again to look at Sylvia with the hope of discovering that the rare bird was one of her acquaintances.

But Sylvia was watching a hop-toad in the narrow footpath.

"You would know the heron if you saw it," the stranger continued eagerly. "A queer tall white bird with soft feathers and long thin legs. And it would have a nest perhaps in the top of a high tree, made of sticks, something like a hawk's nest."

Sylvia's heart gave a wild beat; she knew that strange white bird, and had once stolen softly near where it stood in some bright green swamp grass, away over at the other side of the woods. There was an open place where the sunshine always seemed strangely yellow and hot, where tall, nodding rushes grew, and her grandmother had warned her that she might sink in the soft black mud underneath and never be heard of more. Not far beyond were the salt marshes just this side the sea itself, which Sylvia wondered and dreamed about, but never had seen, whose great voice could sometimes be heard above the noise of the woods on stormy nights.

"I can't think of anything I should like so much as to find that heron's nest," the handsome stranger was saying. "I would give ten dollars to anybody who could show it to me," he added desperately, "and I mean to spend my whole vacation hunting for it if need be. Perhaps it was only migrating, or had been chased out of its own region by some bird of prey."

Mrs. Tilley gave amazed attention to all this, but Sylvia still watched the toad, not divining, as she might have done at some calmer time, that the creature wished to get to its hole under the door-step, and was much hindered by the unusual spectators at that hour of the evening. No amount of thought, that night, could decide how many wished-for treasures the ten dollars, so lightly spoken of, would buy.

The next day the young sportsman hovered about the woods, and Sylvia kept him company, having lost her first fear of the friendly lad, who proved to be most kind and sympathetic. He told her many things about the birds and what they knew and where they lived and what they did with themselves. And he gave her a jack-knife, which she thought as great a treasure as if she were a desert-islander. All day long he did not once make her troubled or afraid except when he brought down some unsuspecting singing creature from its bough. Sylvia would have liked him vastly better without his gun; she could not understand why he killed the very birds he seemed to like so much. But as the day waned, Sylvia still watched the young man with loving admiration. She had never seen anybody so charming and delightful; the woman's heart, asleep in the child, was vaguely thrilled by a dream of love. Some premonition of that great power stirred and swayed these young creatures who traversed the solemn woodlands with soft-footed silent care. They stopped to listen to a bird's song; they pressed forward again eagerly, parting the branches—speaking to each other rarely and in whispers; the young man going first and Sylvia following, fascinated, a few steps behind, with her gray eyes dark with excitement.

She grieved because the longed-for white heron was elusive, but she did not lead the guest, she only followed, and there was no such thing as speaking first. The sound of her own unquestioned voice would have terrified her—it was hard enough to answer yes or no when there was need of that. At last evening began to fall, and they drove the cow together, and Sylvia smiled with pleasure when they came to the place where she heard the whistle and was afraid only the night before.

II

Half a mile from home, at the farther edge of the woods, where the land was highest, a great pine-tree stood, the last of its generation. Whether it was left for a boundary mark, or for what reason, no one could say; the woodchoppers who had felled its mates were dead and gone long ago, and a whole forest of sturdy trees, pines and oaks and maples, had grown again. But the stately head of this old pine towered above them all and made a landmark for sea and shore miles and miles away. Sylvia knew it well. She had always believed that whoever climbed to the top of it could see the ocean; and the little girl had often laid her hand on the great rough trunk and looked up wistfully at those dark boughs that the wind always stirred, no matter how hot and still the air might be below. Now she thought of the tree with a new excitement, for why, if one climbed it at break of day, could not one see all the world, and easily discover from whence the white heron flew, and mark the place, and find the hidden nest?

What a spirit of adventure, what wild ambition! What fancied triumph and delight and glory for the later morning when she could make known the secret! It was almost too real and too great for the childish heart to bear.

All night the door of the little house stood open, and the whippoorwills came and sang upon the very step. The young sportsman and his old hostess were sound asleep, but Sylvia's great design kept her broad awake and watching. She forgot to think of sleep. The short summer night seemed as long as the winter darkness, and at last when the whippoorwills ceased, and she was afraid the morning would after all come too soon, she stole out of the house and followed the pasture path through the woods, hastening toward the open ground beyond, listening with a sense of comfort and companionship to the drowsy twitter of a half-awakened bird, whose perch she had jarred in passing. Alas, if the great wave of human interest which flooded for the first time this dull little life should sweep away the satisfactions of an existence heart to heart with nature and the dumb life of the forest!

There was the huge tree asleep yet in the paling moonlight, and small and silly Sylvia began with utmost bravery to mount to the top of it, with tingling, eager blood coursing the channels of her whole frame, with her bare feet and fingers, that pinched and held like bird's claws to the monstrous ladder reaching up, up, almost to the sky itself. First she must mount the white oak tree that grew alongside, where she was almost lost among the dark branches and the green leaves heavy and wet with dew; a bird fluttered off its nest, and a red squirrel ran to and fro and scolded pettishly at the harmless housebreaker. Sylvia felt her way easily. She had often climbed there, and knew that higher still one of the oak's upper branches chafed against the pine trunk, just where its lower boughs were set close together. There, when she made the dangerous pass from one tree to the other, the great enterprise would really begin.

She crept out along the swaying oak limb at last, and took the daring step across into the old pine-tree. The way was harder than she thought; she must reach far and hold fast, the sharp dry twigs caught and held her and scratched her like angry talons, the pitch make her thin little fingers clumsy and stiff as she went round and round the tree's great stem, higher and higher upward. The sparrows and robins in the woods below were beginning to wake and twitter to the dawn, yet it seemed much lighter there aloft in the pine tree, and the child knew that she must hurry if her project were to be of any use.

The tree seemed to lengthen itself out as she went up, and to reach farther and farther upward. It was like a great main-mast to the voyaging earth; it must truly have been amazed that morning through all its ponderous frame as it felt this determined spark of human spirit wending its way from higher branch to branch. Who knows how steadily the least twigs held themselves to advantage this light, weak creature on her way! The old pine must have loved his new dependent. More than all the hawks, and bats, and moths, and even the sweet voiced thrushes, was the brave, beating heart of the solitary gray-eyed child. And the tree stood still and frowned away the winds that June morning while the dawn grew bright in the east.

Sylvia's face was like a pale star, if one had seen it from the ground, when the last thorny bough was past, and she stood trembling and tired but wholly triumphant, high in the tree-top. Yes, there was the sea with the dawning sun making a golden dazzle over it, and toward that glorious east flew two hawks with slow-moving pinions. How low they looked in the air from that height when one had only seen them before far up, and dark against the blue sky. Their gray feathers were as soft as moths; they seemed only a little way from the tree, and Sylvia felt as if she too could go flying away among the clouds. Westward, the woodlands and farms reached miles and miles into the distance; here and there were church steeples, and white villages; truly it was a vast and awesome world!

The birds sang louder and louder. At last the sun came up bewilderingly bright. Sylvia could see the white sails of ships out at sea, and the clouds that were purple and rose-colored and yellow at first began to fade away. Where was the white heron's nest in the sea of green branches, and was this wonderful sight and pageant of the world the only reward for having climbed to such a giddy height? Now look down again, Sylvia, where the green marsh is set among the shining birches and dark hemlocks; there where you saw the white heron once you will see him again; look, look! a white spot of him like a single floating feather comes up from the dead hemlock and grows larger, and rises, and comes close at last, and goes by the landmark pine with steady sweep of wing and outstretched slender neck and crested head. And wait! wait! do not move a foot or a finger, little girl, do not send an arrow of light and conscious-ness from your two eager eyes, for the heron has perched on a pine bough not far beyond yours, and cries back to his mate on the nest and plumes his feathers for the new day!

The child gives a long sigh a minute later when a company of shouting cat-birds comes also to the tree, and vexed by their fluttering and lawlessness the solemn heron goes away. She knows his secret now, the wild, light, slender bird that floats and wavers, and goes back like an arrow presently to his home in the green world beneath. Then Sylvia, well satisfied, makes her perilous way down again, not daring to look far below the branch she stands on, ready to cry sometimes because her fingers ache and her lamed feet slip. Wondering over and over again what the stranger would say to her, and what he would think when she told him how to find his way straight to the heron's nest.

"Sylvy, Sylvy!" called the busy old grandmother again and again, but nobody answered, and the small husk bed was empty, and Sylvia had disappeared.

The guest waked from a dream, and remembering his day's pleasure hurried to dress himself that it might sooner begin. He was sure from the way the shy little girl looked once or twice yesterday that she had at least seen the white heron, and now she must really be made to tell. Here she comes now, paler than ever, and her worn old frock is torn and tattered, and smeared with pine pitch. The grandmother and the sportsman stand in the door together and question her, and the splendid moment has come to speak of the dead hemlock-tree by the green marsh.

But Sylvia does not speak after all, though the old grandmother fretfully rebukes her, and the young man's kind appealing eyes are looking straight in her own. He can make them rich with money; he has promised it, and they are poor now. He is so well worth making happy, and he waits to hear the story she can tell.

No, she must keep silence! What is it that suddenly forbids her and makes her dumb? Has she been nine years growing, and now, when the great world for the first time puts out a hand to her, must she thrust it aside for a bird's sake? The murmur of the pine's green branches is in her ears, she remembers how the white heron came flying through the golden air and how they watched the sea and the morning together, and Sylvia cannot speak; she cannot tell the heron's secret and give its life away.

Dear loyalty, that suffered a sharp pang as the guest went away disappointed later in the day, that could have served and followed him and loved him as a dog loves! Many a night Sylvia heard the echo of his whistle haunting the pasture path as she came home with the loitering cow. She forgot even her sorrow at the sharp report of his gun and the piteous sight of thrushes and sparrows dropping silent to the ground, their songs hushed and their pretty feathers stained and wet with blood. Were the birds better friends than their hunter might have been,—who can tell? Whatever treasures were lost to her, woodlands and summertime, remember! Bring your gifts and graces and tell your secrets to this lonely country child!

THE DULHAM LADIES

To be leaders of society in the town of Dulham was as satisfactory to Miss Dobin and Miss Lucinda Dobin as if Dulham were London itself. Of late years, though they would not allow themselves to suspect such treason, the most ill-bred of the younger people in the village made fun of them behind their backs, and laughed at their treasured summer mantillas, their mincing steps, and the shape of their parasols.

They were always conscious of the fact that they were the daughters of a once eminent Dulham minister; but beside this unanswerable claim to the respect of the First Parish, they were aware that their mother's social position was one of superior altitude. Madam Dobin's grandmother was a Greenaple, of Boston. In her younger days she had often visited her relatives, the Greenaples and Hightrees, and in seasons of festivity she could relate to a select and properly excited audience her delightful experiences of town life. Nothing could be finer than her account of having taken tea at Governor Clovenfoot's on Beacon Street in company with an English lord, who was indulging himself in a brief vacation from his arduous duties at the Court of St. James.

"He exclaimed that he had seldom seen in England so beautiful and intelligent a company of ladies," Madam Dobin would always say in conclusion. "He was decorated with the blue ribbons of the Knights of the Garter." Miss Dobin and Miss Lucinda thought for many years that this famous blue ribbon was tied about the noble gentleman's leg. One day they even discussed the question openly; Miss Dobin placing the decoration at his knee, and Miss Lucinda locating it much lower down, according to the length of the short gray socks with which she was familiar.

"You have no imagination, Lucinda," the elder sister replied impatiently. "Of course, those were the days of small-clothes and long silk stockings!"—whereat Miss Lucinda was rebuked, but not persuaded.

"I wish that my dear girls could have the outlook upon society which fell to my portion," Madam Dobin sighed, after she had set these ignorant minds to rights, and enriched them by communicating the final truth about the blue ribbon. "I must not chide you for the absence of opportunities, but if our cousin Harriet Greenaple were only living you would not lack enjoyment or social education."

Madam Dobin had now been dead a great many years. She seemed an elderly woman to her daughters some time before she left them; later they thought that she had really died comparatively young, since their own years had come to equal the record of hers. When they visited her tall white tombstone in the orderly Dulham burying-ground, it was a strange thought to both the daughters that they were older women than their mother had been when she died. To be sure, it was the fashion to appear older in her day,—they could remember the sober effect of really youthful married persons in cap and frisette; but, whether they owed it to the changed times or to their own qualities, they felt no older themselves than ever they had. Beside upholding the ministerial dignity of their father, they were obliged to give a lenient sanction to the ways of the world for their mother's sake; and they combined the two duties with reverence and impartiality.

Madam Dobin was, in her prime, a walking example of refinements and courtesies. If she erred in any way, it was by keeping too strict watch and rule over her small kingdom. She acted with great dignity in all matters of social administration and etiquette, but, while it must be owned that the parishioners felt a sense of freedom for a time after her death, in their later years they praised and valued her more and more, and often lamented her generously and sincerely.

Several of her distinguished relatives attended Madam Dobin's funeral, which was long considered the most dignified and elegant pageant of that sort which had ever taken place in Dulham. It seemed to mark the close of a famous epoch in Dulham history, and it was increasingly difficult forever afterward to keep the tone of society up to the old standard. Somehow, the distinguished relatives had one by one disappeared, though they all had excellent reasons for the discontinuance of their visits. A few had left this world altogether, and the family circle of the Greenaples and Hightrees was greatly reduced in circumference. Sometimes, in summer, a stray connection drifted Dulham-ward, and was displayed to the townspeople (not to say paraded) by the gratified hostesses. It was a disappointment if the guest could not be persuaded to remain over Sunday and appear at church. When household antiquities became fashionable, the ladies remarked a surprising interest in their corner cupboard and best chairs, and some distant relatives revived their almost forgotten custom of paying a summer visit to Dulham. They were not long in finding out with what desperate affection Miss Dobin and Miss Lucinda clung to their mother's wedding china and other inheritances, and were allowed to depart without a single teacup. One graceless descendant of the Hightrees prowled from garret to cellar, and admired the household belongings diligently, but she was not asked to accept even the dislocated cherry-wood footstool that she had discovered in the far corner of the parsonage pew.

Some of the Dulham friends had long suspected that Madam Dobin made a social misstep when she chose the Reverend Edward Dobin for her husband. She was no longer young when she married, and though she had gone through the wood and picked up a crooked stick at last, it made a great difference that her stick possessed an ecclesiastical bark. The Reverend Edward was, moreover, a respectable graduate of Harvard College, and to a woman of her standards a clergyman was by no means insignificant. It was impossible not to respect his office, at any rate, and she must have treated him with proper veneration for the sake of that, if for no other reason, though his early advantages had been insufficient, and he was quite insensible to the claims of the Greenaple pedigree, and preferred an Indian pudding to pie crust that was, without exaggeration, half a quarter high. The delicacy of Madam Dobin's touch and preference in everything, from hymns to cookery, was quite lost upon this respected preacher, yet he was not without pride or complete confidence in his own decisions.

The Reverend Mr. Dobin was never very enlightening in his discourses, and was providentially stopped short by a stroke of paralysis in the middle of his clerical career. He lived on and on through many dreary years, but his children never accepted the fact that he was a tyrant, and served him humbly and patiently. He fell at last into a condition of great incapacity and chronic trembling, but was able for nearly a quarter of a century to be carried to the meeting-house from time to time to pronounce farewell discourses. On high days of the church he was always placed in the pulpit, and held up his shaking hands when the benediction was pronounced, as if the divine gift were exclusively his own, and the other minister did but say empty words. Afterward, he was usually tired and displeased and hard to cope with, but there was always a proper notice taken of these too often recurring events. For old times' and for pity's sake and from natural goodness of heart, the elder parishioners rallied manfully about the Reverend Mr. Dobin; and whoever his successor or colleague might be, the Dobins were always called the minister's folks, while the active laborer in that vineyard was only Mr. Smith or Mr. Jones, as the case might be. At last the poor old man died, to everybody's relief and astonishment; and after he was properly preached about and lamented, his daughters, Miss Dobin and Miss Lucinda, took a good look at life from a new standpoint, and decided that now they were no longer constrained by home duties they must make themselves a great deal more used to the town.

Sometimes there is such a household as this (which has been perhaps too minutely described), where the parents linger until their children are far past middle age, and always keep them in a too childish and unworthy state of subjection. The Misses Dobin's characters were much influenced by such an unnatural prolongation of the filial relationship, and they were amazingly slow to suspect that they were not so young as they used to be. There was nothing to measure themselves by but Dulham people and things. The elm-trees were growing yet, and many of the ladies of the First Parish were older than they, and called them, with pleasant familiarity, the Dobin girls. These elderly persons seemed really to be growing old, and Miss Lucinda lamented the change in society; she thought it a freak of nature and too sudden blighting of earthly hopes that several charming old friends of her mother's were no longer living. They were advanced in age when Miss Lucinda was a young girl, though time and space are but relative, after all.

Their influence upon society would have made a great difference in many ways. Certainly, the new parishioners, who had often enough been instructed to pronounce their pastor's name as if it were spelled with one "b," would not have boldly returned again and again to their obnoxious habit of saying Dobbin. Miss Lucinda might carefully speak to the neighbor and new-comers of "my sister, Miss Do-bin"; only the select company of intimates followed her lead, and at last there was something humiliating about it, even though many persons spoke of them only as "the ladies."

"The name was originally *D'Aubigne*, we think," Miss Lucinda would say coldly and patiently, as if she had already explained this foolish mistake a thousand times too often. It was like the sorrows in many a provincial château in the Reign of Terror. The ladies looked on with increasing dismay at the retrogression in society. They felt as if they were a feeble garrison, to whose lot it had fallen to repulse a noisy, irreverent mob, an increasing band of marauders who would overthrow all land-marks of the past, all etiquette and social rank. The new minister himself was a round-faced, unspiritual-looking young man, whom they would have instinctively ignored if he had not been a minister. The new people who came to Dulham were not like the older residents, and they had no desire to be taught better. Little they cared about the Greenaples or the Hightrees; and once, when Miss Dobin essayed to speak of some detail of her mother's brilliant opportunities in Boston high life, she was interrupted, and the new-comer who sat next her at the parish sewing society began to talk about something else. We cannot believe that it could have been the tea-party at Governor Clovenfoot's which the rude creature so disrespectfully ignored, but some persons are capable of showing any lack of good taste.

The ladies had an unusual and most painful sense of failure, as they went home together that evening. "I have always made it my object to improve and interest the people at such times; it would seem so possible to elevate their thoughts and direct them into higher channels," said Miss Dobin sadly. "But as for that Woolden woman, there is no use in casting pearls before swine!"

Miss Lucinda murmured an indignant assent. She had a secret suspicion that the Woolden woman had heard the story in question oftener than had pleased her. She was but an ignorant creature; though she had lived in Dulham twelve or thirteen years, she was no better than when she came. The mistake was in treating sister Harriet as if she were on a level with the rest of the company. Miss Lucinda had observed more than once, lately, that her sister sometimes repeated herself, unconsciously, a little oftener than was agreeable. Perhaps they were getting a trifle dull; toward spring it might be well to pass a few days with some of their friends, and have a change.

"If I have tried to do anything," said Miss Dobin in an icy tone, "it has been to stand firm in my lot and place, and to hold the standard of cultivated mind and elegant manners as high as possible. You would think it had been a hundred years since our mother's death, so completely has the effect of her good breeding and exquisite hospitality been lost sight of, here in Dulham. I could wish that our father had chosen to settle in a larger and more appreciative place. They would like to put us on the shelf, too. I can see that plainly."

"I am sure we have our friends," said Miss Lucinda anxiously, but with a choking voice. "We must not let them think we do not mean to keep up with the times, as we always have. I do feel as if perhaps—our hair"—

And the sad secret was out at last. Each of the sisters drew a long breath of relief at this beginning of a confession.

It was certain that they must take some steps to retrieve their lost ascendency. Public attention had that evening been called to their fast-disappearing locks, poor ladies; and Miss Lucinda felt the discomfort most, for she had been the inheritor of the Hightree hair, long and curly, and chestnut in color. There used to be a waviness about it, and sometimes pretty escaping curls, but these were gone long ago. Miss Dobin resembled her father, and her hair had not been luxuriant, so that she was less changed by its absence than one might suppose. The straightness and thinness had increased so gradually that neither sister had quite accepted the thought that other persons would particularly notice their altered appearance.

They had shrunk, with the reticence born of close family association, from speaking of the cause even to each other, when they made themselves pretty little lace and dotted muslin caps. Breakfast caps, they called them, and explained that these were universally worn in town; the young Princess of Wales originated them, or at any rate adopted them. The ladies offered no apology for keeping the breakfast caps on until bedtime, and in spite of them a forward child had just spoken, loud and shrill, an untimely question in the ears of the for once silent sewing society. "Do Miss Dobbineses wear them great caps because their bare heads is cold?" the little beast had said; and everybody was startled and dismayed.

Miss Dobin had never shown better her good breeding and valor, the younger sister thought.

"No, little girl," replied the stately Harriet, with a chilly smile. "I believe that our headdresses are quite in the fashion for ladies of all ages. And you must remember that it is never polite to make such personal remarks." It was after this that Miss Dobin had been reminded of Madam Somebody's unusual headgear at the evening entertainment in Boston. Nobody but the Woolden woman could have interrupted her under such trying circumstances.

Miss Lucinda, however, was certain that the time had come for making some effort to replace her lost adornment. The child had told an unwelcome truth, but had paved the way for further action, and now was the time to suggest something that had slowly been taking shape in Miss Lucinda's mind. A young grand-nephew of their mother and his bride had passed a few days with them, two or three summers before, and the sisters had been quite shocked to find that the pretty young woman wore a row of frizzes, not originally her own, over her smooth forehead. At the time, Miss Dobin and Miss Lucinda had spoken severely with each other of such bad taste, but now it made a great difference that the wearer of the frizzes was not only a relative by marriage and used to good society, but also that she came from town, and might be supposed to know what was proper in the way of toilet.

"I really think, sister, that we had better see about having some— arrangements, next time we go anywhere," Miss Dobin said unexpectedly, with a slight tremble in her voice, just as they reached their own door. "There seems to be quite a fashion for them nowadays. For the parish's sake we ought to recognize"—and Miss Lucinda responded with instant satisfaction. She did not like to complain, but she had been troubled with neuralgic pains in her forehead on suddenly meeting the cold air. The sisters felt a new bond of sympathy in keeping this secret with and for each other; they took pains to say to several acquaintances that they were thinking of going to the next large town to do a few errands for Christmas.

A bright, sunny morning seemed to wish the ladies good-fortune. Old Hetty Downs, their faithful maid-servant and protector, looked after them in affectionate foreboding. "Dear sakes, what devil's wiles may be played on them blessed innocents afore they 're safe home again!" she murmured, as they vanished round the corner of the street that led to the railway station.

Miss Dobin and Miss Lucinda paced discreetly side by side down the main street of Westbury. It was nothing like Boston, of course, but the noise was slightly confusing, and the passers-by sometimes roughly pushed against them. Westbury was a consequential manufacturing town, but a great convenience at times like this. The trifling Christmas gifts for their old neighbors and Sunday-school scholars were purchased and stowed away in their neat Fayal basket before the serious commission of the day was attended to. Here and there, in the shops, disreputable frizzes were displayed in unblushing effrontery, but no such vulgar shopkeeper merited the patronage of the Misses Dobin. They pretended not to observe the unattractive goods, and went their way to a low, one-storied building on a side street, where an old tradesman lived. He had been useful to the minister while he still remained upon the earth and had need of a wig, sandy in hue and increasingly sprinkled with gray, as if it kept pace with other changes of existence. But old Paley's shutters were up, and a bar of rough wood was nailed firmly across the one that had lost its fastening and would rack its feeble hinges in the wind. Old Paley had always been polite and bland; they really had looked forward to a little chat with him; they had heard a year or two before of his wife's death, and meant to offer sympathy. His business of hair-dressing had been carried on with that of parasol and umbrella mending, and the condemned umbrella which was his sign cracked and swung in the rising wind, a tattered skeleton before the closed door. The ladies sighed and turned away; they were beginning to feel tired; the day was long, and they had not met with any pleasures yet. "We might walk up the street a little farther," suggested Miss Lucinda; "that is, if you are not tired," as they stood hesitating on the corner after they had finished a short discussion of Mr. Paley's disappearance. Happily it was only a few minutes before they came to a stop together in front of a new, shining shop, where smirking waxen heads all in a row were decked with the latest fashions of wigs and frizzes. One smiling fragment of a gentleman stared so straight at Miss Lucinda with his black eyes that she felt quite coy and embarrassed, and was obliged to feign not to be conscious of his admiration. But Miss Dobin, after a brief delay, boldly opened the door and entered; it was better to be sheltered in the shop then exposed to public remark as they gazed in at the windows. Miss Lucinda felt her heart beat and her courage give out; she, coward like, left the transaction of their business to her sister, and turned to contemplate the back of the handsome model. It was a slight shock to find that he was not so attractive from this point of view. The wig he wore was well made all round, but his shoulders were roughly finished in a substance that looked like plain plaster of Paris.

"What can I have ze pleasure of showing you young ladees?" asked a person who advanced; and Miss Lucinda faced about to discover a smiling, middle-aged Frenchman, who rubbed his hands together and looked at his customers, first one and then the other, with delightful deference. He seemed a very civil, nice person, the young ladies thought.

"My sister and I were thinking of buying some little arrangements to wear above the forehead," Miss Dobin explained, with pathetic dignity; but the Frenchman spared her any further words. He looked with eager interest at the bonnets, as if no lack had attracted his notice before. "Ah, yes. *Je comprends*; ze high foreheads are not now ze mode. Je prefer them, moi, yes, yes, but ze ladies must accept ze fashions; zay must now cover ze forehead with ze frizzes, ze bangs, you say. As you wis', as you wis'!" and the tactful little man, with many shrugs and merry gestures at such girlish fancies, pulled down one box after another.

It was a great relief to find that this was no worse, to say the least, than any other shopping, though the solemnity and secrecy of the occasion were infringed upon by the great supply of "arrangements" and the loud discussion of the color of some crimps a noisy girl was buying from a young saleswoman the other side of the shop.

Miss Dobin waved aside the wares which were being displayed for her approval. "Something—more simple, if you please,"—she did not like to say "older."

"But these are *très simple*," protested the Frenchman. "We have nothing younger;" and Miss Dobin and Miss Lucinda blushed, and said no more. The Frenchman had his own way; he persuaded them that nothing was so suitable as some conspicuous forelocks that matched their hair as it used to be. They would have given anything rather than leave their breakfast caps at home, if they had known that their proper winter bonnets must come off. They hardly listened to the wig merchant's glib voice as Miss Dobin stood revealed before the merciless mirror at the back of the shop.

He made everything as easy as possible, the friendly creature, and the ladies were grateful to him. Beside, now that the bonnet was on again there was a great improvement in Miss Dobin's appearance. She turned to Miss Lucinda, and saw a gleam of delight in her eager countenance. "It really is very becoming. I like the way it parts over your forehead." said the younger sister, "but if it were long enough to go behind the ears"—"Non, non," entreated the Frenchman. "To make her the old woman at once would be cruelty!" And Lucinda who was wondering how well she would look in her turn, succumbed promptly to such protestations. Yes, there was no use in being old before their time. Dulham was not quite keeping pace with the rest of the world in these days, but they need not drag behind everybody else, just because they lived there.

The price of the little arrangements was much less than the sisters expected, and the uncomfortable expense of their reverend father's wigs had been, it was proved, a thing of the past. Miss Dobin treated her polite Frenchman with great courtesy; indeed, Miss Lucinda had more than once whispered to her to talk French, and as they were bowed out of the shop the gracious *Bong-sure* of the elder lady seemed to act like the sting of a shower-bath, and bring down an awesome torrent of foreign words upon the two guileless heads. It was impossible to reply; the ladies bowed again, however, and Miss Lucinda caught a last smile from the handsome wax countenance in the window. He appeared to regard her with fresh approval, and she departed down the street with mincing steps.

"I feel as if anybody might look at me now, sister," said gentle Miss Lucinda. "I confess, I have really suffered sometimes, since I knew I looked so distressed."

"Yours is lighter than I thought it was in the shop," remarked Miss Dobin, doubtfully, but she quickly added that perhaps it would change a little. She was so perfectly satisfied with her own appearance that she could not bear to dim the pleasure of any one else. The truth remained that she never would have let Lucinda choose that particular arrangement if she had seen it first in a good light. And Lucinda was thinking exactly the same of her companion.

"I am sure we shall have no more neuralgia," said Miss Dobin. "I am sorry we waited so long, dear," and they tripped down the main street of Westbury, confident that nobody would suspect them of being over thirty. Indeed, they felt quite girlish, and unconsciously looked sideways as they went along, to see their satisfying reflections in the windows. The great panes made excellent mirrors, with not too clear or lasting pictures of these comforted passers-by.

The Frenchman in the shop was making merry with his assistants. The two great frisettes had long been out of fashion; he had been lying in wait with them for two unsuspecting country ladies, who could be cajoled into such a purchase.

"Sister," Miss Lucinda was saying, "you know there is still an hour to wait before our train goes. Suppose we take a little longer walk down the other side of the way"; and they strolled slowly back again. In fact, they nearly missed the train, naughty girls! Hetty would have been so worried, they assured each other, but they reached the station just in time.

"Lutie," said Miss Dobin, "put up your hand and part it from your forehead; it seems to be getting out of place a little;" and Miss Lucinda, who had just got breath enough to speak, returned the information that Miss Dobin's was almost covering her eyebrows. They might have to trim them a little shorter; of course it could be done. The darkness was falling; they had taken an early dinner before they started, and now they were tired and hungry after the exertion of the afternoon, but the spirit of youth flamed afresh in their hearts, and they were very happy. If one's heart remains young, it is a sore trial to have the outward appearance entirely at variance. It was the ladies' nature to be girlish, and they found it impossible not to be grateful to the flimsy, ineffectual disguise which seemed to set them right with the world. The old conductor, who had known them for many years, looked hard at them as he took their tickets, and, being a man of humor and compassion, affected not to notice anything remarkable in their appearance. "You ladies never mean to grow old, like the rest of us," he said gallantly, and the sisters fairly quaked with joy.

"Bless us!" the obnoxious Mrs. Woolden was saying, at the other end of the car. "There's the old maid Dobbinses, and they've bought 'em some bangs. I expect they wanted to get thatched in a little before real cold weather; but don't they look just like a pair o' poodle dogs."

The little ladies descended wearily from the train. Somehow they did not enjoy a day's shopping as much as they used. They were certainly much obliged to Hetty for sending her niece's boy to meet them, with a lantern; also for having a good warm supper ready when they came in. Hetty took a quick look at her mistresses, and returned to the kitchen. "I knew somebody would be foolin' of 'em," she assured herself angrily, but she had to laugh. Their dear, kind faces were wrinkled and pale, and the great frizzes had lost their pretty curliness, and were hanging down, almost straight and very ugly, into the ladies' eyes. They could not tuck them under their caps, as they were sure might be done.

Then came a succession of rainy days, and nobody visited the rejuvenated household. The frisettes looked very bright chestnut by the light of day, and it must be confessed that Miss Dobin took the scissors and shortened Miss Lucinda's half an inch, and Miss Lucinda returned the compliment quite secretly, because each thought her sister's forehead lower than her own. Their dear gray eyebrows were honestly displayed, as if it were the fashion not to have them match with wigs. Hetty at last spoke out, and begged her mistresses, as they say at breakfast, to let her take the frizzes back and change them. Her sister's daughter worked in that very shop, and, though in the work-room, would be obliging, Hetty was sure.

But the ladies looked at each other in pleased assurance, and then turned together to look at Hetty, who stood already a little apprehensive near the table, where she had just put down a plateful of smoking drop-cakes. The good creature really began to look old.

"They are worn very much in town," said Miss Dobin. "We think it was quite fortunate that the fashion came in just as our hair was growing a trifle thin. I dare say we may choose those that are a shade duller in color when these are a little past. Oh, we shall not want tea this evening, you remember, Hetty. I am glad there is likely to be such a good night for the sewing circle." And Miss Dobin and Miss Lucinda nodded and smiled.

"Oh, my sakes alive!" the troubled handmaiden groaned. "Going to the circle, be they, to be snickered at! Well, the Dobbin girls they was born, and the Dobbin girls they will remain till they die; but if they ain't innocent Christian babes to those that knows 'em well, mark me down for an idjit myself! They believe them front-pieces has set the clock back forty year or more, but if they 're pleased to think so, let 'em!"

Away paced the Dulham ladies, late in the afternoon, to grace the parish occasion, and face the amused scrutiny of their neighbors. "I think we owe it to society to observe the fashions of the day," said Miss Lucinda. "A lady cannot afford to be unattractive. I feel now as if we were prepared for anything!"

THE KING OF
FOLLY ISLAND

he September afternoon was nearly spent, and the
sun was already veiled in a thin cloud of haze that
hinted at coming drought and dustiness rather
than rain. Nobody could help feeling sure of just
such another golden day on the morrow; this was as good weather as heart
could wish. There on the Maine coast, where it was hard to distinguish the
islands from the irregular outline of the main-land, where the summer
greenness was just beginning to change into all manner of yellow and
russet and scarlet tints, the year seemed to have done its work and begun
its holidays.

Along one of the broad highways of the bay, in the John's Island
postmaster's boat, came a stranger—a man of forty-two or forty-three
years, not unprosperous but hardly satisfied, and ever on the quest for
entertainment, though he called his pleasure by the hard name of work,
and liked himself the better for such a wrong translation. Fate had made
him a business man of good success and reputation; inclination, at least so
he thought, would have led him another way, but his business ventures
pleased him more than the best of his holidays. Somehow life was more
interesting if one took it by contraries; he persuaded himself that he had
been looking forward to this solitary ramble for many months, but the
truth remained that he had found it provokingly hard to break away from
his city office, his clerks, and his accounts. He had grown much richer in

this last twelve-month, and as he leaned back in the stern of the boat with his arm over the rudder, he was pondering with great perplexity the troublesome question what he ought to do with so much money, and why he should have had it put into his careless hands at all. The bulk of it must be only a sort of reservoir for the sake of a later need and ownership. He thought with scorn of some liberal gifts for which he had been aggravatingly thanked and praised, and made such an impatient gesture with his shoulder that the boat gave a surprised flounce out of its straight course, and the old skipper, who was carefully inspecting the meagre contents of the mail-bag, nearly lost his big silver spectacles overboard. It would have been a strange and awesome calamity. There were no new ones to be bought within seven miles.

"Did a flaw strike her?" asked Jabez Pennell, who looked curiously at the sky and sea and then at his passenger. "I 've known of a porpus h'isting a boat, or mought be you kind o' shifted the rudder?"

Whereupon they both laughed; the passenger with a brilliant smile and indescribably merry sound, and the old postmaster with a mechanical grimace of the face and a rusty chuckle; then he turned to his letters again, and adjusted the rescued spectacles to his weather-beaten nose. He thought the stranger, though a silent young man, was a friendly sort of chap, boiling over with fun, as it were; whereas he was really a little morose—so much for Jabez's knowledge of human nature. "Feels kind o' strange, 't is likely; that 's better than one o' your forrard kind," mused Jabez, who took the visitor for one of the rare specimens of commercial travelers who sometimes visited John's Island—to little purpose it must be confessed. The postmaster cunningly concealed the fact that he kept the only store on John's Island; he might as well get his pay for setting the stranger across the bay, and it was nobody's business to pry into what he wanted when he got there. So Jabez gave another chuckle, and could not help looking again at the canvas-covered gun case with its neat straps, and the well-packed portmanteau that lay alongside it in the bows.

"I suppose I can find some place to stay in overnight?" asked the stranger, presently.

"Do' know 's you can, I 'm sure," replied Mr. Pennell. "There ain't no reg'lar boarding places onto John's Island. Folks keep to theirselves pretty much."

"I suppose money is of some object?" gently inquired the passenger.

"Waal, yes," answered Jabez, without much apparent certainty. "Yes, John's Island folks ain't above nippin' an' squeezin' to get the best of a bargain. They 're pretty much like the rest o' the human race, an' want money, whether they 've got any use for it or not. Take it in cold weather, when you 've got pork enough and potatoes and them things in your sullar, an' it blows an' freezes so 't ain't wuth while to go out, 'most all that money 's good for is to set an' look at. Now I need to have more means than most on 'em," continued the speaker, plaintively, as if to excuse himself for any rumor of his grasping ways which might have reached his companion. "Keeping store as I do, I have to handle"—But here he stopped short, conscious of having taken a wrong step. However, they were more than half across now, and the mail was overdue; he would not be forced into going back when it was ascertained that he refused to even look at any samples.

But the passenger took no notice of the news that he was sailing with the chief and only merchant of John's Island, and even turned slowly to look back at the shore they had left, far away now, and fast growing dim on the horizon. John's Island was, on the contrary, growing more distinct, and there were some smaller fragments of land near it; on one he could already distinguish a flock of sheep that moved slowly down a barren slope. It was amazing that they found food enough all summer in that narrow pasture. The suggestion of winter in this remote corner of the world gave Frankfort a feeling of deep pity for the sheep, as well as for all the other inhabitants. Yet it was worth a cheerless year to come occasionally to such weather as this; and he filled his lungs again and again with the delicious air blown to him from the inland country of bayberry and fir balsams across the sparkling salt-water. The fresh northwest wind carried them straight on their course, and the postmaster's passenger could not have told himself why he was going to John's Island, except that when he had apparently come to the end of everything on an outreaching point of the main-land, he had found that there was still a settlement beyond—John's Island, twelve miles distant, and communication would be that day afforded. "Sheep farmers and fishermen—a real old-fashioned crowd," he had been told. It was odd to go with the postmaster: perhaps he was addressed by fate to some human being who expected him. Yes, he would find out what could be done for the John's-Islanders; then a wave of defeat seemed to chill his desire. It was better to let them work toward what they needed and wanted; besides, "the gift without the giver were dumb." Though after all it would be a kind of satisfaction to take a poor little neighborhood under one's wing, and make it presents of books and various enlightenments. It would n't be a bad thing to send it a Punch and Judy show, or a panorama.

"May I ask your business?" interrupted Jabez Pennell, to whom the long silence was a little oppressive.

"I am a sportsman," responded John Frankfort, the partner in a flourishing private bank, and the merchant-postmaster's face drooped with disappointment. No bargains, then, but perhaps a lucrative boarder for a week or two; and Jabez instantly resolved that for not a cent less than a dollar a day should this man share the privileges and advantages of his own food and lodging. Two dollars a week being the current rate among John's-Islanders, it will be easily seen that Mr. Pennell was a man of far-seeing business enterprise.

II

On shore, public attention was beginning to centre upon the small white sail that was crossing the bay. At the landing there was at first no human being to be seen, unless one had sharp eyes enough to detect the sallow, unhappy countenance of the postmaster's wife. She sat at the front kitchen window of the low-storied farm-house that was perched nearly at the top of a long green slope. The store, of which the post-office department was a small fraction, stood nearer the water, at the head of the little harbor. It was a high, narrow, smartly painted little building, and looked as if it had strayed from some pretentious inland village, but the tumble-down shed near by had evidently been standing for many years, and was well acquainted with the fish business. The landing-place looked still more weather-beaten; its few timbers were barnacled and overgrown with sea-weeds below high-water mark, and the stone-work was rudely put together. There was a litter of drift-wood, of dilapidated boats and empty barrels and broken lobster pots, and a little higher on the shore stood a tar kettle, and, more prominent still, a melancholy pair of high chaise wheels, with their thorough-braces drawn uncomfortably tight by exposure to many seasonings of relentless weather.

The tide was high, and on this sheltered side of the island the low waves broke with a quick, fresh sound, and moved the pebbles gently on the narrow beach. The sun looked more and more golden red, and all the shore was glowing with color. The faint reddening tinge of some small oaks among the hemlocks farther up the island shore, the pale green and primrose of a group of birches, were all glorified with the brilliant contrast of the sea and the shining of the autumn sky. Even the green pastures and browner fields looked as if their covering had been changed to some richer material, like velvet, so soft and splendid they looked. High on a barren pasture ridge that sheltered the landing on its seaward side the huckleberry bushes had been brightened with a touch of carmine. Coming toward John's Island one might be reminded of some dull old picture that had been cleansed and wet, all its colors were suddenly grown so clear and gay.

Almost at the same moment two men appeared from different quarters of the shore, and without apparently taking any notice of each other, even by way of greeting, they seated themselves side by side on a worm-eaten piece of ship timber near the tar pot. In a few minutes a third resident of the island joined them, coming over the high pasture slope, and looking for one moment giant-like against the sky.

"Jabez need n't grumble to-day on account o' no head-wind," said one of the first comers. "I was mendin' a piece o' wall that was overset, an' I see him all of a sudden, most inshore. My woman has been expecting a letter from her brother's folks in Castine. I s'pose ye 've heard? They was all down with the throat distemper last we knew about 'em, an' she was dreadful put about because she got no word by the last mail. Lor', now wa'n't it just like Jabe's contrairiness to go over in that fussin' old dory o' his with no sail to speak of?"

"Would n't have took him half the time in his cat-boat," grumbled the elder man of the three. "Thinks he can do as he 's a mind to, an' we 've got to make the best on 't. Ef I was postmaster I should look out, fust thing, for an abler boat nor any he 's got. He 's gittin nearer every year, Jabe is."

"'T ain't fa'r to the citizens," said the first speaker. "Don't git no mail but twice a week anyhow, an' then he l'iters round long 's he 's a mind to, dickerin' an' spoutin' politics over to the Foreside. Folks may be layin' dyin', an' there 's all kinds o' urgent letters that ought to be in owners' hands direct. Jabe need n't think we mean to put up with him f'rever;" and the irate islander, who never had any letters at all from one year's end to another's looked at both his companions for their assent.

"Don't ye git riled so, Dan'el," softly responded the last-comer, a grizzled little fisherman-farmer, who looked like a pirate, and was really the most amiable man on John's Island—"don't ye git riled. I don' know as, come to the scratch, ary one of us would want to make two trips back an' forrard every week the year round for a hundred an' twenty dollars. Take it in them high December seas, now, an' 'long in Jenoary an' March. Course he accommodates himself, an' it comes in the way o' his business, an' he gits a passenger now an' then. Well, it all counts up, I s'pose."

"There 's somebody or 'nother aboard now," said the opponent. "They may have sent over for our folks from Castine. They was headin' on to be dangerous, three o' the child'n and Wash'n'ton himself. I may have to go up to-night. Dare say they 've sent a letter we ain't got. Darn that Jabe! I 've heard before now of his looking over everything in the bag comin' over—sortin' he calls it, to save time—but 't would n't be no wonder ef a letter blowed out o' his fingers now an' again."

"There 's King George a-layin' off, ain't he?" asked the peace-maker, who was whittling a piece of dry kelp stalk that he had picked up from the pebbles, and all three men took a long look at the gray sail beyond the moorings.

"What a curi's critter that is!" exclaimed one of the group. "I suppose, now, nothin 's goin' to tempt him to set foot on John's Island long 's he lives—do you?" but nobody answered.

"Don' know who he 's spitin' but himself," said the peace-maker. "I was underrunning my trawl last week, an' he come by with his fare o' fish, an' hove to to see what I was gittin'. Me and King George 's al'a's kind of fellowshiped a little by spells. I was off to the Banks, you know, that time he had the gran' flare up an' took himself off, an' so he ain't counted me one o' his enemies."

"I always give my vote that he wa'n't in his right mind; 't wa'n't all ugliness, now. I went to school with him, an' he was a clever boy as there was," said the elder man, who had hardly spoken before. "I never more 'n half blamed him, however 't was, an' it kind o' rankled me that he should ha' been drove off an' outlawed hisself this way. 'T was Jabe Pennell; he thought George was stan'in' in his light 'bout the postmastership, an' he worked folks up, an' set 'em agin him. George's mother's folks did have a kind of a punky spot somewhere in their heads, but he never give no sign o' anything till Jabe Pennell begun to hunt him an' dare him."

"Well, he 's done a good thing sence he bought Folly Island. I hear say King George is gittin' rich," said the peaceful pirate. "'T was a hard thing for his folks, his wife an' the girl. I think he 's been more scattery sence his wife died anyway. Darn! how lonesome they must be in winter! I should think they 'd be afeared a sea would break right over 'em. Pol'tics be hanged, I say, that 'll drive a man to do such things as them—never step foot on any land but his own agin! I tell ye we 've each on us got rights."

This was unusual eloquence and excitement on the speaker's part, and his neighbors stole a furtive look at him and then at each other. He was an own cousin to King George Quint, the recluse owner of Folly Island—an isolated bit of land several miles farther seaward—and one of the listeners reflected that this relationship must be the cause of his bravery.

The post-boat was nearly in now, and the three men rose and went down to the water's edge. The sail was furled, and the old dory slipped about uneasily on the low waves. The postmaster was greeted by friendly shouts from his late maligners, but he was unnecessarily busy with his sail and with his packages amidships, and took his time, as at least one spectator grumbled, about coming in. King George had also lowered his sail and taken to his oars, but just as he would have been alongside, the postmaster caught up his own oars, and pulled smartly toward the landing. This proceeding stimulated his pursuer to a stern-chase, and presently the boats were together, but Pennell pushed straight on through the low waves to the strand, and his pursuer lingered just outside, took in his oars, and dropped his killock over the bow. He knew perfectly well that the representative of the government would go ashore and take all the time he could to sort the contents of the mail-bag in his place of business. It would even be good luck if he did not go home to supper first, and keep everybody waiting all the while. Sometimes his constituents had hailed him from their fishing-boats on the high seas, and taken their weekly newspaper over the boat's side, but it was only in moments of great amiability or forgetfulness that the King of Folly Island was so kindly served. This was tyranny pure and simple. But what could be done? So was winter cold, and so did the dog-fish spoil the trawls. Even the John's-Islanders needed a fearless patriot to lead them to liberty.

The three men on the strand and King George from the harbor were all watching with curious eyes the stranger who had crossed in Jabez Pennell's boat. He was deeply interested in them also; but at that moment such a dazzling glow of sunlight broke from the cloud in the west that Frankfort turned away to look at the strange, remote landscape that surrounded him. He felt as if he had taken a step backward into an earlier age—these men had the look of pioneers or of colonists—yet the little country-side showed marks of long occupancy. He had really got to the outer boundary of civilization.

"Now it 's too bad o' you, Jabez, to keep George Quint a-waitin'," deprecated the peace-maker. "He 's got a good ways to go 'way over to Folly Island, an' like 's not he means to underrun his trawl too. We all expected ye sooner with this fair wind." At which the postmaster gave an unintelligible growl.

"This 'ere passenger was comin' over, calc'latin' to stop a spell, an' wants to be accommodated," he announced presently.

But one of the group on the strand interrupted him. He was considered the wag of that neighborhood. "Ever b'en to Folly Island, stranger?" he asked, with great civility. "There's the King of it, layin' off in his boat. George!" he called lustily, "I want to know ef you can't put up a trav'ler that wants to view these parts o' the airth?"

Frankfort somehow caught the spirit of the occasion, and understood that there was a joke underlying this request. Folly Island had an enticing sound, and he listened eagerly for the answer. It was well known by everybody except himself that Jabez Pennell monopolized the entertainment of the traveling public, and King George roared back, delightedly, that he would do the best he could on short notice, and pulled his boat farther in. Frankfort made ready to transfer his luggage, and laughed again with the men on the shore. He was not sorry to have a longer voyage in that lovely sunset light, and the hospitality of John's Island, already represented by these specimens of householders, was not especially alluring. Jabez Pennell was grumbling to himself, and turned to go to the store. King George reminded him innocently of some groceries which he had promised to have ready, and always fearful of losing one of his few customers, he nodded and went his way. It seemed to be a strange combination of dependence and animosi ty between the men. The King followed his purveyor with a blasting glance of hatred, and turned his boat, and held it so that Frankfort could step in and reach back afterward for his possessions.

In a few minutes Mr. Pennell returned with some packages and a handful of newspapers.

"Have ye put in the cough drops?" asked the fisherman, gruffly, and was answered by a nod of the merchant's head.

"Bring them haddick before Thu'sday," he commanded the island potentate, who was already setting his small sail.

The wind had freshened. They slid out of the bay, and presently the figures on the shore grew indistinct, and Frankfort found himself outward bound on a new tack toward a low island several miles away. It seemed to be at considerable distance from any other land; the light of the sun was full upon it. Now he certainly was as far away as he could get from city life and the busy haunts of men. He wondered at the curious chain of circumstances that he had followed that day. This man looked like a hermit, and really lived in the outermost island of all.

Frankfort grew more and more amused with the novel experiences of the day. He had wished for a long time to see these Maine islands for himself. A week at Mount Desert had served to make him very impatient of the imported society of that renowned watering-place, so incongruous with the native simplicity and quiet. There was a serious look to the dark forests and bleak rocks that seemed to have been broken into fragments by some convulsion of nature, and scattered in islands and reefs along the coast. A strange population clung to these isolated bits of the world, and it was rewarding to Frankfort's sincere interest in such individualized existence that he should now be brought face to face with it.

The boat sailed steadily. A colder air, like the very breath of the great sea, met the voyagers presently. Two or three light-house lamps flashed out their first pale rays like stars, and evening had begun. Yet there was still a soft glow of color over the low seaboard. The western sky was slow to fade, and the islands looked soft and mirage-like in the growing gloom. Frankfort found himself drifting away into dreams as if he were listening to music; there was something lulling in the motion of the boat. As for the King, he took no notice of his passenger, but steered with an oar and tended the sheet and hummed a few notes occasionally of some quaint minor tune, which must have been singing itself more plainly to his own consciousness. The stranger waked from his reverie before very long, and observed with delight that the man before him had a most interesting face, a nobly moulded forehead, and brave, commanding eyes. There was truly an air of distinction and dignity about this King of Folly Island, an uncommon directness and independence. He was the son and heir of the old Vikings who had sailed that stormy coast and discovered its harborage and its vines five hundred years before Columbus was born in Italy, or was beggar to the surly lords and gentlemen of Spain.

The silence was growing strange, and provoking curiosity between the new-made host and guest, and Frankfort asked civilly some question about the distance. The King turned to look at him with surprise, as if he had forgotten his companionship. The discovery seemed to give him pleasure, and he answered, in a good clear voice, with a true fisherman's twang and brogue: "We 're more 'n half there. Be you cold?" And Frankfort confessed to a stray shiver now and then, which seemed to inspire a more friendly relationship in the boat's crew. Quick as thought, the King pulled off his own rough coat and wrapped it about the shoulders of the paler city man. Then he stepped forward along the boat, after handing the oar to his companion, and busied himself ostentatiously with a rope, with the packages that he had bought from Pennell. One would have thought he had freed himself from his coat merely as a matter of convenience; and Frankfort, who was not a little touched by the kindness, paid his new sovereign complete deference. George Quint was evidently a man whom one must be very careful about thanking, however, and there was another time of silence.

"I hope my coming will not make any trouble in your family," ventured the stranger, after a little while.

"Bless ye, no!" replied the host. "There 's only Phebe, my daughter, and nothing would please her better than somebody extra to do for. She 's dreadful folksy for a girl that 's hed to live alone on a far island, Phebe is. 'T ain't every one I 'd pick to carry home, though," said the King, magnificently. "'T has been my plan to keep clear o' humans much as could be. I had my fill o' the John's-Islanders a good while ago."

"Hard to get on with?" asked the listener, humoring the new tone which his ears had caught.

"I could get on with 'em ef 't was anyways wuth while," responded the island chieftain. "I did n't see why there was any need o' being badgered and nagged all my days by a pack o' curs like them John's-Islanders. They 'd hunt ye to death if ye was anyways their master; and I got me a piece o' land as far off from 'em as I could buy, and here I be. I ain't stepped foot on any man's land but my own these twenty-six years. Ef anybody wants to deal with me, he must come to the water's edge."

The speaker's voice trembled with excitement, and Frankfort was conscious of a strange sympathy and exhilaration.

"But why did n't you go ashore and live on the main-land, out of the way of such neighbors altogether?" he asked, and was met by a wondering look.

"I did n't belong there," replied the King, as if the idea had never occurred to him before. "I had my living to get. It took me more than twelve years to finish paying for my island, besides what hard money I laid down. Some years the fish is mighty shy. I always had an eye to the island sence I was a boy; and we 've been better off here, as I view it. I was some sorry my woman should be so fur from her folks when she was down with her last sickness."

The sail was lowered suddenly, and the boat rose and fell on the long waves near the floats of a trawl, which Quint pulled over the bows, slipping the long line by with its empty hooks until he came to a small haddock, which he threw behind him to flop and beat itself about at Frankfort's feet as if imploring him not to eat it for his supper. Then the sprit-sail was hoisted again, and they voyaged toward Folly Island slowly with a failing breeze. The King stamped his feet, and even struck his arms together as if they were chilled, but took no notice of the coat which his guest had taken off again a few minutes before. To Frankfort the evening was growing mild, and his blood rushed through his veins with a delicious thrill. The island loomed high and black, as if it were covered with thick woods; but there was a light ashore in the window of a small house, and presently the pilgrim found himself safe on land, quite stiff in his legs, but very serene in temper. A brisk little dog leaped about him with clamorous barks, a large gray cat also appeared belligerent and curious; then a voice came from the doorway: "Late, ain't you, father?"

Without a word of reply, the King of that isle led the way to his castle, haddock in hand. Frankfort and the dog and cat followed after. Before they reached the open door, the light shone out upon a little wilderness of bright flowers, yellow and red and white. The King stepped carefully up the narrow pathway, and waited on the step for his already loyal subject to enter.

"Phebe," he said, jokingly, "I 've brought ye some company—a gentleman from Lord knows where, who could n't seem to content himself without seeing Folly Island."

Phebe stepped forward with great shyness, but perfect appreciation of the right thing to be done. "I give you welcome," she said, quietly, and offered a thin affectionate hand. She was very plain in her looks, with a hard-worked, New England plainness, but as Frankfort stood in the little kitchen he was immediately conscious of a peculiar delicacy and refinement in his surroundings. There was an atmosphere in this out-of-the-way corner of civilization that he missed in all but a few of the best houses he had ever known.

The ways of the Folly Island housekeeping were too well established to be thrown out of their course by even so uncommon an event as the coming of a stranger. The simple supper was eaten, and Frankfort was ready for his share of it. He was touched at the eagerness of his hostess to serve him, at her wistful questioning of her father to learn whom he had seen and what he had heard that day. There was no actual exile in the fisherman's lot after all; he met his old acquaintances almost daily on the fishing grounds, and it was upon the women of the household that an unmistakable burden of isolation had fallen. Sometimes a man lived with them for a time to help cultivate the small farm, but Phebe was skilled in out-door handicrafts. She could use tools better than her father, the guest was told proudly, and that day she had been digging potatoes—a great pleasure evidently, as anything would have been that kept one out-of-doors in the sunshiny field.

When the supper was over, the father helped his daughter to clear away that table as simply and fondly as could be, and as if it were as much his duty as hers. It was very evident that the cough drops were for actual need; the poor girl coughed now and then with a sad insistence and hollowness. She looked ill already, so narrow-chested and bent-shouldered, while a bright spot of color flickered in her thin cheeks. She had seemed even elderly to Frankfort when he first saw her, but he discovered from something that was said that her age was much less than his own. What a dreary lifetime! he thought, and then reproached himself, for he had never seen a happier smile than poor Phebe gave her father at that moment. The father was evidently very anxious about the cough; he started uneasily at every repetition of it, with a glance at his guest's face to see if he also were alarmed by the foreboding. The wind had risen again, and whined in the chimney. The pine-trees near the house and the wind and sea united in a solemn, deep sound which affected the new-comer strangely. Above this undertone was the lesser, sharper noise of waves striking the pebbly beach and retreating. There was a loneliness, a remoteness, a feeling of being an infinitesimal point in such a great expanse of sea and stormy sky, that was almost too heavy to be borne. Phebe knitted steadily, with an occasional smile at her own thoughts. The tea-kettle sang and whistled away; its cover clicked now and then as if with hardly suppressed cheerfulness, and the King of Folly Island read his newspaper diligently, and doled out bits of information to his companions. Frankfort was surprised at the tenor of these. The reader was evidently a man of uncommon depth of thought and unusual common-sense. It was both less and more surprising that he should have chosen to live alone; one would imagine that his instinct would have led him among people of his own sort. It was no wonder that he had grown impatient of such society as the postmaster's; but at this point of his meditation the traveler's eyes began to feel strangely heavy, and he fell asleep in his high-backed rocking-chair. What peacefulness had circled him in! the rush and clamor of his business life had fallen away as if he had begun another existence, without the fretful troubles of this present world.

"He 's a pretty man," whispered Phebe to her father, and the old fisherman nodded a grave assent, and folded his hands upon the county newspaper while he took a long honest look at the stranger within his gates.

The next morning Frankfort made his appearance in the kitchen at a nobly early hour, to find that the master of the house had been out in his boat since four o'clock, and would not be in for some time yet. Phebe was waiting to give him his breakfast, and soon after he saw her going to the potato field, and joined her. The sun was bright, and the island was gay with color; the asters were in their best pale lavender and royal purple tints; the bay was flecked with sails of fishing-boats, because the mackerel had again struck in; and outside the island, at no great distance, was the highway of the coasting vessels to and from the eastern part of the state and the more distant provinces. There were near two hundred craft in sight, great and small, and John Frankfort dug his potatoes with intermittent industry as he looked off east and west at such a lovely scene. They might have been an *abbé galant* and a dignified *marquise*, he and Phebe—it did not matter what work they toyed with. They were each filled with a charming devotion to the other, a grave reverence and humoring of the mutual desire for quiet and meditation. Toward noon the fishing-boat which Phebe had known constantly and watched with affectionate interest was seen returning deep laden, and she hastened to the little landing. Frankfort had already expressed his disdain of a noonday meal, and throwing down his hoe, betook himself to the highest point of the island. Here was a small company of hemlocks, twisted and bent by the northeast winds, and on the soft brown carpet of their short pins, our pilgrim to the outer boundaries spent the middle of the day. A strange drowsiness, such as he had often felt before in such bracing air, seemed to take possession of him, and to a man who had been perplexing himself with hard business problems and erratic ventures in financiering, potato-digging on a warm September day was not exciting.

The hemlocks stood alone on the summit of the island, and must have been a landmark for the King to steer home by. Before Frankfort stretched a half-cleared pasture, where now and then, as he lazily opened his eyes, he could see a moving sheep's back among the small birches and fern and juniper. Behind him were the cleared fields and the house, and a fringe of forest trees stood all round the rocky shore of the domain. From the water one could not see that there was such a well-arranged farm on Folly Island behind this barrier of cedars, but the inhabitants of that region thriftily counted upon the natural stockade to keep the winter winds away.

The sun had changed its direction altogether when he finally waked, and shone broadly down upon him from a point much nearer the western horizon. At that moment the owner of the island made his appearance, looking somewhat solicitous.

"We did n't know what had become of ye, young man," he said, in a fatherly way. "'T ain't nateral for ye to go without your dinner, as I view it. We 'll soon hearten ye up, Phebe an' me; though she don't eat no more than a chippin'-sparrer, Phebe don't," and his face returned to its sadder lines.

"No," said Frankfort; "she looks very delicate. Don't you think it might be better to take her inland, or to some more sheltered place, this winter?"

The question was asked with hesitation, but the speaker's kind-heartedness was in all his words. The father turned away and snapped a dry hemlock twig with impatient fingers.

"She would n't go withouten me," he answered, in a choked voice, "an' my vow is my vow. I shall never set foot on another man's land while I 'm alive."

The day had been so uneventful, and Folly Island had appeared to be such a calm, not to say prosaic place, that its visitor was already forgetting the thrill of interest with which he had first heard its name. Here again, however, was the unmistakable tragic element in the life of the inhabitants; this man, who should be armed and defended by his common-sense, was yet made weak by some prejudice or superstition. What could have warped him in this strange way? for, indeed, the people of most unenlightened communities were prone to herd together, to follow each other's lead, to need a dictator, no matter how much they might rebel at his example or demands. This city gentleman was moved by a deep curiosity to know for himself the laws and charts of his new-found acquaintance's existence; he had never felt a keener interest in a first day's acquaintance with any human being.

"Society would be at a stand-still," he said with apparent lightness, "if each of us who found his neighbors unsatisfactory should strike out for himself as you have done."

The King of Folly Island gave a long shrewd look at his companion, who was still watching the mackerel fleet; then he blushed like a girl through all the sea-changed color of his cheeks.

"Look out for number one, or else number two 's got to look out for you," he said, with some uncertainty in the tone of his voice.

"Yes," answered Frankfort, smiling. "I have repeated that to myself a great many times. The truth is, I don't belong to my neighbors any more than you do."

"I expect that you have got a better chance nor me; ef I had only been started amon'st Christians, now!" exclaimed Quint, with gathering fury at the thought of his John's-Islanders.

"Human nature is the same the world over," said the guest, quietly, as if more to himself than his listener. "I dare say that the fault is apt to be our own;" but there was no response to this audacious opinion.

Frankfort had risen from the couch of hemlock pins, and the two men walked toward the house together. The cares of modern life could not weigh too heavily on such a day. The shining sea, the white sails, gleaming or gray-shadowed, and the dark green of the nearer islands made a brilliant picture, and the younger man was impatient with himself for thinking the armada of small craft a parallel to the financial ventures which were made day after day in city life. What a question of chance it was, after all, for either herring or dollars—some of these boats were sure to go home disappointed, or worse, at night; but at this point he shrugged his shoulders angrily because he could not forget some still undecided ventures of his own. How degraded a man became who chose to be only a money-maker! The zest of the chase for wealth and the power of it suddenly seemed a very trivial and foolish thing to Frankfort, who confessed anew that he had no purpose in making his gains.

"You ain't a married man; live a bachelor life, don't ye?" asked the King, as if in recognition of these thoughts, and Frankfort, a little startled, nodded assent.

"Makes it a sight easier," was the unexpected response. "You don't feel as if you might be wronging other folks when you do what suits you best. Now my woman was wuth her weight in gold, an' she lays there in the little yard over in the corner of the field—she never fought me, nor argued the p'int again after she found I was sot, but it aged her, fetchin' of her away from all her folks, an' out of where she was wonted. I did n't foresee it at the time."

There was something martyr-like and heroic in the exile's appearance as he spoke, and his listener had almost an admiration for such heroism, until he reminded himself that this withdrawal from society had been willful, and, so far as he knew, quite selfish. It could not be said that Quint had stood in his lot and place as a brave man should, unless he had left John's Island as the Pilgrim Fathers left England, for conscientious scruples and a necessary freedom. How many pilgrims since those have falsely made the same plea for undeserved liberty!

"What was your object in coming here?" the stranger asked, quietly, as if he had heard no reason yet that satisfied him.

"I wanted to be by myself;" and the King rallied his powers of eloquence to make excuses. "I wa'n't one that could stand them folks that overlooked an' harried me, an' was too mean to live. They could go their way, an' I mine; I would n't harm 'em, but I wanted none of 'em. Here, you see, I get my own livin'. I raise my own hog, an' the women-folks have more hens than they want, an' I keep a few sheep a-runnin' over the other side o' the place. The fish o' the sea is had for the catchin', an' I owe no man anything. I should ha' b'en beholden if I 'd stopped where we come from;" and he turned with an air of triumph to look at Frankfort, who glanced at him in return with an air of interest.

"I see that you depend upon the larger islands for some supplies—cough drops, for instance?" said the stranger, with needless clearness. "I cannot help feeling that you would have done better to choose a less exposed island—one nearer the main-land, you know, in a place better sheltered from the winds."

"They do cut us 'most in two," said the King, meekly, and his face fell. Frankfort felt quite ashamed of himself, but he was conscious already of an antagonistic feeling. Indeed, this was an island of folly; this man, who felt himself to be better than his neighbors, was the sacrificer of his family's comfort; he was heaping up riches, and who would gather them? Not the poor pale daughter, that was certain. In this moment they passed the corner of the house, and discovered Phebe herself standing on the doorstep, watching some distant point of sea or sky with a heavy, much battered spy-glass.

She look pleased as she lowered the glass for a moment, and greeted Frankfort with a silent welcome.

"Oh, so 't is; now I forgot 't was this afternoon," said Quint. "She 's a-watchin' the funeral; ain't you, daughter? Old Mis' Danforth, over onto Wall Island, that has been layin' sick all summer—a cousin o' my mother's," he confessed, in a lower tone, and turned away with feigned unconcern as Frankfort took the spy-glass which Phebe offered. He was sure that his hostess had been wishing that she could share in the family gathering. Was it possible that Quint was a tyrant, and had never let this grown woman leave his chosen isle? Freedom, indeed!

He forgot the affairs of Folly Island the next moment, as he caught sight of the strange procession. He could see the coffin with its black pall in a boat rowed by four men, who had pushed out a little way from shore, and other boats near it. From the low gray house near the water came a little group of women stepping down across the rough beach and getting into their boats; then all fell into a rude sort of orderliness, the hearse-boat going first, and the procession went away across the wide bay toward the main-land. He lowered the glass for an instant, and Phebe reached for it eagerly.

"They were just bringing out the coffin before you came," she said, with a little sigh; and Frankfort, who had seen many pageants and ceremonials, rebuked himself for having stolen so much of this rare pleasure from his hostess. He could still see the floating funeral. Though it was only a far-away line of boats, there was a strange awe and fascination in watching them follow their single, steady course.

"Danforth's folks bury over to the Foreside," explained the King of Folly Island; but his guest had taken a little book from his pocket, and seated himself on a rock that made one boundary of the gay, disorderly garden. It was very shady and pleasant at this side of the house, and he was too warm after his walk across the unshaded pastures. It was very hot sunshine for that time of the year, and his holiday began to grow dull. Was he, after all, good for nothing but money-making? The thought fairly haunted him; he had lost his power of enjoyment, and there might be no remedy.

The fisherman had disappeared; the funeral was a dim speck off there where the sun glittered on the water, yet he saw it still, and his book closed over his listless fingers. Phebe sat on the door-step knitting now, with the old glass laid by her side ready for use. Frankfort looked at her presently with a smile.

"Will you let me see your book?" she asked, with a child's eagerness; and he gave it to her.

"It is an old copy of Wordsworth's shorter poems," he said. "It belonged to my mother. Her name was the same as yours."

"She spelled it with the o," said Phebe, radiant with interest in this discovery, and closely examining the flyleaf. "What a pretty hand she wrote! Is it a book you like?"

"I like it best because it was hers, I am afraid," replied Frankfort, honestly. "Yes, it does one good to read such poems; but I find it hard to read anything in these days; my business fills my mind. You know so little, here on your island, of the way the great world beyond pushes and fights and wrangles."

"I suppose there are some pleasant folks," said Phebe, simply. "I used to like to read, but I found it made me lonesome. I used to wish I could go ashore and do all the things that folks in books did. But I don't care now; I would n't go away from the island for anything."

"No," said Frankfort, kindly; "I would n't if I were you. Go on dreaming about the world; that is better. And it does people good to come here and see you so comfortable and contented," he added, with a tenderness in his voice that was quite foreign to it of late years. But Phebe gave one quick look at the far horizon, her thin cheeks grew very rosy, and she looked down again at her knitting.

Presently she went into the house. At tea-time that evening the guest was surprised to find the little table decked out for a festival, with some flowered china, and a straight-backed old mahogany chair from the best room in his own place of honor. Phebe looked gay and excited, and Frankfort wondered at the feast, as well as the master of the house, when they came to take their places.

"You see, you found me unawares last night, coming so unexpected," said the poor pale mistress. "I did n't want you to think that we had forgotten how to treat folks."

And somehow the man whose face was usually so cold and unchanging could hhe brought it to him with a splendid sense of its art, and Frankfort said everything that could be said except that it was beautiful. He even begged to be told exactly how it was done, and they sat by the light together and discussed the poor toy, while the King of Folly Island dozed and waked again with renewed pleasure as he contemplated his daughter's enjoyment. But she coughed very often, poor Phebe, and the guest wondered if the postmaster's supply of drugs were equal to this pitiful illness. Poor Phebe! and winter would be here soon!

Day after day, in the bright weather, Frankfort lingered with his new friends, spending a morning now and then in fishing with his host, and coming into closer contact with the inhabitants of that part of the world.

Before the short visit was over, the guest was aware that he had been tired and out of sorts when he had yielded to the desire to hide away from civilization, and had drifted, under some pilotage that was beyond himself, into this quiet haven. He felt stronger and in much better spirits, and remembered afterward that he had been as merry as a boy on Folly Island in the long evenings when Phebe was busy with her knitting-work, and her father told long and spirited stories of his early experiences along the coast and among the fishermen. But business cares began to fret this holiday-maker, and as suddenly as he had come he went away again on a misty morning that promised rain. He was very sorry when he said good-by to Phebe; she was crying as he left the house, and a great wave of compassion poured itself over Frankfort's heart. He never should see her again, that was certain; he wished that he could spirit her away to some gentler climate, and half spoke his thought as he stood hesitating that last minute on the little beach. The next moment he was fairly in the boat and pushing out from shore. George Quint looked as hardy and ruddy and weather-beaten as his daughter was pale and faded, like some frost-bitten flower that tries to lift itself when morning comes and it feels the warmth of the sun. The tough fisherman, with his pet doctrines and angry aversions, could have no idea of the loneliness of his wife and daughter all these unvarying years on his Folly Island. And yet how much they had been saved of useless rivalries and jealousies, of petty tyranny from narrow souls! Frankfort had a bitter sense of all that, as he leaned back against the side of the boat, and sailed slowly out into the bay, while Folly Island seemed to retreat into the gathering fog and slowly disappear. His thoughts flew before him to his office, to his clerks and accounts; he thought of his wealth which was buying him nothing, of his friends who were no friends at all, for he had pushed away some who might have been near, strangely impatient of familiarity, and on the defense against either mockery or rivalry. He was the true King of Folly Island, not this work-worn fisherman; he had been a lonelier and a more selfish man these many years.

George Quint was watching Frankfort eagerly, as if he had been waiting for this chance to speak to him alone.

"You seem to be a kind of solitary creatur'," he suggested, with his customary frankness. "I expect it never crossed your thought that 't would be nateral to git married?"

"Yes, I thought about it once, some years ago," answered Frankfort, seriously.

"Disapp'inted, was you? Well, 't was better soon nor late, if it had to be," said the sage. "My mind has been dwellin' on Phebe's case. She was a master pooty gal 'arlier on, an' I was dreadful set against lettin' of her go, though I call to mind there was a likely chap as found her out, an' made bold to land an' try to court her. I drove him, I tell you, an' ducked him under when I caught him afterward out a-fishin', an' he took the hint. Phebe did n't know what was to pay, though I dare say she liked to have him follerin' about."

Frankfort made no answer,—he was very apt to be silent when you expected him to speak,—and presently the King resumed his suggestions.

"I 've been thinking that Phebe ought to have some sort o' brightenin' up. She pines for her mother: they was a sight o' company for each other. Now I s'pose you could n't take no sort o' fancy for her in course o' time? I 've got more hard cash stowed away than folks expects, an' you should have everything your own way. I could git a cousin o' mine, a widow woman, to keep the house winters, an' you an' the gal need n't only summer here. I take it you 've got some means?"

Frankfort found himself similing at this pathetic appeal, and was ashamed of himself directly, and turned to look seaward. "I 'm afraid I could n't think of it," he answered. "You don't suppose"—

"Lor' no," said George Quint, sadly, shifting his sail. "*She* ain't give no sign, except that I never see her take to no stranger as she has to you. I thought you might kind of have a feelin' for her, an' I knowed you thought the island was a sightly place; 't would do no harm to speak, leastways."

They were on their way to John's Island, where Frankfort was to take the postmaster's boat to the main-land. Quint found his fog-bound way by some mysterious instinct, and at their journey's end the friends parted with little show of sentiment or emotion. Yet there was much expression in Quint's grasp of his hand, Frankfort thought, and both men turned more than once as the boats separated, to give a kindly glance backward. People are not brought together in this world for nothing, and poor Quint had no idea of the confusion that his theories and his manner of life had brought into the well-regulated affairs of John Frankfort. Jabez Pennell was brimful of curiosity about the visit, but he received little satisfaction. "Phebe Quint was the pootiest gal on these islands some ten years ago," he proclaimed, "an' a born lady. Her mother's folks was ministers over to Castine."

The winter was nearly gone when Frankfort received a letter in a yellow envelope, unbusiness-like in its appearance. The King of Folly Island wrote to say that Phebe had been hoping to get strength enough to thank him for the generous Christmas-box which Frankfort had sent. He had taxed both his imagination and memory to supply the minor wants and fancies of the islanders.

But Phebe was steadily failing in health, and the elderly cousin had already been summoned to take care of her and to manage the house-keeping. The King wrote a crabbed hand, as if he had used a fish-hook instead of a pen, and he told the truth about his sad affairs with simple, unlamenting bravery. Phebe only sent a message of thanks, and an assurance that she liked to think of Frankfort's being there in the fall. She would soon send him a small keepsake.

One morning Frankfort opened a much-crushed bundle which lay upon his desk, and found this keepsake, the shell meeting-house, which looked sadly trivial and astray. He was entirely confused by its unexpected appearance; he did not dare to meet the eyes of an office-boy who stood near; there was an uncomfortable feeling in his throat, but he bravely unfastened a letter from the battered steeple, and read it slowly, without a very clear understanding of the words:—

"DEAR FRIEND" (said poor Phebe),—"I was very thankful for all that you sent in the box—I take such pleasure in the things. I find it hard to write, but I think about you every day. Father sends his best respects. We have had rough weather, and he stays right here with me. You must keep your promise, and come back to the island; he will be lonesome, and you are one that takes father just right. It seems as if I had n't been any use in the world, but it rests me, laying here, to think what a sight of use you must be. And so good-by."

A sudden vision of the poor girl came before his eyes as he saw her stand on the door-step the day they watched the boat funeral. She had worn a dress with a quaint pattern, like gray and yellowish willow leaves as one sees them fallen by the country roadsides. A vision of her thin, stooping shoulders and her simple, pleasant look touched him with real sorrow. "Much use in the world!" Alas! alas! how had her affection made her fancy such a thing!

The day was stormy, and Frankfort turned anxiously to look out of the window beside him, as he thought how the wind must blow across the distant bay. He felt a strange desire to sweep away everything that might vex poor Phebe or make her less comfortable. Yet she must die, at any rate, before the summer came. The King of Folly Island would reign only over his sheep pastures and the hemlock-trees and pines. Much use in the world! The words stung him more and more.

The office-boy still stood waiting, and now Frankfort became unhappily conscious of his presence. "I used to see one o' them shell-works where I come from, up in the country," the boy said, with unexpected forbearance and sympathy; but Frankfort dismissed him with a needless question about the price of certain railroad bonds, and dropped the embarrassing gift, the poor little meeting-house, into a deep lower drawer of his desk. He had hardly thought of the lad before except as a willing, half mechanical errand-runner; now he was suddenly conscious of the hopeful, bright young face. At that moment a whole new future of human interests spread out before his eyes, from which a veil had suddenly been withdrawn, and Frankfort felt like another man, or as if there had been a revivifying of his old, uninterested, self-occupied nature. Was there really such a thing as taking part in the heavenly warfare against ignorance and selfishness? Had Phebe given him in some mysterious way a legacy of all her unsatisfied hopes and dreams?

THE COURTING OF SISTER WISBY

All the morning there had been an increasing temptation to take an out-door holiday, and early in the afternoon the temptation outgrew my power of resistance. A far-away pasture on the long southwestern slope of a high hill was persistently present to my mind, yet there seemed to be no particular reason why I should think of it. I was not sure that I wanted anything from the pasture, and there was no sign, except the temptation, that the pasture wanted anything of me. But I was on the farther side of as many as three fences before I stopped to think again where I was going, and why.

There is no use in trying to tell another person about that afternoon unless he distinctly remembers weather exactly like it. No number of details concerning an Arctic ice-blockade will give a single shiver to a child of the tropics. This was one of those perfect New England days in late summer, when the spirit of autumn takes a first stealthy flight, like a spy, through the ripening country-side, and, with feigned sympathy for those who droop with August heat, puts her cool cloak of bracing air about leaf and flower and human shoulders. Every living thing grows suddenly cheerful and strong; it is only when you catch sight of a horror-stricken little maple in swampy soil,—a little maple that has second sight and foreknowledge of coming disaster to her race,—only then does a distrust of autumn's friendliness dim your joyful satisfaction.

In midwinter there is always a day when one has the first foretaste of spring; in late August there is a morning when the air is for the first time autumn like. Perhaps it is a hint to the squirrels to get in their first supplies for the winter hoards, or a reminder that summer will soon end, and everybody had better make the most of it. We are always looking forward to the passing and ending of winter, but when summer is here it seems as if summer must always last. As I went across the fields that day, I found myself half lamenting that the world must fade again, even that the best of her budding and bloom was only a preparation for another spring-time, for an awakening beyond the coming winter's sleep.

The sun was slightly veiled; there was a chattering group of birds, which had gathered for a conference about their early migration. Yet, oddly enough, I heard the voice of a belated bobolink, and presently saw him rise from the grass and hover leisurely, while he sang a brief tune. He was much behind time if he were still a housekeeper; but as for the other birds, who listened, they cared only for their own notes. An old crow went sagging by, and gave a croak at his despised neighbor, just as a black reviewer croaked at Keats: so hard it is to be just to one's contemporaries. The bobolink was indeed singing out of season, and it was impossible to say whether he really belonged most to this summer or to the next. He might have been delayed on his northward journey; at any rate, he had a light heart now, to judge from his song, and I wished that I could ask him a few questions,—how he liked being the last man among the bobolinks, and where he had taken singing lessons in the South.

Presently I left the lower fields, and took a path that led higher, where I could look beyond the village to the northern country mountainward. Here the sweet fern grew, thick and fragrant, and I also found myself heedlessly treading on pennyroyal. Near by, in a field corner, I long ago made a most comfortable seat by putting a stray piece of board and bit of rail across the angle of the fences. I have spent many a delightful hour there, in the shade and shelter of a young pitch-pine and a wild-cherry tree, with a lovely outlook toward the village, just far enough beyond the green slopes and tall elms of the lower meadows. But that day I still had the feeling of being outward bound, and did not turn aside nor linger. The high pasture land grew more and more enticing.

I stopped to pick some blackberries that twinkled at me like beads among their dry vines, and two or three yellow-birds fluttered up from the leaves of a thistle, and then came back again, as if they had complacently discovered that I was only an overgrown yellow-bird, in strange disguise but perfectly harmless. They made me feel as if I were an intruder, though they did not offer to peck at me, and we parted company very soon. It was good to stand at last on the great shoulder of the hill. The wind was coming in from the sea, there was a fine fragrance from the pines, and the air grew sweeter every moment. I took new pleasure in the thought that in a piece of wild pasture land like this one may get closest to Nature, and subsist upon what she gives of her own free will. There have been no drudging, heavy-shod ploughmen to overturn the soil, and vex it into yielding artificial crops. Here one has to take just what Nature is pleased to give, whether one is a yellow-bird or a human being. It is very good entertainment for a summer wayfarer, and I am asking my reader now to share the winter provision which I harvested that day. Let us hope that the small birds are also faring well after their fashion, but I give them an anxious thought while the snow goes hurrying in long waves across the buried fields, this windy winter night.

I next went farther down the hill, and got a drink of fresh cool water from the brook, and pulled a tender sheaf of sweet flag beside it. The mossy old fence just beyond was the last barrier between me and the pasture which had sent an invisible messenger earlier in the day, but I saw that somebody else had come first to the rendezvous: there was a brown gingham cape-bonnet and a sprigged shoulder-shawl bobbing up and down, a little way off among the junipers. I had taken such uncommon pleasure in being alone that I instantly felt a sense of disappointment; then a warm glow of pleasant satisfaction rebuked my selfishness. This could be no one but dear old Mrs. Goodsoe, the friend of my childhood and fond dependence of my maturer years. I had not seen her for many weeks, but here she was, out on one of her famous campaigns for herbs, or perhaps just returning from a blueberrying expedition. I approached with care, so as not to startle the gingham bonnet; but she heard the rustle of the bushes against my dress, and looked up quickly, as she knelt, bending over the turf. In that position she was hardly taller than the luxuriant junipers themselves.

"I 'm a-gittin' in my mulleins," she said briskly, "an' I 've been thinking o' you these twenty times since I come out o' the house. I begun to believe you must ha' forgot me at last."

"I have been away from home," I explained. "Why don't you get in your pennyroyal too? There 's a great plantation of it beyond the next fence but one."

"Pennyr'yal!" repeated the dear little old woman, with an air of compassion for inferior knowledge; "'t ain't the right time, darlin'. Pennyr'yal's too rank now. But for mulleins this day is prime. I 've got a dreadful graspin' fit for 'em this year; seems if I must be goin' to need 'em extry. I feel like the squirrels must when they know a hard winter's comin'." And Mrs. Goodsoe bent over her work again, while I stood by and watched her carefully cut the best full-grown leaves with a clumsy pair of scissors, which might have served through at least half a century of herb-gathering. They were fastened to her apron-strings by a long piece of list.

"I 'm going to take my jack-knife and help you," I suggested, with some fear of refusal. "I just passed a flourishing family of six or seven heads that must have been growing on purpose for you."

"Now be keerful, dear heart," was the anxious response; "choose 'em well. There 's odds in mulleins same 's there is in angels. Take a plant that 's all run up to stalk, and there ain't but little goodness in the leaves. This one I 'm at now must ha' been stepped on by some creatur' and blighted of its bloom, and the leaves is han'some! When I was small I used to have a notion that Adam an' Eve must a took mulleins fer their winter wear. Ain't they just like flannel, for all the world? I 've had experience, and I know there 's plenty of sickness might be saved to folks if they 'd quit horse-radish and such fiery, exasperating things, and use mullein drarves in proper season. Now I shall spread these an' dry 'em nice on my spare floor in the garrit, an' come to steam 'em for use along in the winter there 'll be the vally of the whole summer's goodness in 'em, sartin." And she snipped away with the dull scissors, while I listened respectfully, and took great pains to have my part of the harvest present a good appearance.

"This is most too dry a head," she added presently, a little out of breath. "There! I can tell you there 's win'rows o' young doctors, bilin' over with book-larnin', that is truly ignorant of what to do for the sick, or how to p'int out those paths that well people foller toward sickness. Book-fools I call 'em, them young men, an' some on 'em never 'll live to know much better, if they git to be Methuselahs. In my time every middle-aged woman, who had brought up a family, had some proper ideas o' dealin' with complaints. I won't say but there was some fools amongst *them*, but I 'd rather take my chances, unless they 'd forsook herbs and gone to dealin' with patent stuff. Now my mother really did sense the use of herbs and roots. I never see anybody that come up to her. She was a meek-looking woman, but very understandin', mother was."

"Then that 's where you learned so much yourself, Mrs. Goodsoe," I ventured to say.

"Bless your heart, I don't hold a candle to her; 't is but little I can recall of what she used to say. No, her l'arnin' died with her," said my friend, in a self-depreciating tone. "Why, there was as many as twenty kinds of roots alone that she used to keep by her, that I forget the use of; an' I 'm sure I should n't know where to find the most of 'em, any. There was an herb"—*airb,* she called it—"an herb called masterwort, that she used to get way from Pennsylvany; and she used to think everything of noble-liverwort, but I never could seem to get the right effects from it as she could. Though I don't know as she ever really did use masterwort where somethin' else would n't a served. She had a cousin married out in Pennsylvany that used to take pains to get it to her every year or two, and so she felt 't was important to have it. Some set more by such things as come from a distance, but I rec'lect mother always used to maintain that folks was meant to be doctored with the stuff that grew right about 'em; 't was sufficient, an' so ordered. That was before the whole population took to livin' on wheels, the way they do now. 'T was never my idee that we was meant to know what 's goin' on all over the world to once. There 's goin' to be some sort of a set-back one o' these days, with these telegraphs an' things, an' letters comin' every hand's turn, and folks leavin' their proper work to answer 'em. I may not live to see it. 'T was allowed to be difficult for folks to git about in old times, or to git word across the country, and they stood in their lot an' place, and were n't all just alike, either, same as pine spills."

We were kneeling side by side now, as if in penitence for the march of progress, but we laughed as we turned to look at each other.

"Do you think it did much good when everybody brewed a cracked quart mug of herb-tea?" I asked, walking away on my knees to a new mullein.

"I 've always lifted my voice against the practice, far 's I could," declared Mrs. Goodsoe; "an' I won't deal out none o' the herbs I save for no such nonsense. There was three houses along our road,—I call no names,—where you could n't go into the livin' room without findin' a mess o' herb-tea drorin' on the stove or side o' the fireplace, winter or summer, sick or well. One was thoroughwut, one would be camomile, and the other, like as not, yellow dock; but they all used to put in a little new rum to git out the goodness, or keep it from spilin'." (Mrs. Goodsoe favored me with a knowing smile.) "Land, how mother used to laugh! But, poor creaturs, they had to work hard, and I guess it never done 'em a mite o' harm; they was all good herbs. I wish you could hear the quawkin' there used to be when they was indulged with a real case o' sickness. Everybody would collect from far an' near; you 'd see 'em coming along the road and across the pastures then; everybody clamorin' that nothin' would n't do no kind o' good but her choice o' teas or drarves to the feet. I wonder there was a babe lived to grow up in the whole lower part o' the town; an' if nothing else 'peared to ail 'em, word was passed about that 't was likely Mis' So-and-So's last young one was goin' to be foolish. Land, how they 'd gather! I know one day the doctor came to Widder Peck's and the house was crammed so 't he could scercely git inside the door; and he says, just as polite, 'Do send for some of the neighbors!' as if there wa'n't a soul to turn to, right or left. You 'd ought to seen 'em begin to scatter."

"But don't you think the cars and telegraphs have given people more to interest them, Mrs. Goodsoe? Don't you believe people's lives were narrower then, and more taken up with little things?" I asked, unwisely, being a product of modern times.

"Not one mite, dear," said my companion stoutly. "There was as big thoughts then as there is now; these times was born o' them. The difference is in folks themselves; but now, instead o' doin' their own housekeepin' and watchin' their own neighbors,—though that was carried to excess,—they git word that a niece's child is ailin' the other side o' Massachusetts, and they drop everything and git on their best clothes, and off they jiggit in the cars. 'T is a bad sign when folks wears out their best clothes faster 'n they do their every-day ones. The other side o' Massachusetts has got to look after itself by rights. An' besides that, Sunday-keepin' 's all gone out o' fashion. Some lays it to one thing an' some another, but some o' them old ministers that folks are all a-sighin' for did preach a lot o' stuff that wa'n't nothin' but chaff; 't wa'n't the word o' God out o' either Old Testament or New. But everybody went to meetin' and heard it, and come home, and was set to fightin' with their next door neighbor over it. Now I 'm a believer, and I try to live a Christian life, but I 'd as soon hear a surveyor's book read out, figgers an' all, as try to get any simple truth out o' most sermons. It's them as is most to blame."

"What was the matter that day at Widow Peck's?" I hastened to ask, for I knew by experience that the good, clear-minded soul beside me was apt to grow unduly vexed and distressed when she contemplated the state of religious teaching.

"Why, there wa'n't nothin' the matter, only a gal o' Miss Peck's had met with a dis'pintment and had gone into screechin' fits. 'T was a rovin' creatur' that had come along hayin' time, and he 'd gone off an' forsook her betwixt two days; nobody ever knew what become of him. Them Pecks was 'Good Lord, anybody!' kind o' gals, and took up with whoever they could get. One of 'em married Heron, the Irishman; they lived in that little house that was burnt this summer, over on the edge o' the plains. He was a good-hearted creatur', with a laughin' eye and a clever word for everybody. He was the first Irishman that ever came this way, and we was all for gettin' a look at him, when he first used to go by. Mother's folks was what they call Scotch-Irish, though; there was an old race of 'em settled about here. They could foretell events, some on 'em, and had the second sight. I know folks used to say mother's grandmother had them gifts, but mother was never free to speak about it to us. She remembered her well, too."

"I suppose that you mean old Jim Heron, who was such a famous fiddler?" I asked with great interest, for I am always delighted to know more about that rustic hero, parochial Orpheus that he must have been!

"Now, dear heart, I suppose you don't remember him, do you?" replied Mrs. Goodsoe, earnestly. "Fiddle! He 'd about break your heart with them tunes of his, or else set your heels flying up the floor in a jig, though you was minister o' the First Parish and all wound up for a funeral prayer. I tell ye there ain't no tunes sounds like them used to. It used to seem to me summer nights when I was comin' along the plains road, and he set by the window playin', as if ther e was bewitched human creatur' in that old red fiddle o' his. He could make it sound just like a woman's voice tellin' somethin' over and over, as if folks could help her out o' her sorrows if she could only make 'em understand. I 've set by the stone-wall and cried as if my heart was broke, and dear knows it wa'n't in them days. How he would twirl off them jigs and dance tunes! He used to make somethin' han'some out of 'em in fall an' winter, playin' at huskins and dancin' parties; but he was unstiddy by spells, as he got along in years, and never knew what it was to be forehanded. Everybody felt bad when he died; you could n't help likin' the creatur'. He 'd got the gift—that 's all you could say about it.

"There was a Mis' Jerry Foss, that lived over by the brook bridge, on the plains road, that had lost her husband early, and was left with three child'n. She set the world by 'em, and was a real pleasant, ambitious little woman, and was workin' on as best she could with that little farm, when there come a rage o' scarlet fever, and her boy and two girls was swept off and laid dead within the same week. Every one o' the neighbors did what they could, but she 'd had no sleep since they was taken sick, and after the funeral she set there just like a piece o' marble, and would only shake her head when you spoke to her. They all thought her reason would go; and 't would certain, if she could n't have shed tears. An' one o' the neighbors— 't was like mother's sense, but it might have been somebody else—spoke o' Jim Heron. Mother an' one or two o' the women that knew her best was in the house with her. 'T was right in the edge o' the woods and some of us younger ones was over by the wall on the other side of the road where there was a couple of old willows,—I remember just how the brook damp felt; and we kept quiet 's we could, and some other folks come along down the road, and stood waitin' on the little bridge, hopin' sombody 'd come out, I suppose, and they 'd git news. Everybody was wrought up, and felt a good deal for her, you know. By an' by Jim Heron come stealin' right out o' the shadows an' set down on the door-step, an' 't was a good while before he heard a sound; then, oh, dear me! 't was what the whole neighborhood felt for that mother all spoke in the notes, an' they told me afterwards that Mis' Foss's face changed in a minute, and she come right over an' got into my mother's lap,—she was a little woman,—an' laid her head down, and there she cried herself into a blessed sleep. After awhile one o' the other women stole out an' told the folks, and we all went home. He only played that one tune.

"But there!" resumed Mrs. Goodsoe, after a silence, during which my eyes were filled with tears. "His wife always complained that the fiddle made her nervous. She never 'peared to think nothin' o' poor Heron after she 'd once got him."

"That 's often the way," said I, with harsh cynicism, though I had no guilty person in my mind at the moment; and we went straying off, not very far apart, up through the pasture. Mrs. Goodsoe cautioned me that we must not get so far off that we could not get back the same day. The sunshine began to feel very hot on our backs, and we both turned toward the shade. We had already collected a large bundle of mullein leaves, which were carefully laid into a clean, calico apron, held together by the four corners, and proudly carried by me, though my companion regarded them with anxious eyes. We sat down together at the edge of the pine woods, and Mrs. Goodsoe proceeded to fan herself with her limp cape-bonnet.

"I declare, how hot it is! The east wind's all gone again," she said. "It felt so cool this forenoon that I overburdened myself with as thick a petticoat as any I've got. I'm despri't afeared of having a chill, now that I ain't so young as once. I hate to be housed up."

"It's only August, after all," I assured her unnecessarily, confirming my statement by taking two peaches out of my pocket, and laying them side by side on the brown pine needles between us.

"Dear sakes alive!" exclaimed the old lady, with evident pleasure. "Where did you get them, now? Doesn't anything taste twice better out-o'-doors? I ain't had such a peach for years. Do le's keep the stones, an' I'll plant 'em; it only takes four year for a peach pit to come to bearing, an' I guess I'm good for four year, 'thout I meet with some accident."

I could not help agreeing, or taking a fond look at the thin little figure, and her wrinkled brown face and kind, twinkling eyes. She looked as if she had properly dried herself, by mistake, with some of her mullein leaves, and was likely to keep her goodness, and to last the longer in consequence. There never was a truer, simple-hearted soul made out of the old-fashioned country dust than Mrs. Goodsoe. I thought, as I looked away from her across the wide country, that nobody was left in any of the farm-houses so original, so full of rural wisdom and reminiscence, so really able and dependable, as she. And nobody had made better use of her time in a world foolish enough to sometimes undervalue medicinal herbs.

When we had eaten our peaches we still sat under the pines, and I was not without pride when I had poked about in the ground with a little twig, and displayed to my crony a long fine root, bright yellow to the eye, and a wholesome bitter to the taste.

"Yis, dear, goldthread," she assented indulgently. "Seems to me there's more of it than anything except grass an' hardhack. Good for canker, but no better than two or three other things I can call to mind; but I always lay in a good wisp of it, for old times' sake. Now, I want to know why you should a bit it, and took away all the taste o' your nice peach? I was just thinkin' what a han'some entertainment we 've had. I 've got so I 'sociate certain things with certain folks, and goldthread was somethin' Lizy Wisby could n't keep house without, no ways whatever. I believe she took so much it kind o' puckered her disposition."

"Lizy Wisby?" I repeated inquiringly.

"You knew her, if ever, by the name of Mis' Deacon Brimblecom," answered my friend, as if this were only a brief preface to further information, so I waited with respectful expectation. Mrs. Goodsoe had grown tired out in the sun, and a good story would be an excuse for sufficient rest. It was a most lovely place where we sat, half-way up the long hillside; for my part, I was perfectly contented and happy. "You 've often heard of Deacon Brimblecom?" she asked, as if a great deal depended upon his being properly introduced.

"I remember him," said I. "They called him Deacon Brimfull, you know, and he used to go about with a witch-hazel branch to show people where to dig wells."

"That 's the one," said Mrs. Goodsoe, laughing. "I did n't know 's you could go so far back. I 'm always divided between whether you can remember everything I can, or are only a babe in arms."

"I have a dim recollection of there being something strange about their marriage," I suggested, after a pause, which began to appear dangerous. I was so much afraid the subject would be changed.

"I can tell you all about it," I was quickly answered. "Deacon Brimblecom was very pious accordin' to his lights in his early years. He lived way back in the country then, and there come a rovin' preacher along, and set everybody up that way all by the ears. I 've heard the old folks talk it over, but I forget most of his doctrin', except some of his followers was persuaded they could dwell among the angels while yet on airth, and this Deacon Brimfull, as you call him, felt sure he was called by the voice of a spirit bride. So he left a good, deservin' wife he had, an' four children, and built him a new house over to the other side of the land he 'd had from his father. They did n't take much pains with the buildin', because they expected to be translated before long, and then the spirit brides and them folks was goin' to appear and divide up the airth amongst 'em, and the world's folks and on-believers was goin' to serve 'em or be sent to torments. They had meetins about in the school-houses, an' all sorts o' goins on; some on 'em went crazy, but the deacon held on to what wits he had, an' by an' by the spirit bride did n't turn out to be much of a housekeeper, an' he had always been used to good livin', so he sneaked home ag'in. One o' mother's sisters married up to Ash Hill, where it all took place; that 's how I come to have the particulars."

"Then how did he come to find his Eliza Wisby?" I inquired. "Do tell me the whole story; you 've got mullein leaves enough."

"There 's all yesterday's at home, if I have n't," replied Mrs. Goodsoe. "The way he come a-courtin' o' Sister Wisby was this: she went a-courtin' o' him.

"There was a spell he lived to home, and then his poor wife died, and he had a spirit bride in good earnest, an' the child'n was placed about with his folks and hers, for they was both out o' good families; and I don't know what come over him, but he had another pious fit that looked for all the world like the real thing. He had n't no family cares, and he lived with his brother's folks, and turned his land in with theirs. He used to travel to every meetin' an' conference that was within reach of his old sorrel hoss's feeble legs; he j'ined the Christian Baptists that was just in their early prime, and he was a great exhorter, and got to be called deacon, though I guess he wa'n't deacon, 'less it was for a spare hand when deacon timber was scercer'n usual. An' one time there was a four days' protracted meetin' to the church in the lower part of the town. 'T was a real solemn time; something more'n usual was goin' forward, an' they collected from the whole country round. Women folks liked it, an' the men too; it give 'em a change, an' they was quartered round free, same as conference folks now. Some on 'em, for a joke, sent Silas Brimblecom up to Lizy Wisby's, though she 'd give out she could n't accommodate nobody, because of expectin' her cousin's folks. Everybody knew 't was a lie; she was amazin' close considerin' she had plenty to do with. There was a streak that wa'n't just right somewheres in Lizy's wits, I always thought. She was very kind in case o' sickness, I 'll say that for her.

"You know where the house is, over there on what they call Windy Hill? There the deacon went, all unsuspectin', and 'stead o' Lizy's resentin' of him she put in her own hoss, and they come back together to evenin' meetin'. She was prominent among the sect herself, an' he bawled and talked, and she bawled and talked, an' took up more 'n the time allotted in the exercises, just as if they was showin' off to each other what they was able to do at expoundin'. Everybody was laughin' at 'em after the meetin' broke up, and that day an' the next, an' all through, they was constant, and seemed to be havin' a beautiful occasion. Lizy had always give out she scorned the men, but when she got a chance at a particular one 't was altogether different, and the deacon seemed to please her somehow or 'nother, and—There! you don't want to listen to this old stuff that 's past an' gone?"

"Oh yes, I do," said I.

"I run on like a clock that 's onset her striking hand," said Mrs. Goodsoe mildly. "Sometimes my kitchen timepiece goes on half the forenoon, and I says to myself the day before yesterday I would let it be a warnin', and keep it in mind for a check on my own speech. The next news that was heard was that the deacon an' Lizy—well, opinions differed which of 'em had spoke first, but them fools settled it before the protracted meetin' was over, and give away their hearts before he started for home. They considered 't would be wise, though, considerin' their short acquaintance, to take one another on trial a spell; 't was Lizy's notion, and she asked him why he would n't come over and stop with her till spring, and then, if they both continued to like, they could git married any time 't was convenient. Lizy, she come and talked it over with mother, and mother disliked to offend her, but she spoke pretty plain; and Lizy felt hurt, an' thought they was showin' excellent judgment, so much harm come from hasty unions and folks comin' to a realizin' sense of each other's failin's when 't was too late.

"So one day our folks saw Deacon Brimfull a-ridin' by with a gre't coopful of hens in the back o' his wagon, and bundles o' stuff tied on top and hitched to the exes underneath; and he riz a hymn just as he passed the house, and was speedin' the old sorrel with a willer switch. 'T was most Thanksgivin' time, an' sooner 'n she expected him. New Year's was the time she set; but he thought he'd better come while the roads was fit for wheels. They was out to meetin' together Thanksgivin' Day, an' that used to be a gre't season for marryin'; so the young folks nudged each other, and some on 'em ventured to speak to the couple as they come down the aisle. Lizy carried it off real well; she wa'n't afraid o' what nobody said or thought, and so home they went. They'd got out her yaller sleigh and her hoss; she never would ride after the deacon's poor old creatur', and I believe it died long o' the winter from stiffenin' up.

"Yes," said Mrs. Goodsoe emphatically, after we had silently considered the situation for a short space of time,—"yes, there was consider'ble talk, now I tell you! The raskil boys pestered 'em just about to death for a while. They used to collect up there an' rap on the winders, and they 'd turn out all the deacon's hens 'long at nine o'clock 'o night, and chase 'em all over the dingle; an' one night they even lugged the pig right out o' the sty, and shoved it into the back entry, an' run for their lives. They 'd stuffed its mouth full o' somethin', so it could n't squeal till it got there. There wa'n't a sign o' nobody to be seen when Lizy hasted out with the light, and she an' the deacon had to persuade the creatur' back as best they could; 't was a cold night, and they said it took 'em till towards mornin'. You see the deacon was just the kind of a man that a hog would n't budge for; it takes a masterful man to deal with a hog. Well, there was no end to the works nor the talk, but Lizy left 'em pretty much alone. She did 'pear kind of dignified about it, I must say!"

"And then, were they married in the spring?"

"I was tryin' to remember whether it was just before Fast Day or just after," responded my friend, with a careful look at the sun, which was nearer the west than either of us had noticed. "I think likely 't was along in the last o' April, any way some of us looked out o' the window one Monday mornin' early, and says, 'For goodness' sake! Lizy's sent the deacon home again!' His old sorrel havin' passed away, he was ridin' in Ezry Welsh's hoss-cart, with his hen-coop and more bundles than he had when he come, and he looked as meechin' as ever you see. Ezry was drivin', and he let a glance fly swiftly round to see if any of us was lookin' out; an' then I declare if he did n't have the malice to turn right in towards the barn, where he see my oldest brother, Joshuay, an' says he real natural, 'Joshuay, just step out with your wrench. I believe I hear my kingbolt rattlin' kind o' loose.' Brother, he went out an' took in the sitooation, an' the deacon bowed kind of stiff. Joshuay was so full o' laugh, and Ezry Welsh, that they could n't look one another in the face. There wa'n't nothing ailed the kingbolt, you know, an' when Josh riz up he says, 'Goin' up country for a spell, Mr. Brimblecom?'

"'I be,' says the deacon, lookin' dreadful mortified and cast down.

"'Ain't things turned out well with you an' Sister Wisby?' says Joshuay. 'You had ought to remember that the woman is the weaker vessel.'

"'Hang her, let her carry less sail, then!' the deacon bu'st out, and he stood right up an' shook his fist there by the hen-coop, he was so mad; an' Ezry's hoss was a young creatur', an' started up an set the deacon right over backwards into the chips. We did n't know but he 'd broke his neck;

but when he see the women folks runnin' out, he jumped up quick as a cat, an' clim' into the cart, an' off they went. Ezry said he told him that he could n't git along with Lizy, she was so fractious in thundery weather; if there was a rumble in the daytime she must go right to bed an' screech, and if 't was night she must git right up an' go an' call him out of a sound sleep. But everybody knew he 'd never a gone home unless she 'd sent him.

"Somehow they made it up agin right away, him an' Lizy, and she had him back. She 'd been countin' all along on not havin' to hire nobody to work about the gardin an' so on, an' she said she wa'n't goin' to let him have a whole winter's board for nothin'. So the old hens was moved back, and they was married right off fair an' square, an' I don't know but they got along well as most folks. He brought his youngest girl down to live with 'em after a while, an' she was a real treasure to Lizy; everybody spoke well o' Phebe Brimblecom. The deacon got over his pious fit, and there was consider'ble work in him if you kept right after him. He was an amazin' cider-drinker, and he airnt the name you know him by in his latter days. Lizy never trusted him with nothin', but she kep' him well. She left everything she owned to Phebe, when she died, 'cept somethin' to satisfy the law. There, they 're all gone now: seems to me sometimes, when I get thinkin', as if I 'd lived a thousand years!"

I laughed, but I found that Mrs. Goodsoe's thoughts had taken a serious turn.

"There, I come by some old graves down here in the lower edge of the pasture," she said as we rose to go. "I could n't help thinking how I should like to be laid right out in the pasture ground, when my time comes; it looked sort o' comfortable, and I have ranged these slopes so many summers. Seems as if I could see right up through the turf and tell when the weather was pleasant, and get the goodness o' the sweet fern. Now, dear, just hand me my apernful o' mulleins out o' the shade. I hope you won't come to need none this winter, but I 'll dry some special for you."

"I 'm going home by the road," said I, "or else by the path across the meadows, so I will walk as far as the house with you. Are n't you pleased with my company?" for she demurred at my going the least bit out of the way.

So we strolled toward the little gray house, with our plunder of mullein leaves slung on a stick which we carried between us. Of course I went in to make a call, as if I had not seen my hostess before; she is the last maker of muster-gingerbread, and before I came away I was kindly measured for a pair of mittens.

"You 'll be sure to come an' see them two peach-trees after I get 'em well growin'?" Mrs. Goodsoe called after me when I had said good-by, and was almost out of hearing down the road.

MISS TEMPY'S
WATCHERS

The time of year was April; the place was a small farming town in New Hampshire, remote from any railroad. One by one the lights had been blown out in the scattered houses near Miss Tempy Dent's; but as her neighbors took a last look out-of-doors, their eyes turned with instinctive curiosity toward the old house where a lamp burned steadily. They gave a little sigh. "Poor Miss Tempy!" said more than one bereft acquaintance; for the good woman lay dead in her north chamber, and the lamp was a watcher's light. The funeral was set for the next day, at one o'clock.

The watchers were two of the oldest friends, Mrs. Crowe and Sarah Ann Binson. They were sitting in the kitchen, because it seemed less awesome than the unused best room, and they beguiled the long hours by steady conversation. One would think that neither topics nor opinions would hold out, at that rate, all through the long spring night; but there was a certain degree of excitement just then, and the two women had risen to an unusual level of expressiveness and confidence. Each had already told the other more than one fact that she had determined to keep secret; they were again and again tempted into statements that either would have found impossible by daylight. Mrs. Crowe was knitting a blue yarn stocking for her husband; the foot was already so long that it seemed as if she must have forgotten to narrow it at the proper time. Mrs. Crowe knew exactly what she was about, however; she was of a much cooler disposition than Sister Binson, who made futile attempts at some sewing, only to drop her work into her lap whenever the talk was most engaging.

Their faces were interesting,—of the dry, shrewd, quick-witted New England type, with thin hair twisted neatly back out of the way. Mrs. Crowe could look vague and benignant, and Miss Binson was, to quote her neighbors, a little too sharp-set; but the world knew that she had need to be, with the load she must carry of supporting an inefficient widowed sister and six unpromising and unwilling nieces and nephews. The eldest boy was at last placed with a good man to learn the mason's trade. Sarah Ann Binson, for all her sharp, anxious aspect, never defended herself, when her sister whined and fretted. She was told every week of her life that the poor children never would have had to lift a finger if their father had lived, and yet she had kept her steadfast way with the little farm, and patiently taught the young people many useful things, for which, as everybody said, they would live to thank her. However pleasureless her life appeared to outward view, it was brimful of pleasure to herself.

Mrs. Crowe, on the contrary, was well to do, her husband being a rich farmer and an easy-going man. She was a stingy woman, but for all that she looked kindly; and when she gave away anything, or lifted a finger to help anybody, it was thought a great piece of beneficence, and a compliment, indeed, which the recipient accepted with twice as much gratitude as double the gift that came from a poorer and more generous acquaintance. Everybody liked to be on good terms with Mrs. Crowe. Socially she stood much higher than Sarah Ann Binson.

They were both old schoolmates and friends of Temperance Dent, who had asked them, one day, not long before she died, if they would not come together and look after the house, and manage everything, when she was gone. She may have had some hope that they might become closer friends in this period of intimate partnership, and that the richer woman might better understand the burdens of the poorer. They had not kept the house the night before; they were too weary with their care of their old friend, whom they had not left until all was over. There was a brook which ran down the hillside very near the house, and the sound of it was much louder than usual. When there was silence in the kitchen, the busy stream had a strange insistence in its wild voice, as if it tried to make the watchers understand something that related to the past.

"I declare, I can't begin to sorrow for Tempy yet. I am so glad to have her at rest," whispered Mrs. Crowe. "It is strange to set here without her, but I can't make it clear that she has gone. I feel as if she had got easy and dropped off to sleep, and I'm more scared about waking her up than knowing any other feeling."

"Yes," said Sarah Ann, "it's just like that, ain't it? But I tell you we are goin' to miss her worse than we expect. She's helped me through with many a trial, has Temperance. I ain't the only one who says the same, neither."

These words were spoken as if there were a third person listening; somebody beside Mrs. Crowe. The watchers could not rid their minds of the feeling that they were being watched themselves. The spring wind whistled in the window crack, now and then, and buffeted the little house in a gusty way that had a sort of companionable effect. Yet, on the whole, it was a very still night, and the watchers spoke in a half-whisper.

"She was the freest-handed woman that ever I knew," said Mrs. Crowe, decidedly. "According to her means, she gave away more than anybody. I used to tell her 't wa'n't right. I used really to be afraid that she went without too much, for we have a duty to ourselves."

Sister Binson looked up in a half-amused, unconscious way, and then recollected herself.

Mrs. Crowe met her look with a serious face. "It ain't so easy for me to give as it is for some," she said simply, but with an effort which was made possible only by the occasion. "I should like to say, while Tempy is laying here yet in her own house, that she has been a constant lesson to me. Folks are too kind, and shame me with thanks for what I do. I ain't such a generous woman as poor Tempy was, for all she had nothin' to do with, as one may say."

Sarah Binson was much moved at this confession, and was even pained and touched by the unexpected humility. "You have a good many calls on you"—she began, and then left her kind little compliment half finished.

"Yes, yes, but I've got means enough. My disposition's more of a cross to me as I grow older, and I made up my mind this morning that Tempy's example should be my pattern henceforth." She began to knit faster than ever.

" 'T ain't no use to get morbid: that's what Tempy used to say herself," said Sarah Ann, after a minute's silence. "Ain't it strange to say 'used to say'?'' and her own voice choked a little. "She never did like to hear folks git goin' about themselves."

" 'T was only because they 're apt to do it so as other folks say 't was n't so, an' praise 'em up," humbly replied Mrs. Crowe, "and that ain't my object. There wa'n't a child but what Tempy set herself to work to see what she could do to please it. One time my brother's folks had been stopping here in the summer, from Massachusetts. The children was all little, and they broke up a sight of toys, and left 'em when they were going away. Tempy come right up after they rode by, to see if she could n't help me set the house to rights, and she caught me just as I was going to fling some of the clutter into the stove. I was kind of tired out, starting 'em off in season. 'Oh, give me them!' says she, real pleading; and she wropped 'em up and took 'em home with her when she went, and she mended 'em up and stuck 'em together, and made some young one or other happy with every blessed one. You 'd thought I 'd done her the biggest favor. 'No thanks to me. I should ha' burnt 'em, Tempy,' says I."

"Some of 'em came to our house, I know," said Miss Binson. "She 'd take a lot o' trouble to please a child, 'stead o' shoving of it out o' the way, like the rest of us when we 're drove."

"I can tell you the biggest thing she ever gave, and I don't know 's there 's anybody left but me to tell it. I don't want it forgot," Sarah Binson went on, looking up at the clock to see how the night was going. "It was that pretty-looking Trevor girl, who taught the Corners school, and married so well afterward, out in New York State. You remember her, I dare say?"

"Certain," said Mrs. Crowe, with an air of interest.

"She was a splendid scholar, folks said, and give the school a great start; but she 'd overdone herself getting her education, and working to pay for it, and she all broke down one spring, and Tempy made her come and stop with her awhile,—you remember that? Well, she had an uncle, her mother's brother, out in Chicago, who was well off and friendly, and used to write to Lizzie Trevor, and I dare say make her some presents; but he was a lively, driving man, and did n't take time to stop and think about his folks. He had n't seen her since she was a little girl. Poor Lizzie was so pale and weakly that she just got through the term o' school. She looked as if she was just going straight off in a decline. Tempy, she cosseted her up awhile, and then, next thing folks knew, she was tellin' round how Miss Trevor had gone to see her uncle, and meant to visit Niagary Falls on the way, and stop over night. Now I happened to know, in ways I won't dwell on to explain, that the poor girl was in debt for her schoolin' when she come here, and her last quarter's pay had just squared it off at last, and left her without a cent ahead, hardly; but it had fretted her thinking of it, so she paid it all; they might have dunned her that she owed it to. An' I taxed Tempy about the girl's goin' off on such a journey till she owned up, rather 'n have Lizzie blamed, that she 'd given her sixty dollars, same 's if she was rolling in riches, and sent her off to have a good rest and vacation."

"Sixty dollars!" exclaimed Mrs. Crowe. "Tempy only had ninety dollars a year that came in to her; rest of her livin' she got by helpin' about, with what she raised off this little piece o' ground, sand one side an' clay the other. An' how often I 've heard her tell, years ago, that she 'd rather see Niagary than any other sight in the world!"

The women looked at each other in silence; the magnitude of the generous sacrifice was almost too great for their comprehension.

"She was just poor enough to do that!" declared Mrs. Crowe at last, in an abandonment of feeling. "Say what you may, I feel humbled to the dust," and her companion ventured to say nothing. She never had given away sixty dollars at once, but it was simply because she never had it to give. It came to her very lips to say in explanation, "Tempy was so situated"; but she checked herself in time, for she would not break in upon her own loyal guarding of her dependent household.

"Folks say a great deal of generosity, and this one 's being public-sperited, and that one free handed about giving," said Mrs. Crowe, who was a little nervous in the silence. "I suppose we can't tell the sorrow it would be to some folks not to give, same 's 't would be to me not to save. I seem kind of made for that, as if 't was what I 'd got to do. I should feel sights better about it if I could make it evident what I was savin' for. If I had a child, now, Sarah Ann," and her voice was a little husky,—"if I had a child, I should think I was heapin' of it up because he was the one trained by the Lord to scatter it again for good. But here 's Crowe and me, we can't do anything with money, and both of us like to keep things same 's they 've always been. Now Priscilla Dance was talking away like a mill-clapper, week before last. She 'd think I would go right off and get one o' them new-fashioned gilt-and-white papers for the best room, and some new furniture, an' a marble-top table. And I looked at her, all struck up. 'Why,' says I, 'Priscilla, that nice old velvet paper ain't hurt a mite. I should n't feel 't was my best room without it. Dan'el says 't is the first thing he can remember rubbin' his little baby fingers on to it, and how splendid he thought them red roses was.' I maintain," continued Mrs. Crowe stoutly, "that folks wastes sights o' good money doin' just such foolish things. Tearin' out the insides o' meetin'-houses, and fixin' the pews different; 't was good enough as 't was with mendin'; then times come, an' they want to put it all back same's 't was before."

This touched upon an exciting subject to active members of that parish. Miss Binson and Mrs. Crowe belonged to opposite parties, and had at one time come as near hard feelings as they could, and yet escape them. Each hastened to speak of other things, and to show her untouched friendliness.

"I do agree with you," said Sister Binson, "that few of us know what use to make of money, beyond every-day necessities. You 've seen more o' the world than I have, and know what 's expected. When it comes to taste and judgment about such things, I ought to defer to others"; and with this modest avowal the critical moment passed when there might have been an improper discussion.

In the silence that followed, the fact of their presence in a house of death grew more clear than before. There was something disturbing in the noise of a mouse gnawing at the dry boards of a closet wall near by. Both the watchers looked up anxiously at the clock; it was almost the middle of the night, and the whole world seemed to have left them alone with their solemn duty. Only the brook was awake.

"Perhaps we might give a look up-stairs now," whispered Mrs. Crowe, as if she hoped to hear some reason against their going just then to the chamber of death; but Sister Binson rose, with a serious and yet satisfied countenance, and lifted the small lamp from the table. She was much more used to watching than Mrs. Crowe, and much less affected by it. They opened the door into a small entry with a steep stairway; they climbed the creaking stairs, and entered the cold upper room on tiptoe. Mrs. Crowe's heart began to beat very fast as the lamp was put on a high bureau, and made long, fixed shadows about the walls. She went hesitatingly toward the solemn shape under its white drapery, and felt a sense of remonstrance as Sarah Ann gently, but in a business-like way, turned back the thin sheet.

"Seems to me she looks pleasanter and pleasanter," whispered Sarah Ann Binson impulsively, as they gazed at the white face with its wonderful smile. "To-morrow 't will all have faded out. I do believe they kind of wake up a day or two after they die, and it 's then they go." She replaced the light covering, and they both turned quickly away; there was a chill in this upper room.

"'T is a great thing for anybody to have got through, ain't it?" said Mrs. Crowe softly, as she began to go down the stairs on tiptoe. The warm air from the kitchen beneath met them with a sense of welcome and shelter.

"I don' know why it is, but I feel as near again to Tempy down here as I do up there," replied Sister Binson. "I feel as if the air was full of her, kind of. I can sense things, now and then, that she seems to say. Now I never was one to take up with no nonsense of sperits and such, but I declare I felt as if she told me just now to put some more wood into the stove."

Mrs. Crowe preserved a gloomy silence. She had suspected before this that her companion was of a weaker and more credulous disposition than herself. "'T is a great thing to have got through," she repeated, ignoring definitely all that had last been said. "I suppose you know as well as I that Tempy was one that always feared death. Well, it 's all put behind her now; she knows what 't is." Mrs. Crowe gave a little sigh, and Sister Binson's quick sympathies were stirred toward this other old friend, who also dreaded the great change.

"I 'd never like to forgit almost those last words Tempy spoke plain to me," she said gently, like the comforter she truly was. "She looked up at me once or twice, that last afternoon after I come to set by her, and let Mis' Owen go home; and I says, 'Can I do anything to ease you, Tempy?' and the tears come into my eyes so I could n't see what kind of a nod she gives me. 'No, Sarah Ann, you can't, dear,' says she; and then she got her breath again, and says she, looking at me real meanin', 'I 'm only a-gettin' sleepier and sleepier; that 's all there is,' says she, and smiled up at me kind of wishful, and shut her eyes. I knew well enough all she meant. She 'd been lookin' out for a chance to tell me, and I don' know 's she ever said much afterwards."

Mrs. Crowe was not knitting; she had been listening too eagerly. "Yes, 't will be a comfort to think of that sometimes," she said, in acknowledgment.

"I know that old Dr. Prince said once, in evenin' meetin', that he 'd watched by many a dyin' bed, as we well knew, and enough o' his sick folks had been scared o' dyin' their whole lives through; but when they come to the last, he 'd never seen one but was willin', and most were glad, to go. "'T is as natural as bein' born or livin' on,' he said. I don't know what had moved him to speak that night. You know he wa'n't in the habit of it, and 't was the monthly concert of prayer for foreign missions anyways," said Sarah Ann; "but 't was a great stay to the mind to listen to his words of experience."

"There never was a better man," responded Mrs. Crowe, in a really cheerful tone. She had recovered from her feeling of nervous dread, the kitchen was so comfortable with lamplight and firelight; and just then the old clock began to tell the hour of twelve with leisurely whirring strokes.

Sister Binson laid aside her work, and rose quickly and went to the cupboard. "We 'd better take a little to eat," she explained. "The night will go fast after this. I want to know if you went and made some o' your nice cupcake, while you was home to day?" she asked, in a pleased tone; and Mrs. Crowe acknowledged such a gratifying piece of thoughtfulness for this humble friend who denied herself all luxuries. Sarah Ann brewed a generous cup of tea, and the watchers drew their chairs up to the table presently, and quelled their hunger with good country appetites. Sister Binson put a spoon into a small, old-fashioned glass of preserved quince, and passed it to her friend. She was most familiar with the house, and played the part of hostess. "Spread some o' this on your bread and butter," she said to Mrs. Crowe. "Tempy wanted me to use some three or four times, but I never felt to. I know she 'd like to have us comfortable now, and would urge us to make a good supper, poor dear."

"What excellent preserves she did make!" mourned Mrs. Crowe. "None of us has got her light hand at doin' things tasty. She made the most o' everything, too. Now, she only had that one old quince tree down in the far corner of the piece, but she 'd go out in the spring and tend to it, and look at it so pleasant, and kind of expect the old thorny thing into bloomin'."

"She was just the same with folks," said Sarah Ann. "And she 'd never git more 'n a little apernful o' quinces, but she 'd have every mite o' goodness out o' those, and set the glasses up onto her best-room closet shelf, so pleased. 'T wa'n't but a week ago to-morrow mornin' I fetched her a little taste o' jelly in a teaspoon; and she says 'Thank ye,' and took it, an' the minute she tasted it she looked up at me as worried as could be. 'Oh, I don't want to eat that,' says she. 'I always keep that in case o' sickness.' 'You're goin' to have the good o' one tumbler yourself,' says I. 'I'd just like to know who's sick now, if you ain't!' An' she couldn't help laughin', I spoke up so smart. Oh, dear me, how I shall miss talkin' over things with her! She always sensed things, and got just the p'int you meant."

"She didn't begin to age until two or three years ago, did she?" asked Mrs. Crowe. "I never saw anybody keep her looks as Tempy did. She looked young long after I begun to feel like an old woman. The doctor used to say 't was her young heart, and I don't know but what he was right. How she did do for other folks! There was one spell she wasn't at home a day to a fortnight. She got most of her livin' so, and that made her own potatoes and things last her through. None o' the young folks could get married without her, and all the old ones was disappointed if she wa'n't round when they was down with sickness and had to go. An' cleanin', or tailorin' for boys, or rug-hookin',—there was nothin' but what she could do as handy as most. 'I do love to work,'—ain't you heard her say that twenty times a week?"

Sarah Ann Binson nodded, and began to clear away the empty plates. "We may want a taste o' somethin' more towards mornin'," she said. "There's plenty in the closet here; and in case some comes from a distance to the funeral, we'll have a little table spread after we get back to the house."

"Yes, I was busy all the mornin'. I've cooked up a sight o' things to bring over," said Mrs. Crowe. "I felt 't was the last I could do for her."

They drew their chairs near the stove again, and took up their work. Sister Binson's rocking-chair creaked as she rocked; the brook sounded louder than ever. It was more lonely when nobody spoke, and presently Mrs. Crowe returned to her thoughts of growing old.

"Yes, Tempy aged all of a sudden. I remember I asked her if she felt as well as common, one day, and she laughed at me good. There, when Dan'el begun to look old, I couldn't help feeling as if somethin' ailed him, and like as not 't was somethin' he was goin' to git right over, and I dosed him for it stiddy, half of one summer."

"How many things we shall be wanting to ask Tempy!" exclaimed Sarah Ann Binson, after a long pause. "I can't make up my mind to doin' without her. I wish folks could come back just once, and tell us how 't is where they've gone. Seems then we could do without 'em better."

The brook hurried on, the wind blew about the house now and then; the house itself was a silent place, and the supper, the warm fire, and an absence of any new topics for conversation made the watchers drowsy. Sister Binson closed her eyes first, to rest them for a minute; and Mrs. Crowe glanced at her compassionately, with a new sympathy for the hard-worked little woman. She made up her mind to let Sarah Ann have a good rest, while she kept watch alone; but in a few minutes her own knitting was dropped, and she, too, fell asleep. Overhead, the pale shape of Tempy Dent, the outworn body of that generous, loving-hearted, simple soul, slept on also in its white raiment. Perhaps Tempy herself stood near, and saw her own life and its surroundings with new understanding. Perhaps she herself was the only watcher.

Later, by some hours, Sarah Ann Binson woke with a start. There was a pale light of dawn outside the small windows. Inside the kitchen, the lamp burned dim. Mrs. Crowe awoke, too.

"I think Tempy 'd be the first to say 't was just as well we both had some rest," she said, not without a guilty feeling.

Her companion went to the outer door, and opened it wide. The fresh air was none too cold, and the brook's voice was not nearly so loud as it had been in the midnight darkness. She could see the shapes of the hills, and the great shadows that lay across the lower country. The east was fast growing bright.

"'T will be a beautiful day for the funeral," she said, and turned again, with a sigh, to follow Mrs. Crowe up the stairs. The world seemed more and more empty without the kind face and helpful hands of Tempy Dent.

GOING TO SHREWSBURY

**T**he train stopped at a way station with apparent unwillingness, and there was barely time for one elderly passenger to be hurried on board before a sudden jerk threw her almost off her unsteady old feet and we moved on. At my first glance I saw only a perturbed old countrywoman, laden with a large basket and a heavy bundle tied up in an old-fashioned bundle-handkerchief; then I discovered that she was a friend of mine, Mrs. Peet, who lived on a small farm, several miles from the village. She used to be renowned for good butter and fresh eggs and the earliest cowslip greens; in fact, she always made the most of her farm's slender resources; but it was some time since I had seen her drive by from market in her ancient thorough-braced wagon.

The brakeman followed her into the crowded car, also carrying a number of packages. I leaned forward and asked Mrs. Peet to sit by me; it was a great pleasure to see her again. The brakeman seemed relieved, and smiled as he tried to put part of his burden into the rack overhead; but even the flowered carpet-bag was much too large, and he explained that he would take care of everything at the end of the car. Mrs. Peet was not large herself, but with the big basket, and the bundle-handkerchief, and some possessions of my own we had very little spare room.

"So this 'ere is what you call ridin' in the cars! Well, I do declare!" said my friend, as soon as she had recovered herself a little. She looked pale and as if she had been in tears, but there was the familiar gleam of good humor in her tired old eyes.

"Where in the world are you going, Mrs. Peet?" I asked.

"Can't be you ain't heared about me, dear?" said she, "Well, the world's bigger than I used to think 't was. I've broke up,—'t was the only thing *to* do,—and I'm a-movin' to Shrewsbury."

"To Shrewsbury? Have you sold the farm?" I exclaimed, with sorrow and surprise. Mrs. Peet was too old and too characteristic to be suddenly transplanted from her native soil.

"'T wa'n't mine, the place wa'n't." Her pleasant face hardened slightly. "He was coaxed an' over-persuaded into signin' off before he was taken away. Is'iah, son of his sister that married old Josh Peet, come it over him about his bein' past work and how he 'd do for him like an own son, an' we owed him a little somethin'. I 'd paid off everythin' but that, an' was fool enough to leave it till the last, on account o' Is'iah's bein' a relation and not needin' his pay much as some others did. It 's hurt me to have the place fall into other hands. Some wanted me to go right to law; but 't would n't be no use. Is'iah's smarter 'n I be about them matters. You see he 's got my name on the paper, too; he said 't was somethin' 'bout bein' responsible for the taxes. We was scant o' money, an' I was wore out with watchin' an' being broke o' my rest. After my tryin' hard for risin' forty-five year to provide for bein' past work, here I be, dear, here I be! I used to drive things smart, you remember. But we was fools enough in '72 to put about everythin' we had safe in the bank into that spool factory that come to nothin'. But I tell ye I could ha' kept myself long's I lived, if I cold ha' held the place. I 'd parted with most o' the woodland, if Is'iah 'd coveted it. He was welcome to that, 'cept what might keep me in ovenwood. I 've always desired to travel an' see somethin' o' the world, but I 've got the chance now when I don't value it no great."

"Shrewsbury is a busy, pleasant place," I ventured to say by way of comfort, though my heart was filled with rage at the trickery of Isaiah Peet, who had always looked like a fox and behaved like one.

"Shrewsbury 's be'n held up consid'able for me to smile at," said the poor old soul, "but I tell ye, dear, it 's hard to go an' live twenty-two miles from where you 've always had your home and friends. It may divert me, but it won't be home. You might as well set out one o' my old apple-trees on the beach, so 't could see the waves come in,—there would n't be no please to it."

"Where are you going to live in Shrewsbury?" I asked presently.

"I don't expect to stop long, dear creatur'. I'm 'most seventy-six year old," and Mrs. Peet turned to look at me with pathetic amusement in her honest wrinkled face. "I said right out to Is'iah, before a roomful o' the neighbors, that I expected it of him to git me home an' bury me when my time come, and do it respectable; but I wanted to airn my livin', if 't was so I could, till then. He 'd made sly talk, you see, about my electin' to leave the farm and go 'long some o' my own folks; but"—and she whispered this carefully—"he did n't give me no chance to stay there without hurtin' my pride and dependin' on him. I ain't said that to many folks, but all must have suspected. A good sight on 'em 's had money of Is'iah, though, and they don't like to do nothin' but take his part an' be pretty soft spoken, fear it'll git to his ears. Well, well, dear, we 'll let it be bygones, and not think of it no more;" but I saw the great tears roll slowly down her cheeks, and she pulled her bonnet forward impatiently, and looked the other way.

"There looks to be plenty o' good farmin' land in this part o' the country," she said, a minute later. "Where be we now? See them handsome farm buildin's; he must be a well-off man." But I had to tell my companion that we were still within the borders of the old town where we had both been born. Mrs. Peet gave a pleased little laugh, like a girl. "I 'm expectin' Shrewsbury to pop up any minute. I 'm feared to be kerried right by. I wa'n't never aboard of the cars before, but I 've so often thought about 'em I don't know but it seems natural. Ain't it jest like flyin' through the air? I can't catch holt to see nothin'. Land! and here 's my old cat goin' too, and never mistrustin'. I ain't told you that I'd fetched her."

"Is she in that basket?" I inquired with interest.

"Yis, dear. Truth was, I calc'lated to have her put out o' the misery o' movin', an spoke to one o' the Barnes boys, an' he promised me all fair; but he wa'n't there in season, an' I kind o' made excuse to myself to fetch her along. She 's an' old creatur', like me, an' I can make shift to keep her some way or 'nuther; there 's probably mice where we 're goin', an' she 's a proper mouser that can about keep herself if there 's any sort o' chance. 'T will be somethin' o' home to see her goin' an' comin', but I expect we 're both on us goin' to miss our old haunts. I 'd love to know what kind o' mousin' there 's goin' to be for me."

"You must n't worry," I answered, with all the bravery and assurance that I could muster. "Your niece will be thankful to have you with her. Is she one of Mrs. Winn's daughters?"

"Oh, no, they ain't able; it's Sister Wayland's darter Isabella, that married the overseer of the gre't carriage-shop. I ain't seen her since just after she was married; but I turned to her first because I knew she was best able to have me, and then I can see just how the other girls is situated and make me some kind of a plot. I wrote to Isabella, though she is ambitious, and said 't was so I 'd got to ask to come an' make her a visit, an' she wrote back she would be glad to have me; but she did n't write right off, and her letter was scented up dreadful strong with some sort o' essence, and I don't feel heartened about no great of a welcome. But there, I 've got eyes, an' I can see *how* 't is when I git *where* 't is. Sister Winn's gals ain't married, an' they 've always boarded, an' worked in the shop on trimmin's. Isabella 's well off; she had some means from her father's sister. I thought it all over by night an' day, an' I recalled that our folks kept Sister Wayland's folks all one winter, when he 'd failed up and got into trouble. I 'm reckonin' on sendin' over to-night an' gittin' the Winn gals to come and see me and advise. Perhaps some on 'em may know of somebody that 'll take me for what help I can give about house, or some clever folks that have been lookin' for a smart cat, any ways; no, I don't know 's I could let her go to strangers."

"There was two or three o' the folks round home that acted real warm-hearted towards me, an' urged me to come an' winter with 'em," continued the exile; "an' this mornin' I wished I 'd agreed to, 't was so hard to break away. But now it 's done I feel more 'n ever it 's best. I could n't bear to live right in sight o' the old place, and come spring I should n't 'prove of nothing Is'iah ondertakes to do with the land. Oh, dear sakes! now it comes hard with me not to have had no child'n. When I was young an' workin' hard and into everything, I felt kind of free an' superior to them that was so blessed, an' their houses cluttered up from mornin' till night, but I tell ye it comes home to me now. I 'd be most willin' to own to even Is'iah, mean 's he is; but I tell ye I 'd took it out of him 'fore he was a grown man, if there 'd be'n any virtue in cow-hidin' of him. Folks don't look like wild creatur's for nothin'. Is'iah 's got fox blood in him, an' p'r'haps 't is his misfortune. His own mother always favored the looks of an old fox, true 's the world; she was a poor tool,—a poor tool! I d' know 's we ought to blame him same 's we do.

"I 've always been a master proud woman, if I was riz among the pastures," Mrs. Peet added, half to herself. There was no use in saying much to her; she was conscious of little beside her own thoughts and the smouldering excitement caused by this great crisis in her simple existence. Yet the atmosphere of her loneliness, uncertainty, and sorrow was so touching that after scolding again at her nephew's treachery, and finding the tears come fast to my eyes as she talked, I looked intently out of the car window, and tried to think what could be done for the poor soul. She was one of the old-time people, and I hated to have her go away; but even if she could keep her home she would soon be too feeble to live there alone, and some definite plan must be made for her comfort. Farms in that neighborhood were not valuable. Perhaps through the agency of the law and quite in secret, Isaiah Peet could be forced to give up his unrighteous claim. Perhaps, too, the Winn girls, who were really no longer young, might have saved something, and would come home again. But it was easy to make such pictures in one's mind, and I must do what I could through other people, for I was just leaving home for a long time. I wondered sadly about Mrs. Peet's future, and the ambitious Isabella, and the favorite Sister Winn's daughters, to whom, with all their kindliness of heart, the care of so old and perhaps so dependent an aunt might seem impossible. The truth about life in Shrewsbury would soon be known; more than half the short journey was already past.

To my great pleasure, my fellow-traveler now began to forget her own troubles in looking about her. She was an alert, quickly interested old soul, and this was a bit of neutral ground between the farm and Shrewsbury, where she was unattached and irresponsible. She had lived through the last tragic moments of her old life, and felt a certain relief, and Shrewsbury might be as far away as the other side of the Rocky Mountains for all the consciousness she had of its real existence. She was simply a traveler for the time being, and began to comment, with delicious phrases and shrewd understanding of human nature, on two or three persons near us who attracted her attention.

"Where do you s'pose they be all goin'?" she asked contemptuously. "There ain't none on 'em but what looks kind o' respectable. I 'll warrant they 've left work to home they 'd ought to be doin'. I knowed, if ever I stopped to think, that cars was hived full o' folks, an' wa'n't run to an' fro for nothin'; but these can't be quite up to the average, be they? Some on 'em 's real thrif'less? guess they 've be'n shoved out o' the last place, an' goin' to try the next one,—*like me*, I suppose you 'll want to say! Jest see that flauntin' old creatur' that looks like a stopped clock. There! everybody can't be o' one goodness, even preachers."

I was glad to have Mrs. Peet amused, and we were as cheerful as we could be for a few minutes. She said earnestly that she hoped to be forgiven for such talk, but there were some kinds of folks in the cars that she never had seen before. But when the conductor came to take her ticket she relapsed into her first state of mind, and was at a loss.

"You 'll have to look after me, dear, when we get to Shrewsbury," she said, after we had spent some distracted moments in hunting for the ticket, and the cat had almost escaped from the basket, and the bundle-handkerchief had become untied and all its miscellaneous contents scattered about our laps and the floor. It was a touching collection of the last odds and ends of Mrs. Peet's housekeeping: some battered books, and singed holders for flatirons, and the faded little shoulder shawl that I had seen her wear many a day about her bent shoulders. There were her old tin match-box spilling all its matches, and a goose-wing for brushing up ashes, and her much-thumbed Leavitt's Almanac. It was most pathetic to see these poor trifles out of their places. At last the ticket was found in her left-hand woolen glove, where her stiff, work-worn hand had grown used to the feeling of it.

"I should n't wonder, now, if I come to like living over to Shrewsbury first-rate," she insisted, turning to me with a hopeful, eager look to see if I differed. "You see 't won't be so tough for me as if I had n't always felt it lurking within me to go off some day or 'nother an' see how other folks did things. I do' know but what the Winn gals have laid up somethin' sufficient for us to take a house, with the little mite I 've got by me. I might keep house for us all, 'stead o' boardin' round in other folks' houses. That I ain't never been demeaned to, but I dare say I should find it pleasant in some ways. Town folks has got the upper hand o' country folks, but with all their work an' pride they can't make a dandelion. I do' know the times when I 've set out to wash Monday mornin's, an' tied out the line betwixt the old pucker-pear tree and the corner o' the barn, an' thought, 'Here I be with the same kind o' week's work right over again.' I 'd wonder kind o' f'erce if I could n't git out of it noways; an' now here I be out of it, and an uprooteder creatur' never stood on the airth. Just as I got to feel I had somethin' ahead come that spool-factory business. There! you know he never was a forehanded man; his health was slim, and he got discouraged pretty nigh before ever he begun. I hope he don't know I 'm turned out o' the old place. 'Is'iah 's well off; he 'll do the right thing by ye,' says he. But my! I turned hot all over when I found out what I 'd put my name to,—me that had always be'n counted a smart woman! I did undertake to read it over, but I could n't sense it. I 've told all the folks so when they laid it off on to me some: but hand-writin' is awful tedious readin' and my head felt that day as if the works was gone.

"I ain't goin' to sag on to nobody," she assured me eagerly, as the train rushed along. "I 've got more work in me now than folks expects at my age. I may be consid'able use to Isabella. She 's got a family, an' I 'll take right holt in the kitchen or with the little gals. She had four on 'em, last I heared. Isabella was never one that liked house-work. Little gals! I do' know now but what they must be about grown, times doos slip away so. I expect I shall look outlandish to 'em. But there! everybody knows me to home, an' nobody knows me to Shrewsbury; 't won't make a mite o' difference, if I take holt willin'."

I hoped, as I looked at Mrs. Peet, that she would never be persuaded to cast off the gathered brown silk bonnet and the plain shawl that she had worn so many years; but Isabella might think it best to insist upon more modern fashions. Mrs. Peet suggested, as if it were a matter of little consequence, that she had kept it in mind to buy some mourning; but there were other things to be thought of first, and so she had let it go until winter, any way, or until she should be fairly settled in Shrewsbury.

"Are your nieces expecting you by this train?" I was moved to ask, though with all the good soul's ready talk and appealing manner I could hardly believe that she was going to Shrewsbury for more than a visit; it seemed as if she must return to the worn old farmhouse over by the sheep-lands. She answered that one of the Barnes boys had written a letter for her the day before, and there was evidently little uneasiness about her first reception.

We drew near the junction where I must leave her within a mile of the town. The cat was clawing indignantly at the basket, and her mistress grew as impatient of the car. She began to look very old and pale, my poor fellow-traveler, and said that she felt dizzy, going so fast. Presently the friendly red-cheeked young brakeman came along, bringing the carpet-bag and other possessions, and insisted upon taking the alarmed cat beside, in spite of an aggressive paw that had worked its way through the wicker prison. Mrs. Peet watched her goods disappear with suspicious eyes, and clutched her bundle-handkerchief as if it might be all that she could save. Then she anxiously got to her feet, much too soon, and when I said good-by to her at the car door she was ready to cry. I pointed to the car which she was to take next on the branch line of railway, and I assured her that it was only a few minutes' ride to Shrewsbury, and that I felt certain she would find somebody waiting. The sight of that worn, thin figure adventuring alone across the platform gave my heart a sharp pang as the train carried me away.

Some of the passengers who sat near asked me about my old friend with great sympathy, after she had gone. There was a look of tragedy about her, and indeed it had been impossible not to get a good deal of her history, as she talked straight on in the same tone, when we stopped at a station, as if the train were going at full speed, and some of her remarks caused pity and amusements by turns. At the last minute she said, with deep self-reproach, "Why, I have n't asked a word about your folks; but you 'd ought to excuse such an old stray hen as I be."

In the spring I was driving by on what the old people of my native town call the sheep-lands road, and the sight of Mrs. Peet's former home brought our former journey freshly to my mind. I had last heard from her just after she got to Shrewsbury, when she had sent me a message.

"Have you ever heard how she got on?" I eagerly asked my companion.

"Did n't I tell you that I met her in Shrewsbury High Street one day?" I was answered. "She seemed perfectly delighted with everything. Her nieces have laid up a good bit of money, and are soon to leave the mill, and most thankful to have old Mrs. Peet with them. Somebody told me that they wished to buy the farm here, and come back to live, but she would n't hear of it, and thought they would miss too many privileges. She has been going to concerts and lectures this winter, and insists that Isaiah did her a good turn."

We both laughed. My own heart was filled with joy, for the uncertain, lonely face of this homeless old woman had often haunted me. The rain-blackened little house did certainly look dreary, and a whole lifetime of patient toil had left few traces. The pucker-pear tree was in full bloom, however, and gave a welcome gayety to the deserted door-yard.

A little way beyond we met Isaiah Peet, the prosperous money-lender, who had cheated the old woman of her own. I fancied that he looked somewhat ashamed, as he recognized us. To my surprise, he stopped his horse in most social fashion.

"Old Aunt Peet 's passed away," he informed me briskly. "She had a shock, and went right off sudden yisterday fore-noon. I 'm about now tendin' to the funeral 'rangements. She 's be'n extry smart, they say, all winter,—out to meetin' last Sabbath; never enjoyed herself so complete as she has this past month. She 'd be'n a very hard-workin' woman. Her folks was glad to have her there, and give her every attention. The place here never was good for nothin'. The old gen'leman,—uncle, you know,—he wore hisself out tryin' to make a livin' off from it."

There was an ostentatious sympathy and half-suppressed excitement from bad news which were quite lost upon us, and we did not linger to hear much more. It seemed to me as if I had known Mrs. Peet better than any one else had known her. I had counted upon seeing her again, and hearing her own account of Shrewsbury life, its pleasures and its limitations. I wondered what had become of the cat and the contents of the faded bundle-handkerchief.

IN DARK
NEW ENGLAND DAYS

 **T**he last of the neighbors was going home; officious
Mrs. Peter Downs had lingered late and sought for
additional housework with which to prolong her
stay. She had talked incessantly, and buzzed like a
busy bee as she helped to put away the best crockery after the funeral
supper, while the sisters Betsey and Hannah Knowles grew every moment
more forbidding and unwilling to speak. They lighted a solitary small oil
lamp at last as if for Sunday evening idleness, and put it on the side table in
the kitchen.

"We ain't intending to make a late evening of it," announced Betsey,
the elder, standing before Mrs. Downs in an expectant, final way, making
an irresistible opportunity for saying good-night. "I 'm sure we 're more
than obleeged to ye,—ain't we, Hannah?—but I don't feel 's if we ought to
keep ye longer. We ain't going to do no more to-night, but set down a
spell and kind of collect ourselves, and then make for bed."

Susan Downs offered one more plea. "I 'd stop all night with ye an'
welcome; 't is gettin' late—an' dark," she added plaintively; but the sisters
shook their heads quickly, and Hannah said that they might as well get
used to staying alone, since they would have to do it first or last. In spite of
herself Mrs. Downs was obliged to put on her funeral best bonnet and
shawl and start on her homeward way.

"Close-mouthed old maids!" she grumbled as the door shut behind her all too soon and denied her the light of the lamp along the foot-path. Suddenly there was a bright ray from the window, as if some one had pushed back the curtain and stood with the lamp close to the sash. "That 's Hannah," said the retreating guest. "She 'd told me somethin' about things, I know, if it had n't 'a' been for Betsey. Catch me workin' myself to pieces again for 'em." But, however grudgingly this was said, Mrs. Downs's conscience told her that the industry of the past two days had been somewhat selfish on her part; she had hoped that in the excitement of this unexpected funeral season she might for once be taken into the sisters' confidence. More than this, she knew that they were certain of her motive, and had deliberately refused the expected satisfaction. "'T ain't as if I was one o' them curious busy-bodies anyway," she said to herself pityingly; "they might 'a' neighbored with somebody for once, I do believe." Everybody would have a question ready for her the next day, for it was known that she had been slaving herself devotedly since the news had come of old Captain Knowles's sudden death in his bed from a stroke, the last of three which had in the course of a year or two changed him from a strong old man to a feeble, chair-bound cripple.

Mrs. Downs stepped bravely along the dark country road; she could see a light in her own kitchen window half a mile away, and did not stop to notice either the penetrating dampness or the shadowy woods at her right. It was a cloudy night, but there was a dim light over the open fields. She had a disposition of mind towards the exciting circumstances of death and burial, and was in request at such times among her neighbors; in this she was like a city person who prefers tragedy to comedy, but not having the semblance within her reach, she made the most of looking on at real griefs and departures.

Some one was walking towards her in the road; suddenly she heard footsteps. The figure stopped, then came forward again.

"Oh, 't is you, ain't it?" with a tone of disappointment. "I cal'lated you 'd stop all night, 't had got to be so late, an' I was just going over to the Knowles gals'; well, to kind o' ask how they be, an'—" Mr. Peter Downs was evidently counting on his visit.

"They never passed me the compliment," replied the wife, "I declare I did n't covet the walk home; I 'm 'most beat out, bein' on foot so much. I was 'most put out with 'em for lettin' of me see quite so plain that my room was better than my company. But I don' know 's I blame 'em; they want to look an' see what they 've got, an' kind of git by their selves, I expect. 'T was natural.''

Mrs. Downs knew that her husband would resent her first statements, being a sensitive and grumbling man. She had formed a pacific habit of suiting her remarks to his point of view to save an outburst. He contented himself with calling the Knowles girls hoggish, and put a direct question as to whether they had let fall any words about their situation, but Martha Downs was obliged to answer in the negative.

"Was Enoch Holt there after the folks come back from the grave?"

"He wa'n't; they never give him no encouragement neither."

"He appeared well, I must say," continued Peter Downs. "He took his place next but one behind us in the procession, 'long of Melinda Dutch, an' walked to an' from with her, give her his arm, and then I never see him after we got back; but I thought he might be somewhere in the house, an' I was out about the barn an' so on."

"They was civil to him. I was by when he come, just steppin' out of the bedroom after we 'd finished layin' the old Cap'n into his coffin. Hannah looked real pleased when she see Enoch, as if she had n't reelly expected him, but Betsey stuck out her hand 's if 't was an eend o' board, an' drawed her face solemner 'n ever. There, they had natural feelin's. He was their own father when all was said, the Cap'n was, an' I don't know but he was clever to 'em in his way, 'ceptin' when he disappointed Hannah about her marryin' Jake Good'in. She l'arned to respect the old Cap'n's foresight, too."

"Sakes alive, Marthy, how you do knock folks down with one hand an' set 'em up with t' other," chuckled Mr. Downs. They next discussed the Captain's appearance as he lay in state in the front room, a subject which, with its endless ramifications, would keep the whole neighborhood interested for weeks to come.

An hour later the twinkling light in the Downs house suddenly disappeared. As Martha Downs took a last look out of doors through her bedroom window she could see no other light; the neighbors had all gone to bed. It was a little past nine, and the night was damp and still.

II

The Captain Knowles place was eastward from the Downses', and a short turn in the road and the piece of hard-wood growth hid one house from the other. At this unwontedly late hour the elderly sisters were still sitting in their warm kitchen; there were bright coals under the singing tea-kettle which hung from the crane by three or four long pothooks. Betsey Knowles objected when her sister offered to put on more wood.

"Father never liked to leave no great of a fire, even though he slept right here in the bedroom. He said this floor was one that would light an' catch easy, you r'member."

"Another winter we can move down and take the bedroom ourselves—'t will be warmer for us," suggested Hannah; but Betsey shook her head doubtfully. The thought of their old father's grave, unwatched and undefended in the outermost dark field, filled their hearts with a strange tenderness. They had been his dutiful, patient slaves, and it seemed like disloyalty to have abandoned the poor shape, to be sitting there disregarding the thousand requirements and services of the past. More than all, they were facing a free future; they were their own mistresses at last, though past sixty years of age. Hannah was still a child at heart. She chased away a dread suspicion, when Betsey forbade the wood, lest this elder sister, who favored their father's looks, might take his place as stern ruler of the household.

"Betsey," said the younger sister suddenly, "we 'll have us a cook stove, won't we, next winter? I expect we 're going to have something to do with?"

Betsey did not answer; it was impossible to say whether she truly felt grief or only assumed it. She had been sober and silent for the most part since she routed neighbor Downs, though she answered her sister's prattling questions with patience and sympathy. Now she rose from the chair and went to one of the windows, and, pushing back the sash curtain, pulled the wooden shutter across and hasped it.

"I ain't going to bed just yet," she explained. "I 've been a-waiting to make sure nobody was coming in. I don't know 's there 'll be any better time to look in the chest and see what we 've got to depend on. We never 'll get no chance to do it by day."

Hannah looked frightened for a moment, then nodded, and turned to the opposite window and pulled that shutter with much difficulty; it had always caught and hitched and been provoking—a warped piece of red oak, when even-grained white pine would have saved strength and patience to three generations of the Knowles race. Then the sisters crossed the kitchen and opened the bedroom door. Hannah shivered a little as the colder air struck her, and her heart beat loudly. Perhaps it was the same with Betsey.

The bedroom was clean and orderly for the funeral guests. Instead of the blue homespun there was a beautifully quilted white coverlet which had been part of their mother's wedding furnishing, and this made the bedstead with its four low posts look unfamiliar and awesome. The lamplight shone through the kitchen door behind them, not very bright at best, but Betsey reached under the bed, and with all the strength she could muster pulled out the end of the great sea chest. The sisters tugged together and pushed, and made the most of their strength before they finally brought it through the narrow door into the kitchen. The solemnity of the deed made them both whisper as they talked, and Hannah did not dare say what was in her timid heart—that she would rather brave discovery by daylight than such a feeling of being disapprovingly watched now in the dead of night. There came a slight sound outside the house which made her look anxiously at Betsey, but Betsey remained tranquil.

"It's nothing but a stick falling down the woodpile," she answered in a contemptuous whisper, and the younger woman was reassured.

Betsey reached deep into her pocket and found a great key which was worn smooth and bright like silver, and never had been trusted willingly into even her own safe hands. Hannah held the lamp, and the two thin figures bent eagerly over the lid as it opened. Their shadows were waving about the low walls, and looked like strange shapes bowing and dancing behind them.

The chest was stoutly timbered, as if it was built in some ship-yard, and there were heavy wrought-iron hinges and a large escutcheon for the keyhole that the ship's blacksmith might have hammered out. On the top somebody had scratched deeply the crossed lines for a game of fox and geese, and this had a trivial, irreverent look, and might have been the unforgiven fault of some idle ship's boy. The sisters had hardly dared look at the chest or to signify their knowledge of its existence at unwary times.

They had swept carefully about it year after year, and wondered if it was indeed full of gold as the neighbors used to hint; but no matter how much found a way in, little had found the way out. They had been hampered all their lives for money, and in consequence had developed a wonderful facility for spinning and weaving, mending and making. Their small farm was an early example of intensive farming; they were allowed to use its products in a niggardly way, but the money that was paid for wool, for hay, for wood, and for summer crops had all gone into the chest. The old captain was a hard master; he rarely commended and often blamed. Hannah trembled before him, but Betsey faced him sturdily, being amazingly like him, with a feminine difference; as like as a ruled person can be to a ruler, for the discipline of life had taught the man to aggress, the woman only to defend. In the chest was a fabled sum of prize-money, besides these slender earnings of many years; all the sisters' hard work and self-sacrifice were there in money and a mysterious largess besides. All their lives they had been looking forward to this hour of ownership.

There was a solemn hush in the house; the two sisters were safe from their neighbors, and there was no fear of interruption at such an hour in that hard-working community, tired with a day's work that had been early begun. If any one came knocking at the door, both door and windows were securely fastened.

The eager sisters bent above the chest, they held their breath and talked in softest whispers. With stealthy tread a man came out of the woods near by.

He stopped to listen, came nearer, stopped again, and then crept close to the old house. He stepped up on the banking, next the window with the warped shutter; there was a knothole in it high above the women's heads, towards the top. As they leaned over the chest an eager eye watched them. If they had turned that way suspiciously the eye might have caught the flicker of the lamp and betrayed itself. No, they were too busy: the eye at the shutter watched and watched.

There was a certain feeling of relief in the sisters' minds because the contents of the chest were so commonplace at first sight. There were some old belongings dating back to their father's early days of seafaring. They unfolded a waistcoat pattern or two of figured stuff which they had seen him fold and put away again and again. Once he had given Betsey a gay China silk handkerchief, and here were two more like it. They had not known what a store of treasures might be waiting for them, but the reality so far was disappointing; there was much spare room to begin with, and the wares within looked pinched and few. There were bundles of papers, old receipts, some letters in two not very thick bundles, some old account books with worn edges, and a blackened silver can which looked very small in comparison with their anticipation, being an heirloom and jealously hoarded and secreted by the old man. The women began to feel as if his lean, angry figure were bending with them over the sea chest.

They opened a package done up in many layers of old soft paper—a worked piece of Indian muslin, and an embroidered scarf which they had never seen before. "He must have brought them home to mother," said Betsey with a great outburst of feeling. "He never was the same man again; he never would let nobody else have them when he found she was dead, poor old father!"

Hannah looked wistfully at the treasures. She rebuked herself for selfishness, but she thought of her pinched girlhood and the delight these things would have been. Ah yes! it was too late now for many things besides the sprigged muslin. "If I was young as I was once there's lots o' things I'd like to do now I'm free," said Hannah with a gentle sigh; but her sister checked her anxiously—it was fitting that they should preserve a semblance of mourning even to themselves.

The lamp stood in a kitchen chair at the chest's end and shone full across their faces. Betsey looked intent and sober as she turned over the old man's treasures. Under the India mull was an antique pair of buff trousers, a waistcoat of strange old-fashioned foreign stuff, and a blue coat with brass buttons, brought home from over seas, as the women knew, for their father's wedding clothes. They had seen him carry them out at long intervals to hang them in the spring sunshine; he had been very feeble the last time, and Hannah remembered that she had longed to take them from his shaking hands.

"I declare for 't I wish 't we had laid him out in 'em, 'stead o' the robe," she whispered; but Betsey made no answer. She was kneeling still, but held herself upright and looked away. It was evident that she was lost in her own thoughts.

"I can't find nothing else by eyesight," she muttered.
"This chest never 'd be so heavy with them old clothes. Stop! Hold that light down, Hannah; there's a place underneath here. Them papers in the till takes a shallow part. Oh, my gracious! See here, will ye? Hold the light, hold the light!"

There was a hidden drawer in the chest's side—a long, deep place, and it was full of gold pieces. Hannah had seated herself in the chair to be out of her sister's way. She held the lamp with one hand and gathered her apron on her lap with the other, while Betsey, exultant and hawk-eyed, took out handful after handful of heavy coins, letting them jingle and chink, letting them shine in the lamp's rays, letting them roll across the floor—guineas, dollars, doubloons, old French and Spanish and English gold!

Now, now! Look! The eye at the window!

At last they have found it all; the bag of silver, the great roll of bank bills, and the heavy weight of gold—the prize-money that had been like Robinson Crusoe's in the cave. They were rich women that night; their faces grew young again as they sat side by side and exulted while the old kitchen grew cold. There was nothing they might not do within the range of their timid ambitions; they were women of fortune now and their own mistresses. They were beginning at last to live.

The watcher outside was cramped and chilled. He let himself down softly and crept towards the barn, where he might bury himself in the hay and think. His fingers were quick to find the peg that opened the little barn door; the beasts within were startled and stumbled to their feet, then went back to their slumbers. The night wore on; the light spring rain began to fall, and the sound of it on the house roof close down upon the sisters' bed lulled them quickly to sleep. Twelve, one, two o'clock passed by.

They had put back the money and the clothes and the minor goods and treasures and pulled the chest back into the bedroom so that it was out of sight from the kitchen; the bedroom door was always shut by day. The younger sister wished to carry the money to their own room, but Betsey disdained such precaution. The money had always been safe in the old chest, and there it should stay. The next week they would go to Riverport and put it into the bank; it was no use to lose the interest any longer. Because their father had lost some invested money in his early youth it did not follow that every bank was faithless. Betsey's self-assertion was amazing, but they still whispered to each other as they got ready for bed. With strange forgetfulness Betsey had laid the chest key on the white coverlet in the bedroom and left it there.

III

In August of that year the whole country side turned out to go to court.

The sisters had been rich for one night; in the morning they waked to find themselves poor with a bitter pang of poverty of which they had never dreamed. They had said little, but they grew suddenly pinched and old. They could not tell how much money they had lost, except that Hannah's lap was full of gold, a weight she could not lift nor carry. After a few days of stolid misery they had gone to the chief lawyer of their neighborhood to accuse Enoch Holt of the robbery. They dressed in their best and walked solemnly side by side across the fields and along the road, the shortest way to the man of law. Enoch Holt's daughter saw them go as she stood in her doorway and felt a cold shiver run through her frame as if in foreboding. Her father was not at home; he had left for Boston late on the afternoon of Captain Knowles's funeral. He had had notice the day before of the coming in of a ship in which he owned a thirty-second; there was talk of selling the ship, and the owners' agent had summoned him. He had taken pains to go to the funeral because he and the old captain had been on bad terms ever since they had bought a piece of woodland together and the captain declared himself wronged at the settling of accounts. He was growing feeble even then, and had left the business to the younger man. Enoch Holt was not a trusted man, yet he had never before been openly accused of dishonesty. He was not a professor of religion, but foremost on the secular side of church matters. Most of the men in that region were hard men; it was difficult to get money, and there was little real comfort in a community where the sterner, stingier, forbidding side of New England life was well exemplified.

The proper steps had been taken by the officers of the law, and in answer to the writ Enoch Holt appeared, much shocked and very indignant, and was released on bail which covered the sum his shipping interest had brought him. The weeks had dragged by, June and July were long in passing, and here was court day at last, and all the townsfolk hastening by high-roads and by-roads to the court-house. The Knowles girls themselves had risen at break of day and walked the distance steadfastly, like two of the three Fates: who would make the third, to cut the thread for their enemy's disaster? Public opinion was divided. There were many voices ready to speak on the accused man's side; a sharp-looking acquaintance left his business in Boston to swear that Holt was in his office before noon on the day following the robbery, and that he had spent most of the night in Boston, as proved by several minor details of their interview. As for Holt's young married daughter, she was a favorite with the townsfolk, and her husband was away at sea overdue these last few weeks. She sat on one of the hard court benches with a young child in her arms, born since its father sailed; they had been more or less unlucky, the Holt family, though Enoch himself was a man of brag and bluster.

All the hot August morning until the noon recess, and all the hot August afternoon, fly teased and wretched with the heavy air, the crowd of neighbors listened to the trial. There was not much evidence brought; everybody knew that Enoch Holt left the funeral procession hurriedly and went away on horseback towards Boston. His daughter knew no more than this. The Boston man gave his testimony impatiently, and one or two persons insisted that they saw the accused on his way at nightfall several miles from home.

As the testimony came out it all tended to prove his innocence, though public opinion was to the contrary. The Knowles sisters looked more stern and gray hour by hour; their vengeance was not to be satisfied; their accusation had been listened to and found wanting, but their instinctive knowledge of the matter counted for nothing. They must have been watched through the knothole of the shutter; nobody had noticed it until some years before Enoch Holt himself had spoken of the light's shining through on a winter's night as he came towards the house. The chief proof was that nobody else could have done the deed. But why linger over *pros* and *cons?* The jury returned directly with a verdict of "not proven," and the tired audience left the court-house.

But not until Hannah Knowles with angry eyes had risen to her feet.

The sterner elder sister tried to pull her back; every one said that they should have looked to Betsey to say the awful words that followed, not to her gentler companion. It was Hannah, broken and disappointed, who cried in a strange high voice as Enoch Holt was passing by without a look:

"You stole it, you thief! You know it in your heart!"

The startled man faltered, then he faced the women. The people who stood near seemed made of eyes as they stared to see what he would say.

"I swear by my right hand I never touched it."

"Curse your right hand then!" cried Hannah Knowles, growing tall and thin like a white flame drawing upward. "Curse your right hand, yours and all your folks' that follow you! May I live to see the day!"

The people drew back while for a moment accused and accuser stood face to face. Then Holt's flushed face turned white, and he shrank from the fire in those wild eyes, and walked away clumsily down the court-room. Nobody followed him, nobody shook hands with him or told the acquitted man that they were glad of his release. Half an hour later Betsey and Hannah Knowles took their homeward way, to begin their hard round of work again. The horizon that had widened with such glory for one night had closed round them again like an iron wall.

Betsey was alarmed and excited by her sister's uncharacteristic behavior, and she looked at her anxiously from time to time. Hannah had become the harder-faced of the two. Her disappointment was the keener, for she had kept more of the unsatisfied desires of her girlhood until that dreary morning when they found the sea chest rifled and the treasure gone.

Betsey said inconsequently that it was a pity she did not have that black silk gown that would stand alone. They had planned for it over the open chest, and Hannah's was to be a handsome green. They might have worn them to court. But even the pathetic facetiousness of her elder sister did not bring a smile to Hannah Knowles's face, and the next day one was at the loom and the other at the wheel again. The neighbors talked about the curse with horror; in their minds a fabric of sad fate was spun from the bitter words.

The Knowles sisters never had worn silk gowns and they never would. Sometimes Hannah or Betsey would stealthily look over the chest in one or the other's absence. One day when Betsey was very old and her mind had grown feeble she tied her own India silk handkerchief about her neck, but they never used the other two. They aired the wedding suit once every spring as long as they lived. They were both too old and forlorn to make up the India mull. Nobody knows how many times they took everything out of the heavy old clamped box and peered into every nook and corner to see if there was not a single gold piece left. They never answered any one who made bold to speak of their misfortune.

IV

Enoch Holt had been a seafaring man in his early days, and there was news that the owners of a Salem ship in which he held a small interest wished him to go out as super-cargo. He was brisk and well in health, and his son-in-law, an honest but an unlucky fellow, had done less well than usual, so that nobody was surprised when Enoch made ready for his voyage. It was nearly a year after the theft, and nothing had come so near to restoring him to public favor as his apparent lack of ready money. He openly said that he put great hope in his adventure to the Spice Islands, and when he said farewell one Sunday to some members of the dispersing congregation more than one person wished him heartily a pleasant voyage and safe return. He had an insinuating tone of voice and an imploring look that day, and this fact, with his probable long absence and the dangers of the deep, won him much sympathy. It is a shameful thing to accuse a man wrongfully, and Enoch Holt had behaved well since the trial; and, what is more, had shown no accession to his means of living. So away he went with a fair amount of good wishes, though one or two persons assured remonstrating listeners that they thought it likely Enoch would make a good voyage, better than common, and show himself forwarded when he came to port. Soon after his departure Mrs. Peter Downs and an intimate acquaintance discussed the ever-exciting subject of the Knowles robbery over a friendly cup of tea.

They were in the Downs kitchen and quite by themselves. Peter Downs himself had been drawn as a juror, and had been for two days at the county town. Mrs. Downs was giving herself to social interests in his absence, and Mrs. Forder, an asthmatic but very companionable person, had arrived by two o'clock that afternoon with her knitting work, sure of being welcome. The two old friends had first talked over varied subjects of immediate concern, but when supper was nearly finished they fell back upon the lost Knowles gold, as has been already said.

"They got a dreadful blow, poor gals," wheezed Mrs. Forder with compassion. "'T was harder for them than for most folks; they 'd had a long stent with the ol' gentleman; very arbitrary, very arbitrary."

"Yes," answered Mrs. Downs, pushing back her tea-cup, then lifting it again to see if it was quite empty. "Yes, it took holt o' Hannah the most.

I should 'a' said Betsey was a good deal the most set in her ways an' would 'a' been most tore up, but 't wa'n't so.''

"Lucky that Holt's folks sets on the other aisle in the meetin' house, I do consider, so 't they need n't face each other sure as Sabbath comes round.''

I see Hannah an' him come face to face two Sabbaths afore Enoch left. So happened he dallied to have a word 'long o' Deacon Good'in, an' him an' Hannah stepped front of each other 'fore they knowed what they 's about. I sh'd thought her eyes 'd looked right through him. No one of 'em took the word; Enoch he slinked off pretty quick.''

"I see 'em too," said Mrs. Forder; "made my blood run cold.''

"Nothin' ain't come of the curse yit,"—Mrs. Downs lowered the tone of her voice,—"least, folks says so. It kind o' worries pore Phoebe Holt—Miss Dow, I would say. She was narved all up at the time o' the trial, an' when her next baby come into the world first thin' she made out t' ask me was whether it seemed likely, an' she gived me a pleadin' look as if I 'd got to tell her what she had n't heart to ask. 'Yes, dear,' says I, 'put up his little hands to me kind of wonted': an' she turned a look on me like another creatur' , so pleased an' contented.''

"I s'pose you don't see no great of the Knowles gals?" inquired Mrs. Forder, who lived two miles away in the other direction.

"They stepped to the door yisterday when I was passin' by, an' I went in an' set a spell long of 'em," replied the hostess. "They 'd got pestered with that ol' loom o' theirn. 'Fore I thought, says I, ''T is all worn out, Betsey,' says I; 'why on airth don't ye git somebody to git some o' your own wood an' season it well so 't won't warp, same 's mine done, an' build ye a new one?' But Betsey muttered an' twitched away; 't wa'n't like her, but they 're dis'p'inted at every turn, I s'pose, an' feel poor where they 've got the same 's ever to do with. Hannah's a-coughin' this spring 's if somethin' ailed her. I asked her if she had bad feelin's in her pipes, an' she said yis, she had, but not to speak of 't before Betsey. I 'm goin' to fix her up some hoarhound an' elecampane quick 's the ground 's nice an' warm an' roots livens up a grain more. They 're limp an' wizened 'long to the fust of the spring. Them would be service'ble, simmered away to a syrup 'long o' molasses; now don't you think so, Miss Forder?''

"Excellent," replied the wheezing dame. "I covet a portion myself, now you speak. Nothin' cures my complaint, but a new remedy takes holt clever sometimes, an' eases me for a spell." And she gave a plaintive sign, and began to knit again.

Mrs. Downs rose and pushed the supper table to the wall and drew her chair nearer to the stove. The April nights were chilly.

"The folks is late comin' after me," said Mrs. Forder, ostentatiously. "I may 's well confess that I told 'em if they was late with the work they might let go o' fetchin' o' me an' I 'd walk home in the mornin'; take it easy when I was fresh. Course I mean ef 't would n't put you out: I knowed you was all alone, an' I kind o' wanted a change."

"Them words was in my mind to utter while we was to table," avowed Mrs. Downs, hospitably. "I ain't reelly afeared, but 't is sort o' creepy fastenin' up an' goin' to bed alone. Nobody can't help hearkin', an' every common noise starts you. I never used to give nothin' a thought till the Knowleses was robbed, though."

"'T was mysterious, I do maintain," acknowledged Mrs. Forder. "Comes over me sometimes p'raps 't was n't Enoch; he'd 'a' branched out more in course o' time. I 'm waitin' to see if he does extry well to sea 'fore I let my mind come to bear on his bein' clean-handed."

"Plenty thought 't was the old Cap'n come back for it an' sperited it away. Enough said that 't was n't no honest gains; most on 't was prize-money o' slave ships, an' all kinds o' devil's gold was mixed in. I s'pose you've heard that said?"

"Time an' again," responded Mrs. Forder; "an' the worst on 't was simple old Pappy Flanders went an' told the Knowles gals themselves that folks thought the old Cap'n come back an' got it, and Hannah done wrong to cuss Enoch Holt an' his ginerations after him the way she done."

"I think it took holt on her ter'ble after all she'd gone through," said Mrs. Downs, compassionately. "He ain't near so simple as he is ugly, Pappy Flanders ain't. I 've seen him set here an' read the paper sober's anybody when I 've been goin' about my mornin's work in the shed-room, an' when I 'd come in to look about he 'd twist it with his hands an' roll his eyes an' begin to git off some o' his gabble. I think them wanderin' cheap-wits likes the fun on 't an' 'scapes stiddy work, an' gits the rovin' habits so fixed it sp'iles 'em."

"My gran'ther was to the South Seas in his young days," related Mrs. Forder, impressively, "an' he said cussin' was common there. I mean sober spitin' with a cuss. He seen one o' them black folks git a gredge against another an' go an' set down an' look stiddy at him in his hut an' cuss him in his mind an' set there an' watch, watch, until the other kind o' took sick an' died, all in a fortnight, I believe he said; 't would make your blood run cold to hear gran'ther describe it, 't would so. He never done nothin' but set an' look, an' folks would give him somethin' to eat now an' then, as if they thought 't was all right, an' the other one'd try to go an' come, an' at last he hived away altogether an' died. I don't know what you 'd call it that ailed him. There 's suthin' in cussin' that 's bad for folks, now I tell ye, Miss Downs."

"Hannah's eyes always makes me creepy now," Mrs. Downs confessed uneasily. "They don't look pleadin' an' childish same 's they used to. Seems to me as if she 'd had the worst on 't."

"We ain't seen the end on 't yit," said Mrs. Forder, impressively. "I feel it within me, Marthy Downs, an' it 's a terrible thing to have happened right amon'st us in Christian times. If we live long enough we 're goin' to have plenty to talk over in our old age that 's come o' that cuss. Some seed 's shy o' sproutin' till a spring when the s'ile 's jist right to breed it."

"There 's lobeely now," agreed Mrs. Downs, pleased to descend to prosaic and familiar levels. "They ain't a good crop one year in six, and then you find it in a place where you never observed none to grow afore, like 's not: ain't it so, reelly?" And she rose to clear the table, pleased with the certainty of a guest that night. Their conversation was not reassuring to the heart of a timid woman alone in an isolated farm-house on a dark spring evening, especially so near the anniversary of old Captain Knowles's death.

V

Later in these rural lives by many years two aged women were crossing a wide field together, following a foot-path such as one often finds between widely separated homes of the New England country. Along these lightly traced thoroughfares the children go to play, and lovers to plead, and older people to companion one another in work and pleasure, in sickness and sorrow; generation after generation comes and goes again by these country by-ways.

The foot-path led from Mrs. Forder's to another farm-house half a mile beyond, where there had been a wedding. Mrs. Downs was there, and in the June weather she had been easily persuaded to go home to tea with Mrs. Forder with the promise of being driven home later in the evening. Mrs. Downs's husband had been dead three years, and her friend's large family was scattered from the old nest; they were lonely at times in their later years, these old friends, and found it very pleasant now to have a walk together. Thin little Mrs. Forder, with all her wheezing, was the stronger and more active of the two; Mrs. Downs had grown heavier and weaker with advancing years.

They paced along the foot-path slowly, Mrs. Downs rolling in her gait like a sailor, and availing herself of every pretext to stop and look at herbs in the pasture ground they crossed, and at the growing grass in the mowing fields. They discussed the wedding minutely, and then where the way grew wider they walked side by side instead of following each other, and their voices sank to the low tone that betokens confidence.

"You don't say that you really put faith in all them old stories?"

"It ain't accident altogether, noways you can fix it in your mind," maintained Mrs. Downs. "Need n't tell me that cussin' don't do neither good nor harm. I should n't want to marry amon'st the Holts if I was young ag'in! I r'member when this young man was born that 's married to-day, an' the fust thing his poor mother wanted to know was about his hands bein' right. I said yes they was, but las' year he was twenty year old and come home from the frontier with one o' them hands—his right one—shot off in a fight. They say 't happened to sights o' other fellows, an' their laigs gone too, but I count 'em over on my fingers, them Holts, an' he 's the third. May say that 't was all an accident his mother's gittin' throwed out o' her waggin comin' home from meetin', an' her wrist not bein' set good, an' she, bein' run down at the time, 'most lost it altogether, but thar' it is stiffened up an' no good to her. There was the second. An' Enoch Holt hisself come home from the Chiny seas, made a good passage an' a sight o' money in the pepper trade, jest 's we expected, an' goin' to build him a new house, an' the frame gives a kind o' lurch when they was raisin' of it an' surges over on to him an' nips him under. 'Which arm?' says everybody along the road when they was comin' an' goin' with the doctor. 'Right one—got to lose it,' says the doctor to 'em, an' next time Enoch Holt got out to meetin' he stood up in the house o' God with the hymn-book in his left hand, an' no right hand to turn his leaf with. He knowed what we was all a-thinkin'."

"Well," said Mrs. Forder, very short-breathed with climbing the long slope of the pasture hill, "I don't know but I 'd as soon be them as the Knowles gals. Hannah never knowed no peace again after she spoke them words in the co't-house. They come back an' harnted her, an' you know, Miss Downs, better 'n I do, being door-neighbors as one may say, how they lived their lives out like wild beasts into a lair."

"They used to go out some night to git the air," pursued Mrs. Downs with interest. "I used to open the door an' step right in, an' I used to take their yarn an' stuff 'long o' mine an' sell 'em, an' do for the poor stray creatur's long 's they 'd let me. They 'd be grateful for a mess o' early pease or potatoes as ever you see, an' Peter he allays favored 'em with pork, fresh an' salt, when we slaughtered. The old Cap'n kept 'em child'n long as he lived, an' then they was too old to l'arn different. I allays liked Hannah the best till that change struck her. Betsey she held out to the last jest about the same. I don't know, now I come to think of it, but what she felt it the most o' the two."

"They 'd never let me s' much as git a look at 'em," complained Mrs. Forder. "Folks got awful stories a-goin' one time. I've heard it said, an' it allays creeped me cold all over, that there was somethin' come an' lived with 'em—a kind o' black shadder, a cobweb kind o' a man-shape that followed 'em about the house an' made a third to them; but they got hardened to it theirselves, only they was afraid 't would follow if they went anywheres from home. You don't believe no such a piece o' nonsense?—But there, I 've asked ye times enough before."

"They 'd got shadders enough, poor creatur's," said Mrs. Downs with reserve. "Was n't no kind o' need to make 'em up no spooks, as I know on. Well, here 's these young folks a-startin'; I wish 'em well, I 'm sure. She like him with his one hand better than most gals likes them as has a good sound pair. They looked prime happy; I hope no curse won't foller 'em."

The friends stopped again—poor, short-winded bodies—on the crest of the low hill and turned to look at the wide landscape, bewildered by the marvelous beauty and the sudden flood of golden sunset light that poured out of the western sky. They could not remember that they had ever observed the wide view before; it was like a revelation or an outlook towards the celestial country, the sight of their own green farms and the country-side that bounded them. It was a pleasant country indeed, their own New England: their petty thoughts and vain imaginings seemed futile and unrelated to so fair a scene of things. But the figure of a man who was crossing the meadow below looked like a malicious black insect. It was an old man, it was Enoch Holt; time had worn and bent him enough to have satisfied his bitterest foe. The women could see his empty coat-sleeve flutter as he walked slowly and unexpectantly in that glorious evening light.

MISS ESTHER'S GUEST

Old Miss Porley put on her silk shawl, and arranged it carefully over her thin shoulders, and pinned it with a hand that shook a little as if she were much excited. She bent forward to examine the shawl in the mahogany-framed mirror, for there was a frayed and tender spot in the silk where she had pinned it so many years. The shawl was very old; it had been her mother's, and she disliked to wear it too often, but she never could make up her mind to go out into the street in summer, as some of her neighbors did, with nothing over her shoulders at all. Next she put on her bonnet and tried to set it straight, allowing for a wave in the looking-glass that made one side of her face appear much longer than the other; then she drew on a pair of well-darned silk gloves; one had a wide crack all the way up the back of the hand, but they were still neat and decent for every-day wear, if she were careful to keep her left hand under the edge of the shawl. She had discussed the propriety of drawing the raveled silk together, but a thick seam would look very ugly, and there was something accidental about the crack.

Then, after hesitating a few moments, she took a small piece of folded white letter-paper from the table and went out of the house, locking the door and trying it, and stepped away bravely down the village street. Everybody said, "How do you do, Miss Porley?" or "Good-mornin', Esther." Every one in Daleham knew the good woman; she was one of the unchanging persons, always to be found in her place, and always pleased and friendly and ready to take an interest in old and young. She and her mother, who had early been left a widow, had been for many years the village tailoresses and makers of little boys' clothes. Mrs. Porley had been dead three years, however, and her daughter "Easter," as old friends called our heroine, had lived quite alone. She was made very sorrowful by her loneliness, but she never could be persuaded to take anybody to board: she could not bear to think of any one's taking her mother's place.

It was a warm summer morning, and Miss Porley had not very far to walk, but she was still more shaky and excited by the time she reached the First Church parsonage. She stood at the gate undecidedly, and, after she pushed it open a little way, she drew back again, and felt a curious beating at her heart and a general reluctance of mind and body. At that moment the minister's wife, a pleasant young woman with a smiling, eager face, looked out of the window and asked the tremulous visitor to come in. Miss Esther straightened herself and went briskly up the walk; she was very fond of the minister's wife, who had only been in Daleham a few months.

"Won't you take off your shawl?" asked Mrs. Wayton affectionately; "I have just been making gingerbread, and you shall have a piece as soon as it cools."

"I don't know 's I ought to stop," answered Miss Esther, flushing quickly. "I came on business; I won't keep you long."

"Oh, please stay a little while," urged the hostess. "I 'll take my sewing, if you don't mind; there are two or three things that I want to ask you about."

"I 've thought and flustered a sight over taking this step," said good old Esther abruptly. "I had to conquer a sight o' reluctance, I must say. I 've got so used to livin' by myself that I sha'n't know how to consider another. But I see I ain't got common feelin' for others unless I can set my own comfort aside once in a while. I 've brought you my name as one of those that will take one o' them city folks that needs a spell o' change. It come straight home to me how I should be feeling it by this time, if my lot had been cast in one o' them city garrets that the minister described so affecting. If 't had n't been for kind consideration somewheres, mother an' me might have sewed all them pleasant years away in the city that we enjoyed so in our own home, and our garding to step right out into when our sides set in to ache. And I ain't rich, but we was able to save a little something, and now I 'm eatin' of it all up alone. It come to me I should like to have somebody take a taste out o' mother's part. Now, don't you let 'em send me no rampin' boys like them Barnard's folks had come last year, that vexed dumb creatur's so; and I don't know how to cope with no kind o' men-folks or strange girls, but I should know how to do for a woman that 's getting well along in years, an' has come to feel kind o' spent. P'raps we ain't no right to pick an' choose, but I should know best how to make that sort comfortable on 'count of doin' for mother and studying what she preferred.''

Miss Esther rose with quaint formality and put the folded paper, on which she had neatly written her name and address, into Mrs. Wayton's hand. Mrs. Wayton rose soberly to receive it, and then they both sat down again.

"I 'm sure that you will feel more than repaid for your kindness, dear Miss Esther," said the minister's wife. "I know one of the ladies who have charge of the arrangements for the Country Week, and I will explain as well as I can the kind of guest you have in mind. I quite envy her; I have often thought, when I was busy and tired, how much I should like to run along the street and make you a visit in your dear old-fashioned little house."

"I should be more than pleased to have you, I'm sure," said Miss Esther, startled into a bright smile and forgetting her anxiety. "Come any day, and take me just as I am. We used to have a good deal o' company years ago, when there was a number o' mother's folks still livin' over Ashfield way. Sure as we had a pile o' work on hand and was hurrying for dear life an' limb, a wagonload would light down at the front gate to spend the day an' have an early tea. Mother never was one to get flustered same 's I do 'bout everything. She was a lovely cook, and she 'd fill 'em up an' cheer 'em, and git 'em off early as she could, an' then we 'd be kind o' waked up an' spirited ourselves, and would set up late sewin' and talkin' the company over, an' I 'd have things saved to tell her that had been said while she was out o' the room. I make such a towse over everything myself, but mother was waked right up and felt pleased an' smart, if anything unexpected happened. I miss her more every year," and Miss Esther gave a great sigh. "I s'pose 't wa'n't reasonable to expect that I could have her to help me through with old age, but I 'm a poor tool, alone."

"Oh, no, you must n't say that!" exclaimed the minister's wife. "Why, nobody could get along without you. I wish I had come to Daleham in time to know your mother too."

Miss Esther shook her head sadly. "She would have set everything by you and Mr. Wayton. Now I must be getting back in case I 'm wanted, but you let 'em send me somebody right away, while my bush beans is so nice. An' if any o' your little boy's clothes wants repairin', just give 'em to me; 't will be a real pleasant thing to set a few stitches. Or the minister's; ain't there something needed for him?"

Mrs. Wayton was about to say no, when she became conscious of the pleading old face before her. "I 'm sure you are most kind, dear friend," she answered, "and I do have a great deal to do. I 'll bring you two or three things to-night that are beyond my art, as I go to evening meeting. Mr. Wayton frayed out his best coat sleeve yesterday, and I was disheartened, for we had counted upon his not having a new one before the fall."

"'T would be mere play to me," said Miss Esther, and presently she went smiling down the street.

II

The Committee for the Country Week in a certain ward of Boston were considering the long list of children, and mothers with babies, and sewing-women, who were looking forward, some of them for the first time in many years, to a country holiday. Some were to go as guests to hospitable, generous farmhouses that opened their doors willingly now and then to tired city people; for some persons board could be paid.

The immediate arrangements of that time were settled at last, except that Mrs. Belton, the chairman, suddenly took a letter from her pocket. "I had almost forgotten this," she said; "it is another place offered in dear quiet old Daleham. My friend, the minister's wife there, writes me a word about it: 'The applicant desires especially an old person, being used to the care of an aged parent and sure of her power of making such a one comfortable, and she would like to have her guest come as soon as possible.' My friend asks me to choose a person of some refinement,— 'one who would appreciate the delicate simplicity and quaint ways of the hostess.'"

Mrs. Belton glanced hurriedly down the page. "I believe that's all," she said. "How about that nice old sewing-woman, Mrs. Connolly, in Bantry Street?"

"Oh, no!" some one entreated, looking up from her writing. "Why is n't it just the place for my old Mr. Rill, the dear old Englishman who lives alone up four flights in Town Court and has the bullfinch. He used to engrave seals, and his eyes gave out, and he is so thrifty with his own bit of savings and an atom of a pension. Some one pays his expenses to the country, and this sounds like a place he would be sure to like. I 've been watching for the right chance."

"Take it, then," said the busy chairman, and there was a little more writing and talking, and then the committee meeting was over which settled Miss Esther Porley's fate.

III

The journey to Daleham was a great experience to Mr. Rill. He was a sensible old person, who knew well that he was getting stiffer and clumsier than need be in his garret, and that, as certain friends had said, a short time spent in the country would cheer and invigorate him. There had been occasional propositions that he should leave his garret altogether and go to the country to live, or at least to the suburbs of the city. He could not see things close at hand so well as he could take a wide outlook, and as his outlook from the one garret window was a still higher brick wall and many chimneys, he was losing a great deal that he might have had. But so long as he was expected to take an interest in the unseen and unknown he failed to accede to any plans about the country home, and declared that he was well enough in his high abode. He had lost a sister a few years before who had been his mainstay, but with his hands so well used to delicate work he had been less bungling in his simple house-hold affairs than many another man might have been. But he was very lonely and was growing anxious; as he was rattled along in the train toward Daleham he held the chirping bull-finch's cage fast with both hands, and said to himself now and then, "This may lead to something; the country air smells very good to me."

The Daleham station was not very far out of the village, so that Miss Esther Porley put on her silk shawl and bonnet and everyday gloves just before four o'clock that afternoon, and went to meet her Country Week guest. Word had come the day before that the person for Miss Porley's would start two days in advance of the little company of children and help-less women, and since this message had come from the parsonage Miss Esther had worked diligently, late and early, to have her house in proper order. Whatever her mother had liked was thought of and provided. There were going to be rye short-cakes for tea, and there were some sprigs of thyme and sweet-balm in an old-fashioned wine glass on the keeping-room table; mother always said they were so freshening. And Miss Esther had taken out a little shoulder-shawl and folded it over the arm of the rocking-chair by the window that looked out into the small garden where the London-pride was in full bloom, and the morning-glories had just begun to climb. Miss Esther was sixty-four herself, but still looked upon age as well in the distance.

She was always a prompt person, and had some minutes to wait at the station; then the time passed and the train was late. At last she saw the smoke far in the distance, and her heart began to sink. Perhaps she would not find it easy to get on with the old lady, and—well it was only for a week, and she had thought it right and best to take such a step, and now it would soon be over.

The train stopped, and there was no old lady at all.

Miss Esther had stood far back to get away from the smoke and roar,—she was always as afraid of the cars as she could be,—but as they moved away she took a few steps forward to scan the platform. There was no black bonnet with a worn lace veil, and no old lady with a burden of bundles; there were only the station master and two or three men, and an idle boy or two, and one clean-faced, bent old man with a bird-cage in one hand and an old carpet-bag in the other. She thought of the rye short-cakes for supper and all that she had done to make her small home pleasant, and her fire of excitement suddenly fell into ashes.

The old man with the bird-cage suddenly turned toward her. "Can you direct me to Miss Esther Porley's?" said he.

"I can," replied Miss Esther, looking at him with curiosity.

"I was directed to her house," said the pleasant old fellow, "by Mrs. Belton, of the Country Week Committee. My eyesight is poor. I should be glad if anybody would help me to find the place."

"You step this way with me, sir," said Miss Esther. She was afraid that the men on the platform heard every word they said but nobody took particular notice, and off they walked down the road together. Miss Esther was enraged with the Country Week Committee.

"*You* were sent to—Miss Porley's?" she asked grimly, turning to look at him.

"I was, indeed," said Mr. Rill.

"I am Miss Porley, and I expected an old lady," she managed to say, and they both stopped and looked at each other with apprehension.

"I do declare!" faltered the old seal-cutter anxiously. "What had I better do, ma'am? They most certain give me your name. May be you could recommend me somewheres else, an' I can get home to-morrow if 't ain't convenient."

They were standing under a willow-tree in the shade; Mr. Rill took off his heavy hat,—it was a silk hat of by-gone shape; a golden robin began to sing, high in the willow, and the old bullfinch twittered and chirped in the cage. Miss Esther heard some footsteps coming behind them along the road. She changed color; she tried to remember that she was a woman of mature years and considerable experience.

"'T ain't a mite o' matter, sir," she said cheerfully. "I guess you 'll find everything comfortable for you;" and they turned, much relieved, and walked along together.

"That 's Lawyer Barstow's house," she said calmly, a minute afterward, "the handsomest place in town, we think 't is," and Mr. Rill answered politely that Daleham was a pretty place; he had not been out of the city for so many years that everything looked beautiful as a picture.

IV

Miss Porley rapidly recovered her composure, and bent her energies to the preparing of an early tea. She showed her guest to the snug bedroom under the low gambrel roof, and when she apologized for his having to go upstairs, he begged her to remember that it was nothing but a step to a man who was used to four long flights. They were both excited at finding a proper nail for the bird-cage outside the window, though Miss Esther said that she should love to have the pretty bird downstairs where they could see it and hear it sing. She said to herself over and over that if she could have her long-lost brother come home from sea, she should like to have him look and behave as gentle and kind as Mr. Rill. Somehow she found herself singing a cheerful hymn as she mixed and stirred the short-cakes. She could not help wishing that her mother were there to enjoy this surprise, but it did seem very odd, after so many years, to have a man in the house. It had not happened for fifteen years, at least, when they had entertained Deacon Sparks and wife, delegates from the neighboring town of East Wilby to the County Conference.

The neighbors did not laugh at Miss Esther openly or cause her to blush with self-consciousness, however much they may have discussed the situation and smiled behind her back. She took the presence of her guest with delighted simplicity, and the country week was extended to a fortnight, and then to a month. At last, one day Miss Esther and Mr. Rill were seen on their way to the railroad station, with a large bundle apiece beside the carpet-bag, though some one noticed that the bullfinch was left behind. Miss Esther came back alone, looking very woebegone and lonely, and if the truth must be known, she found her house too solitary. She looked into the woodhouse where there was a great store of kindlings, neatly piled, and her water-pail was filled to the brim, her garden-paths were clean of weeds and swept, and yet everywhere she looked it seemed more lonely than ever. She pinned on her shawl again and went along the street to the parsonage.

"My old lady 's just gone," she said to the minister's wife. "I was so lonesome I could not stay in the house."

"You found him a very pleasant visitor, did n't you, Miss Esther?" asked Mrs. Wayton, laughing a little.

"I did so; he wa'n't like other men,—kind and friendly and fatherly, and never stayed round when I was occupied, but entertained himself down street considerable, an' was as industrious as a bee, always asking me if there wa'n't something he could do about house. He and a sister some years older used to keep house together, and it was her long sickness used up what they 'd saved, and yet he 's got a little somethin', and there are friends he used to work for, jewelers, a big firm, that gives him somethin' regular. He 's goin to see,"—and Miss Esther blushed crimson,—"he 's goin' to see if they 'd be willin' to pay it just the same if he come to reside in Daleham. He thinks the air agrees with him here."

"Does he indeed?" inquired the minister's wife, with deep interest and a look of amusement.

"Yes 'm," said Miss Esther simply; "but don't you go an' say nothin' yet. I don't want folks to make a joke of it. Seems to me if he does feel to come back, and remains of the same mind he went away, we might be judicious to take the step"—

"Why, Miss Esther!" exclaimed the listener.

"Not till fall,—not till fall," said Miss Esther hastily. "I ain't going to count on it too much anyway. I expect we could get along; there 's considerable goodness left in me, and you can always work better when you 've got somebody beside yourself to work for. There, now I 've told you I feel as if I was blown away in a gale."

"Why, I don't know what to say at such a piece of news!" exclaimed Mrs. Wayton again.

"I don't know 's there 's anything to say," gravely answered Miss Esther. "But I did laugh just now coming in the gate to think what a twitter I got into the day I fetched you that piece of paper."

"Why, I must go right and tell Mr. Wayton!" said the minister's wife.

"Oh, don't you, Mis' Wayton; no, no!" begged Miss Esther, looking quite coy and girlish. "I really don't know 's it 's quite settled,—it don't seem 's if it could be. I 'm going to hear from him in the course of a week. But I suppose *he* thinks it 's settled; he 's left the bird."

THE FLIGHT OF
BETSEY LANE

O ne windy morning in May, three old women sat together near an open window in the shed chamber of Byfleet Poor-house. The wind was from the northwest, but their window faced the southeast, and they were only visited by an occasional pleasant waft of fresh air. They were close together, knee to knee, picking over a bushel of beans, and commanding a view of the dandelion-starred, green yard below, and of the winding, sandy road that led to the village, two miles away. Some captive bees were scolding among the cobwebs of the rafters overhead, or thumping against the upper panes of glass; two calves were bawling from the barnyard, where some of the men were at work loading a dump-cart and shouting as if every one were deaf. There was a cheerful feeling of activity, and even an air of comfort, about the Byfleet Poor-house. Almost every one was possessed of a most interesting past, though there was less to be said about the future. The inmates were by no means distressed or unhappy; many of them retired to this shelter only for the winter season, and would go out presently, some to begin such work as they could still do, others to live in their own small houses; old age had impoverished most of them by limiting their power of endurance; but far from lamenting the fact that they were town charges, they rather liked the change and excitement of a winter residence on the poor-farm. There was a sharp-faced, hard-worked young widow with seven children, who was an exception to the general level of society, because she deplored the change in her fortunes. The older women regarded her with suspicion, and were apt to talk about her in moments like this, when they happened to sit together at their work.

The three bean-pickers were dressed alike in stout brown ginghams, checked by a white line, and all wore great faded aprons of blue drilling, with sufficient pockets convenient to the right hand. Miss Peggy Bond was a very small, belligerent-looking person, who wore a huge pair of steel-bowed spectacles, holding her sharp chin well up in air, as if to supplement an inadequate nose. She was more than half blind, but the spectacles seemed to face upward instead of square ahead, as if their wearer were always on the sharp lookout for birds. Miss Bond had suffered much personal damage from time to time, because she never took heed where she planted her feet, and so was always tripping and stubbing her bruised way through the world. She had fallen down hatchways and cellarways, and stepped composedly into deep ditches and pasture brooks; but she was proud of stating that she was upsighted, and so was her father before her. At the poor-house, where an unusual malady was considered a distinction, upsightedness was looked upon as a most honorable infirmity. Plain rheumatism, such as afflicted Aunt Lavina Dow, whose twisted hands found even this light work difficult and tiresome,—plain rheumatism was something of every-day occurrence, and nobody cared to hear about it. Poor Peggy was a meek and friendly soul, who never put herself forward; she was just like other folks, as she always loved to say, but Mrs. Lavina Dow was a different sort of person altogether, of great dignity and, occasionally, almost aggressive behavior. The time had been when she could do a good day's work with anybody: but for many years now she had not left the town-farm, being too badly crippled to work; she had no relations or friends to visit, but from an innate love of authority she could not submit to being one of those who are forgotten by the world. Mrs. Dow was the hostess and social lawgiver here, where she remembered every inmate and every item of interest for nearly forty years, besides an immense amount of town history and biography for three or four generations back.

She was the dear friend of the third woman, Betsey Lane; together they led thought and opinion—chiefly opinion—and held sway, not only over Byfleet Poor-farm, but also the selectmen and all others in authority. Betsey Lane had spent most of her life as aid-in-general to the respected household of old General Thornton. She had been much trusted and valued, and, at the breaking up of that once large and flourishing family, she had been left in good circumstances, what with legacies and her own comfortable savings; but by sad misfortune and lavish generosity everything had been scattered, and after much illness, which ended in a stiffened arm and more uncertainty, the good soul had sensibly decided that it was easier for the whole town to support her than for a part of it. She had always hoped to see something of the world before she died; she came of an adventurous, seafaring stock, but had never made a longer journey than to the towns of Danby and Northville, thirty miles away.

They were all old women; but Betsey Lane, who was sixty-nine, and looked much older, was the youngest. Peggy Bond was far on in the seventies, and Mrs. Dow was at least ten years older. She made a great secret of her years; and as she sometimes spoke of events prior to the Revolution with the assertion of having been an eye-witness, she naturally wore an air of vast antiquity. Her tales were an inexpressible delight to Betsey Lane, who felt younger by twenty years because her friend and comrade was so unconscious of chronological limitations.

The bushel basket of cranberry beans was within easy reach, and each of the pickers had filled her lap from it again and again. The shed chamber was not an unpleasant place in which to sit at work, with its traces of seed corn hanging from the brown cross-beams, its spare churns, and dusty loom, and rickety wool-wheels, and a few bits of old furniture. In one far corner was a wide board of dismal use and suggestion, and close beside it an old cradle. There was a battered chest of drawers where the keeper of the poor-house kept his garden-seeds, with the withered remains of three seed cucumbers ornamenting the top. Nothing beautiful could be discovered, nothing interesting, but there was something usable and homely about the place. It was the favorite and untroubled bower of the bean-pickers, to which they might retreat unmolested from the public apartments of this rustic institution.

Betsey Lane blew away the chaff from her handful of beans. The spring breeze blew the chaff back again, and sifted it over her face and shoulders. She rubbed it out of her eyes impatiently, and happened to notice old Peggy holding her own handful high, as if it were an oblation, and turning her queer, up-tilted head this way and that, to look at the beans sharply, as if she were first cousin to a hen.

"There, Miss Bond, 't is kind of botherin' work for you, ain't it?" Betsey inquired compassionately.

"I feel to enjoy it, anything that I can do my own way so," responded Peggy. "I like to do my part. Ain't that old Mis' Fales comin' up the road? It sounds like her step."

The others looked, but they were not far-sighted, and for a moment Peggy had the advantage. Mrs. Fales was not a favorite.

"I hope she ain't comin' here to put up this spring. I guess she won't now, it 's gettin' so late," said Betsey Lane. "She likes to go rovin' soon as the roads is settled."

"'T is Mis' Fales!" said Peggy Bond, listening with solemn anxiety. "There, do let 's pray her by!"

"I guess she 's headin' for her cousin's folks up Beech Hill way," said Betsey presently. "If she 'd left her daughter's this mornin', she 'd have got just about as far as this. I kind o' wish she had stepped in just to pass the time o' day, long 's she wa'n't going to make no stop."

There was a silence as to further speech in the shed chamber; and even the calves were quiet in the barnyard. The men had all gone away to the field where corn-planting was going on. The beans clicked steadily into the wooden measure at the pickers' feet. Betsey Lane began to sing a hymn, and the others joined in as best they might, like autumnal crickets; their voices were sharp and cracked, with now and then a few low notes of plaintive tone. Betsey herself could sing pretty well, but the others could only make a kind of accompaniment. Their voices ceased altogether at the higher notes.

"Oh my! I wish I had the means to go to the Centennial," mourned Betsey Lane, stopping so suddenly that the others had to go on croaking and shrilling without her for a moment before they could stop. "It seems to me as if I can't die happy 'less I do," she added; "I ain't never seen nothin' of the world, an' here I be."

"What if you was as old as I be?" suggested Mrs. Dow pompously. "You 've got time enough yet, Betsey; don't you go an' despair. I knowed of a woman that went clean round the world four times when she was past eighty, an' enjoyed herself real well. Her folks followed the sea; she had three sons an' a daughter married,—all ship-masters, and she 'd been with her own husband when they was young. She was left a widder early, and fetched up her family herself,—a real stirrin', smart woman. After they 'd got married off, an' settled, an' was doing well, she come to be lonesome;

and first she tried to stick it out alone, but she wa'n't one that could; an' she got a notion she had n't nothin' before her but her last sickness, and she wa'n't a person that enjoyed havin' other folks do for her. So one on her boys—I guess 't was the oldest—said he was going to take her to sea; there was ample room, an' he was sailin' a good time o' year for the Cape o' Good Hope an' way up to some o' them tea-ports in the Chiny Seas. She was all high to go, but it made a sight o' talk at her age; an' the minister made it a subject o' prayer the last Sunday, and all the folks took a last leave; but she said to some she 'd fetch 'em home something real pritty, and so did. An' then they come home t' other way, round the Horn, an' she done so well, an' was such a sight o' company, the other child'n was jealous, an' she promised she 'd go a v'y'ge long o' each on 'em. She was as sprightly a person as ever I see; an' could speak well o' what she 'd seen."

"Did she die to sea?" asked Peggy, with interest.

"No, she died to home between v'y'ges, or she 'd gone to sea again. I was to her funeral. She liked her son George's ship the best; 't was the one she was going on to Callao. They said the men aboard all called her 'gran'ma'am,' an' she kep' 'em mended up, an' would go below and tend to 'em if they was sick. She might 'a' been alive an' enjoyin' of herself a good many years but for the kick of a cow; 't was a new cow out of a drove, a dreadful unruly beast."

Mrs. Dow stopped for breath, and reached down for a new supply of beans; her empty apron was gray with soft chaff. Betsey Lane, still pondering on the Centennial, began to sing another verse of her hymn, and again the old women joined her. At this moment some strangers came driving round into the yard from the front of the house. The turf was soft, and our friends did not hear the horses' steps. Their voices cracked and quavered; it was a funny little concert, and a lady in an open carriage just below listened with sympathy and amusement.

II

"Betsey! Betsey! Miss Lane!" a voice called eagerly at the foot of the stairs that led up from the shed. "Betsey! There 's a lady here wants to see you right away."

Betsey was dazed with excitement, like a country child who knows the rare pleasure of being called out of school. "Lor', I ain't fit to go down, be I?" she faltered, looking anxiously at her friends; but Peggy was gazing even nearer to the zenith than usual, in her excited effort to see down into the yard, and Mrs. Dow only nodded somewhat jealously, and said that she guessed 't was nobody would do her any harm. She rose ponderously, while Betsey hesitated, being, as they would have said, all of a twitter. "It is a lady, certain," Mrs. Dow assured her; "'t ain't often there's a lady comes here."

"While there was any of Mis' Gen'ral Thornton's folks left, I wa'n't without visits from the gentry," said Betsey Lane, turning back proudly at the head of the stairs, with a touch of old-world pride and sense of high station. Then she disappeared, and closed the door behind her at the stair-foot with a decision quite unwelcome to the friends above.

"She need n't 'a' been so dreadful 'fraid anybody was goin' to listen. I guess we've got folks to ride an' see us, or had once, if we hain't now," said Miss Peggy Bond, plaintively.

"I expect 't was only the wind shoved it to," said Aunt Lavina. "Betsey is one that gits flustered easier than some. I wish 't was somebody to take her off an' give her a kind of a good time; she's young to settle down 'long of old folks like us. Betsey's got a notion o' rovin' such as ain't my natur', but I should like to see her satisfied. She 'd been a very understandin' person, if she had the advantages that some does."

"'T is so," said Peggy Bond, tilting her chin high. "I suppose you can't hear nothin' they 're saying? I feel my hearin' ain't up to whar it was. I can hear things close to me well as ever; but there, hearin' ain't everything; 't ain't as if we lived where there was more goin' on to hear. Seems to me them folks is stoppin' a good while."

"They surely be," agreed Lavina Dow.

"I expect it's somethin' particular. There ain't none of the Thornton folks left, except one o' the gran'darters, an' I 've often heard Betsey remark that she should never see her more, for she lives to London. Strange how folks feels contented in them strayaway places off to the ends of the airth."

The flies and bees were buzzing against the hot window-panes; the handfuls of beans were clicking into the brown wooden measure. A bird came and perched on the window-sill, and then flitted away toward the blue sky. Below, in the yard, Betsey Lane stood talking with the lady. She had put her blue drilling apron over her head, and her face was shining with delight.

"Lor', dear," she said, for at least the third time, "I remember ye when I first see ye; an awful pritty baby you was, an' they all said you looked just like the old gen'ral. Be you goin' back to foreign parts right away?"

"Yes, I'm going back; you know that all my children are there. I wish I could take you with me for a visit," said the charming young guest. "I'm going to carry over some of the pictures and furniture from the old house; I did n't care half so much for them when I was younger as I do now. Perhaps next summer we shall all come over for a while. I should like to see my girls and boys playing under the pines."

"I wish you re'lly was livin' to the old place," said Betsey Lane. Her imagination was not swift; she needed time to think over all that was being told her, and she could not fancy the two strange houses across the sea. The old Thornton house was to her mind the most delightful and elegant in the world.

"Is there anything I can do for you?" asked Mrs. Strafford kindly,— "anything that I can do for you myself, before I go away? I shall be writing to you, and sending some pictures of the children, and you must let me know how you are getting on."

"Yes, there is one thing, darlin'. If you could stop in the village an' pick me out a pritty, little, small lookin'-glass, that I can keep for me own an' have to remember you by. 'T ain't that I want to set me above the rest o' the folks, but I was always used to havin' my own when I was to your grandma's. There's very nice folks here, some on 'em, and I'm better off than if I was able to keep house; but sence you ask me, that's the only thing I feel cropin' about. What be you goin' right back for? ain't you goin' to see the great fair for Pheladelphy, that everybody talks about?"

"No," said Mrs. Strafford, laughing at this eager and almost convicting question. "No; I'm going back next week. If I were, I believe that I should take you with me. Good-by, dear old Betsey; you make me feel as if I were a little girl again; you look just the same."

For full five minutes the old woman stood out in the sunshine, dazed with delight, and majestic with a sense of her own consequence. She held something tight in her hand, without thinking what it might be; but just as the friendly mistress of the poor-farm came out to hear the news, she tucked the roll of money into the bosom of her brown gingham dress. "'T was my dear Mis' Katy Strafford," she turned to say proudly. "She come way over from London; she 's been sick; they thought the voyage would do her good. She said most the first thing she had on her mind was to come an' find me, and see how I was, an' if I was comfortable; an' now she 's goin' right back. She 's got two splendid houses; an' said how she wished I was there to look after things,—she remembered I was always her gran'ma's right hand. Oh, it does so carry me back, to see her! Seems if all the rest on 'em must be there together to the old house. There, I must go right up an' tell Mis' Dow an' Peggy."

"Dinner 's all ready; I was just goin' to blow the horn for the men-folks," said the keeper's wife. "They 'll be right down. I expect you 've got along smart with them beans,—all three of you together;" but Betsey's mind roved so high and so far at that moment that no achievements of bean-picking could lure it back.

III

The long table in the great kitchen soon gathered its company of waifs and strays,—creatures of improvidence and misfortune, and the irreparable victims of old age. The dinner was satisfactory, and there was not much delay for conversation. Peggy Bond and Mrs. Dow and Betsey Lane always sat together at one end, with an air of putting the rest of the company below the salt. Betsey was still flushed with excitement; in fact, she could not eat as much as usual, and she looked up from time to time expectantly, as if she were likely to be asked to speak of her guest; but everybody was hungry, and even Mrs. Dow broke in upon some attempted confidences by asking inopportunely for a second potato. There were nearly twenty at the table, counting the keeper and his wife and two children, noisy little persons who had come from school with the small flock belonging to the poor widow, who sat just opposite our friends. She finished her dinner before any one else, and pushed her chair back; she always helped with the housework,—a thin, sorry, bad-tempered-looking poor soul, whom grief had sharpened instead of softening. "I expect you feel too fine to set with common folks," she said enviously to Betsey.

"Here I be a-settin'," responded Betsey calmly. "I don' know 's I behave more unbecomin' than usual." Betsey prided herself upon her good and proper manners; but the rest of the company, who would have liked to hear the bit of morning news, were now defrauded of that pleasure. The wrong note had been struck; there was a silence after the clatter of knives and plates, and one by one the cheerful town charges disappeared. The bean-picking had been finished, and there was a call for any of the women who felt like planting corn; so Peggy Bond, who could follow the line of hills pretty fairly, and Betsey herself, who was still equal to anybody at that work, and Mrs. Dow, all went out to the field together. Aunt Lavina labored slowly up the yard, carrying a light splint-bottomed kitchen chair and her knitting-work, and sat near the stone wall on a gentle rise, where she could see the pond and the green country, and exchange a word with her friends as they came and went up and down the rows. Betsey vouchsafed a word now and then about Mrs. Strafford, but you would have thought that she had been suddenly elevated to Mrs. Strafford's own cares and the responsibilities attending them, and had little in common with her old associates. Mrs. Dow and Peggy knew well that these high-feeling times never lasted long, and so they waited with as much patience as they could muster. They were by no means without that true tact which is only another word for unselfish sympathy.

The strip of corn land ran along the side of a great field; at the upper end of it was a field-corner thicket of young maples and walnut saplings, the children of a great nut-tree that marked the boundary. Once, when Betsey Lane found herself alone near this shelter at the end of her row, the other planters having lagged behind beyond the rising ground, she looked stealthily about, and then put her hand inside her gown, and for the first time took out the money that Mrs. Strafford had given her. She turned it over and over with an astonished look: there were new bank-bills for a hundred dollars. Betsey gave a funny little shrug of her shoulders, came out of the bushes, and took a step or two on the narrow edge of turf, as if she were going to dance; then she hastily tucked away her treasure, and stepped discreetly down into the soft harrowed and hoed land, and began to drop corn again, five kernels to a hill. She had seen the top of Peggy Bond's head over the knoll, and now Peggy herself came entirely into view, gazing upward to the skies, and stumbling more or less, but counting the corn by touch and twisting her head about anxiously to gain advantage over her uncertain vision. Betsey made a friendly, inarticulate little sound as they passed; she was thinking that somebody said once that Peggy's eyesight might be remedied if she could go to Boston to the hospital; but that was so remote and impossible an undertaking that no one had ever taken the first step. Betsey Lane's brown old face suddenly worked with excitement, but in a moment more she regained her usual firm expression, and spoke carelessly to Peggy as she turned and came alongside.

The high spring wind of the morning had quite fallen; it was a lovely May afternoon. The woods about the field to the northward were full of birds, and the young leaves scarcely hid the solemn shapes of a company of crows that patiently attended the corn-planting. Two of the men had finished their hoeing, and were busy with the construction of a scarecrow; they knelt in the furrows, chuckling, and looking over some forlorn, discarded garments. It was a time-honored custom to make the scarecrow resemble one of the poor-house family; and this year they intended to have Mrs. Lavina Dow protect the field in effigy; last year it was the counterfeit of Betsey Lane who stood on guard, with an easily recognized quilted hood and the remains of a valued shawl that one of the calves had found airing on a fence and chewed to pieces. Behind the men was the foundation for this rustic attempt at statuary,—an upright stake and bar in the form of a cross. This stood on the highest part of the field; and as the men knelt near it, and the quaint figures of the corn-planters went and came, the scene gave a curious suggestion of foreign life. It was not like New England; the presence of the rude cross appealed strangely to the imagination.

IV

Life flowed so smoothly, for the most part, at the Byfleet Poor-farm, that nobody knew what to make, later in the summer, of a strange disappearance. All the elder in-mates were familiar with illness and death, and the poor pomp of a town-pauper's funeral. The comings and goings and the various misfortunes of those who composed this strange family, related only through its disasters, hardly served for the excitement and talk of a single day. Now that the June days were at their longest, the old people were sure to wake earlier than ever; but one morning, to the astonishment of every one, Betsey Lane's bed was empty; the sheets and blankets, which were her own, and guarded with jealous care, were carefully folded and placed on a chair not too near the window, and Betsey had flown. Nobody had heard her go down the creaking stairs. The kitchen door was unlocked, and the old watch-dog lay on the step outside in the early sunshine, wagging his tail and looking wise, as if he were left on guard and meant to keep the fugitive's secret.

"Never knowed her to do nothin' afore 'thout talking it over a fortnight, and paradin' off when we could all see her," ventured a spiteful voice. "Guess we can wait till night to hear 'bout it."

Mrs. Dow looked sorrowful and shook her head. "Betsey had an aunt on her mother's side that went and drownded of herself; she was a pritty-appearing woman as ever you see."

"Perhaps she 's gone to spend the day with Decker's folks," suggested Peggy Bond. "She always takes an extra early start; she was speakin' lately o' going up their way;" but Mrs. Dow shook her head with a most melancholy look. "I 'm impressed that something 's befell her," she insisted. "I heard her a-groanin' in her sleep. I was wakeful the forepart o' the night,—'t is very unusual with me, too."

"'T wa'n't like Betsey not to leave us any word," said the other old friend, with more resentment than melancholy. They sat together almost in silence that morning in the shed chamber. Mrs. Dow was sorting and cutting rags, and Peggy braided them into long ropes, to be made into mats at a later date. If they had only known where Betsey Lane had gone, they might have talked about it until dinner-time at noon; but failing this new subject, they could take no interest in any of their old ones. Out in the field the corn was well up, and the men were hoeing. It was a hot morning in the shed chamber, and the woolen rags were dusty and hot to handle.

V

Byfleet people knew each other well, and when this mysteriously absent person did not return to the town-farm at the end of a week, public interest became much excited; and presently it was ascertained that Betsey Lane was neither making a visit to her friends the Deckers on Birch Hill, nor to any nearer acquaintances; in fact, she had disappeared altogether from her wonted haunts. Nobody remembered to have seen her pass, hers had been such an early flitting; and when somebody thought of her having gone away by train, he was laughed at for forgetting that the earliest morning train from South Byfleet, the nearest station, did not start until long after eight o'clock; and if Betsey had designed to be one of the passengers, she would have started along the road at seven, and been seen and known of all women. There was not a kitchen in that part of Byfleet that did not have windows toward the road. Conversation rarely left the level of the neighborhood gossip: to see Betsey Lane, in her best clothes, at that hour in the morning, would have been the signal of much exercise of imagination; but as day after day went by without news, the curiosity of those who knew her best turned slowly into fear, and at last Peggy Bond again gave utterance to the belief that Betsey had either gone out in the early morning and put an end to her life, or that she had gone to the Centennial. Some of the people at table were moved to loud laughter,—it was at supper-time on a Sunday night,—but others listened with great interest.

"She never 'd put on her good clothes to drownd herself," said the widow. "She might have thought 't was good as takin' 'em with her, though. Old folks has wandered off an' got lost in the woods afore now."

Mrs. Dow and Peggy resented this impertinent remark, but deigned to take no notice of the speaker. "She would n't have wore her best clothes to the Centennial, would she?" mildly inquired Peggy, bobbing her head toward the ceiling. "'T would be a shame to spoil your best things in such a place. An' I don't know of her havin' any money; there 's the end o' that."

"You 're bad as old Mis' Bland, that used to live neighbor to our folks," said one of the old men. "She was dreadful precise; an' she so begretched to wear a good alpaca dress that was left to her, that it hung in a press forty year, an' baited the moths at last."

"I often seen Mis' Bland a-goin' in to meetin' when I was a young girl," said Peggy Bond approvingly. "She was a good-appearin' woman, an' she left property."

"Wish she 'd left it to me, then," said the poor soul opposite, glancing at her pathetic row of children: but it was not good manners at the farm to deplore one's situation, and Mrs. Dow and Peggy only frowned. "Where do you suppose Betsey can be?" said Mrs. Dow, for the twentieth time. "She did n't have no money. I know she ain't gone far, if it 's so that she 's yet alive. She 's b'en real pinched all the spring."

"Perhaps that lady that come one day give her some," the keeper's wife suggested mildly.

"Then Betsey would have told me," said Mrs. Dow, with injured dignity.

<h1 style="text-align:center">VI</h1>

On the morning of her disappearance, Betsey rose even before the pewee and the English sparrow, and dressed herself quietly, though with trembling hands, and stole out of the kitchen door like a plunderless thief. The old dog licked her hand and looked at her anxiously; the tortoise-shell cat rubbed against her best gown, and trotted away up the yard, then she turned anxiously and came after the old woman, following faithfully until she had to be driven back. Betsey was used to long country excursions afoot. She dearly loved the early morning; and finding that there was no dew to trouble her, she began to follow pasture paths and short cuts across the fields, surprising here and there a flock of sleepy sheep, or a startled calf that rustled out from the bushes. The birds were pecking their breakfast from bush and turf; and hardly any of the wild inhabitants of that rural world were enough alarmed by her presence to do more than flutter away if they chanced to be in her path. She stepped along, light-footed and eager as a girl, dressed in her neat old straw bonnet and black gown, and carrying a few belongings in her best bundle-handkerchief, one that her only brother had brought home from the East Indies fifty years before. There was an old crow perched as sentinel on a small, dead pine-tree, where he could warn friends who were pulling up the sprouted corn in a field close by; but he only gave a contemptuous caw as the adventurer appeared, and she shook her bundle at him in revenge, and laughed to see him so clumsy as he tried to keep his footing on the twigs.

"Yes, I be," she assured him. "I'm a-goin' to Pheladelphy, to the Centennial, same's other folks. I'd jest as soon tell ye's not, old crow;" and Betsey laughed aloud in pleased content with herself and her daring, as she walked along. She had only two miles to go to the station at South Byfleet, and she felt for the money now and then, and found it safe enough. She took great pride in the success of her escape, and especially in the long concealment of her wealth. Not a night had passed since Mrs. Strafford's visit that she had not slept with the roll of money under her pillow by night, and buttoned safe inside her dress by day. She knew that everybody would offer advice and even commands about the spending or saving of it; and she brooked no interference.

The last mile of the foot-path to South Byfleet was along the railway track; and Betsey began to feel in haste, though it was still nearly two hours to train time. She looked anxiously forward and back along the rails every few minutes, for fear of being run over; and at last she caught sight of an engine that was apparently coming toward her, and took flight into the woods before she could gather courage to follow the path again. The freight train proved to be at a standstill, waiting at a turnout; and some of the men were straying about, eating their early breakfast comfortably in this time of leisure. As the old woman came up to them, she stopped too, for a moment of rest and conversation.

"Where be ye goin'?" she asked pleasantly; and they told her. It was to the town where she had to change cars and take the great through train; a point of geography which she had learned from evening talks between the men at the farm.

"What 'll ye carry me there for?"

"We don't run no passenger cars," said one of the young fellows, laughing. "What makes you in such a hurry?"

"I 'm startin' for Pheladelphy, an' it's a gre't ways to go."

"So 't is; but you 're consid'able early, if you 're makin' for the eight-forty train. See here! you have n't got a needle an' thread 'long of you in that bundle, have you? If you 'll sew me on a couple o' buttons, I 'll give ye a free ride. I 'm in a sight o' distress, an' none o' the fellows is provided with as much as a bent pin."

"You poor boy! I 'll have you seen to, in half a minute. I 'm troubled with a stiff arm, but I 'll do the best I can."

The obliging Betsey seated herself stiffly on the slope of the embankment, and found her thread and needle with utmost haste. Two of the train-men stood by and watched the careful stitches, and even offered her a place as spare brakeman, so that they might keep her near; and Betsey took the offer with considerable seriousness, only thinking it necessary to assure them that she was getting most too old to be out in all weathers. An express went by like an earthquake, and she was presently hoisted on board an empty box-car by two of her new and flattering acquaintances, and found herself before noon at the end of the first stage of her journey, without having spent a cent, and furnished with any amount of thrifty advice. One of the young men, being compassionate of her unprotected state as a traveler, advised her to find out the widow of an uncle of his in Philadelphia, saying despairingly that he could n't tell her just how to find the house; but Miss Betsey Lane said that she had an English tongue in her head, and should be sure to find whatever she was looking for. This unexpected incident of the freight train was the reason why everybody about the South Byfleet station insisted that no such person had taken passage by the regular train that same morning, and why there were those who persuaded themselves that Miss Betsey Lane was probably lying at the bottom of the poor-farm pond.

VII

"Land sakes!" said Miss Betsey Lane, as she watched a Turkish person parading by in his red fez, "I call the Centennial somethin' like the day o' judgment! I wish I was goin' to stop a month, but I dare say 't would be the death o' my poor old bones."

She was leaning against the barrier of a patent pop-corn establishment, which had given her a sudden reminder of home, and of the winter nights when the sharp-kerneled little red and yellow ears were brought out, and Old Uncle Eph Flanders sat by the kitchen stove, and solemnly filled a great wooden chopping-tray for the refreshment of the company. She had wandered and loitered and looked until her eyes and head had grown numb and unreceptive; but it is only unimaginative persons who can be really astonished. The imagination can always outrun the possible and actual sights and sounds of the world; and this plain old body from Byfleet rarely found anything rich and splendid enough to surprise her. She saw the wonders of the West and the splendors of the East with equal calmness and satisfaction; she had always known that there was an amazing world outside the boundaries of Byfleet. There was a piece of paper in her pocket on which was marked, in her clumsy handwriting, "If Betsey Lane should meet with accident, notify the selectmen of Byfleet;" but having made this slight provision for the future, she had thrown herself boldly into the sea of strangers, and then had made the joyful discovery that friends were to be found at every turn.

There was something delightfully companionable about Betsey; she had a way of suddenly looking up over her big spectacles with a reassuring and expectant smile, as if you were going to speak to her, and you generally did. She must have found out where hundreds of people came from, and whom they had left at home, and what they thought of the great show, as she sat on a bench to rest, or leaned over the railings where free luncheons were afforded by the makers of hot waffles and molasses candy and fried potatoes; and there was not a night when she did not return to her lodgings with a pocket crammed with samples of spool cotton and nobody knows what. She had already collected small presents for almost everybody she knew at home, and she was such a pleasant, beaming old country body, so unmistakably appreciative and interested, that nobody ever thought of wishing that she would move on. Nearly all the busy people of the Exhibition called her either Aunty or Grandma at once, and made little pleasures for her as best they could. She was a delightful contrast to the indifferent, stupid crowd that drifted along, with eyes fixed at the same level, and seeing, even on that level, nothing for fifty feet at a time. "What be you making here, dear?" Betsey Lane would ask joyfully, and the most perfunctory guardian hastened to explain. She squandered money as she had never had the pleasure of doing before, and this hastened the day when she must return to Byfleet. She was always inquiring if there were any spectacle-sellers at hand, and received occasional directions; but it was a difficult place for her to find her way about in, and the very last day of her stay arrived before she found an exhibitor of the desired sort, and oculist and instrument-maker.

"I called to get some specs for a friend that's upsighted," she gravely informed the salesman, to his extreme amusement. "She's dreadful troubled, and jerks her head up like a hen a-drinkin'. She's got a blur a-growin' an' spreadin', an' sometimes she can see out to one side on 't, and more times she can't."

"Cataracts," said a middle-aged gentleman at her side; and Betsey Lane turned to regard him with approval and curiosity.

"'T is Miss Peggy Bond I was mentioning, of Byfleet Poor-farm," she explained. "I count on gettin' some glasses to relieve her trouble, if there's any to be found."

"Glasses won't do her any good," said the stranger. "Suppose you come and sit down on this bench, and tell me all about it. First, where is Byfleet?" and Betsey gave the directions at length.

"I thought so," said the surgeon. "How old is this friend of yours?"

Betsey cleared her throat decisively, and smoothed her gown over her knees as if it were an apron; then she turned to take a good look at her new acquaintance as they sat on the rustic bench together. "Who be you, sir, I should like to know?" she asked, in a friendly tone.

"My name 's Dunster."

"I take it you 're a doctor," continued Betsey, as if they had overtaken each other walking from Byfleet to South Byfleet on a summer morning.

"I 'm a doctor; part of one at least," said he. "I know more or less about eyes; and I spend my summers down on the shore at the mouth of your river; some day I 'll come up and look at this person. How old is she?"

"Peggy Bond is one that never tells her age; 't ain't come quite up to where she 'll begin to brag of it, you see," explained Betsey reluctantly; "but I know her to be nigh to seventy-six, one way or t' other. Her an' Mrs. Mary Ann Chick was same year's child'n, and Peggy knows I know it, an' two or three times when we 've be'n in the buryin'-ground where Mary Ann lays an' had her dates right on her headstone, I could n't bring Peggy to take no sort o' notice. I will say she makes, at times, a convenience of being upsighted. But there, I feel for her,—everybody does; it keeps her stubbin' an' trippin' against everything, beakin' and gazin' up the way she has to."

"Yes, yes," said the doctor, whose eyes were twinkling. "I 'll come and look after her, with your town doctor, this summer,—some time in the last of July or first of August."

"You 'll find occupation," said Betsey, not without an air of patronage. "Most of us to the Byfleet Farm has got our ails, now I tell ye. You ain't got no bitters that 'll take a dozen years right off an ol' lady's shoulders?"

The busy man smiled pleasantly, and shook his head as he went away. "Dunster," said Betsey to herself, soberly committing the new name to her sound memory. "Yes, I must n't forget to speak of him to the doctor, as he directed. I do' know now as Peggy would vally herself quite so much accordin' to, if she had her eyes fixed same as other folks. I expect there would n't been a smarter woman in town, though, if she 'd had a proper chance. Now I 've done what I set to do for her, I do believe, an' 't wa'n't glasses, neither. I 'll git her a pritty little shawl with that money I laid aside. Peggy Bond ain't got a pritty shawl. I always wanted to have a real good time, an' now I 'm havin' it."

VIII

Two or three days later, two pathetic figures might have been seen crossing the slopes of the poor-farm field, toward the low shores of Byfield pond. It was early in the morning, and the stubble of the lately mown grass was wet with rain and hindering to old feet. Peggy Bond was more blundering and liable to stray in the wrong direction than usual; it was one of the days when she could hardly see at all. Aunt Lavina Dow was unusually clumsy of movement, and stiff in the joints; she had not been so far from the house for three years. The morning breeze filled the gathers of her wide gingham skirt, and aggravated the size of her unwieldy figure. She supported herself with a stick, and trusted beside to the fragile support of Peggy's arm. They were talking together in whispers.

"Oh, my sakes!" exclaimed Peggy, moving her small head from side to side. "Hear you wheeze, Mis' Dow! This may be the death o' you; there, do go slow! You set here on the side-hill, an' le' me go try if I can see."

"It needs more eyesight than you 've got," said Mrs. Dow, panting between the words. "Oh! to think how spry I was in my young days, an' here I be now, the full of a door, an' all my complaints so aggravated by my size. 'T is hard! 't is hard! but I 'm a-doin' of all this for pore Betsey's sake. I know they 've all laughed, but I look to see her ris' to the top o' the pond this day,—'t is just nine days since she departed; an' say what they may, I know she hove herself in. It run in her family; Betsey had an aunt that done just so, an' she ain't be'n like herself, a-broodin' an' hivin' away alone, an' nothin' to say to you an' me that was always sich good company all together. Somethin' sprung her mind, now I tell ye, Mis' Bond."

"I feel to hope we sha'n't find her, I must say," faltered Peggy. It was plain that Mrs. Dow was the captain of this doleful expedition. "I guess she ain't never thought o' drowndin' of herself, Mis' Dow; she 's gone off a-vistin' way over to the other side of South Byfleet; some thinks she 's gone to the Centennial even now!''

"She had n't no proper means, I tell ye," wheezed Mrs. Dow indignantly; ''an' if you prefer that others should find her floatin' to the top this day, instid of us that 's her best friends, you can step back to the house.''

They walked on in aggrieved silence. Peggy Bond trembled with excitement, but her companion's firm grasp never wavered, and so they came to the narrow, gravelly margin and stood still. Peggy tried in vain to see the glittering water and the pond-lilies that starred it; she knew that they must be there; once, years ago, she had caught fleeting glimpses of them, and she never forgot what she had once seen. The clear blue sky overhead, the dark pine-woods beyond the pond, were all clearly pictured in her mind. "Can't you see nothin'?" she faltered; "I believe I 'm wuss 'n upsighted this day. I 'm going to be blind.''

"No," said Lavina Dow solemnly; "no, there ain't nothin' whatever, Peggy. I hope to mercy she ain't"—

"Why, whoever 'd expected to find you 'way out here!" exclaimed a brisk and cheerful voice. There stood Betsey Lane herself, close behind them, having just emerged from a thicket of alders that grew close by. She was following the short way homeward from the railroad.

"Why, what 's the matter, Mis' Dow? You ain't overdoin', be ye? an' Peggy 's all of a flutter. What in the name of natur' ails ye?''

"There ain't nothin' the matter, as I knows on," responded the leader of this fruitless expedition. "We only thought we 'd take a stroll this pleasant mornin'," she added, with sublime self-possession. "Where 've you be'n, Betsey Lane?''

"To Pheladelphy, ma'am," said Betsey, looking quite young and gay, and wearing a townish and unfamiliar air that upheld her words. "All ought to go that can; why, you feel 's if you 'd be'n all round the world. I guess I 've got enough to think of and tell ye for the rest o' my days. I 've always wanted to go somewheres. I wish you 'd be'n there, I do so. I 've talked with folks from Chiny an' the back o' Pennsyl-vany: and I see folks way from Australy that 'peared as well as anybody; an' I see how they made spool cotton, an' sights o' other things; an' I spoke with a doctor that lives down to the beach in the summer, an' he offered to come up 'long in the first of August, an' see what he can do for Peggy's eyesight. There was di'monds there as big as pigeon's eggs; an' I met with Mis' Abby

Fletcher from South Byfleet depot; an' there was hogs there that weighed risin' thirteen hundred"—

"I want to know," said Mrs. Lavina Dow and Peggy Bond, together.

"Well, 't was a great exper'ence for a person," added Lavina, turning ponderously, in spite of herself, to give a last wistful look at the smiling waters of the pond.

"I don't know how soon I be goin' to settle down," proclaimed the rustic sister of Sindbad. "What 's for the good o' one 's for the good of all. You just wait till we're setting together up in the old shed chamber! You know, my dear Mis' Katy Strafford give me a han'some present o' money that day she come to see me; and I 'd be'n a-dreamin' by night an' day o' seein' that Centennial; and when I come to think on 't I felt sure somebody ought to go from this neighborhood, if 't was only for the good o' the rest; and I thought I 'd better be the one. I wa'n't goin' to ask the selec'men neither. I 've come back with one-thirty-five in money, and I see everything there, an' I fetched ye all a little somethin'; but I 'm full o' dust now, an' pretty nigh beat out. I never see a place more friendly than Pheladelphy; but 't ain't natural to a Byfleet person to be always walkin' on a level. There, now, Peggy, you take my bundle-handkerchief and the basket, and let Mis' Dow sag on to me. I 'll git her along twice as easy."

With this the small elderly company set forth triumphant toward the poor-house, across the wide green field.

THE ONLY ROSE

ust where the village abruptly ended, and the green mowing fields began, stood Mrs. Bickford's house, looking down the road with all its windows, and topped by two prim chimneys that stood up like ears. It was placed with an end to the road, and fronted southward; you could follow a straight path from the gate past the front door and find Mrs. Bickford sitting by the last window of all in the kitchen, unless she were solemnly stepping about, prolonging the stern duties of her solitary housekeeping.

One day in early summer, when almost every one else in Fairfield had put her house plants out of doors, there were still three flower pots on a kitchen window-sill. Mrs. Bickford spent but little time over her rose and geranium and Jerusalem cherry-tree, although they had gained a kind of personality born of long association. They rarely undertook to bloom, but had most courageously maintained life in spite of their owner's unsympathetic but conscientious care. Later in the season she would carry them out of doors, and leave them, until the time of frosts, under the shade of a great apple-tree, where they might make the best of what the summer had to give.

The afternoon sun was pouring in, the Jerusalem cherry-tree drooped its leaves in the heat and looked pale, when a neighbor, Miss Pendexter, came in from the next house but one to make a friendly call. As she passed the parlor with its shut blinds, and the sitting-room, also shaded carefully from the light, she wished, as she had done many times before, that somebody beside the owner might have the pleasure of living in and using so good and pleasant a house. Mrs. Bickford always complained of having so much care, even while she valued herself intelligently upon having the right to do as she pleased with one of the best houses in Fairfield. Miss Pendexter was a cheerful, even gay little person, who always brought a pleasant flurry of excitement, and usually had a genuine though small piece of news to tell, or some new aspect of already received information.

Mrs. Bickford smiled as she looked up to see this sprightly neighbor coming. She had no gift at entertaining herself, and was always glad, as one might say, to be taken off her own hands.

Miss Pendexter smiled back, as if she felt herself to be equal to the occasion.

"How be you to-day?" the guest asked kindly, as she entered the kitchen. "Why, what a sight o' flowers, Mis' Bickford! What be you goin' to do with 'em all?"

Mrs. Bickford wore a grave expression as she glanced over her spectacles. "My sister's boy fetched 'em over," she answered. "You know my sister Parson's a great hand to raise flowers, an' this boy takes after her. He said his mother thought the gardin never looked handsomer, and she picked me these to send over. They was sendin' a team to Westbury for some fertilizer to put on the land, an' he come with the men, an' stopped to eat his dinner 'long o' me. He's been growin' fast, and looks peaked. I expect sister 'Liza thought the ride, this pleasant day, would do him good. 'Liza sent word for me to come over and pass some days next week, but it ain't so that I can."

"Why, it's a pretty time of year to go off and make a little visit," suggested the neighbor encouragingly.

"I ain't got my sitting-room chamber carpet taken up yet," sighed Mrs. Bickford. "I do feel condemned. I might have done it to-day, but 't was all at end when I saw Tommy coming. There, he's a likely boy, an' so relished his dinner; I happened to be well prepared. I don't know but he's my favorite o' that family. Only I've been sittin' here thinkin', since he went, an' I can't remember that I ever was so belated with my spring cleaning."

"'T was owin' to the weather," explained Miss Pendexter. "None of us could be so smart as common this year, not even the lazy ones that always get one room done the first o' March, and brag of it to others' shame, and then never let on when they do the rest."

The two women laughed together cheerfully. Mrs. Bickford had put up the wide leaf of her large table between the windows and spread out the flowers. She was sorting them slowly into three heaps.

"Why, I do declare if you have n't got a rose in bloom yourself!" exclaimed Miss Pendexter abruptly, as if the bud had not been announced weeks before, and its progress regularly commented upon. "Ain't it a lovely rose? Why, Mis' Bickford!"

"Yes'm, it 's out to-day," said Mrs. Bickford, with a somewhat plaintive air. "I 'm glad you come in so as to see it."

The bright flower was like a face. Somehow, the beauty and life of it were surprising in the plain room, like a gay little child who might suddenly appear in a doorway. Miss Pendexter forgot herself and her hostess and the tangled mass of garden flowers in looking at the red rose. She even forgot that it was incumbent upon her to carry forward the conversation. Mrs. Bickford was subject to fits of untimely silence which made her friends anxiously sweep the corners of their minds in search of something to say, but any one who looked at her now could easily see that it was not poverty of thought that made her speechless, but an overburdening sense of the inexpressible.

"Goin' to make up all your flowers into bo'quets? I think the short-stemmed kinds is often pretty in a dish," suggested Miss Pendexter compassionately.

"I thought I should make them into three bo'quets. I wish there wa'n't quite so many. Sister Eliza 's very lavish with her flowers; she 's always been a kind sister, too," said Mrs. Bickford vaguely. She was not apt to speak with so much sentiment, and as her neighbor looked at her narrowly she detected unusual signs of emotion. It suddenly became evident that the three nosegays were connected in her mind with her bereavement of three husbands, and Miss Pendexter's easily roused curiosity was quieted by the discovery that her friend was bent upon a visit to the burying-ground. It was the time of year when she was pretty sure to spend an afternoon there, and sometimes they had taken the walk in company. Miss Pendexter expected to receive the usual invitation, but there was nothing further said at the moment, and she looked again at the pretty rose.

Mrs. Bickford aimlessly handled the syringas and flowering almond sprays, choosing them out of the fragrant heap only to lay them down again. She glanced out of the window; then gave Miss Pendexter a long expressive look.

"I expect you 're going to carry 'em over to the burying-ground?" inquired the guest, in a sympathetic tone.

"Yes 'm," said the hostess, now well started in conversation and in quite her every-day manner. "You see I was goin' over to my brother's folks to-morrow in South Fairfield, to pass the day; they said they were goin' to send over to-morrow to leave a wagon at the blacksmith's, and they 'd hitch that to their best chaise, so I could ride back very comfortable. You know I have to avoid bein' out in the mornin' sun?"

Miss Pendexter smiled to herself at this moment; she was obliged to move from her chair at the window, the May sun was so hot on her back, for Mrs. Bickford always kept the curtains rolled high up, out of the way, for fear of fading and dust. The kitchen was a blaze of light. As for the Sunday chaise being sent, it was well known that Mrs. Bickford's married brothers and sisters comprehended the truth that she was a woman of property, and had neither chick nor child.

"So I thought 't was a good opportunity to just stop an' see if the lot was in good order,—last spring Mr. Wallis's stone hove with the frost; an' so I could take these flowers." She gave a sigh. "I ain't one that can bear flowers in a close room,—they bring on a headache; but I enjoy 'em as much as anybody to look at, only you never know what to put 'em in. If I could be out in the mornin' sun, as some do, and keep flowers in the house, I should have me a gardin, certain," and she sighed again.

"A gardin 's a sight o' care, but I don't begrudge none o' the care I give to mine. I have to scant on flowers so 's to make room for pole beans," said Miss Pendexter gayly. She had only a tiny strip of land behind her house, but she always had something to give away, and made riches out of her narrow poverty. "A few flowers gives me just as much pleasure as more would," she added. "You get acquainted with things when you 've only got one or two roots. My sweet-williams is just like folks."

"Mr. Bickford was partial to sweet-williams," said Mrs. Bickford. "I never knew him to take notice of no other sort of flowers. When we 'd be over to Eliza's, he 'd walk down her gardin, an' he 'd never make no comments until he come to them, and then he 'd say, 'Those is sweet-williams.' How many times I 've heard him!"

"You ought to have a sprig of 'em for his bo'quet," suggested Miss Pendexter.

"Yes, I 've put a sprig in," said her companion.

At this moment Miss Pendexter took a good look at the bouquets, and found that they were as nearly alike as careful hands could make them. Mrs. Bickford was evidently trying to reach absolute impartiality.

"I don't know but you think it 's foolish to tie 'em up this afternoon," she said presently, as she wound the first with a stout string. "I thought I could put 'em in a bucket o' water out in the shed, where there 's a draught o' air, and then I should have all my time in the morning. I shall have a good deal to do before I go. I always sweep the setting-room and front entry Wednesdays. I want to leave everything nice, goin' away for all day so. So I meant to get the flowers out o' the way this afternoon. Why, it 's most half past four, ain't it? But I sha'n't pick the rose till mornin'; 't will be blowed out better then."

"The rose?" questioned Miss Pendexter. "Why, are you goin' to pick that, too?"

"Yes, I be. I never like to let 'em fade on the bush. There, that 's just what 's a-troublin' me," and she turned to give a long, imploring look at the friend who sat beside her. Miss Pendexter had moved her chair before the table in order to be out of the way of the sun. "I don't seem to know which of 'em ought to have it," said Mrs. Bickford despondently. "I do so hate to make a choice between 'em; they all had their good points, especially Mr. Bickford, and I respected 'em all. I don't know but what I think of one on 'em 'most as much as I do of the other."

"Why, 't is difficult for you, ain't it?" responded Miss Pendexter. "I don't know 's I can offer advice."

"No, I s'pose not," answered her friend slowly, with a shadow of disappointment coming over her calm face. "I feel sure you would if you could, Abby."

Both of the women felt as if they were powerless before a great emergency.

"There 's one thing,—they 're all in a better world now," said Miss Pendexter, in a self-conscious and constrained voice; "they can't feel such little things or take note o' slights same 's we can."

"No; I suppose 't is myself that wants to be just," answered Mrs. Bickford. "I feel under obligations to my last husband when I look about and see how comfortable he left me. Poor Mr. Wallis had his great projects, an' perhaps if he 'd lived longer he 'd have made a record; but when he died he 'd failed all up, owing to that patent corn-sheller he 'd put everything into, and, as you know, I had to get along 'most any way I could for the next few years. Life was very disappointing with Mr. Wallis, but he meant well, an' used to be an amiable person to dwell with, until his temper got spoilt makin' so many hopes an' havin' 'em turn out failures. He had consider'ble of an air, an' dressed very handsome when I was first acquainted with him, Mr. Wallis did. I don't know 's you ever knew Mr. Wallis in his prime?"

"He died the year I moved over here from North Denfield," said Miss Pendexter, in a tone of sympathy. "I just knew him by sight. I was to his funeral. You know you lived in what we call the Wells house then, and I felt it would n't be an intrusion, we was such near neighbors. The first time I ever was in your house was just before that, when he was sick, an' Mary 'Becca Wade an' I called to see if there was anything we could do."

"They used to say about town that Mr. Wallis went to an' fro like a mail-coach an' brought nothin' to pass," announced Mrs. Bickford without bitterness. "He ought to have had a better chance then he did in this little neighborhood. You see, he had excellent ideas, but he never 'd learned the machinist's trade, and there was somethin' the matter with every model he contrived. I used to be real narrow-minded when he talked about moving 'way up to Lowell, or some o' them places; I hated to think of leaving my folks; and now I see that I never done right by him. His ideas was good. I know once he was on a jury, and there was a man stopping to the tavern where he was, near the court house, a man that traveled for a firm to Lowell; and they engaged in talk, an' Mr. Wallis let out some o' his notions an' contrivances, an' he said that man would n't hardly stop to eat, he was so interested, an' said he 'd look for a chance for him up to Lowell. It all sounded so well that I kind of begun to think about goin' myself. Mr. Wallis said we 'd close the house here, and go an' board through the winter. But he never heard a word from him, and the disappointment was one he never got over. I think of it now different from what I did then. I often used to be kind of disapproving to Mr. Wallis; but there, he used to be always tellin' over his great projects. Somebody told me once that a man by the same name of the one he met while he was to court had got some patents for the very things Mr. Wallis used to be workin' over; but 't was after he died, and I don't know 's 't was in him to ever really set things up so other folks could ha' seen their value. His machines always used to work kind of rickety, but folks used to come from all round to see 'em; they was curiosities if they wa'n't nothin' else, an' gave him a name."

Mrs. Bickford paused a moment, with some geranium leaves in her hand, and seemed to suppress with difficulty a desire to speak even more freely.

"He was a dreadful notional man," she said at last, regretfully, and as if this fact were a poor substitute for what had just been in her mind. "I recollect one time he worked all through the early winter over my churn, an' got it so it would go three quarters of an hour all of itself if you wound it up; an' if you 'll believe it, he went an' spent all that time for nothin' when the cow was dry, an' we was with difficulty borrowin' a pint o' milk a day somewheres in the neighborhood just to get along with." Mrs. Bickford flushed with displeasure, and turned to look at her visitor. "Now what do you think of such a man as that, Miss Pendexter?" she asked.

"Why, I don't know but 't was just as good for an invention," answered Miss Pendexter timidly; but her friend looked doubtful, and did not appear to understand.

"Then I asked him where it was, one day that spring when I 'd got tired to death churnin', an' the butter would n't come in a churn I 'd had to borrow, and he 'd gone an' took ours all to pieces to get the works to make some other useless contrivance with. He had no sort of a business turn, but he was well meanin', Mr. Wallis was, an' full o' divertin' talk; they used to call him very good company. I see now that he never had no proper chance. I 've always regretted Mr. Wallis," said she who was now the widow Bickford.

"I 'm sure you always speak well of him," said Miss Pendexter. "'T was a pity he had n't got among good business men, who could push his inventions an' do all the business part."

"I was left very poor an' needy for them next few years," said Mrs. Bickford mournfully; "but he never 'd give up but what he should die worth his fifty thousand dollars. I don't see now how I ever did get along them next few years without him; but there, I always managed to keep a pig, an' sister Eliza gave me my potatoes, and I made out somehow. I could dig me a few greens, you know, in spring, and then 't would come strawberry-time, and other berries a-followin' on. I was always decent to go to meetin' till within the last six months, an' then I went in bad weather, when folks would n't notice; but 't was a rainy summer, an' I managed to get considerable preachin' after all. My clothes looked proper enough when 't was a wet Sabbath. I often think o' them pinched days now, when I 'm left so comfortable by Mr. Bickford.''

"Yes 'm, you 've everything to be thankful for," said Miss Pendexter, who was as poor herself at that moment as her friend had ever been, and who could never dream of venturing upon the support and companionship of a pig. "Mr. Bickford was a very personable man," she hastened to say, the confidences were so intimate and interesting.

"Oh, very," replied Mrs. Bickford; "there was something about him that was very marked. Strangers would always ask who he was as he come into meetin'. His words counted; he never spoke except he had to. 'T was a relief at first after Mr. Wallis's being so fluent; but Mr. Wallis was splendid company for winter evenings,—'t would be eight' o'clock before you knew it. I did n't use to listen to it all, but he had a great deal of information. Mr. Bickford was dreadful dignified; I used to be sort of meechin' with him along at the first, for fear he 'd disapprove of me; but I found out 't wa'n't no need; he was always just that way, an' done everything by rule an' measure. He had n't the mind of my other husbands, but he was a very dignified appearing man; he used 'most always to sleep in the evenin's, Mr. Bickford did.''

"Them is lovely bo'quets, certain!" exclaimed Miss Pendexter. "Why, I could n't tell 'em apart; the flowers are comin' out just right, are n't they?"

Mrs. Bickford nodded assent, and then, startled by sudden recollection, she cast a quick glance at the rose in the window.

"I always seem to forget about your first husband, Mr. Fraley," Miss Pendexter suggested bravely. "I 've often heard you speak of him, too, but he 'd passed away long before I ever knew you."

"He was but a boy," said Mrs. Bickford. "I thought the world was done for me when he died, but I 've often thought since 't was a mercy for him. He come of a very melancholy family, and all his brothers an' sisters enjoyed poor health; it might have been his lot. Folks said we was as pretty a couple as ever come into church; we was both dark, with black eyes an' a good deal o' color,—you would n't expect it to see me now. Albert was one that held up his head, and looked as if he meant to own the town, an' he had a good word for everybody. I don't know what the years might have brought."

There was a long pause. Mrs. Bickford leaned over to pick up a heavy-headed Guelder-rose that had dropped on the floor.

"I expect 't was what they call fallin' in love," she added, in a different tone; "he wa'n't nothin' but a boy, an' I wa'n't nothin' but a girl, but we was dreadful happy. He did n't favor his folks,—they all had hay-colored hair and was faded-looking, except his mother; they was alike, and looked alike, an' set everything by each other. He was just the kind of strong, hearty young man that goes right off if they get a fever. We was just settled on a little farm, an' he 'd have done well if he 'd had time; as it was, he left debts. He had a hasty temper, that was his great fault, but Albert had a lovely voice to sing; they said there wa'n't no such tenor voice in this part o' the State. I could hear him singin' to himself right out in the field a-ploughin' or hoein', an' he did n't know it half o' the time, no more 'n a common bird would. I don't know 's I valued his gift as I ought to, but there was nothin' ever sounded so sweet to me. I ain't one that ever had much fancy, but I knowed Albert had a pretty voice."

Mrs. Bickford's own voice trembled a little, but she held up the last bouquet and examined it critically. "I must hurry now an' put these in water," she said, in a matter of fact tone. Little Miss Pendexter was so quiet and sympathetic that her hostess felt no more embarrassed than if she had been talking only to herself.

"Yes, they do seem to droop some; 't is a little warm for them here in the sun," said Miss Pendexter; "but you 'll find they 'll all come up if you give them their fill o' water. They 'll look very handsome to-morrow; folks 'll notice them from the road. You 've arranged them very tasty, Mis' Bickford."

"They do look pretty, don't they?" Mrs. Bickford regarded the three in turn. "I want to have them all pretty. You may deem it strange, Abby."

"Why, no, Mis' Bickford," said the guest sincerely, although a little perplexed by the solemnity of the occasion. "I know how 't is with friends,—that having one don't keep you from wantin' another; 't is just like havin' somethin' to eat, and then wantin' somethin' to drink just the same. I expect all friends find their places."

But Mrs. Bickford was not interested in this figure, and still looked vague and anxious as she began to brush the broken stems and wilted leaves into her wide calico apron. "I done the best I could while they was alive," she said, "and mourned 'em when I lost 'em, an' I feel grateful to be left so comfortable now when all is over. It seems foolish, but I'm still at a loss about that rose."

"Perhaps you'll feel sure when you first wake up in the morning," answered Miss Pendexter solicitously. "It's a case where I don't deem myself qualified to offer you any advice. But I'll say one thing, seeing's you've been so friendly spoken and confiding with me. I never was married myself, Mis' Bickford, because it wa'n't so that I could have the one I liked."

"I suppose he ain't livin', then? Why, I wa'n't never aware you had met with a disappointment, Abby," said Mrs. Bickford instantly. None of her neighbors had ever suspected little Miss Pendexter of a romance.

"Yes 'm, he's livin'," replied Miss Pendexter humbly. "No 'm, I never have heard that he died."

"I want to know!" exclaimed the woman of experience.

"Well, I'll tell you this, Abby: you may have regretted your lot, and felt lonesome and hardshipped, but they all have their faults, and a single woman's got her liberty, if she ain't got other blessin's."

"'T wouldn't have been my choice to live alone," said Abby, meeker than before. "I feel very thankful for my blessin's, all the same. You've always been a kind neighbor, Mis' Bickford."

"Why can't you stop to tea?" asked the elder woman, with unusual cordiality; but Miss Pendexter remembered that her hostess often expressed a dislike for unexpected company, and promptly took her departure after she had risen to go, glancing up at the bright flower as she passed outside the window. It seemed to belong most to Albert, but she had not liked to say so. The sun was low; the green fields stretched away southward into the misty distance.

II

Mrs. Bickford's house appeared to watch her out of sight down the road, the next morning. She had lost all spirit for her holiday. Perhaps it was the unusual excitement of the afternoon's reminiscences, or it might have been simply the bright moonlight night which had kept her broad awake until dawn, thinking of the past, and more and more concerned about the rose. By this time it had ceased to be merely a flower, and had become a definite symbol and assertion of personal choice. She found it very difficult to decide. So much of her present comfort and well-being was due to Mr. Bickford; still, it was Mr. Wallis who had been most unfortunate, and to whom she had done least justice. If she owed recognition to Mr. Bickford, she certainly owed amends to Mr. Wallis. If she gave him the rose, it would be for the sake of affectionate apology. And then there was Albert, to whom she had no thought of being either indebted or forgiving. But she could not escape from the terrible feeling of indecision.

It was a beautiful morning for a drive, but Mrs. Bickford was kept waiting some time for the chaise. Her nephew, who was to be her escort, had found much social advantage at the blacksmith's shop, so that it was after ten when she finally started with the three large flat-backed bouquets, covered with a newspaper to protect them from the sun. The petals of the almond flowers were beginning to scatter, and now and then little streams of water leaked out of the newspaper and trickled down the steep slope of her best dress to the bottom of the chaise. Even yet she had not made up her mind; she had stopped trying to deal with such an evasive thing as decision, and leaned back and rested as best she could.

"What an old fool I be!" she rebuked herself from time to time, in so loud a whisper that her companion ventured a respectful "What, ma'am?" and was astonished that she made no reply. John was a handsome young man, but Mrs. Bickford could never cease thinking of him as a boy. He had always been her favorite among the younger members of the family, and now returned this affectionate feeling, being possessed of an instinctive confidence in the sincerities of his prosaic aunt.

As they drove along, there had seemed at first to be something unsympathetic and garish about the beauty of the summer day. After the shade and shelter of the house, Mrs. Bickford suffered even more from a contracted and assailed feeling out of doors. The very trees by the roadside had a curiously fateful, trying way of standing back to watch her, as she passed in the acute agony of indecision, and she was annoyed and startled by a bird that flew too near the chaise in a moment of surprise. She was conscious of a strange reluctance to the movement of the Sunday chaise, as if she were being conveyed against her will; but the companionship of her nephew John grew every moment to be more and more a reliance. It was very comfortable to sit by his side, even though he had nothing to say; he was manly and cheerful, and she began to feel protected.

"Aunt Bickford," he suddenly announced, "I may 's well out with it! I 've got a piece o' news to tell you, if you won't let on to nobody. I expect you 'll laugh, but you know I 've set everything by Mary Lizzie Gifford ever since I was a boy. Well, sir!"

"Well, sir!" exclaimed aunt Bickford in her turn, quickly roused into most comfortable self-forgetfulness. "I am really pleased. She 'll make you a good, smart wife, John. Ain't all the folks pleased, both sides?"

"Yes, they be," answered John soberly, with a happy, important look that became him well.

"I guess I can make out to do something for you to help along, when the right time comes," said aunt Bickford impulsively, after a moment's reflection. "I 've known what it is to be starting out in life with plenty o' hope. You ain't calculatin' on gettin' married before fall,—or be ye?"

"'Long in the fall," said John regretfully. "I wish t' we could set up for ourselves right away this summer. I ain't got much ahead, but I can work well as anybody, an' now I 'm out o' my time."

"She 's a nice, modest, pretty girl. I thought she like you, John," said the old aunt. "I saw her over to your mother's, last day I was there. Well, I expect you 'll be happy."

"Certain," said John, turning to look at her affectionately, surprised by this outspokenness and lack of embarrassment between them. "Thank you, aunt," he said simply; "you 're a real good friend to me;" and he looked away again hastily, and blushed a fine scarlet over his sun-browned face. "She 's coming over to spend the day with the girls," he added. "Mother thought of it. You don't get over to see us very often."

Mrs. Bickford smiled approvingly. John's mother looked for her good opinion, no doubt, but it was very proper for John to have told his prospects himself, and in such a pretty way. There was no shilly-shallying about the boy.

"My gracious!" said John suddenly. "I 'd like to have drove right by the burying-ground. I forgot we wanted to stop."

Strange as it may appear, Mrs. Bickford herself had not noticed the burying-ground, either, in her excitement and pleasure; now she felt distressed and responsible again, and showed it in her face at once. The young man leaped lightly to the ground, and reached for the flowers.

"Here, you just let me run up with 'em," he said kindly. "'T is hot in the sun to-day, an' you 'll mind it risin' the hill. We 'll stop as I fetch you back to-night, and you can go up comfortable an' walk the yard after sundown when it 's cool, an' stay as long as you 're a mind to. You seem sort of tired, aunt."

"I don't know but what I will let you carry 'em," said Mrs. Bickford slowly.

To leave the matter of the rose in the hands of fate seemed weakness and cowardice, but there was not a moment for consideration. John was a smiling fate, and his proposition was a great relief. She watched him go away with a terrible inward shaking, and sinking of pride. She had held the flowers with so firm a grasp that her hands felt weak and numb, and as she leaned back and shut her eyes she was afraid to open them again at first for fear of knowing the bouquets apart even at that distance, and giving instructions which she might regret. With a sudden impulse she called John once or twice eagerly; but her voice had a thin and piping sound, and the meditative early crickets that chirped in the fresh summer grass probably sounded louder in John's ears. The bright light on the white stones dazzled Mrs. Bickford's eyes; and then all at once she felt light-hearted, and the sky seemed to lift itself higher and wider from the earth, and she gave a sigh of relief as her messenger came back along the path. "I know who I do hope 's got the right one," she said to herself. "There, what a touse I be in! I don't see what I had to go and pick the old rose for, anyway."

"I declare, they did look real handsome, aunt," said John's hearty voice as he approached the chaise. "I set 'em up just as you told me. This one fell out, an' I kept it. I don't know 's you 'll care. I can give it to Lizzie."

He faced her now with a bright, boyish look. There was something gay in his buttonhole,—it was the red rose.

Aunt Bickford blushed like a girl. "Your choice is easy made," she faltered mysteriously, and then burst out laughing, there in front of the burying-ground. "Come, get right in, dear," she said. "Well, well! I guess the rose was made for you; it looks very pretty in your coat, John."

She thought of Albert, and the next moment the tears came into her old eyes. John was a lover, too.

"My first husband was just such a tall, straight young man as you be," she said as they drove along. "The flower he first give me was a rose."

AUNT CYNTHY DALLETT

"N o," said Mrs. Hand, speaking wistfully,—"no, we never were in the habit of keeping Christmas at our house. Mother died when we were all young; she would have been the one to keep up with all new ideas, but father and grandmother were old-fashioned folks, and— well, you know how 't was then, Miss Pendexter: nobody took much notice of the day except to wish you a Merry Christmas."

"They did n't do much to make it merry, certain," answered Miss Pendexter. "Sometimes nowadays I hear folks complainin' o' bein' overtaxed with all the Christmas work they have to do."

"Well, others think that it makes a lovely chance for all that really enjoys givin'; you get an opportunity to speak your kind feelin' right out," answered Mrs. Hand, with a bright smile. "But there! I shall always keep New Year's Day, too; it won't do no hurt to have an extra day kept an' made pleasant. And there 's many of the real old folks have got pretty things to remember about New Year's Day."

"Aunt Cynthy Dallett 's just one of 'em," said Miss Pendexter. "She 's always very reproachful if I don't get up to see her. Last year I missed it, on account of a light fall o' snow that seemed to make the walkin' too bad, an' she sent a neighbor's boy 'way down from the mount'in to see if I was sick. Her lameness confines her to the house altogether now, an' I have her on my mind a good deal. How anybody does get thinkin' of those that lives alone, as they get older! I waked up only last night with a start, thinkin' if Aunt Cynthy's house should get afire or anything, what she would do, 'way up there all alone. I was half dreamin', I s'pose, but I couldn't seem to settle down until I got up an' went upstairs to the north garret window to see if I could see any light; but the mountains was all dark an' safe, same's usual. I remember noticin' last time I was there that her chimney needed pointin', and I spoke to her about it,—the bricks looked poor in some places."

"Can you see the house from your north gable window?" asked Mrs. Hand, a little absently.

"Yes 'm; it's a great comfort that I can," answered her companion. "I have often wished we were near enough to have her make me some sort o' signal in case she needed help. I used to plead with her to come down and spend the winters with me, but she told me one day I might as well try to fetch down one o' the old hemlocks, an' I believe 't was true."

"Your aunt Dallett is a very self-contained person," observed Mrs. Hand.

"Oh, very!" exclaimed the elderly niece, with a pleased look. "Aunt Cynthy laughs, an' says she expects the time will come when age 'll compel her to have me move up an' take care of her; and last time I was there she looked up real funny, an' says, 'I do know, Abby; I'm most afeard sometimes that I feel myself beginnin' to look for'ard to it!' 'T was a good deal, comin' from Aunt Cynthy, an' I so esteemed it."

"She ought to have you there now," said Mrs. Hand. "You'd both make a savin' by doin' it; but I don't expect she needs to save as much as some. There! I know just how you both feel. I like to have my own home an' do everything just my way too." And the friends laughed, and looked at each other affectionately.

"There was old Mr. Nathan Dunn,—left no debts an' no money when he died," said Mrs. Hand. "'T was over to his niece's last summer. He had a little money in his wallet, an' when the bill for funeral expenses come in there was just exactly enough; some item or other made it come to so many dollars an' eighty-four cents, and, lo an' behold! there was eighty-four cents in a little separate pocket beside the neat fold o' bills, as if the old gentleman had known beforehand. His niece couldn't help laughin', to save her; she said the old gentleman died as methodical as he lived. She didn't expect he had any money, an' was prepared to pay for everything herself; she's very well off."

"'T was funny, certain," said Miss Pendexter. "I expect he felt comfortable, knowin' he had that money by him. 'T is a comfort, when all 's said and done, 'specially to folks that 's gettin' old."

A sad look shadowed her face for an instant, and then she smiled and rose to take leave, looking expectantly at her hostess to see if there were anything more to be said.

"I hope to come out square myself," she said, by way of farewell pleasantry; "but there are times when I feel doubtful."

Mrs. Hand was evidently considering something, and waited a moment or two before she spoke. "Suppose we both walk up to see your aunt Dallett, New Year's Day, if it ain't too windy and the snow keeps off?" she proposed. "I could n't rise the hill if 't was a windy day. We could take a hearty breakfast an' start in good season; I 'd rather walk than ride, the road 's so rough this time o' year."

"Oh, what a person you are to think o' things! I did so dread goin' 'way up there all alone," said Abby Pendexter. "I 'm no hand to go off alone, an' I had it before me, so I really got to dread it. I do so enjoy it after I get there, seein' Aunt Cynthy, an' she 's always so much better than I expect to find her."

"Well, we 'll start early," said Mrs. Hand cheerfully; and so they parted. As Miss Pendexter went down the foot-path to the gate, she sent grateful thoughts back to the little sitting-room she had just left.

"How doors are opened!" she exclaimed to herself. "Here I 've been so poor an' distressed at beginnin' the year with nothin', as it were, that I could n't think o' even goin' to make poor old Aunt Cynthy a friendly call. I 'll manage to make some kind of a little pleasure too, an' somethin' for dear Mis' Hand. 'Use what you 've got,' mother always used to say when every sort of an emergency come up, an' I may only have wishes to give, but I 'll make,'em good ones!"

II

The first day of the year was clear and bright, as if it were a New Year's pattern of what winter can be at its very best. The two friends were prepared for changes of weather, and met each other well wrapped in their winter cloaks and shawls, with sufficient brown barége veils tied securely over their bonnets. They ignored for some time the plain truth that each carried something under her arm; the shawls were rounded out suspiciously, especially Miss Pendexter's, but each respected the other's air of secrecy. The narrow road was frozen in deep ruts, but a smooth-trodden little foot-path that ran along its edge was very inviting to the wayfarers. Mrs. Hand walked first and Miss Pendexter followed, and they were talking busily nearly all the way, so that they had to stop for breath now and then at the tops of the little hills. It was not a hard walk; there were a good many almost level stretches through the woods, in spite of the fact that they should be a very great deal higher when they reached Mrs. Dallett's door.

"I do declare, what a nice day 't is, an' such pretty footin'!" said Mrs. Hand, with satisfaction. "Seems to me as if my feet went o' themselves; gener'lly I have to toil so when I walk that I can't enjoy nothin' when I get to a place."

"It 's partly this beautiful bracin' air," said Abby Pendexter. "Sometimes such nice air comes just before a fall of snow. Don't it seem to make anybody feel young again and to take all your troubles away?"

Mrs. Hand was a comfortable, well-to-do soul, who seldom worried about anything, but something in her companion's tone touched her heart, and she glanced sidewise and saw a pained look in Abby Pendexter's thin face. It was a moment for confidence.

"Why, you speak as if something distressed your mind, Abby," said the elder woman kindly.

"I ain't one that has myself on my mind as usual thing, but it does seem now as if I was goin' to have it very hard," said Abby. "Well, I 've been anxious before."

"Is it anything wrong about your property?" Mrs. Hand ventured to ask.

"Only that I ain't got any," answered Abby, trying to speak gayly. "'T was all I could do to pay my last quarter's rent, twelve dollars. I sold my hens, all but this one that had run away at the time, an' now I 'm carryin' her up to Aunt Cynthy, roasted just as nice as I know how."

"I thought you was carrying somethin'," said Mrs. Hand, in her usual tone. "For me, I 've got a couple o' my mince pies. I thought the old lady might like 'em; one we can eat for our dinner, and one she shall have to keep. But were n't you unwise to sacrifice your poultry, Abby? You always need eggs, and hens don't cost much to keep."

"Why, yes, I shall miss 'em," said Abby; "but, you see, I had to do every way to get my rent-money. Now the shop 's shut down I have n't got any way of earnin' anything, and I spent what little I 've saved through the summer."

"Your aunt Cynthy ought to know it an' ought to help you," said Mrs. Hand. "You 're a real foolish person, I must say. I expect you do for her when she ought to do for you."

"She 's old, an' she 's all the near relation I 've got," said the little woman. "I 've always felt the time would come when she 'd need me, but it 's been her great pleasure to live alone an' feel free. I shall get along somehow, but I shall have it hard. Somebody may want help for a spell this winter, but I 'm afraid I shall have to give up my house. 'T ain't as if I owned it. I don't know just what to do, but there 'll be a way."

Mrs. Hand shifted her two pies to the other arm, and stepped across to the other side of the road where the ground looked a little smoother.

"No, I would n't worry if I was you, Abby," she said. "There, I suppose if 't was me I should worry a good deal more! I expect I should lay awake nights." But Abby answered nothing, and they came to a steep place in the road and found another subject for conversation at the top.

"Your aunt don't know we 're coming?" asked the chief guest of the occasion.

"Oh, no, I never send her word," said Miss Pendexter. "She 'd be so desirous to get everything ready, just as she used to."

"She never seemed to make any trouble o' havin' company; she always appeared so easy and pleasant, and let you set with her while she made her preparations," said Mrs. Hand, with great approval. "Some has such a dreadful way of making you feel inopportune, and you can't always send word you 're comin'. I did have a visit once that 's always been a lesson to me; 't was years ago; I don't know 's I ever told you?"

"I don't believe you ever did," responded the listener to this somewhat indefinite prelude.

"Well, 't was one hot summer afternoon. I set forth an' took a great long walk 'way over to Mis' Eben Fulham's, on the crossroad between the cranberry ma'sh and Staples's Corner. The doctor was drivin' that way, an' he give me a lift that shortened it some at the last; but I never should have started, if I 'd known 't was so far. I had been promisin' all summer to go, and every time I saw Mis' Fulham, Sundays, she 'd say somethin' about it. We wa'n't very well acquainted, but always friendly. She moved here from Bedford Hill."

"Oh, yes; I used to know her," said Abby, with interest.

"Well, now, she did give me a beautiful welcome when I got there," continued Mrs. Hand. "'T was about four o'clock in the afternoon, an' I told her I 'd come to accept her invitation if 't was convenient, an' the doctor had been called several miles beyond and expected to be detained, but he was goin' to pick me up as he returned about seven; 't was very kind of him. She took me right in, and she did appear so pleased, an' I must go right into the best room where 't was cool, and then she said she 'd have tea early, and I should have to excuse her a short time. I asked her not to make any difference, and if I could n't assist her; but she said no, I must just take her as I found her; and she give me a large fan, and off she went.

"There. I was glad to be still and rest where 't was cool, an' I set there in the rockin'-chair an' enjoyed it for a while, an' I heard her clacking at the oven door out beyond, an' gittin' out some dishes. She was a brisk-actin' little woman, an' I thought I 'd caution her when she come back not to make up a great fire, only for a cup o' tea, perhaps. I started to go right out in the kitchen, an' then somethin' told me I 'd better not, we never 'd been so free together as that; I did n't know how she 'd take it, an' there I set an' set. 'T was sort of a greenish light in the best room, an' it begun to feel a little damp to me,—the s'rubs outside grew close up to the windows. Oh, it did seem dreadful long! I could hear her busy with the dishes an' beatin' eggs an' stirrin', an' I knew she was puttin' herself out to get up a great supper, and I kind o' fidgeted about a little an' even stepped to the door, but I thought she 'd expect me to remain where I was. I saw everything in that room forty times over, an' I did divert myself killin' off a brood o' moths that was in a worsted-work mat on the table. It all fell to pieces. I never saw such a sight o' moths to once. But occupation failed after that, an' I begun to feel sort o' tired an' numb. There was one o' them late crickets got into the room an' begun to chirp, an' it sounded kind o' fallish. I could n't help sayin' to myself that Mis' Fulham had forgot all about my bein' there. I thought of all the beauties of hospitality that ever I see!"—

"Did n't she ever come back at all, not whilst things was in the oven, nor nothin'?" inquired Miss Pendexter, with awe.

"I never see her again till she come beamin' to the parlor door an' invited me to walk out to tea," said Mrs. Hand. "'T was 'most a quarter past six by the clock; I thought 't was seven. I 'd thought o' everything, an' I 'd counted, an' I 'd trotted my foot, an' I 'd looked more 'n twenty times to see if there was any more moth-millers."

"I s'pose you did have a very nice tea?" suggested Abby, with interest.

"Oh, a beautiful tea! She could n't have done more if I 'd been the Queen," said Mrs. Hand. "I don't know how she could ever have done it all in the time, I 'm sure. The table was loaded down; there was cup-custards and custard pie, an' cream pie, an' two kinds o' hot biscuits, an' black tea as well as green, an' elegant cake,—one kind she 'd just made new, and called it quick cake; I 've often made it since—an' she 'd opened her best preserves, two kinds. We set down together, an' I 'm sure I appreciated what she 'd done; but 't wa'n't no time for real conversation whilst we was to the table, and before we got quite through the doctor come hurryin' along, an' I had to leave. He asked us if we 'd had a good talk, as we come out, an' I could n't help laughing to myself; but she said quite hearty that she 'd had a nice visit from me. She appeared well satisfied, Mis' Fulham did; but for me, I was disappointed; an' early that fall she died."

Abby Pendexter was laughing like a girl; the speaker's tone had grown more and more complaining. "I do call that a funny experience," she said. "'Better a dinner o' herbs.' I guess that text must ha' risen to your mind in connection. You must tell that to Aunt Cynthy, if conversation seems to fail." And she laughed again, but Mrs. Hand still looked solemn and reproachful.

"Here we are; there 's Aunt Cynthy's land right ahead, there by the great yellow birch," said Abby, "I must say, you 've made the way seem very short, Mis' Hand."

III

Old Aunt Cynthia Dallett sat in her high-backed rocking-chair by the little north window, which was her favorite dwelling-place.

"New Year's Day again," she said, aloud,—"New Year's Day again!" And she folded her old bent hands, and looked out at the great woodland view and the hills without really seeing them, she was lost in so deep a reverie. "I 'm gittin' to be very old," she added, after a little while.

It was perfectly still in the small gray house. Outside in the apple-tree there were some blue-jays flitting about and calling noisily, like school-boys fighting at their games. The kitchen was full of pale winter sunshine. It was more like late October than the first of January, and the plain little room seemed to smile back into the sun's face. The outer door was standing open into the green dooryard, and a fat small dog lay asleep on the step. A capacious cupboard stood behind Mrs. Dallett's chair and kept the wind away from her corner. Its doors and drawers were painted a clean lead-color, and there were places round the knobs and buttons where the touch of hands had worn deep into the wood. Every braided rug was straight on the floor. The square clock on its shelf between the front windows looked as if it had just had its face washed and been wound up for a whole year to come. If Mrs. Dallett turned her head she could look into the bedroom, where her plump feather bed was covered with its dark blue homespun winter quilt. It was all very peaceful and comfortable, but it was very lonely. By her side, on a light-stand, lay the religious newspaper of her denomination, and a pair of spectacles whose jointed silver bows looked like a funny two-legged beetle cast helplessly upon its back.

"New Year's Day again," said old Cynthia Dallett. Time had left nobody in her house to wish her a Happy New Year,—she was the last one left in the old nest. "I 'm gittin' to be very old," she said for the second time; it seemed to be all there was to say.

She was keeping a careful eye on her friendly clock, but it was hardly past the middle of the morning, and there was no excuse for moving; it was the long hour between the end of her new slow morning work and the appointed time for beginning to get dinner. She was so stiff and lame that this hour's rest was usually most welcome, but to-day she sat as if it were Sunday, and did not take up her old shallow splint basket of braiding-rags from the side of her footstool.

"I do hope Abby Pendexter 'll make out to git up to see me this afternoon as usual," she continued. "I know 't ain't so easy for her to get up the hill as it used to be, but I do seem to want to see some o' my own folks. I wish 't I 'd thought to send her word I expected her when Jabez Hooper went back after he came up here with the flour. I 'd like to have had her come prepared to stop two or three days."

A little chickadee perched on the window-sill outside and bobbed his head sideways to look in, and then pecked impatiently at the glass. The old woman laughed at him with childish pleasure and felt companioned; it was pleasant at that moment to see the life in even a bird's bright eye.

"Sign of a stranger," she said, as he whisked his wings and flew away in a hurry. "I must throw out some crumbs for 'em; it 's getting to be hard pickin' for the stayin'-birds." She looked past the trees of her little orchard now with seeing eyes, and followed the long forest slopes that led downward to the lowland country. She could see the two white steeples of Fairfield Village, and the map of fields and pastures along the valley beyond, and the great hills across the valley to the westward. The scattered houses looked like toys that had been scattered by children. She knew their lights by night, and watched the smoke of their chimneys by day. Far to the northward were higher mountains, and these were already white with snow. Winter was already in sight, but to-day the wind was in the south, and the snow seemed only part of a great picture.

"I do hope the cold 'll keep off a while longer," thought Mrs. Dallett. "I don't know how I 'm going to get along after the deep snow comes."

The little dog suddenly waked, as if he had had a bad dream, and after giving a few anxious whines he began to bark outrageously. His mistress tried, as usual, to appeal to his better feelings.

"'T ain't nobody, Tiger," she said. "Can't you have some patience? Maybe it 's some foolish boys that 's rangin' about with their guns." But Tiger kept on, and even took the trouble to waddle in on his short legs, barking all the way. He looked warningly at her, and then turned and ran out again. Then she saw him go hurrying down to the bars, as if it were an occasion of unusual interest.

"I guess somebody is comin'; he don't act as if 't were a vagrant kind o' noise; must really be somebody in our lane." And Mrs. Dallett smoothed her apron and gave an anxious housekeeper's glance round the kitchen. None of her state visitors, the minister or the deacons, ever came in the morning. Country people are usually too busy to go visiting in the forenoons.

Presently two figures appeared where the road came out of the woods,—the two women already known to the story, but very surprising to Mrs. Dallett; the short, thin one was easily recognized as Abby Pendexter, and the taller, stout one was soon discovered to be Mrs. Hand. Their old friend's heart was in a glow. As the guests approached they could see her pale face with its thin white hair framed under the close black silk handkerchief.

"There she is at her window smilin' away!" exclaimed Mrs. Hand; but by the time they reached the doorstep she stood waiting to meet them.

"Why, you two dear creatur's!" she said, with a beaming smile. "I don't know when I 've ever been so glad to see folks comin'. I had a kind of left-all-alone feelin' this mornin', an' I did n't even make bold to be certain o' you, Abby, though it looked so pleasant. Come right in an' set down. You 're all out o' breath, ain't you, Mis' Hand?"

Mrs. Dallett led the way with eager hospitality. She was the tiniest little bent old creature, her handkerchiefed head was quick and alert, and her eyes were bright with excitement and feeling, but the rest of her was much the worse for age; she could hardly move, poor soul, as if she had only a make-believe framework of a body under a shoulder-shawl and thick petticoats. She got back to her chair again, and the guests took off their bonnets in the bedroom, and returned discreet and sedate in their black woolen dresses. The lonely kitchen was blest with society at last, to its mistress's heart's content. They talked as fast as possible about the weather, and how warm it had been walking up the mountain, and how cold it had been a year ago, that day when Abby Pendexter had been kept at home by a snowstorm and missed her visit. "And I ain't seen you now, aunt, since the twenty-eighth of September, but I 've thought of you a great deal, and looked forward to comin' more 'n usual," she ended, with an affectionate glance at the pleased old face by the window.

"I 've been wantin' to see you, dear, and wonderin' how you was gettin' on," said Aunt Cynthy kindly. "And I take it as a great attention to have you come to-day, Mis' Hand," she added, turning again towards the more distinguished guest. "We have to put one thing against another. I should hate dreadfully to live anywhere except on a high hill farm, 'cordin' as I was born an' raised. But there ain't the chance to neighbor that townfolks has, an' I do seem to have more lonely hours than I used to when I was younger. I don't know but I shall soon be gittin' too old to live alone." And she turned to her niece with an expectant, lovely look, and Abby smiled back.

"I often wish I could run in an' see you every day, aunt," she answered. "I have been sayin' so to Mrs. Hand."

"There, how anybody does relish company when they don't have but a little of it!" exclaimed Aunt Cynthia. "I am all alone to-day; there is going to be a shootin'-match somewhere the other side o' the mountain, an' Johnny Foss, that does my chores, begged off to go when he brought the milk unusual early this mornin'. Gener'lly he 's about here all the fore part of the day; but he don't go off with the boys very often, and I like to have him have a little sport; 't was New Year's Day, anyway; he 's a good, stiddy boy for my wants."

"Why, I wish you Happy New Year, aunt!" said Abby, springing up with unusual spirit. "Why, that 's just what we come to say, and we like to have forgot all about it!" She kissed her aunt, and stood a minute holding her hand with a soft, affectionate touch. Mrs. Hand rose and kissed Mrs. Dallett too, and it was a moment of ceremony and deep feeling.

"I always like to keep the day," said the old hostess, as they seated themselves and drew their splint-bottomed chairs a little nearer together than before. "You see, I was brought up to it, and father made a good deal of it; he said he liked to make it pleasant and give the year a fair start. I can see him now, how he used to be standing there by the fireplace when we came out o' the two bedrooms early in the morning, an' he always made out, poor 's he was, to give us some little present, and he 'd heap 'em up on the corner o' the mantelpiece, an' we 'd stand front of him in a row, and mother be bustling about gettin' breakfast. One year he give me a beautiful copy o' the 'Life o' General Lafayette,' in a green cover,—I 've got it now, but we child'n 'bout read it to pieces,—an' one year a nice piece o' blue ribbon, an' Abby—that was your mother, Abby—had a pink one. Father was real kind to his child'n. I thought o' them early days when I first waked up this mornin', and I could n't help lookin' up then to the corner o' the shelf just as I used to look."

"There 's nothin' so beautiful as to have a bright childhood to look back to," said Mrs. Hand. "Sometimes I think child'n has too hard a time now,—all the responsibility is put on to 'em, since they take the lead o' what to do an' what they want, and get to be so toppin' an' knowin'. 'T was happier in the old days, when the fathers an' mothers done the rulin'."

"They say things have changed," said Aunt Cynthy; "but staying right here, I don't know much of any world but my own world."

Abby Pendexter did not join in this conversation, but sat in her straight backed chair with folded hands and the air of a good child. The little old dog had followed her in, and now lay sound asleep again at her feet. The front breadth of her black dress looked rusty and old in the sunshine that slanted across it, and the aunt's sharp eyes saw this and saw the careful darns. Abby was as neat as wax, but she looked as if the frost had struck her. "I declare, she's gittin' along in years," thought Aunt Cynthia compassionately. "She begins to look sort o' set and dried up, Abby does. She ought n't to live all alone; she's one that needs company."

At this moment Abby looked up with new interest. "Now, aunt," she said, in her pleasant voice, "I don't want you to forget to tell me if there ain't some sewin' or mendin' I can do whilst I'm here. I know your hands trouble you some, an' I may's well tell you we're bent on stayin' all day an' makin' a good visit, Mis' Hand an' me."

"Thank ye kindly," said the old woman; "I do want a little sewin' done before long, but 't ain't no use to spile a good holiday." Her face took a resolved expression. "I'm goin' to make other arrangements," she said. "No, you need n't come up here to pass New Year's Day an' be put right down to sewin'. I make out to do what mendin' I need, an' to sew on my hooks an' eyes. I get Johnny Ross to thread me up a good lot o' needles every little while, an' that helps me a good deal. Abby, why can't you step into the best room an' bring out the rockin' chair? I seem to want Mis' Hand to have it."

"I opened the window to let the sun in awhile," said the niece, as she returned. "It felt cool in there an' shut up."

"I thought of doin' it not long before you come," said Mrs. Dallett, looking gratified. Once the taking of such a liberty would have been very provoking to her. "Why, it does seem good to have somebody think o' things an' take right hold like that!"

"I'm sure you would, if you were down at my house," said Abby, blushing. "Aunt Cynthy, I don't suppose you could feel as if 't would be best to come down an' pass the winter with me,—just durin' the cold weather, I mean. You'd see more folks to amuse you, an'—I do think of you so anxious these long winter nights."

There was a terrible silence in the room, and Miss Pendexter felt her heart begin to beat very fast. She did not dare to look at her aunt at first.

Presently the silence was broken. Aunt Cynthia had been gazing out of the window, and she turned towards them a little paler and older than before, and smiling sadly.

"Well, dear, I'll do just as you say," she answered. "I'm beat by age at last, but I've had my own way for eighty-five years, come the month o' March, an' last winter I did use to lay awake an' worry in the long storms.

I 'm kind o' humble now about livin' alone to what I was once." At this moment a new light shone in her face. "I don't expect you 'd be willin' to come up here an' stay till spring,—not if I had Foss's folks stop for you to ride to meetin' every pleasant Sunday, an' take you down to the Corners plenty o' other times besides?" she said beseechingly. "No, Abby, I 'm too old to move now; I should be homesick down to the village. If you 'll come an' stay with me, all I have shall be yours. Mis' Hand hears me say it."

"Oh, don't you think o' that; you 're all I 've got near to me in the world, an' I 'll come an' welcome," said Abby, though the thought of her own little home gave a hard tug at her heart. "Yes, Aunt Cynthy, I 'll come, an' we 'll be real comfortable together. I 've been lonesome sometimes"—

"'T will be best for both," said Mrs. Hand judicially. And so the great question was settled, and suddenly, without too much excitement, it became a thing of the past.

"We must be thinkin' o' dinner," said Aunt Cynthia gayly. "I wish I was better prepared; but there 's nice eggs an' pork an' potatoes, an' you girls can take hold an' help." At this moment the roast chicken and the best mince pies were offered and kindly accepted, and before another hour had gone they were sitting at their New Year feast, which Mrs. Dallett decided to be quite proper for the Queen.

Before the guests departed, when the sun was getting low, Aunt Cynthia called her niece to her side and took hold of her hand.

"Don't you make it too long now, Abby," said she. "I shall be wantin' ye every day till you come; but you must n't forget what a set old thing I be."

Abby had the kindest of hearts, and was always longing for somebody to love and care for; her aunt's very age and helplessness seemed to beg for pity.

"This is Saturday; you may expect me the early part of the week; and thank you, too, aunt," said Abby.

Mrs. Hand stood by with deep sympathy. "It 's the proper thing," she announced calmly. "You 'd both of you be a sight happier; and truth is, Abby 's wild an' reckless, an' needs somebody to stand right over her, Mis' Dallett. I guess she 'll try an' behave, but there—there's no knowin'!" And they all laughed. Then the New Year guests said farewell and started off down the mountain road. They looked back more than once to see Aunt Cynthia's face at the window as she watched them out of sight. Miss

Abby Pendexter was full of excitement; she looked as happy as a child.

"I feel as if we 'd gained the battle of Waterloo," said Mrs. Hand. "I 've really had a most beautiful time. You an' your aunt must n't forgit to invite me up some time again to spend another day."

MARTHA'S LADY

One day, many years ago, the old Judge Pyne house wore an unwonted look of gayety and youthfulness. The high-fenced green garden was bright with June flowers. Under the elms in the large shady front yard you might see some chairs placed near together, as they often used to be when the family were all at home and life was going on gayly with eager talk and pleasure-making; when the elder judge, the grandfather, used to quote that great author, Dr. Johnson, and say to his girls, "Be brisk, be splendid, and be public."

One of the chairs had a crimson silk shawl thrown carelessly over its straight back, and a passer-by, who looked in through the latticed gate between the tall gate-posts with their white urns, might think that this piece of shining East Indian color was a huge red lily that had suddenly bloomed against the syringa bush. There were certain windows thrown wide open that were usually shut, and their curtains were blowing free in the light wind of a summer afternoon; it looked as if a large household had returned to the old house to fill the prim best rooms and find them full of cheer.

It was evident to every one in town that Miss Harriet Pyne, to use the village phrase, had company. She was the last of her family, and was by no means old; but being the last, and wonted to live with people much older than herself, she formed all the habits of a serious elderly person. Ladies of her age, something past thirty, often wore discreet caps in those days, especially if they were married, but being single, Miss Harriet clung to youth in this respect, making one concession of keeping her waving chestnut hair as smooth and stiffly arranged as possible. She had been the dutiful companion of her father and mother in their latest years, all her elder brothers and sisters having married and gone, or died and gone, out of the old house. Now that she was left alone it seemed quite the best thing frankly to accept the fact of age, and to turn more resolutely than ever to the companionship of duty and serious books. She was more serious and given to routine then her elders themselves, as sometimes happened when the daughters of New England gentlefolks were brought up wholly in the society of their elders. At thirty-five she had more reluctance than her mother to face an unforeseen occasion, certainly more than her grandmother, who had preserved some cheerful inheritance of gayety and worldliness from colonial times.

There was something about the look of the crimson silk shawl in the front yard to make one suspect that the sober customs of the best house in a quiet New England village were all being set at defiance, and once when the mistress of the house came to stand in her own doorway, she wore the pleased but somewhat apprehensive look of a guest. In these days New England life held the necessity of much dignity and discretion of behavior; there was the truest hospitality and good cheer in all occasional festivities, but it was sometimes a self-conscious hospitality, followed by an inexorable return to asceticism both of diet and of behavior. Miss Harriet Pyne belonged to the very dullest days of New England, those which perhaps held the most priggishness for the learned professions, the most limited interpretation of the word "evangelical," and the pettiest indifference to large things. The outbreak of a desire for larger religious freedom caused at first a most determined reaction toward formalism, especially in small and quiet villages like Ashford, intently busy with their own concerns. It was high time for a little leaven to begin its work, in this moment when the great impulses of the war for liberty had died away and those of the coming war for patriotism and a new freedom had hardly yet begun.

The dull interior, the changed life of the old house, whose former activities seemed to have fallen sound asleep, really typified these larger conditions, and a little leaven had made its easily recognized appearance in the shape of a light-hearted girl. She was Miss Harriet's young Boston cousin, Helena Vernon, who, half-amused and half-impatient at the unnecessary sober-mindedness of her hostess and of Ashford in general, had set herself to the difficult task of gayety. Cousin Harriet looked on at a succession of ingenious and, on the whole, innocent attempts at pleasure, as she might have looked on at the frolics of a kitten who easily substitutes a ball of yarn for the uncertainties of a bird or a wind-blown leaf, and who may at any moment ravel the fringe of a sacred curtain-tassel in preference to either.

Helena, with her mischievous appealing eyes, with her enchanting old songs and her guitar, seemed the more delightful and even reasonable because she was so kind to everybody, and because she was a beauty. She had the gift of most charming manners. There was all the unconscious lovely ease and grace that had come with the good breeding of her city home, where many pleasant people came and went; she had no fear, one had almost said no respect, of the individual, and she did not need to think of herself. Cousin Harriet turned cold with apprehension when she saw the minister coming in at the front gate, and wondered in agony if Martha were properly attired to go to the door, and would by any chance hear the knocker; it was Helena who, delighted to have anything happen, ran to the door to welcome the Reverend Mr. Crofton as if he were a congenial friend of her own age. She could behave with more or less propriety during the stately first visit, and even contrive to lighten it with modest mirth, and to extort the confession that the guest had a tenor voice, though sadly out of practice; but when the minister departed a little flattered, and hoping that he had not expressed himself too strongly for a pastor upon the poems of Emerson, and feeling the unusual stir of gallantry in his proper heart, it was Helena who caught the honored hat of the late Judge Pyne from its last resting-place in the hall, and holding it securely in both hands, mimicked the minister's self-conscious entrance. She copied his pompous and anxious expression in the dim parlor in such delicious fashion that Miss Harriet, who could not always extinguish a ready spark of the original sin of humor, laughed aloud.

"My dear!" she exclaimed severely the next moment, "I am ashamed of your being so disrespectful!" and then laughed again, and took the affecting old hat and carried it back to its place.

"I would not have had any one else see you for the world," she said sorrowfully as she returned, feeling quite self-possessed again, to the parlor doorway; but Helena still sat in the minister's chair, with her small feet placed as his stiff boots had been, and a copy of his solemn expression before they came to speaking of Emerson and of the guitar. "I wish I had asked him if he would be so kind as to climb the cherry-tree," said Helena, unbending a little at the discovery that her cousin would consent to laugh no more. "There are all those ripe cherries on the top branches. I can climb as high as he, but I can't reach far enough from the last branch that will bear me. The minister is so long and thin"—

"I don't know what Mr. Crofton would have thought of you; he is a very serious young man," said cousin Harriet, still ashamed of her laughter. "Martha will get the cherries for you, or one of the men. I should not like to have Mr. Crofton think you were frivolous, a young lady of your opportunities"—but Helena had escaped through the hall and out at the garden door at the mention of Martha's name. Miss Harriet Pyne sighed anxiously, and then smiled, in spite of her deep convictions, as she shut the blinds and tried to make the house look solemn again.

The front door might be shut, but the garden door at the other end of the broad hall was wide open upon the large sunshiny garden, where the last of the red and white peonies and the golden lilies, and the first of the tall blue larkspurs lent their colors in generous fashion. The straight box borders were all in fresh and shining green of their new leaves, and there was a fragrance of the old garden's inmost life and soul blowing from the honeysuckle blossoms on a long trellis. It was now late in the afternoon, and the sun was low behind great apple-trees at the garden's end, which threw their shadows over the short turf of the bleaching-green. The cherry-trees stood at one side in full sunshine, and Miss Harriet, who presently came to the garden steps to watch like a hen at the water's edge, saw her cousin's pretty figure in its white dress of India muslin hurrying across the grass. She was accompanied by the tall, ungainly shape of Martha the new maid, who, dull and indifferent to every one else, showed a surprising willingness and allegiance to the young guest.

"Martha ought to be in the dining-room, already, slow as she is; it wants but half an hour of tea-time," said Miss Harriet as she turned and went into the shaded house. It was Martha's duty to wait at table, and there had been many trying scenes and defeated efforts toward her education. Martha was certainly very clumsy, and she seemed the clumsier because she had replaced her aunt, a most skillful person, who had but lately married a thriving farm and its prosperous owner. It must be confessed that Miss Harriet was a most bewildering instructor, and that her pupil's brain was easily confused and prone to blunders. The coming of Helena had been somewhat dreaded by reason of this incompetent service, but the guest took no notice of frowns or futile gestures at the first tea-table, except to establish friendly relations with Martha on her own account by a reassuring smile. They were about the same age, and next morning, before cousin Harriet came down, Helena showed by a word and a quick touch the right way to do something that had gone wrong and been impossible to understand the night before. A moment later the anxious mistress came in without suspicion, but Martha's eyes were as affectionate as a dog's, and there was a new look of hopefulness on her face; this dreaded guest was a friend after all, and not a foe come from proud Boston to confound her ignorance and patient efforts.

The two young creatures, mistress and maid, were hurrying across the bleaching-green.

"I can't reach the ripest cherries," explained Helena politely, "and I think that Miss Pyne ought to send some to the minister. He has just made us a call. Why Martha, you have n't been crying again!"

"Yes 'm," said Martha sadly. "Miss Pyne always loves to send something to the minister," she acknowledged with interest, as if she did not wish to be asked to explain these latest tears.

"We 'll arrange some of the best cherries in a pretty dish. I 'll show you how, and you shall carry them over to the parsonage after tea," said Helena cheerfully, and Martha accepted the embassy with pleasure. Life was beginning to hold moments of something like delight in the last few days.

"You 'll spoil your pretty dress, Miss Helena," Martha gave shy warning, and Miss Helena stood back and held up her skirts with unusual care while the country girl, in her heavy blue checked gingham, began to climb the cherry-tree like a boy.

Down came the scarlet fruit like bright rain into the green grass.

"Break some nice twigs with the cherries and leaves together; oh, you 're a duck, Martha!" and Martha, flushed with delight, and looking far more like a thin and solemn blue heron, came rustling down to earth again, and gathered the spoils into her clean apron.

That night at tea, during her handmaiden's temporary absence, Miss Harriet announced, as if by way of apology, that she thought Martha was beginning to understand something about her work. "Her aunt was a treasure, she never had to be told anything twice; but Martha has been as clumsy as a calf," said the precise mistress of the house. "I have been afraid sometimes that I never could teach her anything. I was quite ashamed to have you come just now, and find me so unprepared to entertain a visitor."

"Oh, Martha will learn fast enough because she cares so much," said the visitor eagerly. "I think she is a dear good girl. I do hope that she will never go away. I think she does things better every day, cousin Harriet," added Helena pleadingly, with all her kind young heart. The china-closet door was open a little way, and Martha heard every word. From that moment, she not only knew what love was like, but she knew love's dear ambitions. To have come from a stony hill-farm and a bare small wooden house, was like a cave-dweller's coming to make a permanent home in an art museum, such had seemed the elaborateness and elegance of Miss Pyne's fashion of life; and Martha's simple brain was slow enough in its processes and recognitions. But with this sympathetic ally and defender, this exquisite Miss Helena who believed in her, all difficulties appeared to vanish.

Later that evening, no longer homesick or hopeless, Martha returned from her polite errand to the minister, and stood with a sort of triumph before the two ladies, who were sitting in the front doorway, as if they were waiting for visitors, Helena still in her white muslin and red ribbons, and Miss Harriet in a thin black silk. Being happily self-forgetful in the greatness of the moment, Martha's manners were perfect, and she looked for once almost pretty and quite as young as she was.

"The minister came to the door himself, and returned his thanks. He said that cherries were always his favorite fruit, and he was much obliged to both Miss Pyne and Miss Vernon. He kept me waiting a few minutes, while he got this book ready to send to you, Miss Helena."

"What are you saying, Martha? I have sent him nothing!" exclaimed Miss Pyne, much astonished. "What does she mean, Helena?"

"Only a few cherries," explained Helena. "I thought Mr. Crofton would like them after his afternoon of parish calls. Martha and I arranged them before tea, and I sent them with our compliments."

"Oh, I am very glad you did," said Miss Harriet, wondering, but much relieved. "I was afraid"—

"No, it was none of my mischief," answered Helena daringly. "I did not think that Martha would be ready to go so soon. I should have shown you how pretty they looked among their green leaves. We put them in one of your best white dishes with the openwork edge. Martha shall show you to-morrow; mamma always likes to have them so." Helena's fingers were busy with the hard knot of a parcel.

"See this, cousin Harriet!" she announced proudly, as Martha disappeared round the corner of the house, beaming with the pleasures of adventure and success. "Look! the minister has sent me a book: Sermons on *what?* Sermons—it is so dark that I can't quite see."

"It must be his 'Sermons on the Seriousness of Life;' they are the only ones he has printed, I believe," said Miss Harriet, with much pleasure. "They are considered very fine discourses. He pays you a great compliment, my dear. I feared that he noticed your girlish levity."

"I behaved beautifully while he stayed," insisted Helena. "Ministers are only men," but she blushed with pleasure. It was certainly something to receive a book from its author, and such a tribute made her of more value to the whole reverent household. The minister was not only a man, but a bachelor, and Helena was at the age that best loves conquest; it was at any rate comfortable to be reinstated in cousin Harriet's good graces.

"Do ask the kind gentleman to tea! He needs a little cheering up," begged the siren in India muslin, as she laid the shiny black volume of sermons on the stone doorstep with an air of approval, but as if they had quite finished their mission.

"Perhaps I shall, if Martha improves as much as she has within the last day or two," Miss Harriet promised hopefully. "It is something I always dread a little when I am all alone, but I think Mr. Crofton likes to come. He converses so elegantly."

II

These were the days of long visits, before affectionate friends thought it quite worth while to take a hundred miles' journey merely to dine or to pass a night in one another's houses. Helena lingered through the pleasant weeks of early summer, and departed unwillingly at last to join her family at the White Hills, where they had gone, like other households of high social station, to pass the month of August out of town. The happy-hearted young guest left many lamenting friends behind her, and promised each that she would come back again next year. She left the minister a rejected lover, as well as the preceptor of the academy, but with their pride unwounded, and it may have been with wider outlooks upon the world and a less narrow sympathy both for their own work in life and for their neighbors' work and hindrances. Even Miss Harriet Pyne herself had lost some of the unnecessary provincialism and prejudice which had begun to harden a naturally good and open mind and affectionate heart. She was conscious of feeling younger and more free, and not so lonely. Nobody had ever been so gay, so fascinating, or so kind as Helena, so full of social resource, so simple and undemanding in her friendliness. The light of her young life cast no shadow on either young or old companions, her pretty clothes never seemed to make other girls look dull or out of fashion. When she went away up the street in Miss Harriet's carriage to take the slow train toward Boston and the gayeties of the new Profile House, where her mother waited impatiently with a group of Southern friends, it seemed as if there would never be any more picnics or parties in Ashford, and as if society had nothing left to do but to grow old and get ready for winter.

Martha came into Miss Helena's bedroom that last morning, and it was easy to see that she had been crying; she looked just as she did in that first sad week of homesickness and despair. All for love's sake she had been learning to do many things, and to do them exactly right; her eyes had grown quick to see the smallest chance for personal service. Nobody could be more humble and devoted; she looked years older than Helena, and wore already a touching air of caretaking.

"You spoil me, you dear Martha!" said Helena from the bed. "I don't know what they will say at home, I am so spoiled."

Martha went on opening the blinds to let in the brightness of the summer morning, but she did not speak.

"You are getting on splendidly, are n't you?" continued the little mistress. "You have tried so hard that you make me ashamed of myself. At first you crammed all the flowers together, and now you make them look beautiful. Last night cousin Harriet was so pleased when the table was so charming, and I told her that you did everything yourself, every bit. Won't you keep the flowers fresh and pretty in the house until I come back? It 's so much pleasanter for Miss Pyne, and you 'll feed my little sparrows, won't you? They 're growing so tame."

"Oh, yes, Miss Helena!" and Martha looked almost angry for a moment, then she burst into tears and covered her face with her apron. "I could n't understand a single thing when I first came. I never had been anywhere to see anything, and Miss Pyne frightened me when she talked. It was you made me think I could ever learn. I wanted to keep the place, 'count of mother and the little boys; we 're dreadful hard pushed. Hepsy has been good in the kitchen; she said she ought to have patience with me, for she was awkward herself when she first came."

Helena laughed; she looked so pretty under the tasseled white curtains.

"I dare say Hepsy tells the truth," she said. "I wish you had told me about your mother. When I come again, some day we 'll drive up country, as you call it, to see her. Martha! I wish you would think of me sometimes after I go away. Won't you promise?" and the bright young face suddenly grew grave. "I have hard times myself; I don't always learn things that I ought to learn, I don't always put things straight. I wish you would n't forget me ever, and would just believe in me. I think it does help more than anything."

"I won't forget," said Martha slowly. "I shall think of you every day." She spoke almost with indifference, as if she had been asked to dust a room, but she turned aside quickly and pulled the little mat under the hot water jug quite out of its former straightness; then she hastened away down the long white entry, weeping as she went.

III

To lose out of sight the friend whom one has loved and lived to please is to lose joy out of life. But if love is true, there comes presently a higher joy of pleasing the ideal, that is to say, the perfect friend. The same old happiness is lifted to a higher level. As for Martha, the girl who stayed behind in Ashford, nobody's life could seem duller to those who could not understand; she was slow of step, and her eyes were almost always downcast as if intent upon incessant toil; but they startled you when she looked up, with their shining light. She was capable of the happiness of holding fast to a great sentiment, the ineffable satisfaction of trying to please one whom she truly loved. She never thought of trying to make other people pleased with herself; all she lived for was to do the best she could for others, and to conform to an ideal, which grew at last to be like a saint's vision, a heavenly figure painted upon the sky.

On Sunday afternoons in summer, Martha sat by the window of her chamber, a low-storied little room, which looked into the side yard and the great branches of an elm tree. She never sat in the old wooden rocking-chair except on Sundays like this; it belonged to the day of rest and to happy meditation. She wore her plain black dress and a clean white apron, and held in her lap a little wooden box, with a brass ring on top for a handle. She was past sixty years of age and looked even older, but there was the same look on her face that it had sometimes worn in girlhood. She was the same Martha; her hands were old-looking and work-worn, but her face still shone. It seemed like yesterday that Helena Vernon had gone away, and it was more than forty years.

War and peace had brought their changes and great anxieties, the face of the earth was furrowed by floods and fire, the faces of mistress and maid were furrowed by smiles and tears, and in the sky the stars shone on as if nothing had happened. The village of Ashford added a few pages to its unexciting history, the minister preached, the people listened; now and then a funeral crept along the street, and now and then the bright face of a little child rose above the horizon of a family pew. Miss Harriet Pyne lived on in the large white house, which gained more and more distinction because it suffered no changes, save successive repaintings and new railing about its stately roof. Miss Harriet herself had moved far beyond the uncertainties of an anxious youth. She had long ago made all her decisions, and settled all necessary questions; her scheme of life was as faultless as the miniature landscape of a Japanese garden, and as easily kept in order. The only important change she would ever be capable of making was the final change to another and a better world; and for that nature itself would gently provide, and her own innocent life.

Hardly any great social event had ruffled the easy current of life since Helena Vernon's marriage. To this Miss Pyne had gone, stately in appearance and carrying gifts of some old family silver which bore the Vernon crest, but not without some protest in her heart against the uncertainties of married life. Helena was so equal to a happy independence and even to the assistance of other lives grown strangely dependent upon her quick sympathies and instinctive decisions, that it was hard to let her sink her personality in the affairs of another. Yet a brilliant English match was not without its attractions to an old-fashioned gentle-woman like Miss Pyne, and Helena herself was amazingly happy; one day there had come a letter to Ashford, in which her very heart seemed to beat with love and self-forgetfulness, to tell cousin Harriet of such new happiness and high hope. "Tell Martha all that I say about my dear Jack," wrote the eager girl; "please show my letter to Martha, and tell her that I shall come home next summer and bring the handsomest and best man in the world to Ashford. I have told him all about the dear house and the dear garden; there never was such a lad to reach for cherries with his six-foot-two." Miss Pyne, wondering a little, gave the letter to Martha, who took it deliberately and as if she wondered too, and went away to read it slowly by herself. Martha cried over it, and felt a strange sense of loss and pain; it hurt her heart a little to read about the cherry-picking. Her idol seemed to be less her own since she had become the idol of a stranger. She never had taken such a letter in her hands before, but love at last prevailed, since Miss Helena was happy, and she kissed the last page where her name was written, feeling overbold, and laid the envelope on Miss Pyne's secretary without a word.

The most generous love cannot but long for reassurance, and Martha had the joy of being remembered. She was not forgotten when the day of the wedding drew near, but she never knew that Miss Helena had asked if cousin Harriet would not bring Martha to town; she should like to have Martha there to see her married. "She would help about the flowers," wrote the happy girl; "I know she will like to come, and I'll ask mamma to plan to have some one take her all about Boston and make her have a pleasant time after the hurry of the great day is over."

Cousin Harriet thought it was very kind and exactly like Helena, but Martha would be out of her element; it was most imprudent and girlish to have thought of such a thing. Helena's mother would be far from wishing for any unnecessary guest just then, in the busiest part of her household, and it was best not to speak of the invitation. Some day Martha should go to Boston if she did well, but not now. Helena did not forget to ask if

Martha had come, and was astonished by the indifference of the answer. It was the first thing which reminded her that she was not a fairy princess having everything her own way in that last day before the wedding. She knew that Martha would have loved to be near, for she could not help understanding in that moment of her own happiness the love that was hidden in another heart. Next day this happy young princess, the bride, cut a piece of a great cake and put it into a pretty box that had held one of her wedding presents. With eager voices calling her, and her mother's face growing more and more wistful at the thought of parting, she still lingered and ran to take one or two trifles from her dressing-table, a little mirror and some tiny scissors that Martha would remember, and one of the pretty handkerchiefs marked with her maiden name. These she put in the box too; it was half a girlish freak and fancy, but she could not help trying to share her happiness, and Martha's life was so plain and dull. She whispered a message, and put the little package into cousin Harriet's hand for Martha as she said good-by. She was very fond of cousin Harriet. She smiled with a gleam of her old fun; Martha's puzzled look and tall awkward figure seemed to stand suddenly before her eyes, as she promised to come again to Ashford. Impatient voices called to Helena, her lover was at the door, and she hurried away, leaving her old home and her girlhood gladly. If she had only known it, as she kissed cousin Harriet good-by, they were never going to see each other again until they were old women. The first step that she took out of her father's house that day, married, and full of hope and joy, was a step that led her away from the green elms of Boston Common and away from her own country and those she loved best, to a brilliant, much-varied foreign life, and to nearly all the sorrows and nearly all the joys that the heart of one woman could hold or know.

On Sunday afternoons Martha used to sit by the window in Ashford and hold the wooden box which a favorite young brother, who afterward died at sea, had made for her, and she used to take out of it the pretty little box with a gilded cover that had held the piece of wedding-cake, and the small scissors, and the blurred bit of a mirror in its silver case; as for the handkerchief with the narrow lace edge, once in two or three years she sprinkled it as if it were a flower, and spread it out in the sun on the old bleaching-green, and sat near by in the shrubbery to watch lest some bold robin or cherry-bird should seize it and fly away.

IV

Miss Harriet Pyne was often congratulated upon the good fortune of having such a helper and friend as Martha. As time went on this tall, gaunt woman, always thin, always slow, gained a dignity of behavior and simple affectionateness of look which suited charm and dignity of the ancient house. She was unconsciously beautiful like a saint, like the picturesqueness of a lonely tree which lives to shelter unnumbered lives and to stand quietly in its place. There was such rustic homeliness and constancy belonging to her, such beautiful powers of apprehension, such reticence, such gentleness for those who were troubled or sick; all these gifts and graces Martha hid in her heart. She never joined the church because she thought she was not good enough, but life was such a passion and happiness of service that it was impossible not to be devout, and she was always in her humble place on Sundays, in the back pew next the door. She had been educated by a remembrance; Helena's young eyes forever looked at her reassuringly from a gay girlish face. Helena's sweet patience in teaching her own awkwardness could never be forgotten.

"I owe everything to Miss Helena," said Martha, half aloud, as she sat alone by the window; she had said it to herself a thousand times. When she looked in the little keepsake mirror she always hoped to see some faint reflection of Helena Vernon, but there was only her own brown old New England face to look back at her wonderingly.

Miss Pyne went less and less often to pay visits to her friends in Boston; there were very few friends left to come to Ashford and make long visits in the summer, and life grew more and more monotonous. Now and then there came news from across the sea and messages of remembrance, letters that were closely written on thin sheets of paper, and that spoke of lords and ladies, of great journeys, of the death of little children and the proud successes of boys at school, of the wedding of Helena Dysart's only daughter; but even that had happened years ago. These things seemed far away and vague, as if they belonged to a story and not to life itself; the true links with the past were quite different. There was the unvarying flock of ground-sparrows that Helena had begun to feed; every morning Martha scattered crumbs for them from the side doorsteps while Miss Pyne watched from the dining-room window, and they were counted and cherished year by year.

Miss Pyne herself had many fixed habits, but little ideality or imagination, and so at last it was Martha who took thought for her mistress, and gave freedom to her own good taste. After a while, without any one's observing the change, the every-day ways of doing things in the house came to be the stately ways that had once belonged only to the entertainment of guests. Happily both mistress and maid seized all possible chances for hospitality, yet Miss Harriet nearly always sat alone at her exquisitely served table with its fresh flowers, and the beautiful old china which Martha handled so lovingly that there was no good excuse for keeping it hidden on closet shelves. Every year when the old cherry-trees were in fruit, Martha carried the round white English dish with a fretwork edge, full of pointed green leaves and scarlet cherries, to the minister, and his wife never quite understood why every year he blushed and looked so conscious of the pleasure, and thanked Martha as if he had received a very particular attention. There was no pretty suggestion toward the pursuit of the fine art of housekeeping in Martha's limited acquaintance with newspapers that she did not adopt; there was no refined old custom of the Pyne house-keeping that she consented to let go. And every day, as she had promised, she thought of Miss Helena,—oh, many times in every day: whether this thing would please her, or that be likely to fall in with her fancy or ideas of fitness. As far as was possible the rare news that reached Ashford through an occasional letter or the talk of guests was made part of Martha's own life, the history of her own heart. A worn old geography often stood open at the map of Europe on the light-stand in her room, and a little old-fashioned gilt button, set with a bit of glass like a ruby, that had broken and fallen from the trimming of one of Helena's dresses, was used to mark the city of her dwelling-place. In the changes of a diplomatic life Martha followed her lady all about the map. Sometimes the button was at Paris, and sometimes at Madrid; once, to her great anxiety, it remained long at St. Petersburg. For such a slow scholar Martha was not unlearned at last, since everything about life in these foreign towns was of interest to her faithful heart. She satisfied her own mind as she threw crumbs to the tame sparrows; it was all part of the same thing and for the same affectionate reasons.

V

One Sunday afternoon in early summer Miss Harriet Pyne came hurrying along the entry that led to Martha's room and called two or three times before its inhabitant could reach the door. Miss Harriet looked unusually cheerful and excited, and she held something in her hand. "Where are you, Martha?" she called again. "Come quick, I have something to tell you!"

"Here I am, Miss Pyne," said Martha, who had only stopped to put her precious box in the drawer, and to shut the geography.

"Who do you think is coming this very night at half-past six? We must have everything as nice as we can; I must see Hannah at once. Do you remember my cousin Helena who has lived abroad so long? Miss Helena Vernon,—the Honorable Mrs. Dysart, she is now."

"Yes, I remember her," answered Martha, turning a little pale.

"I knew that she was in this country, and I had written to ask her to come for a long visit," continued Miss Harriet, who did not often explain things, even to Martha, though she was always conscientious about the kind messages that were sent back by grateful guests. "She telegraphs that she means to anticipate her visit by a few days and come to me at once. The heat is beginning in town, I suppose. I daresay, having been a foreigner so long, she does not mind traveling on Sunday. Do you think Hannah will be prepared? We must have tea a little later."

"Yes, Miss Harriet," said Martha. She wondered that she could speak as usual, there was such a ringing in her ears. "I shall have time to pick some fresh strawberries; Miss Helena is so fond of our strawberries."

"Why, I had forgotten," said Miss Pyne, a little puzzled by something quite unusual in Martha's face. "We must expect to find Mrs. Dysart a good deal changed, Martha; it is a great many years since she was here; I have not seen her since her wedding, and she has had a great deal of trouble, poor girl. You had better open the parlor chamber, and make it ready before you go down."

"It is all ready," said Martha. "I can carry some of those little sweet-brier roses upstairs before she comes."

"Yes, you are always thoughtful," said Miss Pyne, with unwonted feeling.

Martha did not answer. She glanced at the telegram wistfully. She had never really suspected before that Miss Pyne knew nothing of the love that had been in her heart all these years; it was half a pain and half a golden joy to keep such a secret; she could hardly bear this moment of surprise.

Presently the news gave wings to her willing feet. When Hannah, the cook, who never had known Miss Helena, went to the parlor an hour later on some errand to her old mistress, she discovered that this stranger guest must be a very important person. She had never seen the tea-table look exactly as it did that night, and in the parlor itself there were fresh blossoming boughs in the old East India jars, and lilies in the paneled hall, and flowers everywhere, as if there were some high festivity.

Miss Pyne sat by the window watching, in her best dress, looking stately and calm; she seldom went out now, and it was almost time for the carriage. Martha was just coming in from the garden with the strawberries, and with more flowers in her apron. It was a bright cool evening in June, the golden robins sang in the elms, and the sun was going down behind the apple-trees at the foot of the garden. The beautiful old house stood wide open to the long-expected guest.

"I think that I shall go down to the gate," said Miss Pyne, looking at Martha for approval, and Martha nodded and they went together slowly down the broad front walk.

There was a sound of horses and wheels on the roadside turf; Martha could not see at first; she stood back inside the gate behind the white lilac-bushes as the carriage came. Miss Pyne was there; she was holding out both arms and taking a tired, bent little figure in black to her heart. "Oh, my Miss Helena is an old woman like me!" and Martha gave a pitiful sob; she had never dreamed it would be like this; this was the one thing she could not bear.

"Where are you, Martha?" called Miss Pyne. "Martha will bring these in; you have not forgotten my good Martha, Helena?" Then Mrs. Dysart looked up and smiled just as she used to smile in the old days. The young eyes were there still in the changed face, and Miss Helena had come.

That night Martha waited in her lady's room just as she used, humble and silent, and went through with the old unforgotten loving services. The long years seemed like days. At last she lingered a moment trying to think of something else that might be done, then she was going silently away, but

Helena called her back. She suddenly knew the whole story and could hardly speak.

"Oh, my dear Martha!" she cried, "won't you kiss me good-night? Oh, Martha, have you remembered like this, all these long years!"

THE FOREIGNER

One evening, at the end of August, in Dunnet Landing, I heard Mrs. Todd's firm footstep crossing the small front entry outside my door, and her conventional cough which served as a herald's trumpet, or a plain New England knock, in the harmony of our fellowship.

"Oh, please come in!" I cried, for it had been so still in the house that I supposed my friend and hostess had gone to see one of her neighbors. The first cold northeasterly storm of the season was blowing hard outside. Now and then there was a dash of great raindrops and a flick of wet lilac leaves against the window, but I could hear that the sea was already stirred— to its dark depths and the great rollers were coming in heavily against the shore. One might well believe that Summer was coming to a sad end that night, in the darkness and rain and sudden access of autumnal cold. It seemed as if there must be danger offshore among the outer islands.

"Oh, there!" exclaimed Mrs. Todd, as she entered. "I know nothing ain't ever happened out to Green Island since the world began, but I always do worry about mother in these great gales. You know those tidal waves occur sometimes down to the West Indies, and I get dwellin' on 'em so I can't set still in my chair, nor knit a common row to a stocking. William might get mooning, out in his small bo't, and not observe how the sea was making, an' meet with some accident. Yes, I thought I 'd come in and set with you if you wa'n't busy. No, I never feel any concern about 'em in winter 'cause then they 're prepared, and all ashore and everything snug. William ought to keep help, as I tell him; yes, he ought to keep help."

I hastened to reassure my anxious guest by saying that Elijah Tilley had told me in the afternoon, when I came along the shore past the fish houses, that Johnny Bowden and the Captain were out at Green Island; he had seen them beating up the bay, and thought they must have put into Burnt Island cove, but one of the lobstermen brought word later that he saw them hauling out at Green Island as he came by, and Captain Bowden pointed ashore and shook his head to say that he did not mean to try to get in. "The old Miranda just managed it, but she will have to stay at home a day or two and put new patches in her sail," I ended, not without pride in so much circumstantial evidence.

Mrs. Todd was alert in a moment. "Then they 'll all have a very pleasant evening," she assured me, apparently dismissing all fears of tidal waves and other sea-going disasters. "I was urging Alick Bowden to go ashore some day and see mother before cold weather. He 's her own nephew; she sets a great deal by him. And Johnny 's a great chum o' William's; don't you know the first day we had Johnny out 'long of us, he took an' give William his money to keep for him that he 'd been a-savin', and William showed it to me an' was so affected I thought he was goin' to shed tears? 'T was a dollar an' eighty cents; yes, they 'll have a beautiful evenin' all together, and like 's not the sea 'll be flat as a doorstep come morning."

I had drawn a large wooden rocking-chair before the fire, and Mrs. Todd was sitting there jogging herself a little, knitting fast, and wonderfully placid of countenance. There came a fresh gust of wind and rain, and we could feel the small wooden house rock and hear it creak as if it were a ship at sea.

"Lord, hear the great breakers!" exclaimed Mrs. Todd. "How they pound!—there, there! I always run of an idea that the sea knows anger these nights and gets full o' fight. I can hear the note o' them old black ledges way down the thoroughfare. Calls up all those stormy verses in the Book o' Psalms; David he knew how old sea-goin' folks have to quake at the heart."

I thought as I had never thought before of such anxieties. The families of sailors and coastwise adventurers by sea must always be worrying about somebody, this side of the world or the other. There was hardly one of Mrs. Todd's elder acquaintances, men or women, who had not at some time or other made a sea voyage, and there was often no news until the voyagers themselves came back to bring it.

"There's a roaring high overhead, and a roaring in the deep sea," said Mrs. Todd solemnly, "and they battle together nights like this. No, I could n't sleep; some women folks always goes right to bed an' to sleep, so 's to forget, but 't ain't my way. Well, it 's a blessin' we don't all feel alike; there 's hardly any of our folks at sea to worry about, nowadays, but I can't help my feelin's, an' I got thinking of mother all alone, if William had happened to be out lobsterin' and could n't make the cove gettin' back."

"They will have a pleasant evening," I repeated. "Captain Bowden is the best of good company."

"Mother 'll make him some pancakes for his supper, like 's not," said Mrs. Todd, clicking her knitting needles and giving a pull at her yarn. Just then the old cat pushed open the unlatched door and came straight toward her mistress's lap. She was regarded severely as she stepped about and turned on the broad expanse, and then made herself into a round cushion of fur, but was not openly admonished. There was another great blast of wind overhead, and a puff of smoke came down the chimney.

"This makes me think o' the night Mis' Cap'n Tolland died," said Mrs. Todd, half to herself. "Folks used to say these gales only blew when somebody 's a-dyin', or the devil was a-comin' for his own, but the worst man I ever knew died a real pretty mornin' in June."

"You have never told me any ghost stories," said I; and such was the gloomy weather and the influence of the night that I was instantly filled with reluctance to have this suggestion followed. I had not chosen the best of moments; just before I spoke we had begun to feel as cheerful as possible. Mrs. Todd glanced doubtfully at the cat and then at me, with a strange absent look, and I was really afraid that she was going to tell me something that would haunt my thoughts on every dark stormy night as long as I lived.

"Never mind now; tell me to-morrow by daylight, Mrs. Todd," I hastened to say, but she still looked at me full of doubt and deliberation.

"Ghost stories!" she answered. "Yes, I don't know but I 've heard a plenty of 'em first an' last. I was just sayin' to myself that this is like the night Mis' Cap'n Tolland died. 'T was the great line storm in September all of thirty, or maybe forty, year ago. I ain't one that keeps much account o' time."

"Tolland? That 's a name I have never heard in Dunnet," I said.

"Then you have n't looked well about the old part o' the buryin' ground, no'theast corner," replied Mrs. Todd. "All their women folks lies there; the sea 's got most o' the men. They were a known family o' shipmasters in early times. Mother had a mate, Ellen Tolland, that she mourns to this day; died right in her bloom with quick consumption, but the rest o' that family was all boys but one, and older than she, an' they lived hard seafarin' lives an' all died hard. They were called very smart seamen. I 've heard that when the youngest went into one o' the old shippin' houses in Boston, the head o' the firm called out to him: 'Did you say Tolland from Dunnet? That 's recommendation enough for any vessel!' There was some o' them old shipmasters as tough as iron, an' they had the name o' usin' their crews very severe, but there wa'n't a man that would n't rather sign with 'em an' take his chances, than with the slack ones that did n't know how to meet accidents."

II

There was so long a pause, and Mrs. Todd still looked so absent-minded, that I was afraid she and the cat were growing drowsy together before the fire, and I should have no reminiscences at all. The wind struck the house again, so that we both started in our chairs and Mrs. Todd gave a curious, startled look at me. The cat lifted her head and listened too, in the silence that followed, while after the wind sank we were more conscious than ever of the awful roar of the sea. The house jarred now and then, in a strange, disturbing way.

"Yes, they 'll have a beautiful evening out to the island," said Mrs. Todd again; but she did not say it gayly. I had not seen her before in her weaker moments.

"Who was Mrs. Captain Tolland?" I asked eagerly, to change the current of our thoughts.

"I never knew her maiden name; if I ever heard it, I 've gone an' forgot; 't would mean nothing to me," answered Mrs. Todd.

"She was a foreigner, an' he met with her out in the Island o' Jamaica. They said she 'd been left a widow with property. Land knows what become of it; she was French born, an' her first husband was a Portugee, or somethin'."

I kept silence now, a poor and insufficient question being worse than none.

"Cap'n John Tolland was the least smartest of any of 'em, but he was full smart enough, an' commanded a good brig at the time, in the sugar trade; he 'd taken out a cargo o' pine lumber to the islands from somewheres up the river, an' had been loadin' for home in the port o' Kingston, an' had gone ashore that afternoon for his papers, an' remained afterwards 'long of three friends o' his, all shipmasters. They was havin' their suppers together in a tavern; 't was late in the evenin' an' they was more lively than usual, an' felt boyish; and over opposite was another house full o' company, real bright and pleasant lookin', with a lot o' lights, an' they heard somebody singin' very pretty to a guitar. They wa'n't in no go-to-meetin' condition, an' one of 'em, he slapped the table an' said, 'Le' 's go over an' hear that lady sing!' an' over they all went, good honest sailors, but three sheets in the wind, and stepped in as if they was invited, an' made their bows inside the door, an' asked if they could hear the music; they were all respectable well-dressed men. They saw the woman that had the guitar, an' there was a company a-listenin', regular highbinders all of 'em; an' there was a long table all spread out with big candlesticks like little trees o' light, and a sight o' glass an' silver ware; an' part o' the men was young officers in uniform, an' the colored folks was steppin' round servin' 'em, an' they had the lady singin'. 'T was a wasteful scene, an' a loud talkin' company, an' though they was three sheets in the wind themselves there wa'n't one o' them cap'ns but had sense to perceive it. The others had pushed back their chairs, an' their decanters an' glasses was standin' thick about, an' they was teasin' the one that was singin' as if they 'd just got her in to amuse 'em. But they quieted down; one o' the young officers had beautiful manners, an' invited the four cap'ns to join 'em, very polite; 't was a kind of public house, and after they 'd all heard another song, he come to consult with 'em whether they would n't git up and dance a hornpipe or somethin' to the lady's music.

"They was all elderly men an' shipmasters, and owned property; two of 'em was church members in good standin'," continued Mrs. Todd loftily, "an' they would n't lend theirselves to no such kick-shows as that, an' spite o' bein' three sheets in the wind, as I have once observed; they waved aside the tumblers of wine the young officer was pourin' out for 'em so freehanded, and said they should rather be excused. An' when they all rose, still very dignified, as I 've been well informed, and made their partin' bows and was goin' out, them young sports got round 'em an' tried to prevent 'em, and they had to push an' strive considerable, but out they come. There was this Cap'n Tolland and two Cap'n Bowdens, and the fourth was my own father." (Mrs. Todd spoke slowly, as if to impress the value of her authority.) "Two of them was very religious, upright men, but they would have their night off sometimes, all o' them old-fashioned cap'ns, when they was free of business and ready to leave port.

"An' they went back to their tavern an' got their bills paid, an' set down kind o' mad with everybody by the front windows, mistrusting some o' their tavern charges, like 's not, by that time, an' when they got tempered down, they watched the house over across, where the party was.

"There was a kind of a grove o' trees between the house an' the road, an' they heard the guitar a-goin' an' a-stoppin' short by turns, and pretty soon somebody began to screech, an' they saw a white dress come runnin' out through the bushes, an' tumbled over each other in their haste to offer help; an' out she come, with the guitar, cryin' into the street, and they just walked off four square with her amongst 'em, down toward the wharves where they felt more to home. They couldn't make out at first what 't was she spoke,—Cap'n Lorenzo Bowden was well acquainted in Havre an' Bordeaux, an' spoke a poor quality o' French, an' she knew a little mite o' English, but not much; and they come somehow or other to discern that she was in real distress. Her husband and her children had died o' yellow fever; they 'd all come up to Kingston from one o' the far Wind'ard Islands to get passage on a steamer to France, an' a negro had stole their money off her husband while he lay sick o' the fever, an' she had been befriended some, but the folks that knew about her had died too; it had been a dreadful run o' the fever that season, an' she fell at last to playin' an' singin' for hire, and for what money they 'd throw to her round them harbor houses.

"'T was a real hard case, an' when them cap'ns made out about it, there wa'n't one that meant to take leave without helpin' of her. They was pretty mellow, an' whatever they might lack o' prudence they more 'n made up with charity: they did n't want to see nobody abused, an' she was sort of a pretty woman, an' they stopped in the street then an' there an' drew lots who should take her aboard, bein' all bound home. An' the lot fell to Cap'n Jonathan Bowden who did act discouraged; his vessel had but small accommodations, though he could stow a big freight, an' she was a dreadful slow sailer through bein' square as a box, an' his first wife, that was livin' then, was a dreadful jealous woman. He threw himself right onto the mercy o' Cap'n Tolland."

Mrs. Todd indulged herself for a short time in a season of calm reflection.

"I always thought they 'd have done better, and more reasonable, to give her some money to pay her passage home to France, or wherever she may have wanted to go," she continued.

I nodded and looked for the rest of the story.

"Father told mother," said Mrs. Todd confidentially, "that Cap'n Jonathan Bowden an' Cap'n John Tolland had both taken a little more than usual; I would n't have you think, either, that they both was n't the best o' men, an' they was solemn as owls, and argued the matter between 'em, an' waved aside the other two when they tried to put their oars in. An' spite o' Cap'n Tolland's bein' a settled old bachelor they fixed it that he was to take the prize on his brig; she was a fast sailer, and there was a good spare cabin or two where he 'd sometimes carried passengers, but he 'd filled 'em with bags o' sugar on his own account an' was loaded very heavy beside. He said he 'd shift the sugar an' get along somehow, an' the last the other three cap'ns saw of the party was Cap'n John handing the lady into his bo't, guitar and all, an' off they all set tow'ds their ships with their men rowin' 'em in the bright moonlight down to Port Royal where the anchorage was, an' they all lay, goin' out with the tide an' mornin' wind at break o' day. An' the others thought they heard music of the guitar, two o' the bo'ts kept well together, but it may have come from another source."

"Well; and then?" I asked eagerly after a pause. Mrs. Todd was almost laughing aloud over her knitting and nodding emphatically. We had forgotten all about the noise of the wind and sea.

"Lord bless you! he come sailing into Portland with his sugar, all in good time, an' they stepped right afore a justice o' the peace, and Cap'n John Tolland come paradin' home to Dunnet Landin' a married man. He owned one o' them thin, narrow-lookin' houses with one room each side o' the front door, and two slim black spruces spindlin' up against the front windows to make it gloomy inside. There was no horse nor cattle of course, though he owned pasture land, an' you could see rifts o' light right through the barn as you drove by. And there was a good excellent kitchen, but his sister reigned over that; she had a right to two rooms, and took the kitchen an' a bedroom that led out of it; an' bein' given no rights in the kitchen had angered the cap'n so they were n't on no kind o' speakin' terms. He preferred his old brig for comfort, but now and then, between voyages, he 'd come home for a few days, just to show he was master over his part o' the house, and show Eliza she could n't commit no trespass.

"They stayed a little while; 't was pretty spring weather, an' I used to see Cap'n John rollin' by with his arms full o' bundles from the store, lookin' as pleased and important as a boy; an' then they went right off to sea again, an' was gone a good many months. Next time he left her to live there alone, after they 'd stopped at home together some weeks, an' they said she suffered from bein' at sea, but some said that the owners would n't have a woman aboard. 'T was before father was lost on that last voyage of his, an' he and mother went up once or twice to see them. Father said there wa'n't a mite o' harm in her, but somehow or other a sight o' prejudice arose; it may have been caused by the remarks of Eliza an' her feelin's tow'ds her brother. Even my mother had no regard for Eliza Tolland. But mother asked the cap'ns wife to come with her one evenin' to a social circle that was down to the meetin'-house vestry, so she 'd get acquainted a little, an' she appeared very pretty until they started to have some singin' to the melodeon. Mari' Harris an' one o' the younger Caplin girls undertook to sing a duet, an' they sort o' flatted, an' she put her hands right up to her ears, and give a little squeal, an' went quick as could be an' give 'em the right notes, for she could read the music like plain print, an' made 'em try it over again. She was real willin' an' pleasant, but that did n't suit, an' she made faces when they got it wrong. An' then there fell a dead calm, an' we was all settin' round prim as dishes, an' my mother, that never expects ill feelin', asked her if she would n't sing somethin', an' up she got,—poor creatur', it all seems so different to me now,—an' sung a lovely little song standin' in the floor; it seemed to have something gay about it that kept a-repeatin', an' nobody could help keepin' time, an' all of a sudden she looked round at the tables and caught up a tin plate that somebody 'd fetched a Washin'ton pie in, an' she begun to drum on it with her fingers like one o' them tambourines, an' went right on singin' faster an' faster, and next minute she begun to dance a little pretty dance between the verses, just as light and pleasant as a child. You could n't help seein' how pretty 't was; we all got to trottin' a foot, an' some o' the men clapped their hands quite loud, a-keepin' time, 't was so catchin', an' seemed so natural to her. There wa'n't one of 'em but enjoyed it; she just tried do her part, an' some urged her on, till she stopped with a little twirl of her skirts an' went to her place again by mother. And I can see mother now, reachin' over an' smilin' an' pattin' her hand.

"But next day there was an awful scandal goin' in the parish, an' Mari' Harris reproached my mother to her face, an' I never wanted to see her since, but I 've had to a good many times. I said Mis' Tolland did n't intend no impropriety,—I reminded her of David's dancin' before the Lord; but she said such a man as David never would have thought o' dancin' right there in the Orthodox vestry, and she felt I spoke with irreverence.

"And next Sunday Mis' Tolland come walkin' into our meeting, but I must say she acted like a cat in a strange garret, and went right out down the aisle with her head in air, from the pew Deacon Caplin had showed her into. 'T was just in the beginning of the long prayer. I wish she 'd stayed through, whatever her reasons were. Whether she 'd expected somethin' different, or misunderstood some o' the pastor's remarks, or what 't was, I don't really feel able to explain, but she kind o' declared war, at least folks thought so, an' war 't was from that time. I see she was cryin', or had been, as she passed by me; perhaps bein' in meetin' was what had power to make her feel homesick and strange.

"Cap'n John Tolland was away fittin' out; that next week he come home to see her and say farewell. He was lost with his ship in the Straits of Malacca, and she lived there alone in the old house a few months longer till she died. He left her well off; 't was said he hid his money about the house and she knew where 't was. Oh, I expect you 've heard that story told over an' over twenty times, since you 've been here at the Landin'?"

"Never one word," I insisted.

"It was a good while ago," explained Mrs. Todd, with reassurance. "Yes, it all happened a great while ago."

III

At this moment, with a sudden flaw of the wind, some wet twigs outside blew against the window panes and made a noise like a distressed creature trying to get in. I started with sudden fear, and so did the cat, but Mrs. Todd knitted away and did not even look over her shoulder.

"She was a good-looking woman; yes, I always thought Mis' Tolland was good-looking, though she had, as was reasonable, a sort of foreign cast, and she spoke very broken English, no better than a child. She was always at work about her house, or settin' at a front window with her sewing; she was a beautiful hand to embroider. Sometimes, summer evenings, when the windows was open, she 'd set an' drum on her guitar, but I don't know as I ever heard her sing but once after the cap'n went away. She appeared very happy about havin' him, and took on dreadful at partin' when he was down here on the wharf, going back to Portland by boat to take ship for that last v'y'ge. He acted kind of ashamed, Cap'n John did; folks about here ain't so much accustomed to show their feelings. The whistle had blown an' they was waitin' for him to get aboard, an' he was put to it to know what to do and treated her very affectionate in spite of all impatience; but mother happened to be there and she went an' spoke, and I remember what a comfort she seemed to be. Mis' Tolland clung to her then, and she would n't give a glance after the boat when it had started, though the captain was very eager a-wavin' to her. She wanted mother to come home with her an' would n't let go her hand, and mother had just come in to stop all night with me an' had plenty o' time ashore, which did n't always happen, so they walked off together, an' 't was some considerable time before she got back.

" 'I want you to neighbor with that poor lonesome creatur',' says mother to me, lookin' reproachful. 'She 's a stranger in a strange land,' says mother. 'I want you to make her have a sense that somebody feels kind to her.'

" 'Why, since that time she flaunted out o' meetin', folks have felt she liked other ways better 'n our'n,' says I. I was provoked, because I 'd had a nice supper ready, an' mother 'd let it wait so long 't was spoiled. 'I hope you 'll like your supper!' I told her. I was dreadful ashamed afterward of speakin' so to mother.

" 'What consequence is my supper?' says she to me; mother can be very stern,—'or your comfort or mine, beside letting a foreign person an' a stranger feel so desolate; she 's done the best a woman could do in her lonesome place, and she asks nothing of anybody except a little common kindness. Think if 't was you in a foreign land!'

"And mother set down to drink her tea, an' I set down humbled enough over by the wall to wait till she finished. An' I did think it all over, an' next day I never said nothin', but I put on my bonnet, and went to see Mis' Cap'n Tolland, if 't was only for mother's sake. 'T was about three quarters of a mile up the road here, beyond the schoolhouse. I forgot to tell you that the cap'n had bought out his sister's right at three or four times what 't was worth, to save trouble, so they 'd got clear o' her, an' I went round into the side yard sort o' friendly an' sociable, rather than stop an' deal with the knocker an' the front door. It looked so pleasant an' pretty I was glad I come; she had set a little table for supper, though 't was still early, with a white cloth on it, right out under an old apple tree close by the house. I noticed 't was same as with me at home, there was only one plate. She was just coming out with a dish; you could n't see the door nor the table from the road.

"In the few weeks she 'd been there she 'd got some bloomin' pinks an' other flowers next the doorstep. Somehow it looked as if she 'd known how to make it homelike for the cap'n. She asked me to set down; she was very polite, but she looked very mournful, and I spoke of mother, an' she put down her dish and caught holt o' me with both hands an' said my mother was an angel. When I see the tears in her eyes 't was all right between us, and we were always friendly after that, and mother had us come out to make a little visit that summer; but she come a foreigner and she went a foreigner, and never was anything but a stranger among our folks. She taught me a sight o' things about herbs I never knew before nor since; she was well acquainted with the virtues o' plants. She 'd act awful secret about some things too, an' used to work charms for herself sometimes, an' some o' the neighbors told to an' fro after she died that they knew enough not to provoke her, but 't was all nonsense; 't is the believin' in such things that causes 'em to be any harm, an' so I told 'em," confided Mrs. Todd contemptuously. "That first night I stopped to tea with her she 'd cooked some eggs with some herb or other sprinkled all through, and 't was she that first led me to discern mushrooms; an' she went right down on her knees in my garden here when she saw I had my different officious herbs. Yes, 't was she that learned me the proper use o' parsley too; she was a beautiful cook."

Mrs. Todd stopped talking, and rose, putting the cat gently in the chair, while she went away to get another stick of apple-tree wood. It was not an evening when one wished to let the fire go down, and we had a splendid bank of bright coals. I had always wondered where Mrs. Todd had got such an unusual knowledge of cookery, of the varieties of mushrooms, and the use of sorrel as a vegetable, and other blessings of that sort. I had long ago learned that she could vary her omelettes like a child of France, which was indeed a surprise in Dunnet Landing.

IV

All these revelations were of the deepest interest, and I was ready with a question as soon as Mrs. Todd came in and had well settled the fire and herself and the cat again.

"I wonder why she never went back to France, after she was left alone?"

"She come here from the French islands," explained Mrs. Todd. "I asked her once about her folks, an' she said they were all dead; 't was the fever took 'em. She made this her home, lonesome as 't was; she told me she had n't been in France since she was 'so small,' and measured me off a child o' six. She 'd lived right out in the country before, so that part wa'n't unusual to her. Oh yes, there was something very strange about her, and she had n't been brought up in high circles nor nothing o' that kind. I think she 'd been really pleased to have the cap'n marry her an' give her a good home, after all she 'd passed through, and leave her free with his money an' all that. An' she got over bein' so strange-looking to me after a while, but 't was a very singular expression: she wore a fixed smile that wa'n't a smile; there wa'n't no light behind it, same 's a lamp can't shine if it ain't lit. I don't know just how to express it, 't was a sort of made countenance."

One could not help thinking of Sir Philip Sidney's phrase, "A made countenance, between simpering and smiling."

"She took it hard, havin' the captain go off on that last voyage," Mrs. Todd went on. "She said somethin' told her when they was partin' that he would never come back. He was lucky to speak a home-bound ship this side o' the Cape o' Good Hope, an' got a chance to send her a letter, an' that cheered her up. You often felt as if you was dealin' with a child's mind, for all she had so much information that other folks had n't. I was a sight younger than I be now, and she made me imagine new things, and I got interested watchin' her an' findin' out what she had to say, but you could n't get to no affectionateness with her. I used to blame me sometimes; we used to be real good comrades goin' off for an afternoon, but I never give her a kiss till the day she laid in her coffin and it come to my heart there wa'n't no one else to do it."

"And Captain Tolland died," I suggested after a while.

"Yes, the cap'n was lost," said Mrs. Todd, "and of course word did n't come for a good while after it happened. The letter come from the owners to my uncle, Cap'n Lorenzo Bowden, who was in charge of Cap'n Tolland's affairs at home, and he come right up for me an' said I must go with him to the house. I had known what it was to be a widow, myself, for near a year, an' there was plenty o' widow women along this coast that the sea had made desolate, but I never saw a heart break as I did then.

"'T was this way: we walked together along the road, me an' uncle Lorenzo. You know how it leads straight from just above the schoolhouse to the brook bridge, and their house was just this side o' the brook bridge on the left hand; the cellar 's there now, and a couple or three good-sized gray birches growin' in it. And when we come near enough I saw that the best room, this way, where she most never set, was all lighted up, and the curtains up so that the light shone bright down the road, and as we walked, those lights would dazzle and dazzle in my eyes, and I could hear the guitar a-goin', an' she was singin'. She heard our steps with her quick ears and come running to the door with her eyes a-shinin', an' all that set look gone out of her face, an' begun to talk French, gay as a bird, an' shook hands and behaved very pretty an' girlish, sayin' 't was her fête day. I did n't know what she meant then. And she had gone an' put a wreath o' flowers on her hair an' wore a handsome gold chain that the cap'n had given her; an' there she was, poor creatur', makin' believe have a party all alone in her best room; 't was prim enough to discourage a person, with too many chairs set close to the walls, just as the cap'n's mother had left it, but she had put sort o' long garlands on the walls, droopin' very graceful, and a sight of green boughs in the corners, till it looked lovely, and all lit up with a lot o' candles."

"Oh dear!" I sighed. "Oh, Mrs. Todd, what did you do?"

"She beheld our countenances," answered Mrs. Todd solemnly. "I expect they was telling everything plain enough, but Cap'n Lorenzo spoke the sad words to her as if he had been her father; and she wavered a minute and then over she went on the floor before we could catch hold of her, and then we tried to bring her to herself and failed, and at last we carried her upstairs, an' I told uncle to run down and put out the lights, and then go fast as he could for Mrs. Begg, being very experienced in sickness, an' he so did. I got off her clothes and her poor wreath, and I cried as I done it. We both stayed there that night, and the doctor said 't was a shock when he come in the morning; he'd been over to Black Island an' had to stay all night with a very sick child."

"You said that she lived alone some time after the news came," I reminded Mrs. Todd then.

"Oh yes, dear," answered my friend sadly, "but it wa'n't what you'd call livin'; no, it was only dyin', though at a snail's pace. She never went out again those few months, but for a while she could manage to get about the house a little, and do what was needed, an' I never let two days go by without seein' her or hearin' from her. She never took much notice as I came an' went except to answer if I asked her anything. Mother was the one who gave her the only comfort."

"What was that?" I asked softly.

"She said that anybody in such trouble ought to see their minister, mother did, and one day she spoke to Mis' Tolland, and found that the poor soul had been believin' all the time that there were n't any priests here. We 'd come to know she was a Catholic by her beads and all, and that had set some narrow minds against her. And mother explained it just as she would to a child; and uncle Lorenzo sent word right off somewheres up river by a packet that was bound up the bay, and the first o' the week a priest come by the boat, an' uncle Lorenzo was on the wharf 'tendin' to some business; so they just come up for me, and I walked with him to show him the house. He was a kind-hearted old man; he looked so benevolent an' fatherly I could ha' stopped an' told him my own troubles; yes, I was satisfied when I first saw his face, an' when poor Mis' Tolland beheld him enter the room, she went right down on her knees and clasped her hands together to him as if he 'd come to save her life, and he lifted her up and blessed her, an' I left 'em together, and slipped out into the open field and walked there in sight so if they needed to call me, and I had my own thoughts. At last I saw him at the door; he had to catch the return boat. I meant to walk back with him and offer him some supper, but he said no, and said he was comin' again if needed, and signed me to go into the house to her, and shook his head in a way that meant he understood everything. I can see him now; he walked with a cane, rather tired and feeble; I wished somebody would come along, so 's to carry him down to the shore.

"Mis' Tolland looked up at me with a new look when I went in, an' she even took hold o' my hand and kept it. He had put some oil on her forehead, but nothing anybody could do would keep her alive very long; 't was his medicine for the soul rather 'n the body. I helped her to bed, and next morning she could n't get up to dress her, and that was Monday, and she began to fail, and 't was Friday night she died." (Mrs. Todd spoke with unusual haste and lack of detail.) "Mrs. Begg and I watched with her, and made everything nice and proper, and after all the ill will there was a good number gathered to the funeral. 'T was in Reverend Mr. Bascom's day, and he done very well in his prayer, considering he could n't fill in with mentioning all the near connections by name as was his habit. He spoke very feeling about being a stranger and twice widowed, and all he said about her being reared among the heathen was to observe that there might be roads leadin' up to the New Jerusalem from various points. I says to myself that I guessed quite a number must ha' reached there that wa'n't able to set out from Dunnet Landin'!"

Mrs. Todd gave an odd little laugh as she bent toward the firelight to pick up a dropped stitch in her knitting, and then I heard a heartfelt sigh.

"'T was most forty years ago," she said; "most everybody 's gone a'ready that was there that day."

V

Suddenly Mrs. Todd gave an energetic shrug of her shoulders, and a quick look at me, and I saw that the sails of her narrative were filled with a fresh breeze.

"Uncle Lorenzo, Cap'n Bowden that I have referred to"—

"Certainly!" I agreed with eager expectation.

"He was the one that had been left in charge of Cap'n John Tolland's affairs, and had now come to be of unforeseen importance.

"Mrs. Begg an' I had stayed in the house both before an' after Mis' Tolland's decease, and she was now in haste to be gone, having affairs to call her home; but uncle come to me as the exercises was beginning, and said he thought I 'd better remain at the house while they went to the buryin' ground. I could n't understand his reasons, an' I felt disappointed, bein' as near to her as most anybody; 't was rough weather, so mother could n't get in, and did n't even hear Mis' Tolland was gone till next day. I just nodded to satisfy him, 't wa'n't no time to discuss anything. Uncle seemed flustered; he 'd gone out deep-sea fishin' the day she died, and the storm I told you of rose very sudden, so they got blown off way down the coast beyond Monhegan, and he'd just got back in time to dress himself and come.

"I set there in the house after I 'd watched her away down the straight road far 's I could see from the door; 't was a little short walkin' funeral an' a cloudy sky, so everything looked dull an' gray, an' it crawled along all in one piece, same 's walking funerals do, an' I wondered how it ever come to the Lord's mind to let her begin down among them gay islands all heat and sun, and end up here among the rocks with a north wind blowin'. 'T was a gale that begun the afternoon before she died, and had kept blowin' off an' on ever since. I 'd thought more than once how glad I should be to get home an' out o' sound o' them black spruces a-beatin' an' scratchin' at the front windows.

"I set to work pretty soon to put the chairs back, an' set outdoors some that was borrowed, an' I went out in the kitchen, an' I made up a good fire in case somebody come an' wanted a cup o' tea; but I did n't expect any one to travel way back to the house unless 't was uncle Lorenzo. 'T was growin' so chilly that I fetched some kindlin' wood and made fires in both the fore rooms. Then I set down an' begun to feel as usual, and I got my knittin' out of a drawer. You can't be sorry for a poor creatur' that 's come to the end o' all her troubles; my only discomfort was I thought I 'd ought to feel worse at losin' her than I did; I was younger then than I be now. And as I set there, I begun to hear some long notes o' dronin' music from upstairs that chilled me to the bone."

Mrs. Todd gave a hasty glance at me.

"Quick 's I could gather me, I went right upstairs to see what 't was," she added eagerly, "an' 't was just what I might ha' known. She 'd always kept her guitar hangin' right against the wall in her room; 't was tied by a blue ribbon, and there was a window left wide open; the wind was veerin' a good deal, an' it slanted in and searched the room. The strings was jarrin' yet.

"'T was growin' pretty late in the afternoon, an' I begun to feel lonesome as I should n't now, and I was disappointed at having to stay there, the more I thought it over, but after a while I saw Cap'n Lorenzo polin' back up the road all alone, and when he come nearer I could see he had a bundle under his arm and had shifted his best black clothes for his every-day ones. I run out and put some tea into the teapot and set it back on the stove to draw, an' when he come in I reached down a little jug o' spirits,—Cap'n Tolland had left his house well provisioned as if his wife was goin' to put to sea same 's himself, an' there she 'd gone an' left it. There was some cake that Mis' Begg an' I had made the day before. I thought that uncle an' me had a good right to the funeral supper, even if there wa'n't any one to join us. I was lookin' forward to my cup o' tea; 't was beautiful tea out of a green lacquered chest that I 've got now."

"You must have felt very tired," said I, eagerly listening.

"I was 'most beat out, with watchin' an' tendin' and all," answered Mrs. Todd, with as much sympathy in her voice as if she were speaking of another person. "But I called out to uncle as he came in, 'Well, I expect it 's all over now, an' we 've all done what we could. I thought we 'd better have some tea or somethin' before we go home. Come right out in the kitchen, sir,' says I, never thinking but we only had to let the fires out and lock up everything safe an' eat our refreshment, an' go home.

" 'I want both of us to stop here to-night,' says uncle, looking at me very important.

" 'Oh, what for?' says I, kind o' fretful.

" 'I 've got my proper reasons,' says uncle. 'I 'll see you well satisfied, Almira. Your tongue ain't so easy-goin' as some o' the women folks, an' there 's property here to take charge of that you don't know nothin' at all about.'

" 'What do you mean?' says I.

" 'Cap'n Tolland acquainted me with his affairs; he had n't no sort o' confidence in nobody but me an' his wife, after he was tricked into signin' that Portland note, an' lost money. An' she did n't know nothin' about business; but what he did n't take to sea to be sunk with him he 's hid somewhere in this house. I expect Mis' Tolland may have told you where she kept things?' said uncle.

"I see he was dependin' a good deal on my answer," said Mrs. Todd, "but I had to disappoint him; no, she had never said nothin' to me.

" 'Well, then, we 've got to make a search,' says he, with considerable relish; but he was all tired and worked up, and we set down to the table, an' he had somethin', an' I took my desired cup o' tea, and then I begun to feel more interested.

" 'Where you goin' to look first?' says I, but he give me a short look an' made no answer, and begun to mix me a very small portion out of the jug, in another glass. I took it to please him; he said I looked tired, speakin' real fatherly, and I did feel better for it, and we set talkin' a few minutes, an' then he started for the cellar, carrying an old ship's lantern he fetched out o' the stairway an' lit.

" 'What are you lookin' for, some kind of a chist?' I inquired, and he said yes. All of a sudden it come to me to ask who was the heirs; Eliza Tolland, Cap'n John's own sister, had never demeaned herself to come near the funeral, and uncle Lorenzo faced right about and begun to laugh, sort o' pleased. I thought queer of it; 't wa'n't what he 'd taken, which would be nothin' to an old weathered sailor like him.

" 'Who 's the heir?' says I the second time.

" 'Why, it 's *you*, Almiry,' says he; and I was so took aback I set right down on the turn o' the cellar stairs.

" 'Yes 't is,' said uncle Lorenzo. 'I 'm glad of it too. Some thought she did n't have no sense but foreign sense, an' a poor stock o' that, but she said you was friendly to her, an' one day after she got news of Tolland's death, an' I had fetched up his will that left everything to her, she said she was goin' to make a writin', so 's you could have things after she was gone, an' she give five hundred to me for bein' executor. Square Pease fixed up the paper, an' she signed it; it 's all accordin' to law.' There, I begun to cry," said Mrs. Todd; "I could n't help it. I wished I had her back again to do somethin' for, an' to make her know I felt sisterly to her more 'n I 'd ever showed, an' it come over me 't was all too late, an' I cried the more, till uncle showed impatience, an' I got up an' stumbled along down cellar with my apern to my eyes the greater part of the time.

" 'I 'm goin' to have a clean search,' says he; 'you hold the light.' An' I held it, and he rummaged in the arches an' under the stairs, an' over in some old closet where he reached out bottles an' stone jugs an' canted some kags an' one or two casks, an' chuckled well when he heard there

was somethin' inside,—but there wa'n't nothin' to find but things usual in
a cellar, an' then the old lantern was givin' out an' we come away.

" 'He spoke to me of a chist, Cap'n Tolland did,' says uncle in a
whisper. 'He said a good sound chist was as safe a bank as there was, an' I
beat him out of such nonsense, 'count o' fire an' other risks.' 'There 's no
chist in the rooms above,' says I ; 'no, uncle, there ain't no sea-chist, for
I 've been here long enough to see what there was to be seen.' Yet he
would n't feel contented till he 'd mounted up into the toploft; 't was one
o' them single, hip-roofed houses that don't give proper accommodation
for a real garret, like Cap'n Littlepage's down here at the Landin'. There
was broken furniture and rubbish, an' he let down a terrible sight o' dust
into the front entry, but sure enough there was n't no chist. I had it all to
sweep up next day.

" 'He must have took it away to sea,' says I to the cap'n, an' even then
he did n't want to agree, but we was both beat out. I told him where I 'd
always seen Mis' Tolland get her money from, and we found much as a
hundred dollars there in an old red morocco wallet. Cap'n John had been
gone a good while a'ready, and she had spent what she needed. 'T was in
an old desk o' his in the settin' room that we found the wallet."

"At the last minute he may have taken his money to sea," I suggested.

"Oh yes," agreed Mrs. Todd. "He did take considerable to make his
venture to bring home, as was customary, an' that was drowned with him
as uncle agreed; but he had other property in shipping, and a thousand
dollars invested in Portland in a cordage shop, but 't was about the time
shipping begun to decay, and the cordage shop failed, and in the end I
wa'n't so rich as I thought I was goin' to be for those few minutes on the
cellar stairs. There was an auction that accumulated something. Old Mis'
Tolland, the cap'n's mother, had heired some good furniture from a
sister: there was above thirty chairs in all, and they 're apt to sell well. I got
over a thousand dollars when we come to settle up, and I made uncle take
his five hundred; he was getting along in years and had met with losses in
navigation, and he left it back to me when he died, so I had a real good lift.
It all lays in the bank over to Rockland, and I draw my interest fall an'
spring, with the little Mr. Todd was able to leave me; but that 's kind o'
sacred money; 't was earnt and saved with the hope o' youth, an' I 'm very
particular what I spend it for. Oh yes, what with ownin' my house, I 've
been enabled to get along very well, with prudence!" said Mrs. Todd

contentedly.

"But there was the house and land," I asked,—"what became of that part of the property?"

Mrs. Todd looked into the fire, and a shadow of disapproval flitted over her face.

"Poor old uncle!" she said, "he got childish about the matter. I was hoping to sell at first, and I had an offer, but he always run of an idea that there was more money hid away, and kept wanting me to delay; an' he used to go up there all alone and search, and dig in the cellar, empty an' bleak as 't was in winter weather or any time. An' he 'd come and tell me he 'd dreamed he found gold behind a stone in the cellar wall, or somethin'. And one night we all see the light o' fire up that way, an' the whole Landin' took the road, and run to look, and the Tolland property was all in a light blaze. I expect the old gentleman had dropped fire about; he said he 'd been up there to see if everything was safe in the afternoon. As for the land, 't was so poor that everybody used to have a joke that the Tolland boys preferred to farm the sea instead. It 's 'most all grown up to bushes now, where it ain't poor water grass in the low places. There 's some upland that has a pretty view, after you cross the brook bridge. Years an' years after she died, there was some o' her flowers used to come up and remind me of her, constant as the spring. But I never did want to fetch home that guitar, some way or 'nother; I would n't let it go at the auction, either. It was hangin' right there in the house when the fire took place. I 've got some o' her other little things scattered about the house: that picture on the mantelpiece belonged to her."

I had often wondered where such a picture had come from, and why Mrs. Todd had chosen it; it was a French print of the statue of the Empress Josephine in the Savane at old Fort Royal, in Martinique.

VI

Mrs. Todd drew her chair closer to mine; she held the cat and her knitting with one hand as she moved, but the cat was so warm and so sound asleep that she only stretched a lazy paw in spite of what must have felt like a slight earthquake. Mrs. Todd began to speak almost in a whisper.

"I ain't told you all," she continued; "no, I have n't spoken of all to but very few. The way it came was this," she said solemnly, and then stopped to listen to the wind, and sat for a moment in deferential silence, as if she waited for the wind to speak first. The cat suddenly lifted her head with quick excitement and gleaming eyes, and her mistress was leaning forward toward the fire with an arm laid on either knee, as if they were consulting the glowing coals for some augury. Mrs. Todd looked like an old prophetess as she sat there with the firelight shining on her strong face; she was posed for some great painter. The woman with the cat was as unconscious and as mysterious as any sibyl of the Sistine Chapel.

"There, that 's the last struggle o' the gale," said Mrs. Todd, nodding her head with impressive certainty and still looking into the bright embers of the fire. "You 'll see!" She gave me another quick glance, and spoke in a low tone as if we might be overheard.

" 'T was such a gale as this the night Mis' Tolland died. She appeared more comfortable the first o' the evenin'; and Mrs. Begg was more spent than I, bein' older, and a beautiful nurse that was the first to see and think of everything, but perfectly quiet an' never asked a useless question. You remember her funeral when you first come to the Landing? And she consented to goin' an' havin' a good sleep while she could, and left me one o' those good little pewter lamps that burnt whale oil an' made plenty o' light in the room, but not too bright to be disturbin'.

"Poor Mis' Tolland had been distressed the night before, an' all that day, but as night come on she grew more and more easy, an' was layin' there asleep; 't was like settin' by any sleepin' person, and I had none but usual thoughts. When the wind lulled and the rain, I could hear the seas, though more distant than this, and I don' know·'s I observed any other sound than what the weather made; 't was a very solemn feelin' night. I set close by the bed; there was times she looked to find somebody when she was awake. The light was on her face, so I could see her plain; there was always times when she wore a look that made her seem a stranger you 'd never set eyes on before. I did think what a world it was that her an' me should have come together so, and she have nobody but Dunnet Landin' folks about her in her extremity. 'You 're one o' the stray ones, poor creatur',' I said. I remember those very words passin' through my mind, but I saw reason to be glad she had some comforts, and did n't lack friends at the last, though she 'd seen misery an' pain. I was glad she was quiet; all day she 'd been restless, and we could n't understand what she wanted from her French speech. We had the window open to give her air, an' now an' then a gust would strike that guitar that was on the wall and set it swinging by the blue ribbon, and soundin' as if somebody begun to play it. I come near takin' it down, but you never know what 'll fret a sick person an' put em' on the rack, an' that guitar was one o' the few things she 'd brought with her."

I nodded assent, and Mrs. Todd spoke still lower.

"I set there close by the bed; I 'd been through a good deal for some days back, and I thought I might 's well be droppin' asleep too, bein' a quick person to wake. She looked to me as if she might last a day longer, certain, now she 'd got more comfortable, but I was real tired, an' sort o' cramped as watchers will get, an' a fretful feeling begun to creep over me such as they often do have. If you give way, there ain't no support for the sick person; they can't count on no composure o' their own. Mis' Tolland moved then, a little restless, an' I forgot me quick enough, an' begun to hum out a little part of a hymn tune just to make her feel everything was as usual an' not wake up into a poor uncertainty. All of a sudden she set right up in bed with her eyes wide open, an' I stood an' put my arm behind her; she had n't moved like that for days. And she reached out both her arms toward the door, an' I looked the way she was lookin', an' I see some one was standin' there against the dark. No, 't wa'n't Mis' Begg; 't was somebody a good deal shorter than Mis' Begg. The lamplight struck across the room between us. I could n't tell the shape, but 't was a woman's dark face lookin' right at us; 't wa'n't but an instant I could see. I felt dreadful cold, and my head begun to swim; I thought the light went out; 't wa'n't but an instant, as I say, an' when my sight come back I could n't see nothing there. I was one that did n't know what it was to faint away, no matter what happened; time was I felt above it in others, but 't was somethin' that made poor human natur' quail. I saw very plain while I could see; 't was a pleasant enough face, shaped somethin' like Mis' Tolland's, and a kind of expectin' look.

"No, I don't expect I was asleep," Mrs. Todd assured me quietly, after a moment's pause, though I had not spoken. She gave a heavy sigh before she went on. I could see that the recollection moved her in the deepest way.

"I suppose if I had n't been so spent an' quavery with long watchin', I might have kept my head an' observed much better," she added humbly; "but I see all I could bear. I did try to act calm, an' I laid Mis' Tolland down on her pillow, an' I was a-shakin' as I done it. All she did was to look up to me so satisfied and sort o' questioning, an' I looked back to her.

" 'You saw her, did n't you?' she says to me, speakin' perfectly reasonable. ' 'T is my mother,' she says again, very feeble, but lookin' straight up at me, kind of surprised with the pleasure, and smiling as if she saw I was overcome, an' would have said more if she could, but we had hold of hands. I see then her change was comin', but I did n't call Mis' Begg, nor make no uproar. I felt calm then, an' lifted to somethin' different as I never was since. She opened her eyes just as she was goin'—

" 'You saw her, did n't you?' she said the second time, an' I says, '*Yes, dear, I did; you ain't never goin' to feel strange an' lonesome no more.*' An' then in a few minutes 't was all over. I felt they 'd gone away together. No, I wa'n't alarmed afterward; 't was just that one moment I could n't live under, but I never called it beyond reason I should see the other watcher. I saw plain enough there was somebody there with me in the room."

VII

" 'T was just such a night as this Mis' Tolland died," repeated Mrs. Todd, returning to her usual tone and leaning back comfortably in her chair as she took up her knitting. " 'T was just such a night as this. I 've told the circumstances to but very few; but I don't call it beyond reason. When folks is goin' 't is all natural, and only common things can jar upon the mind. You know plain enough there 's somethin' beyond this world; the doors stand wide open. 'There 's somethin' of us that must still live on; we 've got to join both worlds together an' live in one but for the other.' The doctor said that to me one day, an' I never could forget it; he said 't was in one o' his old doctor's books."

We sat together in silence in the warm little room; the rain dropped heavily from the eaves, and the sea still roared, but the high wind had done blowing. We heard the far complaining fog horn of a steamer up the Bay.

"There goes the Boston boat out, pretty near on time," said Mrs. Todd with satisfaction. "Sometimes these late August storms 'll sound a good deal worse than they really be. I do hate to hear the poor steamers callin' when they 're bewildered in thick nights in winter, comin' on the coast. Yes, there goes the boat; they 'll find it rough at sea, but the storm 's all over."

BIBLIOGRAPHY

SARAH ORNE JEWETT'S BOOKS

Deephaven. Boston: Osgood, 1877.
Old Friends and New. Boston: Houghton, Osgood, 1879.
Country By-Ways. Boston: Houghton, Mifflin, 1881.
The Mate of the Daylight and Friends Ashore. Boston: Houghton, Mifflin, 1884.
A Country Doctor. Boston: Houghton, Mifflin, 1884.
A White Heron and Other Stories. Boston: Houghton, Mifflin, 1886.
The King of Folly Island and Other People. Boston: Houghton, Mifflin, 1888.
Strangers and Wayfarers. Boston: Houghton, Mifflin, 1890.
A Native of Winby and Other Tales. Boston: Houghton, Mifflin, 1893.
The Life of Nancy. Boston: Houghton, Mifflin, 1895.
The Country of the Pointed Firs. Boston: Houghton, Mifflin, 1896.
The Queen's Twin and Other Stories. Boston: Houghton, Mifflin, 1899.
The Tory Lover. Boston: Houghton, Mifflin, 1901.
The Uncollected Short Stories of Sarah Orne Jewett, ed. Richard Cary, Waterville, Maine: Colby College Press, 1971.

Paperback Editions

The Country of the Pointed Firs and Other Short Stories, ed. Willa Cather. Garden City, N.Y.: Doubleday Anchor, 1956.
Deephaven and Other Stories, ed. Richard Cary. New Haven: College and University Press, 1966.
Short Fiction of Sarah Orne Jewett and Mary Wilkins Freeman, ed. Barbara H. Solomon. New York: New American Library, 1979.

The Country of the Pointed Firs and Other Stories, ed. Mary Ellen Chase. New York: Norton, 1982.

A Country Doctor, ed. Joy Gould Boyum and Ann R. Shapiro. New York: New American Library, 1986.

BOOKS ABOUT SARAH ORNE JEWETT

Fields, Annie, ed. *Letters of Sarah Orne Jewett*. Boston: Houghton, Mifflin, 1911.

Cary, Richard, ed. *Sarah Orne Jewett Letters*. Waterville, Maine: Colby College Press, 1967.

Donovan, Josephine. *Sarah Orne Jewett*. New York: Ungar, 1980.

_____. *New England Local Color Literature: A Women's Tradition*. New York: Ungar, 1983.

Matthiessen, F.O. *Sarah Orne Jewett*. Boston: Houghton, Mifflin, 1929.

Nagel, Gwen, ed. *Critical Essays on Sarah Orne Jewett*. Boston: G.K. Hall, 1984.